"A crime story that fascinates through its detailed historical flair."

—*Flug* magazine (North Rhine-Westphalia)

"This crime story is perfect for those who love tension-packed thrills and want to be introduced at the same time to the thinking and beliefs of the Middle Ages. An excellently researched novel about the Middle Ages, [*Death and the Devil*] is relaxing entertainment for all devotees of intelligent crime stories, and it is informative for those interested in reading not only about history but specifically ecclesiastical history as well."

—*Neues Leben*

"In order to survive, this tension-filled crime story demands courage, strength, and fantasy from its hero against his will. Thanks to the author's fluid writing we are luckily kept on the heels of the hunted as he crisscrosses Cologne's Old Town. This not only signifies a special gift for storytelling but tells also of a profound joy for imagining a story."

—*Compact* magazine (North Rhine-Westphalia)

"This first work by Frank Schatzing presents us with a colorful description of this metropolis on the Rhine River in the Middle Ages. It tells the 'behind-the-scenes' story of the battle for supremacy at the top of society, far beyond all other historical writings."

—*Schnüss Bonn*

"Thrills, entertainment, good writing, and so much information! What more could one expect from a crime story?"

—*Koelner Stadt Anzeiger*

Paul Schmitz, Cologne

About the Author

FRANK SCHATZING is the author of the international bestseller *The Swarm*. He is a winner of the Köln Literatur Prize, the Corine Prize, and the German Science Fiction Prize. Frank Schatzing lives and works in Cologne, Germany.

ALSO BY FRANK SCHATZING

The Swarm

DEATH

AND THE

FRANK SCHATZING

TRANSLATED BY MIKE MITCHELL

HARPER

NEW YORK • LONDON • TORONTO • SYDNEY

HARPER

This book is a work of fiction. References to real people, events, establishments, organizations, or locales are intended only to provide a sense of authenticity, and are used fictitiously. All other characters, and all incidents and dialogue, are drawn from the author's imagination and are not to be construed as real.

Originally published in paperback in 2003 in Germany by Goldmann Publishing House.

A hardcover edition of this book was published in 2007 by William Morrow, an imprint of HarperCollins Publishers.

DEATH AND THE DEVIL. Copyright © 2003, 2007 by Hermann-Josef Emons Verlag. English translation copyright © 2007 by Mike Mitchell. All rights reserved. Printed in the United States of America. No part of this book may be used or reproduced in any manner whatsoever without written permission except in the case of brief quotations embodied in critical articles and reviews. For information address HarperCollins Publishers, 10 East 53rd Street, New York, NY 10022.

HarperCollins books may be purchased for educational, business, or sales promotional use. For information please write: Special Markets Department, HarperCollins Publishers, 10 East 53rd Street, New York, NY 10022.

FIRST HARPER PAPERBACK PUBLISHED 2008.

Designed by Kris Tobiassen

Library of Congress Cataloging-in-Publication Data has been applied for.

ISBN 978-0-06-164661-4

08 09 10 11 12 DIX/RRD 10 9 8 7 6 5 4 3 2 1

Language does not veil reality, but expresses it.

—PETER ABELARD

Prologue

✠

The wolf stood on the height, its gaze fixed on the ring of the great wall bathed in the gold of the evening sun.

Its breathing was steady. Its powerful flanks quivered slightly. It had been running all day from the castles of Jülich over the hills and down to this spot where the trees ended, giving a clear view of the distant city. Despite that, it felt no tiredness. As the sun behind it slipped below the horizon in a ball of fire, it threw back its muzzle to take stock of its surroundings.

The odors were intense: the river water, the mud of the banks, the rotting wood of ships' hulls. It sucked in the scent of animals mingling with the smells given off by humans and their artifacts: fragrant wines and excrement, incense, peat and flesh, the salt on sweaty bodies and the fragrance of expensive furs, blood, honey, herbs, ripe fruit, leprosy, and mold. It smelled love and fear, terror, weakness, hatred, and power. Everything down there spoke its own pungent language, telling the wolf of life inside the stone walls, and of death.

It turned its head.

Silence. The only sound the rustling of leaves.

It waited, motionless, until the gold had gone from the walls and all that was left was a shimmer on the topmost battlements of the gate towers. In a short while that would be gone as well, leaving the day to oblivion.

Night would come, clothing the valley in new, dull colors until those too gave way to a darkness in which the gleam of its eyes was the only light.

The time was close when wolves would appear in the dreams of men, a time of change, a time of hunting.

With lithe steps the wolf padded down the slope and disappeared in the tall, dry grass.

Here and there a bird started singing again.

10 September

✠

OUTSIDE THE GATES

"I'm cold."

"You're always cold. You're an arrant coward, that's your problem."

Heinrich drew his cloak tighter around him and shot his companion an angry glance. "You don't really mean that, Matthias. It *is* cold."

Matthias shrugged his shoulders. "Sorry, then. If you insist—it's cold."

"You don't understand. I feel cold inside." Heinrich threw his hands out in a theatrical gesture. "That we have to stoop to such means! As God's my witness, there's no man less inclined to violence, but—"

"God's not your witness," Matthias interrupted.

"What?"

"Why should God waste his precious time on your whining and moaning? To tell the truth, I'm surprised you managed to get on your horse at this time of the night."

"Now you're going too far," Heinrich hissed. "Show a little respect, *if* you please."

"I show everyone the respect they deserve." Matthias steered his horse around an overturned oxcart that suddenly loomed up out of the darkness. The light was fading rapidly. It had been sunny, but it was September and the days were growing shorter, the evenings cooler. Mists rose, shrouding the world in enigmatic gloom. By now the walls of Cologne were almost half a mile behind them and all they had were their flickering torches. Matthias knew well that Heinrich was almost soiling himself with fear, and that fact gave him a grim satisfaction. Heinrich had his good points, but courage was not one of them.

He decided to ignore him and urged his horse forward.

In general no one would think of leaving the city at this hour, unless they had been thrown out. The area was unsafe. There were bands of thieves and robbers everywhere, despite the Pacification proclaimed by the archbishop of Cologne together with the lords of the surrounding district. That was in 1259, scarcely a year ago. It was all drawn up in a document plastered with seals. If you believed it, travelers and merchants could make their way across the Rhineland without being robbed and killed by brigands. But promises that were more or less kept by day, especially when the merchants' contributions toward the rather sparse protection was due, did not extend to the night. Only recently the body of a girl had been found, raped and strangled, in the fields not many yards from the Frisian Gate. Her parents were reputable people from a family of armorers who had lived for generations at the sign of the helmet opposite the archbishop's palace. One rumor had it that the Archfiend himself had cast a spell on the girl to lure her out, others suggested that the farmer in whose field she had been found should be broken on the wheel. It was not so much that they thought he was the murderer, but how did the daughter of respectable burghers come to be lying dead on his land? Especially since no one could explain what she was doing out there so late. Once the first wave of indignation had died down, however, it turned out that it was common knowledge she had been going around with minstrels and worse, lardmongers from Grease Lane and scum that should never have been allowed into the city in the first place. Her own fault, then. It was better not to rely on the Pacification.

"Wait!"

Heinrich was a long way behind. Matthias realized he had given his Arab steed his head and slowed it down to a walk until his companion caught up. They had passed several farms now since leaving the city and reached a small wood. The moon cast only a faint light on the land around.

"Shouldn't we wait somewhere here?" Heinrich's voice was trembling almost as much as his hands.

"No." Matthias was peering through the first trees of the wood. The path disappeared into the darkness. "We have to go to the clearing. Are you sure you wouldn't rather go back?"

"What? By myself?!" Mortified, Heinrich bit his lip, but too late, it was out. For a moment anger overcame his cowardice. "You keep trying to provoke me. As if I'd turn back! As if the thought would even occur to me, here in the darkness with a puffed-up peacock at my side who's always shooting his mouth off—"

"Talking of mouths," Matthias hissed, reining in his horse and grabbing Heinrich by the shoulder, "you'd do better to keep yours shut. If I were the man we've come to meet and heard your wailing I'd have taken off long ago."

Heinrich glared at him in a mixture of fury and humiliation, then pulled himself away and rode on through the trees, crouching low in the saddle. Matthias followed. The shadows of the branches danced in the light from their torches. A few minutes later they reached the clearing and stopped. Apart from the rustling of the wind through the leaves there was nothing to be heard but the monotonous hooting of an owl somewhere above.

They waited in silence.

After a while Heinrich began to twist and turn restlessly in his saddle. "And if he doesn't come?"

"He'll come."

"How can you be so sure? People like that are nothing—here today, gone tomorrow."

"He'll come. William of Jülich recommended him, and that means he'll come."

"The count of Jülich knew nothing at all about him."

"What one knows about these people is not important. It's what they do that counts and this man served William well."

"I hate not knowing who other people are."

"Why? It's easier like that."

"Nevertheless. Perhaps we ought to go back and think everything over again."

"And what will you tell the others? That you pissed your pants and your horse with fear?"

"You'll apologize for that!"

"Just hold your tongue."

"I've not reached my age to have you shut me up all the time!"

"I'm three years older, remember?" Matthias mocked. "The older, the wiser. And since I don't think I've achieved wisdom myself yet, you can tell roughly where you stand. Now keep quiet."

Before Heinrich could reply Matthias had dismounted and sat down in the grass. Nervously Heinrich surveyed the silhouettes of the pines and looked for the moon. It was hidden behind a thin bank of cloud; here and there a few stars peeped through. The night was not to his liking, though to be honest no night was to his liking if he wasn't tucked up in bed or in the arms of a courtesan.

He looked back, screwing up his eyes to make sure no one had followed them.

A shadow flitted through the trees.

Heinrich gave such a start he almost spurred his horse. Suddenly his throat was unpleasantly dry.

"Matthias—"

"What?"

"There's something. There."

In a flash Matthias was on his feet and looking in the same direction.

"I can't see anything."

"But there was something."

"Hmm. Perhaps your fervent desire to perform heroic deeds has conjured up an enemy. They say witches—"

"This is not the time for jokes. Look, there!"

Two faintly gleaming points of light appeared out of the darkness and slowly came nearer. A scarcely perceptible something could just be discerned against the darkness of the bushes, blacker than black, its massive head toward them. It was observing them.

"The Devil!" Heinrich exclaimed in horror. His hand groped wildly for his sword.

"Nonsense." Matthias held up his torch and took a step toward the edge of the wood.

"Are you mad?! Come back, for God's sake!"

Matthias squatted down to get a better view. The two points of light disappeared as quickly as they had come. "A wolf," he declared.

"A wolf?" Heinrich gulped. "What are wolves doing this close to the city?"

"Hunting," a voice said.

Both swung around. Where Matthias had been sitting stood a man. He was tall, and thick blond hair fell over his shoulders in locks that almost coiled down to his waist. His cloak was as black as the night. Neither had heard him approach.

Matthias peered into the darkness. "Urquhart?"

The man nodded.

Heinrich was frozen in the saddle like a pillar of salt, gaping open-mouthed at the stranger. Matthias threw him a contemptuous glance. "You can get down now, O noble knight full of years and valor."

Heinrich's features twitched. He closed his mouth with an audible clack of teeth and slithered out of the saddle.

"Let's sit down," Matthias suggested.

By the time they had seated themselves a little way from the horses, Heinrich had recovered his voice and his dignified manner. "We didn't hear you come," he complained.

"Of course not." Urquhart's smile revealed two gleaming rows of perfect white teeth. "You were busy with your wolf. Wolves are quickly there when you call them. Didn't you know that?"

"What on earth are you talking about?" asked Matthias with a frown. "No one in his right mind would call wolves."

Urquhart smiled. "You could be right. Anyway, it was probably only a dog that was more afraid of you than you of it. If that's any comfort," he added politely, turning toward Heinrich.

Heinrich stared at the ground and started tugging at bits of grass.

"Where's your horse?" Matthias asked.

"Near enough," Urquhart replied. "I won't be needing it in the city."

"Are you sure? Cologne's bigger than most cities."

"And I'm faster than most horses."

Matthias gave him an appraising look. "If you say so. The count of Jülich told you how much we are prepared to pay?"

Urquhart nodded. "William mentioned a thousand silver marks. I'm happy with that."

"We're raising our offer. The requirements have increased. Say twice as much work."

"Agreed. And my wages—say three times as much."

"I'm not happy with that."

"And I'm not happy with this chopping and changing. We're not haggling over a piece of merchandise. Three thousand."

Heinrich cut in sharply. "Are you worth that much?"

Urquhart surveyed him for a while, the corners of his mouth twitching in mild amusement. Then he raised his bushy eyebrows. "Yes."

Matthias nodded. "Agreed then. Three thousand."

"What?" Heinrich objected. "But you yourself just—"

"Agreed!" Matthias turned to Urquhart. "Let's get down to details."

"As your lordship wishes."

A strange fellow, thought Matthias, well mannered and polite. He started to talk, softly, insistently. Urquhart listened, motionless apart from the occasional nod. "Any questions?"

"No."

"Good." Matthias got up, brushing the grass and soil from his clothes. He produced a scroll from the folds of his cloak and handed it to Urquhart. "A letter of recommendation from the abbot of the Greyfriars. There's no need to go and pay your respects; no one's expecting you. I don't think you'll be stopped at the gate, but with a reference like this no town guard will refuse you entry."

Urquhart gave a low whistle. "I don't need papers to get in, but it would interest me to know how you got the abbot to put his seal to your service."

Matthias gave a smug laugh. "Our mutual friend, William of Jülich, is the proud owner of a farm only a stone's throw from the abbey and the abbot owes him various favors. William has made a number of valuable contributions to the sacristy, if you get my meaning."

"I thought the Franciscans were poor and without worldly goods."

"Yes. That means everything on their land belongs to the Lord alone. Of course, until He comes to fetch it, it has to be looked after."

"Or eaten?"

"And drunk."

"Have you two quite finished?" Heinrich kept his voice down but the irritation was audible. "Cock Gate closes at ten on the dot and a night under the stars is the last thing I want."

"Yes, yes." Matthias scrutinized Urquhart. "Work out your plan. We'll meet at the convent of the Ursulines at five tomorrow to discuss any remaining details. I presume I can rely on you to keep low until then?"

"You've no need to worry about me," said Urquhart with a smile. He stretched and looked up at the moon peeping shyly out between the clouds. "You two go now. Time's getting short."

"I see you carry no weapons."

"As I said, you've no need to worry about me. I use my weapons, not wear them for public show. They'll be there when I need them." He gave Matthias a wink. "I even carry a quill and parchment with me."

"Those aren't weapons," Matthias objected.

"Oh, yes, they are. The written word can be a very powerful weapon. Anything can be a weapon for those who know how to use it."

"If you say so."

"I do. Now go."

Heinrich turned away and stumped sulkily over to the horses. Matthias followed. He looked back once, but Urquhart had vanished.

"Did you notice his eyes?" Heinrich whispered.

"What?"

"Urquhart's eyes!"

Matthias was trying to collect his thoughts. "What about his eyes?"

"A dead man's eyes."

Matthias stared at the spot where Urquhart had been standing. "You're dreaming, Heinrich."

"Eyes like a dead man's. He frightens me."

"Not me. Off we go."

They rode as fast as the darkness and the tangle of roots in the wood allowed. Once out in the open countryside they spurred their horses on and reached the city ten minutes later. As they slipped into the safety of the great wall, the gate closed slowly behind them, shutting out the triumphant night.

11 September

✠

HAYMARKET

Jacob the Fox was wandering around the markets assembling his lunch.

The nickname was inevitable. His head blazed like a house on fire. Short and slim, no one would have noticed him had it not been for the uncontrollable mop of red hair sticking out in all directions. Each wiry strand seemed to have a will of its own and yet, or perhaps for that very reason, it exerted a strange power over women. They seemed to feel an irresistible urge to run their fingers through it, to pat and pull at it, as if there were a competition to see who could teach it at least the rudiments of discipline. Up to now there had been no winner, for which Jacob gave heartfelt thanks to the Creator and made sure he kept his red thatch well tousled, maintaining its attraction to the fair sex. Once they had succumbed to the lure of the red mane they were in danger of losing themselves completely in the bright blue of his eyes.

Today, however, with his stomach rumbling angrily, Jacob had abandoned the prospect of further conquests, at least in the short term, and covered his red mane with an old rag that even in its better days would not have deserved the name of hood.

He caught the odor of expensive Dutch cheese and quickly moved away between the crowded stalls, doing his best to ignore it. A vivid picture was forming in his mind of the exposed slice glistening with fat as it melted in the midday sun. However much the Devil might waft the delicious smell under his nose, at the moment things at the cheese market were much too lively for a quick snatch.

There were better opportunities at the vegetable market opposite. The northern end of Haymarket was more attractive to the penniless customer anyway, offering as it did a variety of escape routes. One could slip between the coal merchants' piled-up wares and the salt market and disappear into a thousand alleyways, for example past the hosiers' shops and the bread hall, then up to the poulterers' stands and into Judengasse. Another possibility was to head down toward the Rhine, by Salzgasse or, better still, past the basket weavers to where the fishmongers had their open stalls. There, in the shadow of the great monastery church of St. Martin's, the fishmarket began and with it the stench of herring, eel, and catfish, so that there at the latest pursuers would give up the chase, sparing a sympathetic thought for the venerable brethren of St. Martin's and thanking God that they didn't have to set up their stalls on the banks of the Rhine.

But Jacob didn't want fish. He hated the smell, the sight, in fact everything about it. The danger would have to be extreme before he would even cross the fishmarket.

He squeezed his way between groups of chattering maids and nuns haggling at the tops of their voices over the price of pumpkins, almost drowned out by the melodious cries of the vendors, bumped into a richly clad merchant, and stumbled, gabbling his excuses, against a stall with carrots and celery. The stratagem brought him three oaths, one of which, surprisingly enough, he had never heard before, and a couple of lovely, smooth carrots, bursting with juice. Not a bad haul.

He looked around and thought for a minute. He could go via the crates of apples the farmers sold in Old Market Square. That was the sensible route. Carrots and apples—hunger stilled and thirst quenched.

But it was one of those days. Jacob wanted more. And unfortunately that "more" was on the southern, less safe side of Haymarket, at the part indicated by a higher percentage of clerics among the jostling crowd. On the meat stalls.

The meat stalls...

Only last week a thief had been caught there. He had been caught before, and this time the angry butcher chopped one of his hands off, comforting him with the thought that now he had his piece of flesh. The authorities later expressed their disapproval of this act of retribution but that didn't make his hand grow back. Anyway, it was his own fault. Meat was not for the poor.

And yet had not the dean of St. Cecilia's recently explained that only those among the poor who combined their poverty with honesty enjoyed God's favor? Did that mean Jacob belonged to the ungodly? And could the ungodly be condemned for not resisting the temptations of the flesh? The temptation of St. John was nothing compared to the way the flesh was tempting him at the moment.

But dangerous it certainly was.

There was no crush he could disappear into, as on the north side. Fewer alleyways. After the meat and smoked ham stalls there was nothing but the horse troughs and then that damned square where they'd caught the poor fellow last week.

Apples after all, then? Meat lay heavy on the stomach anyway. On the other hand, better on his stomach than on that of some fat priest, in Jacob's humble opinion.

He cast a look of longing at the stalls where the red slabs with their collars of yellow fat were being sold. He just had to accept that Providence had decreed he would not be a rich patrician. On the other hand Providence had surely not decreed he should die of unsatisfied yearning!

With a heavy heart, if not a heavy stomach, he watched as the objects of his desire briskly changed hands. Among the crowd of burghers' wives in their burgundy dresses with golden clasps and richly embroidered silk bonnets he could see Alexian Brothers, Franciscans and Conradines, Crutched Friars, and Augustinians in their black habits.

Since the archbishop had granted the city the right of staple the previous year, there was no more sumptuous market than that of Cologne. People of every degree met there, no one felt it was beneath them to display their wealth openly by buying up the contents of the stalls. To add to the confusion, the whole square was swarming with children fighting their own private battles or combining to chase pigs across the trampled clay. On the eastern side where the fleshmarket began, opposite the linen-weavers' hall with its ring of beggars, hung sausages, and Jacob would have dearly loved to be able to hop in with the round dozen that were just disappearing into the basket of an expensively dressed old man with a pointed hat.

Or not quite completely disappearing. As the man shuffled on his way one was left dangling enticingly.

Jacob's eyes popped.

It was looking back at him. It promised a foretaste of paradise, the New Jerusalem, heavenly bliss here on earth. Hundreds of tiny lumps of white fat were winking at him from the reddish brown of the smoked flesh under the bulging skin. It seemed to be calling on him to take his courage—and the sausage—in both hands and run for it. He could just picture himself sitting in his lean-to by the city wall gorging on it. The picture became more and more vivid, more and more real, until his legs began to move of their own accord. Danger and fear were forgotten. The world was reduced to one sausage.

Like an eel Jacob weaved his way between the people until he was behind the old man, who had stopped to examine a haunch of horseflesh. His eyesight must have been poor, he had to bend right over the counter.

Jacob came up close behind him, let him poke and sniff for a few seconds, then shouted at the top of his voice, "Thief! Look! Over there! Making off with a fillet of beef, the bastard!"

The people craned their necks. The butchers, naturally assuming the miscreant was behind them, turned around and, there being nothing to see, stood there looking baffled. It was the work of a second for Jacob's fingers to transfer the sausage to his jerkin. Time for a quick exit.

The display on the counter caught his eye. Chops within easy reach. And the butchers still staring at nothing.

He stretched out a hand, hesitated. Enough, enough, whispered a voice, time you were gone.

The temptation was too strong.

He grasped the nearest chop at the same moment as one of the butchers turned around. His look was as sharp as the executioner's axe and his face flushed with indignation. "Villain!" the butcher bellowed.

"Thief! Thief!" squawked the old man. He rolled his eyes, gave a strangled croak, and collapsed between the stalls.

Without a moment's hesitation Jacob threw the chop into the butcher's face. The people around started shrieking and hands grasped his old jerkin, pulling his hood off. His red mop shone forth in all its glory. He kicked out, but they refused to let go. The butcher jumped over the counter with a cry of rage.

Already Jacob could see himself minus one hand, and he didn't like what he saw.

Pulling all his strength together, he threw his arms up and leaped into the crowd. To his astonishment it was easier than he imagined. Then he realized he had jumped out of his jerkin, which the people were tearing to pieces as if the poor garment were the malefactor himself. He hit out in all directions, found he was free, and scampered across the square, the butcher in hot pursuit. And not only the butcher. To judge by the pounding of feet and the angry voices, half the people in Haymarket were after him, all determined to give the executioner the opportunity to try out his sword on Jacob's hand.

He slithered through muddy ruts and gravel, just avoiding the hooves of a startled horse. People turned to watch him, attracted by the spectacle.

"A thief!" roared the others.

"What? Who?"

"Carrot-top there! The fox!"

Reinforcements joined the pursuing throng. They appeared from every street and alleyway. Even the churchgoers seemed to be pouring out of St. Mary's with the sole intent of tearing him limb from limb.

Fear was starting to take over. The only escape route, past the malt mill and through Corn Gate to the Brook, was blocked. Someone had parked a cart in such a stupid fashion across the street that no one could get past.

But perhaps underneath?

Still running, Jacob then dropped to the ground, rolled under the shaft, bounced back onto his feet, and hurried off to the right, along the Brook. The butcher tried to copy him but got stuck and had to be pulled out to a chorus of angry shouts and yells. The bloodhounds had lost valuable seconds.

Finally three of them clambered over the cart and set off after Jacob again.

ON THE BROOK

But Jacob had disappeared.

They ran up and down a few times, then abandoned the chase. Although traffic on the Brook was light and, it being lunchtime, only a few dyers were at work outside, they had lost him. They had a look at the feltmakers' row of houses on the left, but couldn't see anyone suspicious.

"Red hair," muttered one.

"What?"

"Red hair, goddammit! He can't have given us the slip, we'd have seen him."

"That cart held us up," said the third. "Let's go. He won't escape on Judgment Day."

"No!" The speaker had torn his sleeve climbing over the cart and there was an angry glint in his eyes. "Someone must have seen him."

He strode up the Brook, a street that followed the course of the Duffes Brook along the old Roman wall, his reluctant companions in tow. They asked everyone they met until they came to the woad market, but none had seen the redhead.

"Let's call it a day," said one. "He didn't steal anything from me."

"No!" The man with the torn coat looked around desperately. His eye fell on a young woman kneeling down beside the stream rinsing out a large piece of cloth that had been dyed blue. She was pretty, in a rather singular way, with a slightly crooked nose and pouting lips. He planted himself in front of her, threw out his chest, and bellowed, "We're looking for a thief. A serious felony's just been committed."

She glanced up at him, not particularly interested, then went back to her cloth.

"Are you going to help us?" he thundered. "Or do we have to assume good-for-nothings are welcome here?"

The woman glared at him, took a deep breath—which, given her ample chest measurement, made the self-appointed inquisitor forget all about thieves for a moment—put her hands on her hips, and bawled back at him, "What an insulting suggestion! If we'd seen a thief, he'd be in the stocks by now!"

"That's where he belongs. He tore my doublet, stole half a horse—what, a whole one, and rode off on it, and I wouldn't be surprised if he hadn't murdered the odd person on the way."

"Incredible!" The woman shook her head in indignation, sending a mass of dark-brown locks flying to and fro. Her interrogator was finding it more and more difficult to concentrate on the matter at hand.

"What does he look like?" she asked.

"Mop of bright red hair." The man pursed his lips. "Forgive my asking, but doesn't it get a bit lonely here by the Brook?"

A delicious smile spread across the woman's face. "Oh, it does."

"Well—" He tapped his fingertips against each other.

"D'you know," she went on, "I sometimes think it would be nice to have someone who would just sit here and listen to me. When my husband—he's a preacher with the Dominicans, very highly thought of—is giving a sermon, I'm left all by myself. I've got seven children, but they're always out somewhere. Probably looking for the other five."

"The *other* five?" the man stammered. "I thought you had seven?"

"Seven from my first marriage. With the other five I had with the canon that makes twelve hungry mouths to feed and nothing to eat. You wouldn't believe how little the dyeing brings in." The smile became even more radiant. "I've been wondering whether it might not be time to tell the old Antonite to pack his bags."

"Er—wasn't it a Dominican, you said?"

"It *was,* but it's my Antonite I'm talking about now. Limp as a dishrag. Now when I look at you—"

"Just a minute!"

"A man of your size, built like one of the saints, a fount of wisdom, not like that wine merchant I—"

"Yes, I'm sure. Well, I wish you good day." The man hurried after his companions, who were making their way back to Corn Gate, shaking their heads. "And if you should happen to see the thief," he shouted over his shoulder, "then tell him—well—ask him—"

"Yes?"

"That's right. Exactly."

She watched the three disappear.

Then she burst into a fit of laughter.

Her laughter was louder than the bells of St. George's. She laughed until her sides hurt and the tears were running down her cheeks so that she didn't see the blue cloth rise up and slip to one side to reveal a soaking wet Jacob the Fox gasping for breath.

RICHMODIS VON WEIDEN

"So you're a thief?"

He was lying on the ground beside her, still giddy and trying to get the last of the water out of his lungs. It had a somewhat caustic taste. Upstream from the blue-dyers were the red-dyers and some of the substances that got into the stream were better not swallowed.

"Yes," he said, his chest heaving. "One that's just committed a serious felony."

She pursed her lips in a pout. "And you told me it was you who were running away from thieves and murderers."

"I had to think of something. Sorry."

"That's all right." She tried unsuccessfully to repress a giggle. "Pontius Pilate only washed his hands, so I imagine total immersion will do for you."

"Hunger will do for me if I don't get something to eat. My dinner was in that jerkin."

"What jerkin?"

"The one—my jerkin. I had to leave it behind in the market. Force of circumstance."

"Presumably in the form of people trying to recover property you had forgotten to pay for?"

"You could put it that way, yes."

"What was in it?"

"In my jerkin? Oh, carrots, a sausage. Easy come, easy go."

"More easy go in your case, there's not much left at all. At least you've still got your breeches on"—she grinned—"even if it is a pair I wouldn't wish on my worst enemy."

Jacob looked at himself. There was some truth in what his new friend had said. But breeches and jerkin were all the clothes he possessed. Had possessed. He rubbed his eyes and poked his finger around in his left ear, which was still ringing from the water. "Did you believe it?" he asked.

"What?"

"My story."

As she slapped the cloth vigorously up and down, she looked at him from beneath her long lashes with a mocking grin. "Even if your thieving is only half as bad as your lying I'd still advise you to keep away from the market for the next few decades."

Jacob sniffed noisily. "I'm not bad at that kind of thing."

"You just happen to like going for a swim. It might be hot water next time."

"What can I do?" He tried, with limited success, to give himself an air of wounded pride. "Every profession has its risks. Except dyeing perhaps. A very exciting activity: blue dye in the morning, blue dye in the evening, blue—"

Her index finger pinned him to the ground.

"Oh, just listen to Mr. Clever. Here I am, sitting quietly by the stream when like a bolt from the blue this carrot-top appears and begs me to hide him. Then I have to engage that puffed-up codpiece in conversation, just for your sake, only to discover that the real no-good is there in the stream in front of me. And you call that no risk?"

Jacob said nothing. His thoughts were back with his lost dinner.

"Well, then?" she snapped. "Lost your tongue? Grown gills instead after all that time in the water?"

"You're quite right. What can I say?"

"How about thank you?"

In a flash Jacob was on his knees, gazing at her with his devoted-spaniel look. "You want me to show my thanks?"

"At the very least."

"I'll see what I can do."

To her astonishment he began to rummage around in the apparently unfathomable folds of his breeches, muttering and cursing as he turned everything inside out and outside in. Suddenly he beamed, "I've still got it!" and pulled out an object, which he stuck under her nose.

She inspected it with a frown. It appeared to be a thin stick the length of her finger with holes in it. "And what is that supposed to be?"

"Listen."

He put the stick to his lips and blew. A strange, high-pitched tune was heard.

"A whistle!" she exclaimed in delight.

"Yes." Quickly he swapped his devoted-spaniel look for the eyelid-flutter of the irresistible rogue. "I swear by Gabriel and all the archangels that I made up that tune just now for you and you alone. I've never played it to another woman, nor ever will, or may St. Peter send the spirits of the lions from the Circus Maximus to haunt me."

"He knows Roman history, too! For the rest, I don't believe a word of what you say."

"Oh, dear. I'll just have to go on to my next trick." With that Jacob threw the whistle into the air and caught it in his right hand. When he opened his fingers it had disappeared.

Her eyes opened wider and wider until Jacob began to worry they might pop out of their sockets.

"How did you . . . ?"

"Now watch."

Quickly he put his hand to her ear, produced the whistle, took her left hand out of the water, and placed the tiny instrument in her palm.

"For you." He beamed.

She blushed, shook her head, and laughed softly. A nice laugh, Jacob decided and beamed even more.

For a while she looked at her present, then fixed him with a thoughtful gaze, wrinkling her nose at the same time. "Are you really an archcriminal?"

"Of course. I've strangled dozens of men just with my little finger. They call me the Yoke." As if to demonstrate his point he stretched out his little finger, then decided the spiel lacked the air of truth. More joke than yoke. He let his shoulders droop.

She shot him a disapproving look, but there was a twitch of merriment about her lips.

"All right, all right." He threw some stones in the water. "I try to stay alive, that's all. I like life, even if it's not always easy, and I'm sure Him up there can understand that. It's not as if I'm stealing the apples from the Garden of Eden."

"But they're still God's apples."

"Could be. But my hunger's not God's hunger."

"Why am I wasting my time listening to all this? Help me with the cloth."

Together they lifted out the linen, heavy with water, and carried it to the drying poles in front of the house, which was clearly where she lived. Others were already hanging out to dry. There was a smell of woad, the dye from Jülich without which the blue-dyers would not have been able to carry on their trade.

"How about telling me your name, seeing as I've just saved your life?" she asked as she pulled the cloth smooth along the poles and checked that it wasn't touching the ground anywhere.

Jacob bared his teeth. "I'm the Fox!"

"I can see that. Do you have another name?"

"Jacob. And you?"

"Richmodis."

"What a beautiful name!"

"What a corny compliment!"

Jacob had to laugh. "Do you live here alone?"

She shook her head. "No. You're the second man to ask me that already today. How many more stories do I have to invent to get you good-for-nothings to leave me in peace?"

"So you live here with your husband?"

She rolled her eyes. "You don't give up, do you? I live with my father. He's really the dyer, but his back's getting worse and his fingers are bent with rheumatism."

Rheumatism was the typical dyer's disease. It came from having their hands in water all the time, whatever the season. In general the blue-dyers made a good living. The material they dyed was made into the smocks most people wore for work, so there was no shortage of commissions, but they paid for it with their health. But what could one do? Every craft ruined a person's health; even the rich merchants, who earned their money by their wits, suffered from gout almost without exception.

Only recently, so people said, the king of France's doctor had declared that gout came from overindulgence in pork, but the pope's physicians replied that rich people had more opportunity to sin and so needed correspondingly more opportunity to do penance. It simply showed that the gout was one more example of God's grace, encouraging the mortification of the flesh, just as, in His infinite goodness, He had given the gift of bloodletting to medicine. Anyway, they concluded, they could see no point in looking for causes—as if God's will could be used to support arguments in ecclesiastical disputes or even the obduracy of recalcitrant, stiff-necked heretics!

"I feel sorry for your father," said Jacob.

"We have a physician in the family." Richmodis gave the cloth a close inspection and smoothed out a crease. "He's gone to see him just now for some medicine, though I strongly suspect it's medicine derived from the grape that my uncle also prescribes for himself quite a lot."

"You should be glad your father can still hold his glass."

"He can certainly do that. And the rheumatism hasn't affected his throat."

The conversation seemed to have reached a dead end. Each was waiting for the other to think of something to say but for a while all that could be heard was a dog barking.

"May I ask you something, Richmodis?" Jacob said at last.

"You may."

"Why haven't you got a husband?"

"Good question. Why haven't you got a wife?"

"Well—I have got a wife." Jacob felt a surge of embarrassment. "That is, I haven't actually. Call her a girlfriend if you like, but we don't really get on anymore."

"Does she look after you?"

"We look after each other. When we have something to spare."

Jacob had not intended to sound sad but a frown had appeared on Richmodis's face. Her smile had gone and she was looking at him as if considering various ways of reacting to what he had just said. Her gaze wandered up and down the street. One of the neighbors who was outside filling his tub glanced across at them, then quickly looked away.

"Just can't wait to ask each other what Goddert von Weiden's daughter's doing talking to a half-naked redhead," she snorted contemptuously. "And at the first opportunity they'll tell my father."

"I get the message," said Jacob. "You've done more than enough. I'm going now."

"You'll do nothing of the kind," she snapped. "You don't need to worry about my father. Wait there."

Before Jacob could reply she had gone into the house.

So he waited.

Now that he was by himself, more people stared at him, mixing unashamed curiosity with open suspicion. Someone pointed at him and Jacob wondered whether it wouldn't be better simply to disappear.

But what would Richmodis think if he just cleared out? How could he even consider it in view of the prettiest crooked nose a woman had ever pointed in his direction? Lost in thought, he fiddled with the cloth.

Immediately the neighbors' expressions turned threatening and he pulled his hands away. Someone drove a flock of geese past and subjected him to a furtive scrutiny.

Jacob started whistling and took the opportunity to have a better look at the von Weidens' house. It was not the most magnificent he had ever seen, that was for sure. Its first floor with its two tiny windows overhung the street, and beneath its steep roof it seemed to be cowering between the adjoining buildings. But it was well cared for, the timbers had recently been painted, and by the door, under the parlor window, was a bush with waxy yellow flowers. Presumably Richmodis's work.

Richmodis. Who had vanished.

He took a deep breath and shifted from one foot to the other. No point in waiting any longer. He might as well—

"Here." Richmodis reappeared in the doorway, almost completely hidden behind a bundle of clothes. "You may as well take these. The coat's old, but better that than giving all the women a fright. "And there"— before Jacob knew what was happening he felt something placed on his head and pulled down over his eyes—"you have a hat. The brim's a bit droopy but it's good enough keep the rain and snow off."

"A bit is putting it mildly," said Jacob, pushing the hat onto the back of his head, at the same time trying not to drop the other things she was loading onto him.

"Stop moaning. Here's a doublet and hose to go with it. My father'll have me put in the stocks! The boots, too. And now clear out before half of Cologne starts telling the other half you're about to ask for my hand."

Jacob had always thought of himself as fairly unflappable, but for the moment he was speechless. "Why are you doing this?" he asked.

A roguish smile crinkled the corners of her eyes. "No one gives me a whistle and gets away with it."

"Oh?"

"Now you're obliged to teach me how to play it, of course."

Jacob suddenly felt he could have embraced the butchers and everyone else who had chased him to the Brook.

"It's a deal. I won't forget."

"I'd advise you not to."

"Do you know what?" he suddenly blurted out, unable to contain himself. "I love your nose."

She flushed deeply. "That's enough of that. Away with you now."

Jacob gave a broad grin, turned on his naked heel, and trotted off.

Richmodis watched him go, her hands on her hips. A good-looking lad, she thought. The temptation to run her hand through his hair had been quite strong. Pity he wouldn't come back. Men like that were a law unto themselves. His red mop wouldn't be seen on the Brook that soon again. It was with mixed feelings that she went back to the stream.

Little did she know how wrong she was.

RHEINGASSE

The old woman was sitting in the shadow. Only the outline of her hands, an oddly bizarre shape in the slanting rays of the afternoon sun, stood out against the black velvet of her dress.

The room where she was sitting was high and spacious. It ran along the northern side of the first floor and had five arcaded windows close to one another overlooking the street. Apart from the magnificent tapestries on the rear and side walls, it was sparsely furnished. Only a massive black table and a few chairs gave it something of a lived-in look. In general it was used for festivities or official gatherings.

On her right sat a man in his late forties drinking wine from a pewter goblet. A younger man was standing beside him, motionless. Matthias, leaning against the door frame, thoughtfully observed a man in his early twenties who was restlessly pacing up and down by the windows before finally stopping in front of the old woman and the man seated next to her.

"Gerhard won't talk," he said.

"I have no doubt he won't talk," said the man with the goblet after a pause during which only the rasp of the old woman's breathing was to be heard. "The only question is: for how long?"

Matthias pushed himself away from the door frame and slowly walked into the middle of the room. "Kuno, we all know the architect is your friend. I'm as convinced as you are that Gerhard will not betray us. He has more honor in his little finger than is in the fat bodies of all the priests of Cologne put together." He stopped in front of the younger man and looked him straight in the eye. "But what I believe won't necessarily correspond to the facts. We have everything to gain, but also everything to lose."

"It'll all be over in a few days anyway," said Kuno imploringly. "Until then Gerhard won't do anything to harm us."

"And afterward?" The other young man stepped forward, his fist clenched in fury. "What's the use of all our precautions if we end up celebrating the success of our scheme broken on the wheel with the crows gorging themselves on our eyes? On yours, too, Kuno! They'll peck out those dreamy eyes of yours that look at the world with all the sharpness of a newborn baby."

The older man raised his hand. "That's enough, Daniel."

"Enough?!" Daniel's fist crashed down on the table. "While this sentimental fool is exposing us to ruin?"

"I said that's enough!"

Matthias stepped in. "Your father's right, Daniel. Arguing among ourselves is not going to help our cause. It's bad enough having an ass like Heinrich in our ranks."

"That was unavoidable," muttered Daniel.

"Sometimes even idiots have their uses," Matthias admitted, "and his money's a handy ally. As you see, I accept inevitable risks. However"—he placed his index finger to his lips as was his habit when he wasn't a hundred percent certain of something—"we must be sure we can trust Gerhard."

"We are," said Kuno softly.

"Like piss, we are!" Daniel screamed.

"Stop this!" The older man leaped up and slammed his goblet down on the table. "Use your brains instead of blurting out the first thing that comes into your head. Where's the problem? We discussed a matter of common interest and Gerhard, a highly respected citizen and dear friend whose opinion we all value, decided not to join us. As was his right, I say. We should have taken that into account before indulging in such careless talk. If there's a problem, it's of our own making."

"But we're not talking of who's to blame," said Daniel.

"No? Well, anyway, it's happened and Kuno here is ready to vouch for his friend's discretion."

"That's just what he can't do," Daniel exclaimed. "Gerhard made it quite clear what he thought of our plan."

"He rejected our offer to join the group. So what? That doesn't necessarily mean he's going to betray us."

Daniel glowered but said nothing.

"True, Johann," said Matthias. "But it doesn't mean we have a guarantee, either. What do you suggest?"

"We must talk to Gerhard again. Assure ourselves of his loyalty. From what I know of him, I'm sure we'll all be able to sleep soundly after that." Johann looked at Kuno, who couldn't hide his relief. "I think it's in the interest of our young friend here, too."

"Thank you," whispered Kuno. "I'm sure you won't regret it."

Johann inclined his head. "And you can tell your brothers they needn't worry."

Kuno hesitated, then gave a curt nod and left the room.

For some time Johann, Matthias, Daniel, and the woman in the shadows remained in silence. From outside came the scrunch of the wheels of a passing cart, the faint sound of voices, scraps of conversation. A crowd of children ran past, arguing noisily.

Finally Johann said, in an expressionless tone, "What shall we do, Mother?"

Her voice was no more than a rustle of dry leaves.

"Kill him."

THE GREAT WALL

On the way back to the place he called his home, Jacob suddenly decided to visit Tilman, a friend who lived in a somewhat less salubrious neighborhood.

To call where either of them lived a "neighborhood" was a joke. During the last few years, however, a bizarre hierarchy had developed among the poorest of the poor, who didn't even have a place in one of the hospices or convents, and the *status muri*, the "privilege of the Wall," was part of it.

The origin of this privilege went back to the end of the previous century and the conflict between the emperor Frederick Barbarossa and Pope

Alexander III, in which the archbishop of Cologne was involved—on the emperor's side. As far as the peasants were concerned, it made no difference whose army happened to be passing through. Their womenfolk were raped, their children murdered, and they themselves held over a fire until they revealed where they had hidden what few valuables they possessed. Their farms were burned down, their stores requisitioned or consumed on the spot, and, since it was clear to the soldiers that a farmer couldn't survive without his farm, they saved him from starvation by hanging him from the nearest tree.

Nothing for people to get worked up about.

Philip von Heinsberg, the then archbishop of Cologne, joined in the pillaging and plundering with a will and was not above razing the occasional monastery to the ground and massacring the monks. Perhaps surprisingly, this did not stop the pope, when he finally made peace with Barbarossa, from confirming him in his office of archbishop. The only loser in the whole affair, apart from the poor peasants, appeared to be the duke of Saxony, Henry the Lion.

Things started to get critical for Cologne only when the archbishop, having decided to extend his territory at Henry the Lion's expense, made the mistake of squabbling with his allies and found himself facing an angry Lion with only his Cologne foot soldiers. He was forced to retreat, and the ugly mood of his troops threatened to bring disaster down on them all. The Cologne warriors slew everyone and everything that came within range, thus considerably increasing the chances of hostilities spreading to the city's own territory. And if that happened, as everybody was aware, the first to be killed would be those who had nothing to do with this obscenity of a war.

Now they were landed with it.

So far the city council had supported their archbishop, but this was too much. In his absence they started to build new fortifications, which, legally, was the right of the emperor or the archbishop alone. The result was the inevitable bust-up. Philip was furious, forbade the wall, was ignored, appealed to Barbarossa, and in the end was bought off with a payment of two thousand marks. There was nothing to stop the good citizens from building their wall.

Now, in the year of our Lord 1260 and a good eighty years later, it had finally been declared completed. Five miles long, with twelve massive gate towers and fifty-two turrets, it literally dwarfed all other town walls. As well as the city proper, it also enclosed farms and monasteries, productive orchards and vineyards, which until then had lain unprotected outside the city gates, making Cologne an almost self-sufficient world.

For the citizens the great wall was a symbol of their independence and bolstered their self-confidence, much to the disgust of the present archbishop, Conrad von Hochstaden.

For Jacob it was a blessing.

He knew nothing about politics, nor did he want to. However, the men who designed the wall had included an architectural feature of which he and others like him had made good use. At regular intervals along the inside there were arches that were deep and high enough to provide shelter from the worst of the weather and the seasons. Eventually someone had the idea of making a lean-to shack out of planks, branches, and rags, and others followed suit. One of these was an old day-laborer called Richolf Wisterich who managed to keep body and soul together by working in the tread wheel for the hoists on the cathedral building site. When Jacob came back to Cologne a few months previously he had made friends with the old man and, when he died, inherited his shack. Thus he possessed what soon became mockingly referred to as *status muri*, the privilege of a roof—of a kind—over his tousled head.

In contrast to Jacob, who had virtually nothing, Tilman had nothing at all. He usually slept at the Duck Ponds, a miserable patch of ground at the back of a section of old wall left over from the tenth century. It had no arches to shelter under. The moat had more or less filled in and consisted of a series of putrid, stagnant pools where ducks dabbled. Beyond it willows and poplars rose out of the mud, and then began the extensive gardens of the monasteries and convents. The stench was awful. Tilman used to say living there was probably worse than dying out in the open fields, underlining his opinion with a barking cough that sounded as if he was unlikely to be around to reflect on such matters much longer.

When Jacob eventually found him he was sitting with his back to the wall at the Ponds, staring at the sky. His scrawny body was clothed in a long, tattered shirt and his feet wrapped in rags. He could have been an imposing figure of a man, but he was skinny as a rake.

Jacob sat down beside him. For a while they both observed the clouds slowly sailing past.

A dark bank assembled on the horizon.

Tilman coughed and turned toward Jacob, inspecting him from top to toe with his reddened eyes. "Suits you," he said.

Jacob examined himself. In the clothes of his unwitting benefactor he looked more like a simple tradesman than a beggar, if you ignored the monstrosity of a hat. Remembering his bath in the Duffes Brook, he had to laugh.

"I was on the Brook," he said.

"Really?" Tilman gave a weak grin. "Perhaps I should go on the Brook, too."

"Don't you dare! Or, yes, dare if you like. A man needs certain qualities to be given presents like these, if you get my meaning."

"Oh, I do. What's she called?"

"Richmodis," said Jacob proudly. Only respectable girls were called Richmodis.

"What does she do?"

"Her father's a dyer, though she's the one who does the dyeing." Jacob shook his head. "A piece of advice, Tilman. Keep your hands away from the butchers' stalls. There's a curse on all hams and sausages."

"They caught you," said Tilman, not particularly surprised.

"They chased me all around Haymarket. I escaped along the Brook. *Into* the Brook."

"And Goodwife Richmodis fished you out?"

"She's not a goodwife."

"What then?"

"A divine creature."

"Good Lord!"

Jacob pictured her with her crooked nose and her buxom figure under her modest dress. "And she's still available," he added, as if he were announcing his engagement.

"Don't fool yourself, Jacob."

"And why not, I ask?"

Tilman leaned forward. "If I can give *you* a piece of advice, keep away from Haymarket as well as the Brook and stuff your belly somewhere else in future. They can recognize that mop from here to Aachen."

"You're just jealous. I had to pay for these clothes."

"How much?"

"A lot."

"Stop bragging. What have you got to pay with anyway?"

"Had. Three carrots and a beef sausage."

Tilman sighed. "That is a lot."

"Yes. And I almost got torn to pieces for it." Jacob stretched and gave an immense yawn. "Anyway, how's the world been treating you?"

"Very badly. I sat outside St. Mary's Garden, but there were pilgrims there and they took all the pickings, God blast their eyes. The place was teeming with beggars from outside and tricksters faking deformities so that even the most softhearted put their purses away. What can a man do? There were others running around the town with rattles, collecting for the leper colony at Melaten. I left. I don't want to catch leprosy and have my hand drop off when I hold it out for alms."

"Quite right. Had anything to eat?"

"Well, naturally I was invited to the burgomaster's. There were roast pears, wild boar, stuffed pigeons—"

"Nothing at all, then."

"Brilliant. Do I look as if I've had anything to eat?"

Jacob shrugged his shoulders. "Just asking."

"But I'm going to get a drink," Tilman crowed. "Tonight in the Hen."

"The inn?" Jacob asked skeptically.

"The very place."

"Since when have you had money to drink at the inn?"

"I haven't, have I? Otherwise I'd have spent it on food. But someone I know has. Don't ask where he got it, I don't want to know. But he wants to get rid of it. Says you can't drink money, so he's invited me and a couple of others to wet our whistles."

"The man must have gone soft in the head. When?"

"Six o'clock. Why don't you just come along? He'll treat you, too."

It was an attractive idea.

"Don't know," Jacob said, nevertheless. "I must get something solid down me first."

"Aha! You've not eaten either?"

"Not a scrap's passed my lips."

"Why do you have to go for sausages? Why didn't you pay Old Market Square a visit and persuade a few apples to jump into your pocket?"

"Why?" Jacob took a deep breath. "Because I had apples yesterday. Because I had apples the day before yesterday. Because I had apples before that. And before that. Because I'm starting to feel like an apple maggot."

"You're too choosy."

"Oh, thanks very much."

Once more they were silent for a while. The clouds were gathering. The afternoon was making its weary way toward evening.

"Not a bite to eat then." Tilman's summary was matter-of-fact. "As usual."

He coughed.

It was the cough that did it. So casual and so terminal. Jacob jumped up and clenched his fists. "All right, you've persuaded me. Apples it is."

Tilman gave him a long look. Then he smiled. "Apples it is."

MATTHIAS

Matthias had strolled along the Rhine embankment, watching pepper, spices, and barrels of herring being unloaded from Dutch ships, past the Franks Tower and along the Old Bank before turning into Dranckgasse. This ran along the old Roman wall, part of which had been demolished to make way for the new cathedral. On the left in front of him the chapels surrounding the apse towered up into the sky and his heart was filled with misgivings.

He knew Gerhard's plans. This—provided it was ever completed— would be the perfect church, the Holy City here on earth. The plans for the facade alone, with its two mountainous towers, had covered almost fifteen feet of parchment. Matthias had asked Gerhard whether he had forgotten he wouldn't live forever.

Gerhard had patiently tried to explain that having a chancel with five aisles gave him no choice but to set out the whole massive church in one single design, following the precedent of Paris and Bourges. Even if he didn't fully understand, Matthias took the architect at his word. His journeyman years had taken him to the scaffolding of Troyes and the new churches in Paris, including the much-praised Sainte Chapelle rising up in the courtyard of the Palace of Justice. By the time the choir of Amiens cathedral was being built his opinion was valued more highly than that of many a French colleague. Pierre de Montereau, the builder of the abbey church of Saint-Denis, had been his teacher and he was in constant contact with Jean de Chelles, who was supervising the construction of Notre Dame.

Oh, yes, Gerhard Morart had been through a good school, the very best, and above all he had managed to bring together a team of master craftsmen who were familiar with the new style.

For one brief moment he wished he could turn around and forget everything, but it was too late for that now. It had already been too late when the group met for the first time.

He cast his doubts aside and felt his usual calm return. His stoicism was his great virtue. Neither Johann nor Daniel was sufficiently pragmatic to carry their plan through in a businesslike manner. They were liable to outbursts of rage, pangs of conscience, and indecisiveness. The only one he felt at all close to was the old woman. Not emotionally close—God forbid!—but close in their attitude to life.

The bell of St. Mary's-by-the-Steps beyond the cathedral building site struck five.

He quickened his pace, left the chancel of the new cathedral and the old Roman wall behind him, turned right opposite Priest Gate into Marzellenstraße and, after a few hundred yards, left up the lane to the Ursulines' convent.

There was hardly anyone about. The convent grounds were surrounded by a twelve-foot-high wall and had only one narrow entrance, which was usually left open. Matthias went through the low arch into the long court-yard. The rather modest but pretty convent church on the right with its one spire corresponded more to Matthias's own conception of what a church should be like. He knew that, as a person who relied on cold reason, he lacked the imagination to visualize the new cathedral in its completed state. It was a blind spot he at times regretted. At others, however, he saw the titanic enterprise as a symbol of his own ambitions. He would marvel at the way one stone fitted in with the next, obedient to the almost magic power of ruler, square, and plumb line, and watch how the windlasses allowed human muscle to raise a block of Drachenfels stone weighing tons high into the air for the masons to set it precisely edge-to-edge with its neighbor. The cathedral seemed to grow like a living organism, filling him with a sense of his own power and pride at what the future would bring.

Then the image of the old woman suddenly reappeared in his mind, replacing the cathedral with the vision of a gigantic ruin.

He leaned back against the wall, staring at the empty courtyard. Opposite the spire was a well. After some time two nuns came out of the convent building to draw water. They gave him a cursory glance.

If the man he had come to meet did not turn up soon he would have to go. A waste of time.

He swore to himself.

"*Fiat lux*," said Urquhart.

Matthias gave a violent start and scanned the courtyard. No one.

"Up here."

His eye slowly traveled up the wall. Urquhart was sitting on the top, directly above, smiling down at him.

"What the devil are you doing up there?"

"Waiting for you," Urquhart replied with his habitual mixture of politeness and gentle mockery.

"And I for you," Matthias replied sharply. "Perhaps you would have the goodness to come down."

"Why?" Urquhart laughed. "You can come and join me up here, if you like."

Matthias's face was expressionless. "You know very well—" He stopped as he suddenly registered the height of the wall. "How on earth did you manage to get up there?"

"I jumped."

Matthias started to say something, but the words stuck in his throat. What was there to say? No man could jump twelve feet.

"Do you think we could talk?" he asked instead.

"Of course." With a supple twist of his body Urquhart swiveled around and landed on his toes beside Matthias. He had put up his long blond hair in a kind of helmet shape, making him seem taller than ever.

"We'd better wait till those women have gone," Matthias growled. He was irritated that Urquhart had kept him waiting longer than necessary.

His companion raised his eyebrows in surprise. "How complicated you make things! Isn't openness the best disguise? If we were to behave like thieves, keep looking around shiftily and muttering in low voices, then we would deserve to end up in—what do you call that funny tower? Oh, yes, in the Weckschnapp. Just behave naturally. Let us show some courtesy toward the venerable servants of the living God."

He turned to the nuns and gave them a gallant bow. "It's going to rain," he called out. "Better get back inside."

The younger of the two beamed at him. "Rain is also a gift from God," she replied.

"Do you still think that when you're lying alone in your cell and it's hammering against the walls as if the Prince of Darkness himself were demanding entrance?" He wagged his finger at her playfully. "Be on your guard, my little flower."

"Of course," she stammered, gaping at Urquhart as if he were every reason to leave the convent made all-too-solid flesh. Then she hurriedly lowered her gaze and blushed. Fifteen at the most, Matthias guessed.

Her companion shot her a sideways glance and hastily crossed herself. "Come," she commanded. "Quickly!"

She turned on her heel and marched back to the convent with all the grace of a draught horse. The younger one hurried after, looking back over her shoulder several times. Urquhart gave her an even lower bow, combined with a mocking scrutiny from beneath his bushy brows. He seemed to find the whole business amusing.

They were alone in the courtyard.

"That got rid of them," Urquhart stated complacently.

"Is that one of your tactics?" Matthias's voice had a frosty note.

Urquhart nodded. "In a way. Openness is the best concealment, the best way not to be remembered is to make yourself obvious. Neither of them will be able to describe us, not even me. Had we turned away they would have wondered why we didn't salute them and would have had a good look at our faces, our clothes, our posture."

"As far as I'm concerned, I have no reason to hide from anyone."

"But then you're a respectable citizen."

"And I don't want to be seen together with you," Matthias went on, unmoved. "Our next meeting better be somewhere more secluded."

"You suggested we meet here."

"I realize that. Now stop turning the heads of harmless nuns and tell me how you mean to go about your assignment."

Urquhart put his lips to Matthias's ear and spoke quietly to him for a while. The latter's face brightened visibly with every word.

"And the witnesses?" he asked.

"Found and paid."

A smile appeared on Matthias's lips, the first in a long time. "Then I give your plan my blessing."

Urquhart bowed his blond head. "If it is the will of the terrible God."

Matthias frowned and tried to remember where he had heard the expression before, the Old Testament God of vengeance who is terrible to the kings of the earth.

He felt the excruciatingly slow drip of a bead of sweat running down his forehead. Disconcerted, he looked at Urquhart's eyes. Were they really a dead man's eyes, as Heinrich had whispered? At that moment the other gave him an amused wink and Matthias felt a fool. Urquhart was playing with words like a jester. The living were alive, the dead were dead.

"We shouldn't meet at the same place twice. Understood?" he said icily. "Tomorrow at seven o'clock at Greyfriars church."

"As you wish."

"Don't disappoint me." Matthias walked off without a further word and hurried back the way he had come. Just to make it clear who was in charge.

It was only when he was back in Dranckgasse that he was suddenly overcome with the humiliating feeling that he had actually been running away from Urquhart.

THE CATHEDRAL

It was a crazy idea, of course.

But Jacob had set his mind on getting hold of the most noble apples in the whole of Cologne and they happened to belong to Conrad von Hochstaden, lord archbishop of Cologne, who had commanded an army in the service of the emperor and also crowned the anti-king, Henry of Holland. A powerful gentleman and not one to be trifled with.

Getting at these apples necessitated a visit to the archbishop's orchard, which was combined with his zoo. It lay between Conrad's palace and the rising walls of the cathedral choir, or, to be more precise, somewhat behind them. Naturally it had a wall around it and locked gates. Fantastic stories about the animals could be heard in Cologne, for example that the archbishop kept lions and a legendary beast called *elephantus* with a diabolically long nose and legs like tree trunks. In fact, most of the animals lurking among the laden fruit trees were peacocks and pheasants, which were not only a fine sight, but also a fine adornment on the archbishop's table. And that, apart from a dozen squirrels, was that.

The only way into Conrad's private Garden of Eden was over the wall, and the only place where it was worth risking was Große Sparergasse. A misnomer, really. There was nothing "great" about the narrow alleyway, which was little more than a wormhole between the cathedral building site and the orchard. There were walls on either side, too high to climb without a ladder.

But no obstacle to Jacob the Fox.

At this point a few massive, ancient apple trees stretched out from the orchard across the alley and over the building site on the other side. The higher branches pointed straight at the cathedral, but lower, gnarled arms twisted down low enough over the alley for him to be able to grab on to them with both hands and pull himself up.

So he didn't actually need to go into the orchard itself. On the other hand, nature had so arranged things that only an excellent climber could get at the apples. People kept on trying, but most of them ended up dangling from the branches like bats, unable to get their footing before the constables or the archbishop's thugs came to pick them off. But despite the fact that this kept the loss of apples within limits, Conrad had recently announced severe punishments for anyone caught stealing them in the future. Since then the number of thefts had dropped to nil.

Jacob intended to change that.

He stood underneath the branches and waited. By now it was after seven; the sun was just going down. Although heavy rain clouds were approaching inexorably, the setting sun still left enough light in the sky. A gusty wind sprang up. The laborers and craftsmen on the cathedral stopped working and went home. There was no point in continuing once it started to get dark; they only made mistakes and would have to do it all over again the next day.

Suddenly, from one moment to the next, the alley was deserted.

Jacob tensed his muscles, flexed his knees, and pushed off. His hands grasped the lowest branch. Without pausing, he pulled his body up smoothly, did a straddle with his legs and slipped up into the foliage.

It was the work of a moment. And no one had seen him. He clutched the branch above him and swung up onto it. Now he was completely invisible.

But Jacob could see all the better, and what he saw set his heart beating. Nature's bounty was spread out before him. There was nothing in the world to match these apples. Greedily he grabbed one, his teeth tore through the firm green skin, slicing the apple in two. The juice ran down his chin. The apple disappeared, a second followed, and a few moments later all that was left of the third was the stem.

Jacob gave a loud burp. He looked down through the leaves in alarm.

No danger.

He was going to have a terrible stomachache, that he knew. There was nothing for his belly to work on but the acid fruit. But a stomachache would pass. Now that he had stilled the more immediate pangs of hunger, he could set about filling his new and, fortunately, wide coat with further spoils. He thought of Tilman, and of Maria, the woman who sometimes gave him a roof over his head when the winter was too harsh—and her professional commitments permitted. Taking his own needs into consideration as well, he came, after some laborious counting on his fingers, to the figure of thirty.

No time to lose.

First of all he picked the best fruits he could reach from where he was. But he still had nothing like enough when all that was left were smaller, inferior specimens. Cautiously he shuffled along the branch. Now he was right over the middle of the alley. He held on tight with his left hand, while his right was busy among the branches. You could have fed whole families on the fruit growing there.

The most beautiful apples were luring him farther toward the end of the branch. For a brief moment he considered making do with what he had. But given that he was in the archbishop's apple trees, he saw no reason to accept less than Conrad himself.

He screwed up his eyes and crept forward a bit. The branch was getting visibly thinner; now it was jutting out over the cathedral building site. Through the foliage he could see the chancel corseted in scaffolding. There was no one there. In the morning, at cockcrow, the whole area would resound with bustle and hammering, shouts and rumblings, but now it was wrapped in a strange peace.

For a moment Jacob was amazed at how close the horseshoe of soaring windows and pillars seemed to be. Or were his eyes playing tricks on him? Was it just the huge proportions that gave the work a physical presence, as if he could touch it with his hand? And they said it was going to be even bigger? More than twice as high, even without the towers. He could scarcely imagine it.

Nor was it important. He turned back to the apples. A cathedral did nothing for an empty stomach.

At the very moment his fingers were closing around a particularly fine apple, a figure appeared high up on the scaffolding. Jacob jerked back and pressed against the rough bark. Time to be going. But that would be a waste. Better to sit still for a while. In the shadow of the leaves he could see everything without being seen. His eyes followed the man as he made his way along the planks. Even at this distance he could see that he was expensively dressed. His coat had a trimming of rich fur. He held himself erect, like a man who was used to giving orders. At times he shook the scaffolding poles, as if to make sure they were well fixed. At others he placed his hand on the balustrade and just looked down.

Even though Jacob was just an idle good-for-nothing, he knew who the man inspecting the building was. Everyone knew the architect. There was a story doing the rounds that Gerhard Morart had called up the Devil to produce his plans. A stonemason by profession, his appointment had made him one of the most respected and influential burghers. The cathedral chapter had granted him a piece of land on which he had built himself a magnificent stone house in the style of the old established families, the so-called noble houses. He moved in patrician circles, with the Overstolzes, the von Mainzes, the Kones. His advice was sought, his work admired, and at the same time feared, as he was himself. Gerhard was already a legendary figure, and there were those who thought he would, with the help of the Arch-fiend, manage to complete the impossible before his death, at which he would plunge from the topmost spire straight down to hell. Accompanied by that vain and pompous archbishop.

To Jacob, though, the cathedral still seemed more the result of hard labor than of a satanic pact.

In the meantime Gerhard Morart had climbed to the highest level of the scaffolding. His massive silhouette stood out black against what was left of the daylight. The wind tugged fiercely at his coat. Jacob felt the first raindrops splash on his face and shivered. Gerhard could spend the whole night up there, if he wanted. It was time for a few more apples and a quick getaway.

Just then someone else appeared on the scaffolding. He seemed to Jacob to come from nowhere. The second figure was much taller than Gerhard. It materialized so close behind him that for a moment the two shapes seemed to merge.

Then a scream rang out, and Jacob saw Gerhard plummet down, past his scaffolding, pillars, and capitals, past his buttresses and piscinas, his pediments and recesses. His arms were flailing; for one terrible moment it looked as if he were waving to Jacob in his apple tree. Then there was a dull thud as the body hit the ground, rose up, as if grabbed by a giant fist, then came to rest on its back.

Jacob stared at the motionless figure. It was impossible that the architect had survived the fall. Hastily he started to push himself back, but he had gone only a couple of feet when, with a loud crack, the branch gave way. Like a witch on a broomstick, he flew down on the rotten branch and landed with a loud crash in a tangle of leaves and scraps of bark. He kicked his legs to free himself, desperately gasping for breath.

Sweet Jesus! He'd fallen into the cathedral site.

Still panting, he got to his feet. His hat had been pulled off. He stuck the shapeless clump back on his head and looked around wildly.

Out of here, said a voice in his head. Out of here while there's still time. It was the same voice that had warned him in the marketplace that morning.

Out of here!

He caught sight of Gerhard. The twisted body was no more than fifty paces from him. Could that have been a groan he'd heard?

He had another look.

Gerhard's dead, said the voice.

Jacob clenched his fists as the sweat broke out all over his body. There was still time to slip away unnoticed.

Then he saw the movement. Gerhard's arm had twitched. Just slightly, but there was no doubt he was still alive.

A memory surfaced. He pushed it back down.

Get away, Fox!

"Will you never learn, blockhead?" Jacob muttered to himself as he scampered over to the cathedral. The rain, heavier now, was falling into his eyes. He knelt down beside the body.

Gerhard was looking up with a glassy stare. The rain was running over his face and through his thinning hair. His fur-trimmed cap was on the ground beside him. He certainly didn't look like a man who had made a pact with the Devil. It was a gentle, noble-looking face. Or, rather, had been. Now all it showed was the trauma of approaching death.

His chest rose convulsively. His lips quivered.

Jacob brushed the wet hair out of Gerhard's face and bent over him. Gerhard seemed aware of his presence. With an immense effort he turned his head and looked at him. Again his lips moved.

Had he said something?

Voices and steps could be heard from the other side of the cathedral, probably people who had heard the scream. Jacob hesitated, then placed his ear close to Gerhard's lips and closed his eyes.

It was three words.

Without thinking, Jacob grasped his hand and squeezed it.

A trickle of blood came out of Gerhard's mouth.

He was dead.

For Christ's sake, get out of here, the voice urged.

Jacob could hear strange scraping noises above him. He leaped up. Something was coming down the scaffolding. He bent his head back and looked up.

He caught his breath.

The tall black shadow was coming closer, story by story. But it was not climbing down, it was jumping with uncanny speed, springing across the planks as nimbly as an animal, its hair streaming out behind like a comet's tail.

It had almost reached him.

Whoever or whatever it was that was coming, Jacob felt no desire to make its closer acquaintance. He turned on his heel and ran as fast as he could. People were approaching across the cathedral close, shouting and gesticulating. Jacob darted sideways, slipped into the shadow of a workman's shed, and managed to join the crowd from behind. Everybody was talking at once. Someone shouted out the news and already others were carrying it out of the cathedral and into the streets.

No one had seen him. Apart from the shadow.

Oddly enough, it was the apples that came to mind at that moment. He patted his pockets. Some were still there, they'd not all come out when he'd fallen down. Good. He'd saved more than just his skin.

As unobtrusively as possible, he strolled across the close and out by Dragon Gate. He turned around once, but there was no sign of the shadowy being on the scaffold.

Somewhat relieved, he quickened his pace and set off along Bechergasse.

THE SHADOW

Urquhart followed him at a distance. He had pulled his cloak up to cover his hair and, despite his height, was merely a phantom among the busy crush of people, as black and inconspicuous as the night that was falling.

It would have been easy to kill the fellow on the building site. Urquhart knew he had observed the murder. But Gerhard's death was supposed to look like an accident. The shattered body of the architect, and beside it another with a crossbow-bolt in his chest—that wasn't the idea. Nevertheless, he had to dispose of the annoying witness who had so unexpectedly tumbled out of the tree quickly and well away from the cathedral, someplace where there were not many people around. The crossbow under his cloak was ready, but in the crowded market area there was no opportunity for a shot. The head of the fellow kept disappearing among people going home or to vespers, as he hurried on his way out of the city.

What had Gerhard whispered to him? Had he said anything at all or had the only thing to pass his lips before he died been blood? But if he had spoken, then that fellow was carrying a secret, and it was hardly to be expected he would keep it to himself.

He could spoil everything.

Urquhart lengthened his stride while his mind was working out what he knew about his quarry. Observations combined like glass tiles in a colorful mosaic. The man had red hair. When he fell out of the tree his hat had been pulled off. Urquhart had seen his red mane blaze up in the evening sun before he ran over to Gerhard. And he seemed to be in good physical condition. A fast runner. He had to be. Anyone clambering around in the archbishop's orchard at that time of night must be a thief and thieves could either run like the wind or were dangling from the gallows. A clever thief, too. The way he had blended with the crowd suggested an alert mind, as did the fact that he had immediately made for the busiest streets, where it was difficult for someone to follow him.

Though not for Urquhart the Shadow.

There were still too many people in the streets. For the moment all he could do was keep the redhead under observation. With any luck he would have some stolen goods in his coat and would make for his hiding place, perhaps the place where he slept. They were usually quiet places. Thieves kept away from other people.

Unless he had a bed in a monastery. It wasn't easy to get into the friaries and hospices. To follow him there might pose a problem.

There was no time to lose.

Urquhart slipped his hand under his cloak and grasped his crossbow. They were in Minoritenstraße; the Franciscan monastery was there on the right.

And, suddenly, almost all the people seemed to disappear into some house or other. The odd figures still out were hurrying over the slippery ground, heads down against the rain. Then, for a brief second, the street was empty except for the witness hurrying along in his floppy hat. The witness who had seen too much and heard too much.

Urquhart raised his arm.

And quickly lowered it. Too late.

Four men, all of them pretty down-at-heel, had come out of a low tavern opposite the monastery. One greeted the redhead noisily. The others gathered around the two and all Urquhart could see was shoulders and backs.

He crept along in the shadow of the wall of Greyfriars church until he was close enough to hear. Then he waited.

Tilman!" cried Jacob. It was his friend from the Duck Ponds staggering out of the tavern. Jacob was delighted. He had headed for the Hen in the hope of finding Tilman there before the source dried up.

And he needed someone to talk to. He hadn't got over the fright yet.

Tilman grinned. He didn't look any better than he had two hours ago, but there was a feverish gleam in his eyes. The drink was having its effect.

The others were beggars, too. Jacob only knew them by sight. Apart from one, who shared the "privilege of the Wall" with him, an unpleasant tub of lard, with whom he'd exchanged insults now and then. Nothing to get worked up about. They understood each other, that was all. Or, to put it another way, so far neither had smashed the other's skull in for a few scraps of food. Not that there weren't enough smashed skulls around. The fat man had a propensity to violence when there was something to be gotten out of it. The word was, he was getting careless. Jacob gave him six months before his head dropped in the executioner's basket.

The Hen was one of the few ale houses that didn't throw people out just because they were dressed in rags. The landlord was tolerant of the poor, as long as they could pay. Many beggars lived honest, God-fearing—and correspondingly short—lives, and there was no reason why they should not enjoy the blessings of the Cologne brewer's art.

With time, however, the clientele had sunk so low that respectable people no longer went there. The landlord had to put up with local hostility, especially from the Greyfriars, whose monastery was directly opposite. As well as that, the town whores complained it operated as an unofficial brothel for part-time prostitutes, ostensibly respectable ladies who sold themselves, secretly of course, to wealthy gentlemen. Thus they took business away from the licensed whores, which annoyed the town executioner, under whose jurisdiction they were placed and to whom they paid dues.

There had been repeated threats against the Hen, and the landlord had grown cautious. Only recently a brewer in Cleves had been accused of sorcery and burned at the stake. The night that happened, the venerable Franciscan brethren had written the word "Cleves" in pitch on the door; the merchant families in the imposing neighboring houses, at the sign of the Large and the Small Water-Butt, wondered out loud about a denunciation to the Holy Inquisition because their children had seen black cats running out of the Hen while inside two demons, Abigor and Asmodeus, in the form of lecherous women had shouted obscenities and given off sulfurous odors. Jacob wondered how the children knew it was precisely those two demons when there must be at least—how many was it?—at least ten demons, but the Hen had its problems.

And for that, Jacob was told by tub of lard, they'd simply been thrown out.

"Nonsense," whispered Tilman. "The money was finished. You're too late."

"Thrown out!" bellowed the fat man, who had heard and was obviously the one who had been standing the treat.

Tilman coughed his lungs out.

"Doesn't matter," he panted. "Back to the Duck Ponds then."

"Yes, lie down and die." One of the others laughed, slapping him on the shoulder. It wasn't a pleasant laugh.

Jacob felt a wave of disappointment. Why did it have to happen to him? The chance of drinking something other than foul water didn't come his way that often.

Then he remembered the apples and Maria.

"Come on," he said, grabbing Tilman by the arm. The beggars disappeared in the opposite direction, cursing because the money hadn't been sufficient to get properly drunk.

"Did you get any apples?" asked Tilman, out of breath.

"Here." Jacob pulled one out. Tilman bit into it as if it were the first thing his teeth had had to bite on all day. Perhaps it was.

Behind them a late cart rumbled across the street.

"Where are we going, anyway?" Tilman wanted to know. The last syllables turned into a new fit of coughing.

"To Maria."

"See you tomorrow." Tilman tried to pull away, but Jacob kept his arm in a tight grip and continued along the street.

"You're going nowhere. For one thing there's an incredible story I want to tell you and Maria."

"You and your stories. Was there ever one that was true?"

"For another, you're not well. If you don't get a dry bed tonight you soon won't be needing any more apples."

"You know Maria can't stand me," whined Tilman as he scurried along beside Jacob.

"I know she's fed up with giving shelter to all and sundry, but you're my friend. And who isn't to say whether, tonight of all nights, thanks to a happy coincidence—"

"You can forget your happy coincidences."

"You're coming!"

"All right, all right."

The oxcart rattled out of the side street and blocked Urquhart's view. When the redhead and his companion reappeared they were a good way ahead. A few Greyfriars were returning to the monastery from New Market Square, pulling a cartload of thin boards. Urquhart let them pass, then hurried on after the two, but now other people were coming into the street.

He would have to be patient.

Urquhart thought it over. The meeting with the gang of beggars had been too brief for the redhead to have told them anything. The one who was going with him was quite another matter though. Every moment the risk of Gerhard Morart's last words being passed on grew greater.

Of course, it was possible he had not said anything, just groaned and given up the ghost. It was possible, but Urquhart felt it was safer to assume the opposite.

After a few minutes the pair turned off to the right into Berlich, a seedy, sparsely populated district, best known for its pig breeders—which explained the stench. But there were others who went about their business there.

Were they going to the whores?

Urquhart stole along in the shadow of the dilapidated houses. In front he heard someone softly call out, "Maria." A door opened a crack and the two slipped inside.

They had managed to escape.

For the moment.

He briefly considered following them in and settling the matter there and then, but decided against it. He had no idea how many people there were in the building. It was a small house, clearly a brothel. There might be a brothel keeper. Someone staggered out and waddled along toward him. Not one of the men he'd been following. Well dressed and too drunk to notice him. Clearly a merchant. Mumbling to himself, he disappeared behind some pigsties.

Urquhart watched him go, then turned his attention back to the house. A light appeared in a first-floor window and the shutters closed with a crash.

They had to come out again. Eventually.

Urquhart melted into the darkness. He could wait.

BERLICH

It was a whorehouse. The keeper, Clemens Brabanter, was a burly, good-natured fellow. He charged his customers, as a cover charge, so to speak, for four pints of wine, of which only three appeared on the table. A peat fire smoked out the cheap taproom that took in the whole of the ground floor, a grubby curtain dividing off the place where Clemens slept. Fatty, gristly meat was grilled over the fire, usually burned black, unless one of the guests brought a better-quality joint. Then Clemens would sit himself by the fire and keep turning the delicacy. He wanted his guest to enjoy it. The girls only got a taste if the visitor invited them. Since Clemens, as a man of honesty and fairness, did not exempt himself from this rule, the girls respected him, especially as he didn't bother to beat them.

It was similar with the wine. In general Clemens served what in Cologne was known as "wet Ludwig," the product of poor harvests, a sour nothing with neither body nor bouquet that you scarcely tasted but still paid for with excruciating heartburn. On the other hand, there were clients for whom Clemens went down into his cellar to decant a quite different vintage. This lured certain upper-class gentlemen back again and again, and Clemens's most valuable stock, the three women upstairs, were all, apart from one on whom God, for her sins, had bestowed a skinny body and a squint, invitingly plump.

Outside business hours two of the whores, Wilhilde and Margarethe, were married. Their husbands worked as sack holders in the warehouses down by the Rhine. It took four to six of them to hold up the immense sacks while they were being filled with salt. Sack holders earned next to nothing, but then next-to-nothing in the way of skill was demanded of them. They scraped together enough to keep body and soul together; added to their wives' earnings it just about made staying alive worthwhile.

The last of Clemens's threesome was generally considered the most beautiful in the whole of Berlich. Her name was Maria. She was twenty-one, and already had rings under her eyes and a few teeth missing. On the other hand, she had wonderful, silky hair and shining green eyes beneath brows that arched like the Madonna's. Her lips were two rose petals, one of the canons who sneaked away from the cathedral now and then had whispered drunkenly in her ear, her breasts temples of desire, and her womb burned with the fires of purgatory.

Given this, no one was surprised that Maria became prouder and prouder and talked of leaving Berlich at some point to marry a well-situated gentleman with whom she would live a devout and God-fearing life in a neat, solidly built house well away from the stench of pig dung and the grunts and groans from the neighboring rooms.

Her relationship with Jacob suffered accordingly. At first she had been delighted by his every gesture, every little present he brought, indeed, just to see him. Often, when there were no more clients for the night, he had slept in the same bed with her. He brought her any food he could lay his hands on and didn't have to pay, nor to leave afterward. Clemens, whom Jacob never forgot when he was sharing out his spoils, had given his approval, as he had for the husbands of the other two girls. But business came first. If a man in need knocked on the door late at night, Clemens threw the husband out, however much the girl was married.

By now the passion was almost spent. Maria wanted to better herself and there was constant bickering between them, especially since, for some inexplicable reason, Jacob felt responsible for Tilman and was always bringing him along. Sometimes the three of them spent the night together in the tiny bedroom. Tilman did not get a turn with Maria. He couldn't afford her, and Maria would not have shared her bed with him for anything, at least not for anything less than one silver mark. By now the mere mention of Tilman's name made her angry. Jacob knew the relationship was nearing its end.

Perhaps that was why he had insisted on dragging Tilman along with him. If he and Maria were going to argue anyway, it might as well be for a good cause. The way Tilman looked, and with the blood he was coughing up, it would take a miracle to cure him, but at least Jacob didn't want to find him dead at the Duck Ponds one morning, surrounded by crows tearing at his cold, emaciated body.

It was murky in the taproom. Clemens was warming his hands by the fire, over which something indefinable was sizzling. There was a bitter draft coming in through the cracks in the shutters. The brothel keeper was getting more hunched by the day, Jacob thought. Soon he would be a perfect circle and you'd be able to roll him down the street. Margarethe was sitting on the bench by the door and gave them her cross-eyed look. She was always on the lookout for two clients at once, they said, and never saw any at all. Otherwise the room was empty.

"Hi, Jacob," growled Clemens.

Jacob gave Margarethe a quick smile and flopped down on one of the crudely made stools. The bruises from his fall had just started to ache, and they seemed to cover the whole of his body. "Maria in?"

Clemens gave a grim nod. "Can you afford her?"

"There." Jacob took out three apples and put them on the table. Clemens stared, got up from his seat by the fire, and shuffled over. He stroked the smooth skin almost tenderly with his clumsy fingers.

"Where did you get them? You don't get apples like this at the market."

"The Lord has provided, you might say. Can we go up now, Clemens?"

"Well—"

Jacob sighed and took out another apple.

"Of course you can, Jacob." The apples disappeared into a basket. "The client's just gone. You must have seen him."

"Rich?"

"Not poor. But mean. Pays the lowest tariff, so I give him the Ludwig to drink. And he seems to like it, goddammit!"

"And Wilhilde?"

"Customer."

"Good. That smells tasty, too."

"Wouldn't you just like a bit?" snapped Clemens. "It's not for you. Just be glad I don't stuff your lousy apples up your arse."

Jacob was already halfway up the stairs, Tilman in tow.

"I wouldn't say that again," he said, "the archbishop might not like it."

Clemens raised his eyebrows and looked at the contents of the basket.

"Don't you put her in the family way!" he shouted at the retreating Jacob.

Tilman shook his head and followed Jacob. His whole body was quivering with suppressed coughs.

"Could you try not to cough for a while?" Jacob asked.

"Very funny!"

"All right." He opened the door to Maria's room.

She was standing by the window with a grubby sheet around her shoulders, lighting a new candle. Clemens was quite generous with candles. As Jacob and Tilman entered she put the candlestick by her bed, then slammed the shutter.

There was hardly any furniture. A low table, two stools, a crudely made bed full of straw with a matted blanket over it in which, as Jacob well knew, there were at least as many lice as people in Cologne. Under the window was a chest where she kept her belongings. There was a dress in it that a man she liked very much had given her a few months ago. When he came to see her, he mostly just talked. One day he brought the dress, then left and never came back. Maria did not even know his name. But when she wore the dress to church she seemed to Jacob to be just like a respectable woman, and he didn't dare be seen with her. At times like that he felt she would manage to cheat destiny and find a devout and respected husband.

Now the dress was in the chest and the chest was locked. If the great preacher, Berthold of Regensburg, had his way, she would never have worn it again. In a tub-thumping sermon against the evil of fornication, he had demanded that whores should be compelled to wear yellow and ostracized by all good Christians.

There was an empty jug on the table, one beaker on its side. The drunken client had not invited her to share his wine.

"What have you brought?" was her greeting.

Jacob nodded and placed the apples he had left beside the jug.

She smiled and put her arms around him, without drawing him close. Tilman she ignored. The sick man shuddered, sidled over to one of the stools, and sat down as quietly as he could.

"Something odd happened," said Jacob, collapsing onto the bed, which creaked alarmingly.

"And?"

He stared at the ceiling. "The architect who's building the cathedral's dead."

She sat down beside him on the edge of the bed and ran her fingers through his hair, her eyes fixed on the door. Then she looked at him. The rings under her eyes were darker than usual, or perhaps it was just the flickering light from the dim candle that deepened the hollows in her face. She was beautiful, despite it all. Too beautiful for this world.

"Yes," she said softly, "he threw himself to his death."

Jacob levered himself up on his elbows and regarded her thoughtfully. "How do you know?"

She jerked her thumb at the wall. Beyond it was Wilhilde's room.

"The man in her room told her?"

"He arrived just before you, a linen weaver who often goes to Wilhilde. It was the first thing he said. He'd heard it from others who'd seen Gerhard slip and fall. Perhaps the only time in his life"—she shook her head—"and God called him to appear before him for it. How often do we slip and fall? Sometimes I wonder why we're here."

"Just a minute." Jacob sat up. "Which others?"

"What?" said Maria, bewildered.

"You said some others saw Gerhard slip."

"Yes."

"Which others?"

She looked at him as if he were crazy. "Well, the others. People."

"What people?"

"For God's sake, Jacob, what makes it so important?"

Jacob rubbed his eyes. The people . . .

"Maria," he said calmly, "there are people who saw how Gerhard fell to his death through his own carelessness? Is that right?"

"I've already told you."

"No!" Jacob shook his head and jumped up. "That is not right."

"What are you suggesting?" asked Tilman. It made him cough, which produced highly unsavory noises from his insides when he tried to suppress it.

Jacob put his hands to his temples and closed his eyes. In his mind's eye he saw everything again, the shadow, Gerhard's scream, his fall, and his last words, which had burned themselves into his mind.

"That is not right," he repeated. "Gerhard Morart, the cathedral architect, assuming we're talking about the same man, did not die as a result of his own carelessness, he was murdered. And no one saw it but me. There was no one there." He took a deep breath and opened his eyes.

Tilman and Maria were both staring at him.

"I thought I was the one who was drunk, not you," said Tilman.

"Gerhard was killed"—Jacob was getting worked up—"and I was

there. I was sitting in that bloody apple tree when the black thing appeared on the scaffolding and pushed him over."

There was a breathless silence in the room.

"That's what happened, damn it!"

Maria started giggling. "You're crazy."

"Of course," coughed Tilman. "And then the Devil came for him."

"You shut your gob!" Maria snapped at him. "You've no business here anyway, hacking and spewing all the time."

"I—"

"Not here!"

Jacob could hear them, but it was as if he had wadding over his ears. He had expected all sorts of things, but not that they wouldn't believe him.

"I didn't ask to sit around in this den of fornication." Tilman was shouting now. "It was Jacob's idea. Before I accept any favors from you I'd—"

"Jacob wouldn't have thought of it himself," she broke in furiously, "you've just conned him with that ridiculous cough of yours."

"You may call it ridiculous. All I know is it's going to kill me!"

"And the sooner the better! But the truth is, you're in better health than all of us."

"Lord help me! I'm off, Jacob. I'd rather die than listen to your whore bawling me out."

"Don't call me a whore," screeched Maria.

"Well, that's what you are."

"I won't take it from you. I may be one, but I'd rather drink from the cesspit than open my legs for you."

"Good idea, you'd enjoy that, you toothless bitch, you superannuated attempt at a temptress—"

"Oh, don't get your tongue in a twist."

"You old hag. I don't want to hear any more, and certainly not these stories about the Devil."

Tilman leaped up and rushed toward the door, where he collapsed in a heap. Jacob ran over and grabbed him under the armpits.

"Throw him out!" demanded Maria.

"No." Jacob shook his head. "Can't you see, he's ill."

Maria lay on her bed and huddled up. "He's got to go." She was close to tears.

Tilman was breathing heavily. Ice-cold sweat glinted on his upper lip.

"He's ill, Maria," Jacob repeated softly.

She stretched out both arms, her fingers spread like claws. "You can go, too, for all I care. Bugger off."

"Maria—"

"I don't want to see you anymore."

She put her head in her hands and started to sob.

"Maria, I—"

"Out!"

Jacob hung his head.

URQUHART

By now the rain was coming down in torrents. All activity in Berlich had come to a halt. Here and there lights could be seen through the shutters.

Urquhart waited.

Suddenly the whorehouse door opened and a man shot out and up the street toward the city wall. With his head hunched between his shoulders in the downpour, he was nothing but a coat and floppy hat on legs. But Urquhart had made careful note of his quarry's clothing.

It was time to put an end to this tiresome affair. Unhurriedly, he set off after the scampering figure.

Given that he was stumbling over his own feet at every second step, he was showing an astonishing turn of speed. Urquhart decided to follow him until he stopped. He couldn't keep that speed up forever; he'd have to take a rest at some point.

It was less effort to kill him when he wasn't moving so much.

Coat-and-hat crossed the Duck Ponds and headed down a narrow path between the orchards and vineyards. It was so dark you could hardly see your hand in front of your face. But Urquhart could. He could see in the pitch dark. He had the senses of a beast of prey that registered every movement of the man running along the path. With a grunt of satisfaction, he noted that he was getting slower and slower. Good. It would soon be over.

He wondered how many people the redhead had already told. There was the man he had dragged along to the brothel with him, clearly a friend. No problem tracking him down. Urquhart had memorized his features while he was trailing them to Berlich, and he could always get more information out of the whores. Though really it wasn't necessary to bother with him. It was only the witness himself who was a danger. He could almost forget about a beggar with an unlikely story he had from someone else.

But better safe than sorry.

By now they were in Plackgasse. Although it ran along inside the city wall, it was lined with trees and fences and half a dozen scattered farm buildings. It was no more than a country lane, and the rain had turned its surface into a slippery film of mud and pebbles.

The redhead must enjoy the "privilege of the Wall."

Now he was starting to drag his feet. His progress in the lashing, soaking wind was laborious in the extreme. Urquhart was surprised; his assessment of the man's physical capacity had been wrong. The willows bent beneath the black clouds streaming across the sky. Still no house in sight. Not long now and the man would be at the end of his tether.

A moment later he had slipped and was stuck in the mire. Urquhart stood still. The man was so enveloped in the floppy hat and coat, he could have been taken for a rock. Then he moved, tried to stand up.

He almost made it.

He coughed.

With a few steps Urquhart was behind him, aimed his crossbow at the back of his neck, and squeezed the trigger. The force of the bolt threw the body forward onto its knees so that it ended up in a grotesque kneeling position, as if giving thanks to the Lord.

Urquhart looked down at him.

He felt nothing. He was neither proud of his deed nor sorry to have killed a man. He could not understand why others who carried out similar acts had to bemoan them or brag about them afterward. Death was final. This man's life story was over and done with, and that was that. Not worth a further thought.

He turned around and headed back toward Berlich.

The dead man merged into the darkness behind him, a shapeless thing without name or meaning.

BERLICH

Maria calmed down somewhat after Tilman had left, but the atmosphere was still strained. Jacob stared at the candle. For a long time no one spoke.

"What was the point of that?" Maria asked querulously.

"Of what?"

"Giving him your hat and coat and your place under the Wall?"

"It's just for the night, Maria."

She rumpled her nose and wrapped her arms around herself as if she was cold.

"I'm not heartless," she said after a while.

Jacob sighed. "No one says you are."

"Oh, yes, they do!" There was an angry glint in her eyes. "You say it and your horrible friend Tilman says it. Can't you imagine what it's like when you've just about managed to get a roof over your head and then you're expected to share it with any Tom, Dick, or Harry?"

"What do you mean, any Tom, Dick, or Harry?" Jacob spoke sharply. "I look after you as best I can. Sorry I'm not a patrician eating deviled pork with raisins every day and drinking the best wine."

"I wasn't talking about you."

"It sounded very much like it."

"You could have asked who I was talking about. Anyway, what do I do? Lie on my back for God knows who. And why do I do it? So I don't have to sleep in some stinking ditch. You've got to look after yourself. Still I let you come here whenever I'm free. But you don't know when you're onto a good thing. As soon as someone gives you something, you can't wait to give it away. Someone gives you shelter and you drag that riffraff along."

"I'm part of that riffraff, too."

"But it's my room! And it's my business who I let in and who not!"

Jacob said nothing. She was right, really. If he tried to look after everyone he felt sorry for there wouldn't have been enough room in the whole of Berlich.

"Have an apple," he said, somewhat helplessly.

Her hand didn't move, but it was pure pride. Her eyes were fixed on the fruits. "They look good," she admitted.

"Of course. They belong to the archbishop. Belonged."

"I wish you hadn't gone to get them."

"Why?"

"Now you've got it into your head you've seen the Devil. It sends shivers down my spine."

"I don't know if it was the Devil."

"It wasn't anyone. Wilhilde's client said two men were standing opposite the back of the chancel and saw Gerhard slip."

"They're lying."

"Why should they do that? You fell out of the tree and people came and the black shadow chased you. So why didn't all the people see the black shadow, tell me that, then?"

"Maria."

"Because there wasn't one!" she concluded triumphantly.

"So why am I telling you all this? Do you take me for a liar?"

She gave a sly smile. "No. But you might want to attract attention to yourself with your fairy story, so that all sorts of people will want to hear it. And fill your glass to get you to tell it. The next thing, there'll be an investigation and you'll be summoned before the Holy Inquisition." At this she quickly crossed herself. "They'll want to hear what you have to say, and in no time at all the insignificant fox will have turned into a great big bear."

"You're crazy. We don't have the Inquisition in Cologne. Anyway, do you think anyone would listen to me if even you don't believe me?"

She gave him a thoughtful look. "Yes, I do. There are plenty of fools in the world. They'll believe anything as long as the story's spine-chilling enough."

"But it's true!"

"Jacob!" There was a threatening undertone in her voice. "Do you want to make me angry?"

"Christ Almighty!" He was getting angry, too. "Gerhard spoke to me!"

"It gets better all the time."

"He said—"

"I can't wait to hear."

The mocking tone was just too sharp. Jacob had had enough. He stood up and went to the door without a glance at Maria. There he stopped, his eye tracing the grain of the wood in the floorboards.

He was so furious he was trembling all over. "Perhaps you will find your nobleman to take you away from here," he spat out. "Though I can't imagine anyone would stoop so low."

Her speechlessness was tangible.

Jacob didn't wait for a reply. He strode out and down the stairs, swearing he would never set foot in this house again.

Never again.

He was almost at the bottom when he heard her howl of fury. Something flew out of the open door and hit the wall with a crash. She'd probably thrown the candlestick at him. Clenching his teeth, he went out into the rain, while Clemens and Margarethe exchanged bewildered stares before returning to their business with a shrug of the shoulders.

He did not see the shadow that appeared at the far end of the street, and the shadow did not see him.

They missed each other by a heartbeat.

Urquhart went to the whorehouse, thumped on the door with his fist, and entered without waiting. The doorway was so low he had to bend down. He drew back his black hood.

A hunched, greasy fellow roasting something over the fire stared up at him with wrinkled brow. Two women were sitting dozing on a bench. One was quite pretty, the other probably cheap. There was a smell of cabbage, burned meat, and something indefinable it was better not to inquire too closely about.

"Good evening," he said softly.

The old man by the fire started to say something, then stopped. He subjected Urquhart to a thorough scrutiny. A servile smile appeared on his face. He jumped up, as far as his bent back allowed, and shuffled across the room toward him. He had clearly decided that Urquhart might be good business. The prettier of the two women gaped at the blond giant and hastily nudged the other, who started and opened her eyes, revealing a severe squint.

Urquhart slowly moved to the middle of the room and looked round. The landlord regarded him expectantly. "A girl?" he asked tentatively.

Urquhart gave the old man a speculative look. Putting one arm round his crooked shoulders, he took him to one side and whispered, "Later. Perhaps you can help me."

"Perhaps." The landlord drew out the word, grinning up at Urquhart. "And perhaps you will take pity on poor people like us. Otherwise—I mean, you get more forgetful as you get older—"

Urquhart smiled. "Oh, you won't forget my visit, I can promise you that."

"That's different." The hunchbacked landlord put on his most eager-to-please expression. "What can I do for you?"

"Someone, whose name I've forgotten, was here tonight. His hair"— he gave the landlord a confidential wink—"is at least as striking as mine. Though probably less well acquainted with a comb."

A light appeared in the landlord's eyes. "Red? Bright red?"

"Exactly."

"That's Jacob, that is."

"Jacob?"

"Jacob the Fox. That's what they call him." The landlord twirled a finger around his head. "You know." He gave a laugh, as if Urquhart and he were friends.

"Of course." So it was a Jacob he had killed. Why not? One Jacob fewer.

The two women were agog. "See to the food," the old man barked at them. "And you can put those ears down. Do you want the gentleman to think he's in a rabbit hutch?"

"So he was here?" Urquhart asked.

"You can say that again!"

"And what did he say?"

The landlord gave him a bewildered look. "What did he say?"

"That's what I'm asking." Urquhart felt inside his cloak, brought out a coin, and slipped it into the old man's hand. It seemed a physiognomical impossibility, but an even broader grin appeared on his face.

"Well, he dropped hints about the roast," he muttered, with a glance at the lump over that fire that was now identified as a roast. "Thought I might give him a slice. Huh!"

"That was all?"

"He was pretty brusque to me, the swine. Had some poor beggar in tow. No, he didn't say anything. He went straight up to Maria."

"Ah, Maria—" Urquhart pretended to be thinking. "I think he must have mentioned her once or twice."

"Ah, my pride and joy!" The landlord tried to throw out his chest, resulting in a grotesque contortion. Then he plucked at Urquhart's sleeve and whispered, with a conspiratorial grimace, "I could arrange for her to be available." He jerked a contemptuous thumb over his shoulder. "She's much better looking than those two."

"Later. He didn't speak to anyone else?"

Now it was the landlord's turn to put on a show of rummaging around in the depths of his memory, where it appeared to be pitch black. Urquhart let him see the glint of another coin, but closed his hand before he could grasp it.

"No, no, definitely not. He didn't say anything," the old man quickly assured him. "I was down here all the time, Margarethe too, and Wilhilde here— Wilhilde had, er, a visitor."

"What about the other man you mentioned, is he still here?"

"Tilman? No."

"Hmm." Urquhart stared into space for a moment. Tilman? He'd see to him later. He had to sort things out here first.

"Have you heard about Gerhard Morart?" he asked.

Immediately the brothelkeeper's expression changed to one of profound sadness. "Oh, yes, poor Master Gerhard." His sudden grief was supported by a double cry of lamentation from the bench. "What a dreadful accident. Wilhilde's, er, visitor brought the news. Dazzled by his vision of the Kingdom of Heaven, he stepped straight out into the air."

"God rest his soul," said Urquhart solemnly. The old man made a halfhearted attempt to cross himself.

So they knew nothing.

"At such times the love of a beautiful woman is a comfort." The landlord sighed. "Don't you think?"

"Yes," said Urquhart softly, "why not?"

JACOB

The rain had eased off. The moon even appeared now and then.

Without really knowing why, Jacob had kept running until he reached New Market Square. He just felt the need to go somewhere and think things over. Where didn't matter. Best of all would have been a nice tavern, but what would he do in a tavern without any money? So he had just set off at random and eventually found himself in the large meadow between the nunnery of St. Cecilia and the Church of the Apostles. It was where the cattle market was held and during the day it was full of horses and cattle, the cracking of whips, and the haggling of the dealers and customers, everything overlaid with the pungent smell of dung and urine.

Now it was dark and deserted. The only light was the torch at the entrance to the Malt Shovel. Jacob would have loved to be able afford to go in and crawl out on all fours. All the other houses around had an uninhabited air. At this time of night respectable people were in their beds, behind closed shutters.

That night more than ever, Jacob wished he was respectable.

Morosely he trudged across the marshy field to the drinking troughs and sat down by the pump. He tried to feel upset at Maria's anger, but all he could feel was his own hurt pride. She was a whore. So what? At least she was something. Her beauty would find a home with some honest tradesman who didn't feel it was beneath him to take her out of Clemens's rat hole. All Jacob had to offer was what he could steal from others, and then only when he wasn't caught, like this morning, or fell out of the archbishop's tree.

For a moment his thoughts rested on the dyer's daughter.

He and Maria had nothing more to say to each other, so much was clear. Poverty had held them together for a few weeks, but her pride had broken that tie. The worst thing about it was, he could understand her. All she was doing was cutting her coat according to her dreams in the hope of being able to grasp a hand from the world of respectability, from which a number of her clients came. For that she was prepared to forfeit the friendship of all those who had been her companions until now, the sick and downtrodden, beggars and thieves, the doomed and dishonored. Losers. Her friends.

The last will be first, thought Jacob. Why isn't she content with what God has ordained? The poor are poor. The rich are there to give to the poor, and the poor to pray for the salvation of the rich, which in general was very necessary. That was the way of the world. What was wrong with it?

Nothing was wrong.

But, he followed his line of thought, if nothing is wrong, then nothing is right, either. Amazed at the logic of his conclusion, he jumped up. That explained the queasy feeling he got when the clergy started talking about each of us keeping to our proper stations. *Keeping* to them. Why should God object if a poor man tried to rise in the world? Were there not rich people who became poor, like that merchant, Berengar from Salzgasse? His business had gone from bad to worse, and now he went around with a begging bowl.

Perhaps Maria would get nowhere. Perhaps she was being naive with her dreams. But her pride would still be there.

And what about his pride?

He sat down by the pump again, at odds with himself now. Was it

Maria's fault if his ambition ran no higher than eating as much as he could stuff into his slim frame, stealing whenever he had the opportunity, and deflowering the virgins of Cologne?

Was it her fault that he ran away when anything got serious or demanded commitment? What could someone like him offer her that she didn't have more than enough of already? What could he do?

What had he ever tried to do?

He felt in the baggy hose the dyer girl had given him. There was something in the pocket, the only thing he had a surplus of because he kept making new ones to give away.

He pulled out one of his curved whistles.

His tongue snaked over his lips. The next moment the notes of a fast, cheerful tune were buzzing over New Market Square like a swarm of bees. He suddenly felt as if the trees had stopped their rustling just to listen to him, the moon was peeping through the clouds to watch him, and the tall grass was swaying in time to his music. There was one thing he could do! And he made his whistle trill like a skylark, cascades of joy tumbling down—

All at once he stopped.

In his mind's eye he saw the scaffolding and the shadow. The night-dark creature with long, flowing hair. With the figure of a man and the agility and savagery of a beast.

It had murdered Gerhard Morart.

And then it had stared at him.

The Devil!

Jacob shook his head. No, it was a man. A particularly tall and swift man, but a man, for all that. And a murderer.

But why should someone kill Gerhard Morart?

He remembered the supposed witnesses. There were no witnesses. No one had been there apart from him to see Gerhard fall. Whoever said differently was lying. Only he, Jacob, knew the truth. He was the only one who had seen Gerhard's murderer.

And the murderer had seen him.

He suddenly felt cold all over. He drew his knees up to his chest and stared across at the massive facade of the Church of the Apostles.

MARIA

Propped up on her elbows, she explored the furry landscape of Urquhart's chest. Her fingers roamed through the hair, twisting it into little ringlets.

Maria giggled.

"Happy?" asked Urquhart.

"I was wondering how long it would take to deck you out all over like this."

Urquhart grinned. "Your whole life wouldn't be long enough."

"I suppose not." Maria raised her brows. Then she laughed, threw herself on him, and wrapped her arms around his neck. "Well, anyway, I've never come across a man with so much hair on his body before. You almost look like a"—she looked for a suitable comparison—"like a wolf."

Her drew her head down and kissed her. "Wolves are loving," he whispered.

Maria freed herself and jumped up off the bed. She could still feel his weight, his hot breath, could feel him on her and inside her. He had made love to her with a fierce savagery she had found exciting and strangely disturbing.

"Wolves are cruel," she retorted.

She stroked the soft material of his cloak, which was draped over her table.

Urquhart baffled her. She had had lots of men, good lovers and poor lovers, some impatient, some unhurried, some brutal, and some that were like children. Some were kind to her, gave her more money than agreed, which she had to keep from Clemens, and invited her to share their wine, even their food. Others treated her like a thing, an inanimate object. Then there were the lonely ones, who often only wanted to talk, others who were insatiable, worried, exuberant, unscrupulous—or conscience-stricken, tormented by guilt, so that she couldn't tell whether their groans were groans of pleasure or disgust at themselves. And there were others with strange needs, God-forsaken creatures. But even those she took, as long as they paid. Each one she could identify, categorize like an herb or a species of animal. Setting herself above them, studying them from a distance, was her way of dealing with the fact that men came and took her body. Each one left something of himself with her, left a tiny piece of his pride behind in her room, and she gathered these pieces like trophies and locked them away in the dark chamber at the bottom of her heart.

Only Jacob, when he came to Cologne three months ago, had found the key to her heart and had kept his pride.

Now Jacob was past history. She had made up her mind to escape from poverty. Impossible, perhaps, but it meant sacrificing Jacob for the vague chance a decent man might one day come and offer her a better life than staying stuck here in Clemens's stinking hole.

But with each man who came and went, her hope shriveled a little more to a foolish dream, and it became more and more difficult to believe the Blessed Virgin would raise a whore to a respectable burgher's wife. When she was alone, Maria would pray to the Virgin Mary, but then Clemens would bring the men she knew so well. They were like fruit on a market stall—here apples, red or green, ripe or rotten, there quinces, peaches, cherries—each typical of his own kind, each always the same, each cowardly, each a disappointment.

Urquhart was like none of them.

There was something inside him that made her shudder. And yet she wished she could be his forever, follow him everywhere, whether to riches or damnation.

For a moment she felt an urge simply to run away. But what if he was the one she was waiting for?

Wolves are loving. Wolves are cruel.

She turned back to him with a shy smile. Urquhart watched her. "Are you going out?" he asked.

She shrugged her shoulders. "Where would I go?"

Urquhart nodded. His long hair flowed around him like a cloak. "Yes," he said, almost inaudibly, "where would you go?"

He stretched and stood up.

"And you? Are you going?" Maria didn't know whether to feel sorry or relieved.

"Yes." He started to get dressed.

"And will you come again?" she asked hesitantly.

Urquhart threw the cloak over his shoulders. Something was attached to the inside, like a crossbow, only smaller. Then it vanished as he drew the material over his chest.

"Perhaps. It depends what you have to tell me."

"To tell you?"

"There's a man. Called Jacob. You know him."

Maria was bewildered by the sudden change of subject. What had Urquhart to do with Jacob?

"Yes, I know him."

"He needs help."

"What?"

"Our friend talks too much." Urquhart went up to Maria and lifted up her chin. "He's in danger of losing his head, if you understand me. He's been saying strange things about something he claims he saw this evening."

"Oh, God!" Maria exclaimed. "The architect."

"What did he tell you?"

Why should you betray him, she thought, but already it was pouring out. "That Jacob's always got some cock-and-bull story to tell. Huh! He claims he saw the Devil push Gerhard off the scaffolding. He even says he spoke to him."

"To the Devil?"

"Don't be silly." Maria shook her head. She was giving vent to all her annoyance with Jacob. At the same time, surprisingly, she wished he were here with her.

"To Gerhard, then?"

"Yes. At least that's what he claimed."

"And what is Gerhard supposed to have said?"

Careful, a voice inside her whispered, but she ignored the warning.

She was trapped, like an insect, in the amber of his eyes. Strange eyes. You looked into depths, terrifying, unfathomable depths.

"I don't know."

"The priests won't like stories like that."

"Where did you get to know Jacob?"

"Later, Maria. We don't want him to do anything stupid, do we? So he saw the Devil? What did the Devil look like?"

"I don't know. I wasn't interested." She sighed. Poor stupid Jacob. "But I'll ask him the next time he comes," she said softly, more to herself.

The next time he comes...

Urquhart said nothing.

"I shouldn't have treated him like that. Jacob was always good to me. He's good to people all the time, without noticing what he's doing, you know." She shook her head, looked at Urquhart, and didn't know whether to laugh or cry. "He's crazy, he gives away everything he's got. He brings this Tilman with him. I throw him out and Jacob can think of nothing better than to give him his hat and coat—and his place by the Wall as well."

It struck Urquhart like a thunderbolt.

"What did you say?" he whispered. His features were like stone.

"You can imagine how it makes me sorry and livid at the same time. That I screamed at him, wounded his pride, humiliated him. But he has to understand, this isn't an almshouse, I can't just—" She bit her lip. "Sorry. I'm boring you. Sorry."

"When did Jacob leave?" Urquhart asked in a toneless voice.

"Leave? Just before you came. You could almost have bumped into each other."

"Where did he go?"

She lowered her eyes. "I don't know. Perhaps to his shack by the Wall."

"By the Wall?"

She nodded. "By the Eigelstein Gate. Have you never heard of the privilege of the Wall?"

Urquhart's eyes glazed over. "I have to go," he said.

Maria started. Go then, one part of her screamed, go as far away as possible. You're not what I'm looking for; you frighten me. At the same time she felt her heartbeat quicken with the hope he would take her with him.

No, it's better you go—

Instead, "Come back," she blurted out. "Come, whenever you want. I'll be here for you, here for you alone."

Urquhart smiled. "Thank you," he said gently. "That will not be necessary."

JACOB

Jacob was fed up with staring at the church.

An hour must have passed since he left Maria. His anger had subsided and he was starting to find self-pity boring. The best thing to do would be to forget today, wipe it from his memory and try to make it up with Maria. At least they could stay friends.

The damp cold had chilled him to the bone. With a quick prayer to whatever gods were there in the darkness that Clemens would let him sit by the fire, he shook himself like a dog and set off slowly for Berlich. He avoided the shortest way, which would have meant going through Vilsgasse. The latest rumor said there was a butcher there who dragged people in off the street at night and made them into sausages. There was no butcher in Vilsgasse, nor any worse thieves than Jacob himself, but the power of rumor was such that he decided to take the route around by the city wall.

The clouds had gone. The moon dipped the pointed gables of the half-timbered houses on his right in silver. There was no one else out apart from a few drunks whose voices he heard coming from a side street. Somewhere in front two dogs started barking furiously. For a few steps a cat walked beside him along the top of a wall before silently slipping down into the darkness of the garden on the other side.

The hunters of the night were always on the prowl.

Then Berlich lay before him, hushed, silent. A refuge for shabby secrets. Dead souls sitting by cheerful, crackling fires. Hell in miniature. At the other end of the street the wind tugged at a slim tree.

Jacob peered into the darkness. The tree had gone. What he had seen was the silhouette of a man disappearing in the opposite direction. Of an unusually tall man, hair waving in the wind.

Jacob slowed to a halt.

How many tall men, black as night, were there in Cologne?

Annoyed with himself, he hurried on. Ridiculous! Like a timid girl, seeing danger everywhere. He was getting obsessed with this affair at the cathedral. He must put it out of his mind. What had he to do with Gerhard Morart? Or some phantom haunting the scaffolding? His time would be better spent thinking about ways to get something to eat—or drink! Jacob could hardly remember the last time wine had passed his lips. Anyway, he'd get his hands on something, as soon as it was light, so he could make things up with Maria, then go and see what was happening on the Brook with a clear conscience.

If he could make things up with Maria.

Again he stopped. His heart told him Maria wasn't expecting him anymore.

It was one of those moments when Jacob recognized the truth without having looked for it. He had burned his bridges with her. Maybe she had already gone, maybe chance had brought her respectable bridegroom during this last hour. Or, more likely, she was asleep, with her face to the wall, the way she always slept. Had made it clear to Clemens he was to let no one up. Whatever, she wasn't expecting him anymore.

It was a strange feeling. Jacob couldn't say why he was so absolutely sure. They'd quarreled before, more than once, but the one thing you could say about Maria was that she bore a grudge.

Should he try anyway?

He looked at the corner house. Light could be seen in a tiny crack in the shutters. She was still awake.

And he was an idiot if he didn't go straight to her.

He knocked several times and went in. Downstairs everything seemed the same as usual. Clemens was just taking the roast off the fire. On the table was a large bowl of gruel. Margarethe and Wilhilde were just bringing four mugs and a jug of wine.

"You again," said Clemens.

"Me again."

"You've only just gone."

Jacob shrugged his shoulders. His glance rested longingly on the burned meat.

"A banquet?" he said morosely. "What are you celebrating?"

"Business is booming," growled Clemens in a voice that had nothing of booming business in it. "And it's no business of yours what we fill our bellies with here. Think you can get Maria's portion? Huh! Forget it."

"Where is she, anyway, miseryguts?"

Clemens nodded in the direction of the steps.

"Be down soon, I should think. Her last client's just gone. A real gentleman. Knew you too, though it's a mystery to me why he should."

"Who?" Jacob exclaimed in surprise.

"Who, who. I don't ask no names."

"And I don't know no gentlemen," said Jacob, his foot already on the bottom stair. "What did he look like?"

Clemens bared his teeth. It was meant to be a grin. "Better than you, anyway."

"Obviously."

"Twice as tall, I'd say." He gave a hoarse laugh. "No, make that three times. And his hair—"

"Angel's hair," said Margarethe with a dreamy smile.

"Down to the ground," groaned Wilhilde, still drooling over the memory.

Jacob stared at the hand grasping the banister. The knuckles were white. He felt his blood run cold. "Dark clothes?" he asked.

"Black as night."

It can't be, he thought. His mind was racing. It can't be!

He was up the stairs faster than he had ever been before. He stopped at the door.

"Maria?"

No answer.

"Maria!" Louder.

It can't be, it can't be.

In a fever of apprehension, he pushed open the door.

Maria was by the window, her back against the wall, looking at him. She didn't speak.

"Maria, I—" His voice trailed off. There was something wrong with her face. He took a step toward her, a closer look.

His jaw started to quiver.

Maria was looking at him.

But only with one eye.

A small crossbow bolt had gone through the other, shattering her skull and nailing her to the wooden wall.

RHEINGASSE

"I'll slice him into little pieces!"

With a howl, Kuno stormed into the candlelit room, the tears pouring down his cheeks. With his fists he hammered on the massive oak table at which seven people were enjoying a sumptuous dinner. He was quivering all over with fury.

"You'll pay for this," he shouted at Johann, "you and that witch Blithildis."

Matthias threw away the chicken bone he had been gnawing and jumped up. "And you will learn to knock before you enter," he retorted icily.

"Watch what you say!" screamed Kuno. "You deceived me! You gave me your word, your sacred word, nothing would happen to Gerhard and now everyone's saying he's dead."

"He is. But not because of anything we did, but through his own carelessness."

"Falling off the scaffolding?" Kuno laughed hysterically, raising his hands in supplication. "Do you hear that, all ye saints? Do you hear the lies—"

"This is not the moment to call on all the saints!" Johann broke in sharply. "If you must pray, then pray for your own soul, for forgiveness for what we all decided on together. You're no better than we are, and we're no worse than you. D'you understand?"

"Let me throw him out of the window," snarled Daniel, only controlling himself with difficulty.

"Why did you do it?" Kuno sobbed. He sagged and put his face in his hands. Then he stared at each of the others, one after the other. "And it's all my fault," he whispered. "All my fault. That's the worst of all. My fault."

Theoderich took a goblet, filled it with wine, and placed it on the table in front of Kuno. "Who would you be thinking of slicing up into little pieces?" he asked casually.

"Urquhart," Kuno hissed.

Theoderich shook his head. "Have a drink, Kuno. What has Urquhart got to do with it? There are two witnesses who saw Gerhard slip and fall off the scaffolding. We're just as devastated as you are, believe me."

He placed a consoling hand on Kuno's shoulder. Kuno shook it off, stared at the goblet, then took a deep pull at it. "Witnesses," he said with a snort of contempt.

"Yes, witnesses."

"It was Urquhart."

"Urquhart only does what we tell him to and pay him for."

"Then you paid him to kill Gerhard."

"You watch what you say," growled Daniel. "If you dare call my grandmother a witch just once more I won't even give her time to turn you into a toad. I'll split your empty head open, you little turd."

"I'll—"

"Pull yourselves together!" Johann commanded silence. "All of you."

"Dung puncher," Daniel added quietly.

"The time has come to talk openly," Johann went on. "Since this unfortunate affair with Gerhard we've all been at loggerheads. That has got to stop. Yes, it's true, we didn't trust Gerhard. It is also true that it necessitated an unfortunate extension to Urquhart's instructions. The witnesses were his idea. Paid, of course."

"Father!" Daniel gave his father a disbelieving look. "Why are you telling him all this?"

"Because," said Johann, his eyes boring into Kuno's, "he is a man of honor who believes in our cause. Gerhard was like a father to him. I know how he must feel. But I also know that we still have a true friend in Kuno, a staunch friend, who"—his voice cut through the air—"is sufficiently aware of his own sins not to condemn us for something that was necessary." He lowered his voice again. "There are nine of us. I don't count Lorenzo, with him it's the money alone, but the rest of us are in this together. Once we start distrusting and lying to each other we will not succeed. We will fail. So I must insist: no more arguments. Daniel?"

Daniel ground his teeth furiously. Then he nodded.

"Kuno?"

He lowered his eyes. "You can't expect me to jump for joy," he muttered.

"No one feels like jumping for joy," said Matthias. "But think of the day when it'll all be over. Think of that."

"Then we'll jump for joy," said Heinrich. He leaned over toward Kuno, an unctuous smile on his face. "We understand how you feel. But just think what would have happened if Gerhard's conscience had left him no choice but to betray us. Think how we would have felt, Kuno."

"If only Hardefust hadn't killed that butcher," growled Daniel.

"But he did." Matthias shrugged his shoulders as he dipped his fingers into a bowl of sweetmeats. "And even if he hadn't, there would have been occasions enough for the wheel of fortune to turn in that direction. What we are doing is right."

"What we are doing is right." Johann added his voice to Matthias's.

Kuno glowered, but said nothing.

"Tomorrow morning, before the stroke of seven, I'm meeting Lorenzo to go through the details," said Matthias as the silence continued. "Afterward Urquhart will report to me. I'm confident. It looks as if the count of Jülich really has sent us the best."

"He gives me the creeps," said Heinrich in a flat tone.

Matthias had a thousand replies on the tip of his tongue, neat, sharp, biting insults, each more telling than the last. Then he sighed. Their secret alliance had at least three Achilles' heels: Daniel's lack of self-control, Kuno's sentimentality, and Heinrich's constant fear. There was nothing to be done about it. All he could do was hope none of the three would make a mistake.

He sighed resignedly, his hand hovering over the pieces of spicy roast hare.

FLIGHT

Jacob retched. He stumbled backward out of the low-ceilinged room where Maria's dreams had come to such a violent end. He backed into the wall, and still that one eye was looking at him, with a strangely reproachful expression, as if she were asking him why he hadn't been there.

He tried to cross himself, but his arm refused to move.

From the taproom below came the clatter of mugs and the sound of Clemens eating.

"Come on, Maria," he called. "Hurry up, before we've finished the lot. You don't get something like this every day."

The tension slackened. Jacob staggered, stumbled, and fell down the stairs. The women screeched. Clemens turned around ponderously.

"Jacob," Wilhilde gasped, "you're as white as a sheet."

For one terrible moment he didn't know what to do. He glanced feverishly from one to the other. A deep furrow appeared on Clemens's brow. "What's up, Jacob?" His eyes were drawn to the stairs. "Maria?" he shouted.

Jacob's mind went blank. Without thinking, he was out the door and in the street.

"Maria?" He heard Clemens roar a second time.

He started running through Berlich. His mind was in chaos. All he could think was, Get away, away from here, away from Maria, away from that beautiful face with the one eye, still staring at him as he hurried across the Duck Ponds, etched forever on his mind. He ran until the pain in his side was unbearable, and still he kept running, afraid the reality behind would catch up with him. His feet were splashing through a ditch.

Then he fell, facedown in a puddle. Instinctively he rolled over on his back before he swallowed the foul water.

Above, almost close enough to touch, was the moon looking down at him. The moon was Maria's eye. She was following him.

He sat up, turned away from the remorseless gaze, and threw up. Leaning on his elbows, he waited till the retching stopped. Then he felt slightly better, staggered to his feet, and trotted slowly on his way.

Maria killed. Why?

He tried to work out what to do. It was hopeless. His thoughts were whirling around inside his head. At the same time his eyelids were heavy with fatigue. He had to lie down, curl up, go to sleep, and dream. Some beautiful dream, of paradise, God and the angels, Christ and the saints, of a world without misery and evil. He stopped and crossed himself. Again and again. He found his lips were murmuring the Lord's Prayer. It was the only prayer he knew.

Sleep. The Wall.

Automatically his legs set off through the orchards and between the willow trees lining Plackgasse. With any luck Tilman would have left a little room for him under the arch. Assuming he had taken up his offer. Which Jacob doubted.

Sleep.

Maria.

After a while he saw a large lump blocking the track. He came along here almost every day and certainly couldn't remember a boulder of that size. And at the moment he didn't care.

Something was trying to shake him out of his lethargy, to tell him it wasn't a boulder. He ignored it.

Only when his toe bumped into it did he realize it was his coat spread over the thing. And that the thing was not a thing, but a person, crouched in a grotesque position.

His hat was on the ground—

Tilman.

Jacob's mind cleared. Tilman must have collapsed before he even reached the Wall. The coat was still glistening with raindrops.

"Hey," said Jacob. It came out as a vague croaking sound, as if he hadn't spoken for years. He knelt down and stretched out a hand to shake Tilman.

Then he noticed the bolt. The same kind as—

With a shriek he was on his feet and running again. Now there were houses; he was approaching Weidengasse. He saw a man coming with a lantern and slipped into an entrance.

Suddenly his mind started working again, analyzing quickly, almost mechanically, as if a black cloth had been pulled away. He peeped cautiously out from his hiding place. He could still see the man. It wasn't a tall shadow, just the night watchman heading toward Eigelstein.

Maria was dead. Tilman was dead. Both the people Jacob had talked to after coming back from the cathedral were dead. Both killed in the same way.

But why? Why Maria?

Why Tilman?

It struck him like a bolt from the blue.

Because with his coat and hat Tilman looked like Jacob the Fox. *He* was the intended victim. He was the one who should have died. And probably still should.

Very cautiously he stepped out from the doorway. Perhaps it would be best to keep out of sight for the next few days. Stay in his shack under the arch. He thought hard as he jogged along Weidengasse. He could see the arches clearly in front, a deeper black in the dark expanse of the great Wall. There was not enough light to tell if there was anyone there.

He stopped. Anyone? Who would that be?

Maria must have been killed after Tilman. Had the murderer talked to her? Did he realize his mistake?

He stared into the blackness.

The blackness moved. There was something there.

Waiting for him to come near.

Jacob turned tail and ran.

He was right. Whatever it was that had been waiting for him under the arch had given up trying to stay concealed. He could hear the other's steps on the hard surface. Frighteningly rapid steps.

Which were getting closer.

The crossbow! Could Maria's murderer aim while running?

Jacob began twisting and turning, even if that slowed him down. His pursuer had already demonstrated his prowess with the crossbow twice. Jacob's only chance was to make it impossible for him to get a shot at him.

Where was that night watchman with his lantern? Nowhere to be seen, must have turned off somewhere.

The streets were deserted.

Ahead was the crossroads where Weidengasse joined with the lane from the Duck Ponds, then continued into Alter Graben leading down to the Rhine. Before that on the right were the ruins of the old Eigelstein Gate, through which he could get into Marzellenstraße. Three possible escape routes, ignoring the road to the left, which led back to the Wall.

But no time to think. His pursuer was catching up.

Jacob dashed between the towers of the old gate. On the left the spires of St. Machabei rose up above the jagged roofline. The houses seemed to be cowering before the power of the church.

Yes! Keep your head down!

Jacob kept his body low until he was almost scurrying along on all fours like a weasel. He could have laughed at the thought that now his pursuer could at most shoot him in the arse. How humiliating to die because your backside hurt so much you couldn't run. Oddly enough, part of his mind was coolly going through the various ways you could be killed by a crossbow bolt, while he continued to run, stoically ignoring the stitch stabbing into his side like a harbinger of the bolt that would dispatch him.

No more feinting now. Just run as fast as you can.

He'd escaped the crowd in the market. So far he'd managed to shake off every pursuer. If he'd been asked who was the fastest runner in Cologne, he would have nominated himself without hesitation.

He was fast. But did he have the stamina?

The feet of his unknown pursuer were drumming on the cobbles of what had once been a Roman road in a regular, almost relaxed rhythm. As if running caused him not the least exertion, while Jacob's lungs seemed about to burst.

Surely he could have killed me already, he thought. Why hasn't he? Is he waiting for me to collapse? That's it, he's playing with me. He knows I can't escape, so why bother to shoot. He'll just keep after me until I'm so slow he can get a clean shot at me, the lazy, well-fed swine.

The next crossroad appeared in front, the right turn went up to the convent of the Ursulines, the left down to the Rhine. He could choose which street he wanted to die in, both were broad enough.

Fury blazed up inside him. Enough was enough. He was fed up with taking evasive action, running away, spending his whole life on the run. Fed up to here!

Then, just a few yards before the left turn down to the Rhine, he saw a passage open up between the houses.

He had a vague memory that it went to Bethlehem Chapel, a tiny church belonging to one of the neighboring properties. And if his memory was correct, the passageway led to a narrow alley overgrown with weeds and bushes, which branched out into a tangle of footpaths through the convent vineyards. He had been there once. The area around the chapel was neglected, the walls and fences broken in places, so that it was easy to get into the vineyards.

Where he could escape. In the thick undergrowth even this fiendishly swift pursuer couldn't catch Jacob.

He kept running until he was almost past it. Then he suddenly darted to the left and skidded into the passage. He nearly left it too late. As it was, his shoulder scraped painfully along the wall. The regular pounding of the footsteps behind him faltered. The other was having to brake, losing time. Jacob had increased his lead slightly; now everything depended on his sense of direction.

At first all he could see was dense blackness. Then the faint outlines of the trees and the chapel emerged.

And something else.

Jacob couldn't believe it. This wasn't the alley he remembered. It ended in a high wall. There was no way out. His memory had deceived him.

The footsteps behind were swift and regular again. They were getting closer. If something didn't occur to him soon, he might just as well stand there and wait.

Just a minute! That wasn't a bad idea.

Jacob gasped for breath. He could almost feel the bolt in his back. Without looking, he sensed the other raising his crossbow, already celebrating his victory.

With his last ounces of strength he put on a spurt, despite the wall in front.

Then he suddenly braked, swung around, and ran straight at his pursuer.

RHEINGASSE

Johann climbed up the stairs, then stood, irresolute, outside the magnificent door. The flickering light of the candle brought the rich carving to life. As a child he had often stood looking at it, not long after his uncle Gottschalk had found the carved and inlaid wood in a Florentine warehouse and brought it back. It came, so it was said, from Byzantium and had fallen into the hands of Venetian knights during the first Crusade. Often, if the light was right, old ships would sail across an ocean of darkly grained wood, monsters and demons crane mahogany necks, and gargoyles with knotholes for eyes and worm-eaten teeth grin down at him, while cherubim and seraphim, on wings of walnut and ash, flew over them and the Holy City glowed in pure ebony on the horizon, such a glorious sight that he blushed with shame not to be one of those fighting to liberate it.

But then he had been a boy, his head full of ideals.

Now he was getting old, almost fifty. He had not been on a crusade, yet he had seen more of God's creation than many of the self-appointed liberators who lay waste to the world in the name of God, then wasted away themselves in Seljuk prisons or suffered torture in Pecheneg dungeons, their heads impaled on lances lining the entrances to heathen strongholds. Johann's spiritual ideals had taken a backseat to the study of profit and loss, but he never forgot to repeat the Psalm *Have mercy upon me, O God,* and to look on his wealth with due modesty.

He would establish a church, he swore for the nth time, and commission an altarpiece for it, a huge crucifixion on gold leaf. He'd start to make the arrangements as soon as the worries, doubts, and sleepless nights of the next few days were over. At the moment he had other things on his mind.

He knocked and entered the room beyond the door.

The old woman was sitting in the dark, but she was awake. Johann knew she hardly ever truly slept. Blindness was sleep enough for her, a sleep in which she could enjoy again the scenes from her life when she was young and held court with Werner, long since dead and almost forgotten. Their banquets were famous as far away as London, Paris, Rome. She had entertained Roman cardinals, seen rich merchants from Cornwall dancing in the great hall and gentlemen from Flanders with tall hats and full purses go down on their knees before her. She had been admired for her business acumen, respected for her keen mind, and desired for her great beauty.

All that was in the past.

And yet she did not live in the past but in the here and now. Beneath her sunken lids she saw into the future, and sometimes it seemed she saw much more than all the others who had eyes to see.

Johann sat on the edge of the chair opposite her, putting down his silver candlestick. He stared silently at the flame.

After a while she leaned forward slowly. In the glow of the candle her face seemed carved out of marble. Despite the closed eyes and deep furrows, one could still feel the fascination she must have exerted. It was almost like looking at the death mask of a very old, very beautiful woman.

"Something's wrong," she said in a hoarse whisper, all that was left of her rich, melodious voice, dry leaves blown along the walls by the wind.

Johann placed his fingertips together. "Yes."

She gave a sigh, scarcely audible. "You don't believe in our cause anymore?"

He shook his head as if she could see. "That's not it, Mother. I believe in it more strongly than ever. What we are doing is right."

"But you have doubts about the alliance."

"Yes."

"Hmm." The white fingers set off across the black velvet of her dress, sought out and clasped one another. "Gerhard Morart is dead. He had to die. Not because we are cruel—because I am cruel—but because our cause demanded it." She paused. "But there are some in our company who do not seem to understand that. The fools think they can go through fire without getting their feet burned."

"We all come to the fire," said Johann softly. "Sometime or other."

"Of course. But what is pleasing in the sight of God and what is not? Have you ever thought how arrogant it is to claim to know God's will and dispense justice in His name? When not even the pope can prove he is truly a servant of God. If the ways of the Lord are beyond finding out, as the Bible teaches, then perhaps it is the pope who is an abomination in the sight of God. Who, then, is more likely to burn? The man who questions the authority of the holy Catholic Church or the so-called Holy Father?"

"That seems to me a question no mortal can answer."

"Nor can we interpret God's word to suit ourselves. Do not torment yourself unnecessarily, my son. You will not find the answers we are looking for in this world. But since we cannot *know*, does that mean we must not act?"

"We will act," said Johann determinedly.

The parchment skin tautened around the old woman's teeth. She was smiling.

"But I would be happier," he went on, "if I had better troops at my command. I don't share Matthias's fears about Heinrich von Mainz— Matthias sees danger everywhere—but there are others."

"Yes, I know." She lifted up her head and jutted out her chin. Her nostrils quivered as if she were trying to identify some faint odor. "You're worried about Daniel. He's a hothead. He'll kill someone one day."

"Or get killed. Daniel is a risk to the family."

"I'm more concerned about Kuno."

"Yes." Johann sighed wearily. "Kuno's the other one I had in mind."

"But we cannot condemn Kuno because it is his heart speaking. Gerhard Morart dandled him on his knee. Kuno wanted to become a stonemason like him. When Gerhard became a journeyman, Kuno pestered his father to be allowed to accompany him, even though he was only a little boy, a very little boy who had only just learned to speak, never mind think for himself. He loved Gerhard above all else."

"All the worse."

The old woman stretched out her hand, feeling her way to Johann's head. The withered fingers patted his hair. "Kuno's no fool," she said soothingly. "He'll come to his senses soon and stand by us and the oath we all swore."

"And if he doesn't?"

The old woman was silent.

Johann stood up and kissed her gently on the forehead. "Good night, Mother." He took his candle and went to the door.

"Johann."

"Mother?"

"You need to relax. Read the Psalms. I suggest you will find what you need in Psalm one hundred and nine. Verse eight."

"I'm sure you're right, Mother."

He left the room, closing the door quietly behind him, and went to a small English chest of drawers that stood underneath a tapestry showing a hunting scene from Greek mythology. Two candles as thick as a man's arm on either side of the chest gave sufficient light to read. He took out the Bible from one of the drawers and opened the heavy tome.

He heard voices below. Theoderich and Daniel were playing some board game. Hadewig, Johann's wife, was singing an old song with an incredible number of verses.

He smiled.

Now, as the days got shorter and the nights colder, they often sat around the fire together again, telling one another stories. The family was scattered throughout Cologne, but their favorite place was here, at the house in Rheingasse, where the old woman dreamed of days gone by and days to come, weaving her dreams around the whole house, so that they were caught up in them and forgot time and the coldness of the world outside.

He leafed quickly through the pages until he found the passage she had mentioned. Relaxation was not the point. She was well aware that with his knowledge of the Bible, he would have to look it up to understand what she was telling him.

He found the page. His index finger ran along the lines.

For a while he stood there, motionless. Then he closed the book, replaced it, and went downstairs to warm himself by the fire.

JACOB

Jacob flew straight at the Shadow. His pursuer obviously hadn't reckoned on this sudden about-face. He was too close and too astonished to sidestep or stop. They were going to crash into each other like two billy goats. God alone knew which one would get up and leave the alley. But at least it was better than a crossbow bolt between the shoulder blades.

It was strangely satisfying to be able to see his opponent at last. He didn't look as gigantic as he had on the scaffolding, but he was still impressively tall. The weapon in his hand did resemble a crossbow, only a lot smaller. His clothes were as black as a raven's wing, his face hardly recognizable in the darkness. Broad cheekbones, thick eyebrows topped by a high forehead, and flowing hair three feet long. Jacob couldn't have said whether the face was handsome or repulsive. He sensed something untamed, bestial in the way the other moved. The creature before him had killed Gerhard Morart, Tilman, and Maria. And if it was the Devil himself, Jacob did not even have time for one last prayer.

But if it was a man—whoever the witch was who had conceived and brought him up with Satan's aid—then he could be outwitted. Even the Devil had been outwitted sometimes.

And if you're an animal, thought Jacob grimly, then you'll be no match for the Fox!

He waited for the collision.

It didn't come.

His pursuer had spread his arms wide and pushed off the ground. Jacob saw the black cloak rise up in front of his eyes, higher and higher, and felt the roughness of the cloth on his face before the giant had sailed over him in one great leap.

No man could jump that high. No matter.

Breathless, he ran out of the cul-de-sac and around the next corner down toward the Rhine. He heard the other set off after him again. He glanced around, expecting to see him close behind, but he obviously had a greater lead than expected. His trick had worked.

Running as fast as he could, he turned right into a narrow lane he knew led to the cathedral. Trees and walls everywhere. On the left the monastery of St. Maximin was sleeping. The monks' day began at one. He'd renounce the world, he swore, enter the monastery, spend his days in prayer, if he was still alive and breathing at one o'clock. Branches lashed his arms and legs, scratched his face. He didn't notice.

A church appeared, small and nondescript. A man threw something into the lane and started to go back in. His habit billowed in the wind.

"Father!"

Jacob skidded to a halt in front of him and took hold of his sleeve. The monk started and tried to shake him off. He was bald and fat and wheezed.

"Let me in," panted Jacob.

The monk's piggy eyes glinted suspiciously at him. "It's too late," he snapped.

"Too late?"

"Mass finished long ago."

"Let me in, I beg you. Just for a moment. Please."

"But I've told you. It's impossible, my son. Come back in the morn—"

"Your Reverence!" Jacob grasped the man's hands and squeezed them. "Hear my confession. Now! At once! You know you may not refuse me. It is God's will and law that confession should be freely available at all times." Was it God's will and law? Perhaps not, he wasn't particularly well up in church matters. But it was worth a try, all the same.

The monk raised his eyebrows in astonishment. He seemed uncertain. "Well—"

From the end of the lane came the sound of footsteps. Soft, swift, and regular.

"Please, Father."

"All right, then. Otherwise I'll never get rid of you." Somewhat roughly he pushed Jacob into the chapel and closed the door.

Jacob thought feverishly. How come the other was back on his trail already? How did he know what route he had taken?

Like an animal following a scent.

He suddenly had an idea. "Holy water, Father. Where's the holy water?"

The fat monk clasped his hands above his head. "Holy water he wants! Where is the holy water? He's in a church and he asks where the holy water is! Merciful Lord, when was the last time you were in a church? There." His short, fat finger shot out and pointed at a simple stone basin placed on top of a pillar. "There's holy water. But don't imagine you can just— Hey! What are you doing? Has Satan been spitting on your brain? That's not a puddle for you to wash in!"

Turning red as a beetroot, the monk grabbed the bowl out of his hands. "Have you taken leave of your senses?" he shouted, beside himself. "Out you go."

"Wait." Jacob ran over to a tiny window beside the porch.

"I'll—I'll—"

"Shh! The Devil's waiting outside."

The monk was speechless. Eyes wide—as far as the folds of fat would allow—he crossed himself.

Jacob peered out. He started when he saw the Shadow. He came down the lane to the church. Then stood still, turning his head this way and that.

Jacob didn't even dare breathe.

The Shadow took a few more steps, then stopped again and looked toward the church. His pale eyes seemed to be fixed on Jacob. He jerked his head to one side, then the other, to and fro. He looked up at the sky. In the light of the moon his profile stood out against the dark background of trees and walls, his long hair a cascade of silver.

He's confused, thought Jacob in jubilation. He can't understand where I've disappeared to. His mind's telling him I must be somewhere nearby, but his senses are telling him the opposite.

He'll trust his senses. Like every beast of prey.

He waited, tense, until the figure moved hesitantly on his way again. After a while it had merged with the darkness.

The Shadow had lost him.

"Your confession, my son," whispered the monk. There were tiny beads of sweat on his brow. He was trembling.

"Have patience, please. Just a little longer."

Time passed agonizingly slowly in the gloomy church. The monk was obviously so terrified of the Devil he didn't dare move.

When at last Jacob was sure he'd shaken off his pursuer, he sank down against the cold stone wall to the floor, closed his eyes, and sent a short prayer of thanks to St. Ursula. Of all the saints, she was the one he liked best. He made an on-the-spot decision to owe his rescue to her, conveniently forgetting that only a few minutes ago he had been vowing to become a monk in St. Maximin's.

"What was that you were saying about the Devil?" quavered the monk.

Jacob came to with a start. "The Devil? Oh, forget it."

"And confession?"

"Oh, yes, my confession. You know, when I come to think about it, it's not that urgent."

"But—"

"I've just remembered. I went to confession only this morning. Or was it yesterday evening? Tell me, Father, can a simple, honest man commit so many sins in one day that it's worth going to confession?"

The monk stared at him as if he had misheard. Then he pulled himself together. He gave a chilly smile. A moon of a face without any of the moon's charm. "My dear son—"

Jacob was on his feet in a second. That "dear son" did not sound particularly dear.

"—when I was your age I could thump three lads of your size so hard on the head, they ended up looking out through their ribs, like cocks in a cage. Now I'm much too old, and much too pious, of course." He darted over to Jacob and dragged him to the door. "But I imagine I can still manage a godly kick up the backside to get you out of my church."

Jacob thought about it. "Yes," he said, "I imagine you can." Without waiting for a reply, he opened the heavy oak door, glanced outside, and hurried off, his head well down between his shoulders. He just hoped the Shadow wouldn't still be waiting for him.

This time no one followed him.

Shaking his head, the monk came out of the church and put his hands on his hips. Just let that ungodly scoundrel come for confession once again!

Then his anger dissipated. Reverently, he drew in the clear air and muttered a hurried *Ave Maria*.

What a beautiful, peaceful night.

12 September

☩

JACOB

Jacob woke with a mouth as dry as an oven. He'd slept at most three hours and two had been torture, lashed by bad dreams.

But he was alive.

As he sat up, his body protested and he wondered for a moment why he was sore all over, as if he'd been whipped or broken on the wheel. Then he saw the ropes he'd been lying on. They twisted and turned like heavy snakes over the deck of the little boat. The pattern was probably imprinted on his body.

He pulled himself to his feet, wincing with pain. When he pushed up the short sleeve of his jerkin, he saw that his right shoulder was grazed and bruised. He'd scraped it along the stones of the archway as he tried to give his pursuer the slip by St. Peter's. He fingered the spot and groaned. It felt even worse than it looked.

Cautiously he peeped over the rail at the bustle on the quay. Several broad-beamed cargo boats were anchored there. They must have arrived during the night. Porters were transferring their cargoes of slates onto oxcarts. Among them was the harbormaster with his scroll and quill, supervising the work. It was a hive of activity even though, to judge by the sun, it was not yet six. Work at the quayside began before daybreak.

With stiff muscles, he climbed over the rail and dropped to the ground, hoping no one would see him. It was only a small boat in dry dock, clearly it had no goods on board, but the overseers still didn't like beggars and such riffraff sleeping in them. Being caught automatically meant being suspected of having stolen something, which was true more often than not. That for Jacob it had been a matter of life and death was neither here nor there.

He strolled along the harbor like a casual observer. There was a crush at Rhine Gate. It was one of the few places where goods could be brought into the city, also the site of the public weighhouse for grain. Not surprisingly, there was a long queue of wagons and carts. A little farther on at Filzgraben Gate a group of city sheriffs and beadles in their brightly colored robes were checking some tattered-looking individuals. Remembering his unsuccessful attempt to steal a chop, he decided it would be better to avoid being seen. Any other way into the city would be a detour, but probably safer.

As he ambled along outside the city wall, he kept one eye on the workers, gossiping boatmen, overseers, and toll collectors hurrying past. He was ready to take to his heels at a moment's notice. There didn't, however, seem to be any immediate danger. With any luck his pursuer from the previous night had lost his track or, rather, his scent, after he had poured holy water over himself. Which suggested he was dealing with some creature that was only part-human, a demon or perhaps even Satan himself.

Jacob shuddered.

But could you escape from the Devil? The Arch-fiend would have found him anywhere. The Shadow, on the other hand, had lost him.

A man after all?

Suddenly Maria came into his mind. She was dead. He had some difficulty remembering what she had looked like—he had suppressed her image. The things that had happened last night seemed strangely distant, as if all the horrifying experiences belonged to the memory of another person. Jacob was intelligent enough not to be deceived by this. He had a vague feeling the affair wasn't over, that it was only just beginning and he should be prepared for the worst. He couldn't be dousing himself in holy water all the time. Cologne was large but anyone who was determined to find him would do so sooner or later. And the Shadow was looking for him, there was no doubt about that.

He was the quarry, not Tilman.

Perhaps the sensible thing would be to leave Cologne. He had been running away all his life, so why not now? And how many more times would he have to run away?

Jacob didn't feel like running away. Not again.

The next gate was Wash Gate. Not hurrying, Jacob passed under the half-timbered portal, past the toll collectors with their bills of lading, drifting with the crowd. Shortly before Haymarket, he turned off down Rheingasse with the splendid stone-built house of the Overstolz family. Despite the exasperated noises his stomach was making, he decided to avoid the markets. They probably remembered his red hair all too well there, especially at the meat stalls.

His hair!

Could the Shadow have seen his hair? His hat had come off when he fell out of the tree and it hadn't been too dark for someone to see the color of his hair. No problem finding him, then. His lurid mane was a direct invitation to his would-be assassin. And his hat had gone for good. Tilman was wearing it. What was left of Tilman, that is.

Dozens of creepy-crawlies seemed to be wriggling through his intestines. He slipped into the porch of the Overstolz house, took off his jerkin, and started to wind it around his head. Pain stabbed his right shoulder; he could hardly use his right arm. The cloth slid down over his eyes. Cursing, he pulled it off and tried again. It slid to the ground.

"What are you doing here?" a sharp voice behind him asked.

His heart missed a beat.

Slowly he turned around and breathed a sigh of relief. It was no long-haired giant aiming a crossbow at him. The man was wearing a brown coat trimmed with black fur over a pleated burgundy robe and an embroidered hat with earmuffs. His beard was flecked with gray and the eyes fixed on him had a cold gleam.

"Sorry," whispered Jacob.

"This isn't a place to be hanging around, d'you hear? I could set the dogs on you."

"Yes, yes. Of course. Forgive me." Jacob picked up his jerkin and squeezed past the man.

"Hey!"

He froze. There was a lump in his throat that even the most violent swallowing could not get down.

The man came up to him. Jacob saw his hand push back the coat to rest on the pommel of a slim sword hanging from his hip in a gold-mounted sheath.

"I—I was just taking a breather," Jacob assured him.

The other frowned. "You're a beggar," he said. "Why aren't you outside one of the churches begging?"

"I didn't want to beg." Just a moment, why ever not? "It's the hunger, you see, that's all." Jacob assumed his most heartrending expression and pointed at his belly, which, indeed, did not have an ounce of spare fat. "My knees are like wax in the sun, the same sun that's burning my brain. I don't know if I'll survive till the evening. My poor children! My poor wife! But forgive me, your honor, forgive me for having stood in your way, no harm intended. Forgive me, but all I want is a little of God's grace and something in my stomach."

It was a load of soft soap, really, but effective. The man scrutinized him from head to toe. Then he grinned. "What's your name?"

"Jacob, sir. They call me the Fox."

The man felt in his pocket and pressed a coin in Jacob's hand. "Pray for me, Fox."

Jacob nodded vigorously. "That I will, your honor. I promise." Then, closing his fingers around his prize, he hurried off.

"And buy yourself something to eat, Fox, before you steal it," the man shouted after him.

Jacob turned around and watched him go into the big house. A patrician! Jesus Christ! The man must be one of the Overstolzes, the most important family in the whole of Cologne and the surrounding area. That was what he called a piece of luck.

He had a look at the coin. A guilder! That was enough to keep the demons of the night at a distance for a while.

But not enough to make him forget them.

Clutching the cool metal, he turned left into Filzengraben and hurried on, trying at the same time to wrap the blasted jerkin around his head with his left hand so that it covered his hair. He had almost reached the end of the street before he managed it. He didn't dare think what he looked like, even less what Richmodis would say.

Another stab of pain in his shoulder.

Just now she was the only person who could help him. He glanced along the Brook. There were more people there than yesterday.

He devoutly hoped that turning up there would not put Richmodis in danger. He was still alive, but two people had already been killed for something he had seen when he shouldn't have. At least that was the assumption. So far he hadn't had much leisure to think it over.

As he came nearer, he scanned the Duffes Brook. No sign of Richmodis.

He'd have to leave. Either that or knock at her door. But then he risked an earful from her father because he was wearing his jerkin and boots. He might even want them back and report him to the magistrate for theft.

Certainly, Jacob could hear himself saying, take back what is yours. For the hat and coat you'll have to go to Plackgasse. See the man with a crossbow bolt through his neck; he won't cause you any difficulty.

Oho! A crossbow bolt. And you'll be the one who killed him?

Jacob could feel himself breaking out in a cold sweat. He sat down on the narrow strip of grass beside the stream and dipped his hands in the water. That hadn't occurred to him.

It was just too much. He lay on his back, spread his arms wide, and stared up at the sky. The sheriffs, beadles, and magistrates were probably already after him. Plus Gerhard's murderer and the odd butcher.

Great, great.

He closed his eyes. If only he could get some sleep.

"Wake up. Aren't you going to teach me to play the flute?"

"Richmodis!"

Her face was upside down, her hair hanging down and appearing to reach out to him. He shot up and felt the stab of pain in his shoulder, worse than before.

She came around to face him and smiled. She was carrying a basket with a cover. "I didn't expect to see you again so soon."

"I told you, I love your nose." Jacob tried to struggle up.

She noticed his injured shoulder and frowned. "Oh, dear me, where did you do that?"

"Door was too narrow."

He got to his feet, picked up the jerkin, and, with a guilty expression, shook off the dust. Her eyes darted from his shoulder to the jerkin, scrutinized him from head to toe, and returned to his shoulder. She stretched out and squeezed it.

"Ouch!"

"Oh, come on. Squealing like a little piglet."

"Richmodis." He grasped her by the shoulders, then thought better of it and took his hands away. "I know it's asking a lot, but—" He looked around. People were staring at them again.

"What have you done this time?" She sighed.

"You said your uncle's a physician?"

"Not only that, he's dean of St. Mary Magdalene's and knows important people. Why?"

"I need him to— I don't know what I've done to my shoulder. They're trying to get me because I saw everything, all because of that stupid tree, and I'm sorry about the clothes, but I just wanted to help Tilman and—"

Richmodis shook her head and raised her hands. "Stop! Who's trying to get you? What did you see? Who's Tilman? I can't understand a word you're saying."

"Me neither," admitted Jacob.

"Then you'd better come with me." She took his arm and led him to the house. "I don't want to have to drown you under the cloths again, or to invent a story about my dozens of lovers for any would-be ladies' man who happens to turn up." She opened the door and pointed inside. "In you go."

"Won't you get into trouble with your father?" asked Jacob in a low voice.

"You can be a bore with your conscience. Sit down there." She pointed to a bench beside the fireplace. There was a fire crackling in it. The room was simply but comfortably furnished.

Jacob shook his head. "No. I may not exactly be a wealthy burgher, but I do know that respectable young ladies do not take young men into their parlor when the whole neighborhood is watching. I think I'd better go."

"Out of the question."

"I'm serious."

"And so am I," she said emphatically. "You think you can come here handing out pretty little whistles in return for jerkins, and my father's coat and hat—I can't wait to hear what happened to them—and then simply disappear? I'm warning you...." She gave him a stern look, tried a pout, but couldn't stop herself bursting out laughing. "And not a word about my nose."

Jacob spread out his arms in submission and sank down onto the bench. She wagged a finger at him. "And don't you move. I'll be back right away."

He nodded and breathed deeply. It was irresponsible of him to come to see Richmodis, but what else could he have done? He was injured, and there was always the danger Clemens would think he had killed Maria. Running off like that was the stupidest thing he could have done. Running away meant you were guilty. To be accused of her murder, and of Tilman's, was all he needed. Next they would be saying he'd pushed Gerhard off the scaffolding! No, that was one thing they wouldn't suspect him of. There were witnesses to say it had been an accident. Witnesses who hadn't been there to witness it.

Richmodis returned with a pail of water. She came from the back room, which led into the yard. The von Weidens must have their own well. Not everyone did. Most people shared the wells at crossroads or street corners.

She sat astride the bench and started to clean the wound carefully with a cloth. She did it so gently it was almost enjoyable. Under different circumstances Jacob would have invented further injuries just to feel the caress of her soft hands.

"There we are." She dropped the cloth into the pail and inspected her work. "That's the best I can do for the moment."

Jacob squinted down at his shoulder. It was all the colors of the rainbow. "Richmodis—" He took her hand and squeezed it. She didn't pull her hand away, just stared at him with her green eyes and waited. He didn't know what to say.

Eventually she came to his rescue. "You're running away."

"Yes."

"You were doing that yesterday, too."

"Yesterday I'd stolen something. That's different. It's my profession."

"Aha, profession." She raised her eyebrows in mock respect.

"It's not what you're thinking," he said urgently. "I'm a thief and a cheat, I admit it. But this is different. My only mistake was to be in the wrong place at the wrong time. I saw someone being murdered and the murderer saw me—and the two people I told about it are dead." His voice trailed off at the thought of Maria. He cleared his throat noisily and looked away.

She placed her index finger under his chin and turned his head back to face her. "And?"

"And nothing. I'm stuck like a rat in a trap and I don't want to pull you in, too. Believe me, I really did want to see you again—"

"I should hope so, too."

"—but I might be putting your life in danger. That monster chased me all around Cologne last night. I'm surprised I'm still alive."

"Monster?" The line between her brows had reappeared.

"The murderer."

"But you escaped?"

"Yes. For the moment."

"Good. Then there's nothing to worry about. If he had found you again, you'd presumably be dead as mutton by now." She ran her fingers through his hair, then tugged it so hard he couldn't repress a cry of pain. "But from what I hear, you're alive."

She let go, jumped up, and went out of the room. Creaking, rustling noises came from the other side of the door. "And who was it you saw being murdered that makes them so keen to get rid of you as well?"

"Not so loud!" Jacob rolled his eyes and ran over to where she was. The room at the rear appeared to be a mixture of kitchen and ground-level storeroom. She had opened a large chest and was rummaging around among material and other bits and pieces. He slumped against the door frame, then gave a loud groan. His shoulder! Richmodis gave him a brief glance, then returned to the tangle of cloth.

"Oh, I see," she said. "The murderer's in this chest listening to every word we say."

"I can't tell you. I don't want someone else to get killed."

"Here, put these on." She threw him a tan coat and a cap with ear-muffs. "If you won't talk about it, we'll have to do something. What are you waiting for?"

Jacob looked at the clothes. They were good, very good, well made from excellent cloth. He'd never worn anything like them in his life.

Richmodis clapped her hands. "What is it then? Does my lord require to be dressed?"

Jacob quickly put on the coat and pulled the cap so far down that not a red hair was to be seen. Richmodis strutted around, giving a pull here and a tug there, then stepped back, with a satisfied look on her face. Jacob felt stiff and hampered. He would have felt more at ease in the old, used coat.

"And now?"

"Now? We're going for a walk."

"Where?"

"To see my uncle. He'd better have a look at that shoulder and give you something decent to drink. Then you can tell him your story. If you manage to convince him, he'll do everything he can to help you. He likes a little spice in his scholarly existence now and then. If not, he'll throw you out on your backside. Without the hat and coat."

Jacob couldn't think of anything to say. They went out and crossed the stream. He turned around to see if anyone was watching, at which she gave him an irritated nudge and hurried him on. "Don't look," she whispered. "They'll stare anyway."

"And where does your uncle live?" asked Jacob, neatly avoiding a piglet that ran squealing between his legs.

"I told you. He's dean of St. Mary Magdalene's."

"Never heard of it."

"Never heard of it, you heathen?"

"Not heathen, not long in Cologne, that's all."

"Mary Magdalene's is opposite St. Severin's. Rather small, I have to admit. My uncle lives three doors along. That's where he has his study, too."

"There's another thing, Richmodis—"

"Mmm?"

"These clothes—"

"Are my father's, that's right."

Oh, dear!

"Was he angry with you about the other things you gave me?"

"You bet he was! He was furious. He chased me all around the house crying blue murder. The neighbors came to see what was up."

"Christ! A good thing he wasn't there today."

"A good thing indeed."

They passed through the old Roman gate into Severinstraße, which ran straight toward the city wall. It was no mean street. Churches and chapels, monasteries and convents jostled each other for position, not to mention solid patrician houses and inviting inns. Catering to every need, so to speak.

Richmodis was striding out.

"Tell me, fairest nose in the West," he said after a while, "where is he?"

"Who?"

"Your father."

She stopped and looked at him as if that was the silliest question she had ever heard.

"Where would he be? At my uncle's."

A MORNING WALK

Matthias reached the Franciscan monastery punctually at seven. He had to look twice before he recognized Urquhart. The murderer was wearing a black monk's habit with the hood drawn down over his face and his head bowed. He looked as if he were immersed in his devotions.

Matthias walked over to him casually, stopping beside him as if by chance. "Why the disguise?"

"It seemed a good idea for you to accompany one of the good friars on his morning walk," he said. "Yesterday you were not very keen for us to be seen together. You may be right."

"That's perhaps going a little too far," Matthias countered. "After all, no one knows who—"

"Not here. Follow me."

With measured tread the two men walked out and around the corner into one of the city's liveliest streets. It was full of workshops and rang with the sound of hammering, planing, and tapping, mingled with the rumble of carts, the stamp and roar of oxen, with barks, shouts, and the grunt of pigs, constantly interrupted by the bells from the countless churches and chapels. They were passing the harness makers. Matthias had commissioned a saddle that still wasn't finished even though he had laid out so much money that he was contemplating a complaint to the guild.

They strolled past open workshops, splendid town houses, and the Münster Inn, which Daniel was frequenting more and more, much to the annoyance of the family. Then a mansion with extensive grounds.

"Your friend," mocked Matthias.

"Friend?"

"The house of the count of Jülich."

"William is not my friend," said Urquhart in bored tones. "I served him for a while and he benefited from it. Now I am serving you."

"And not without benefit," said Matthias with a patronizing smile. He took a pear out of his coat pocket and bit into it heartily. "Gerhard is dead. Everyone is talking about an accident. Your witnesses were good."

"Two of my witnesses were good."

"But there were only two. Or am I wrong?"

"There were three."

"There were?" Matthias stroked his lips. "I must be getting old. But three is better, of course."

"It is not. The third was not part of the plan."

Matthias stared at the marks of his teeth in the pear. "Tell me."

"There was a thief," explained Urquhart. "Presumably stealing the archbishop's fruit. He saw me push Gerhard off the scaffolding. Too stupid. I had no idea he was stuck in that tree, until he fell out. Presumably from sheer fright." He sucked the air in through his teeth contemptuously.

"What now?" exclaimed Matthias, somewhat horrified.

"Keep your voice down. We have a witness who can tell the good citizens of Cologne the opposite. That Gerhard did not slip."

"Who's going to believe a beggar, a thief?"

"No one, I should imagine." Urquhart stopped. His eyes glinted at Matthias from under the hood. "But do you want to take the chance?"

"What do you mean, me?" spluttered Matthias. "It's your fault."

"No." Urquhart's rejoinder was calm. "You can't know every bird roosting in the branches. Not even I can. But don't start complaining too soon. There's more. It is possible—though I wouldn't swear to it—that Gerhard said something to the man."

"What? I thought Gerhard was dead! This is getting more and more confusing."

Urquhart gave a soft smile. "He died. That is not the same as being dead. Dying men can change their wills or curse God, all in the last moment before they pass away. An architect in his death throes, for example, might well mention your name."

Matthias grasped Urquhart's arm and stood blocking his way. "I do not find that funny," he hissed. "Why didn't you catch the bird?"

"I did attempt to." Urquhart walked on and Matthias had to get out of his way quickly. Furious, he hurled the remains of his pear at a house door and continued on his walk with his presumed spiritual adviser.

"And what was the result of your—attempt?"

"At some point or other I lost track of him."

"Then he's probably been telling his story all over the place." Matthias groaned. "Half of Cologne will have heard it by now."

"Yes, he did tell some. They're dead."

"What?" Matthias thought he must have misheard. They hadn't yet reached the pan makers, so the ringing in his ears couldn't be coming from their constant hammering.

Urquhart shrugged his shoulders. "I did what was necessary."

"Wait." Matthias tried to recover his composure. "You mean you've killed more people?"

"Of course."

"Saints preserve us!"

"Leave the saints out of this," said Urquhart. "What does it matter if I gave Morart a few companions on his road to hell? If I understand you right, you're more interested in the success of your plan than the welfare of your fellow citizens."

He went over to a stall selling smoked honey slices and sweet cakes with nuts. There was an appetizing smell. A coin changed hands. Urquhart started chewing and offered Matthias a piece.

"Like some?"

"No, goddammit."

They walked along in silence. The street was getting crowded with people buying and selling, checking goods, haggling with embroiderers, or simply going about their business. A gang of squealing children came running from the area that echoed with the hammering of the smiths and pan makers. It was one of their favorite games to ask the men, who were all half deaf from the ear-splitting racket, the time, then run away before the inevitable hammer came flying after them.

"You don't need to worry," said Urquhart.

"I don't need to worry!" Matthias gave an angry laugh. "There's someone running around the town who could ruin everything and you're calmly eating cake!"

"We'll find him."

"Who's 'we'?"

"I need a few men. Naturally I wouldn't bother you with this if it weren't so urgent, but I haven't time to go looking for them myself, as I did for the witnesses. Give me three or four of your servants, the fastest, if you don't mind my suggesting it."

"God damn you! Do you at least know who you're looking for?"

"Yes," said Urquhart, stuffing the last piece of cake into his mouth. It made Matthias feel sick just to watch him.

"And? What's he called? What does he look like? Well?"

Urquhart wiped the crumbs from the corners of his mouth. "Short, slim, red hair. Fiery red. Name of Jacob."

Matthias stopped in his tracks, thunderstruck. The ground seemed to tremble under his feet. "Tell me it's not true," he whispered.

In a flash Urquhart's casual air had given way to alert concentration. "Why?"

"Why?" Matthias shook his head. "Because—no, it's just not possible!—because less than an hour ago I gave this Jacob a guilder."

Urquhart's bushy brows contracted. Now he was the one to be flabbergasted. "You did what?" he asked softly.

"One guilder. Jacob the Fox. He was going through strange contortions outside our house in Rheingasse. It almost looked as if he were trying to—trying to cover up his hair."

Of course. What else. It was all so obvious.

"Jacob the Fox," muttered his companion. "A fox indeed."

"And like an ass, I gave him a guilder."

"And now you're getting your just reward," said Urquhart with a malicious sneer.

For one dreadful moment Matthias Overstolz, nephew of the head of one of the richest and most powerful of the noble houses and a man of wealth and influence himself, felt wretched and impotent. Then his fury boiled up. Enough of this wailing and gnashing of teeth; it was time to act.

"Let's get the men," he said, turning back. "I'll give you a dozen of my servants. I'll see if I can find a few soldiers as well. We'll tell them who this Fox is—what he is, a thief in whose capture the Overstolz family has a keen interest."

"I will have to speak to them," said Urquhart.

"Is that unavoidable?"

"Yes."

"It's no problem with the servants. In your habit I can take you into the house. Behave like a real monk, a friend of the family. We were talking about bringing a thief to his God-ordained punishment and you, in your wisdom, had an idea about how it might be done."

Urquhart nodded. "And what is this thief supposed to have stolen?"

Matthias thought. Then he had an idea. An amusing idea. He gave a grim smile. "Let's say he stole some money from me. Yes, that'll do. He stole some money. A gold guilder."

THE PHYSICIAN

St. Mary Magdalene's was, indeed, not a particularly impressive example of ecclesiastical architecture. It even looked somewhat dilapidated. The priests, canons, and suffragans of the city complained often enough that they could not manage on their tithes, so where should they find money for the upkeep of buildings? That was an exaggeration, at least to the extent that, thanks to substantial donations from tradesmen, merchants, and patricians, the big churches were resplendent and there was, after all, sufficient money for a new cathedral. Small parish churches like St. Mary Magdalene's, however, were dependent on their own congregation and funds were naturally not so abundant.

St. Mary Magdalene's looked all the more shabby as it stood opposite St. Severin's, whose imposing stone spire made it clear where God would spend the night if He should happen to be in the district.

Modest as it was, however, the little church was a feast for the eyes compared with the box where Richmodis's uncle lived. It was one of a row of a dozen or so crooked little houses that looked like a line of drunks about to collapse. Her father and uncle, Richmodis told Jacob, would swear blind the houses all stood as upright as the emperor's bodyguard, but that was an optical illusion resulting from the fact that as often as not they were inclined at a similar angle to their architectural environment themselves.

While Jacob was trying to puzzle this out, Richmodis knocked at the door.

"No one at home again?" She strode in. Jacob followed somewhat reluctantly, wishing he wasn't decked out in her father's clothes. If the old man was here, he was in for a hard time.

All there was in the downstairs room, however, was a gray cat. They looked around the back room and in the tiny yard, then went back inside. Richmodis called out a few times, went up to the first floor and then to the attic. She was soon back with a knowing smile on her face.

"Found him?" asked Jacob.

"No. But my father's coat is here, therefore so is my father. And where the one is, the other won't be far away."

She pulled Jacob out into the yard and pointed at a wooden hatch with a rusty ring attached. "What do you think that might be?"

"A cellar?" Jacob conjectured.

"Oh, no. In normal houses there might be a cellar under that. Here it leads straight down to hell. Watch."

She bent down, grasped the ring, and pulled up the hatch. Steep, slippery steps led down. Together with a gust of stale air came some angry words.

"—that in the future I refuse to associate with a man who drinks other people's piss!"

"But I don't, you misbegotten lump," another voice replied. "I'm tasting the urine, something quite different from drinking. Can't you understand that?"

"Piss is still piss."

"Not piss, urine, you piece of excrement. A tiny drop to tell me whether the patient has diabetes mellitus. I can taste it, here, on the tip of my tongue, d'you see? Here."

"Yeuch. Take that yellow pig's tongue out of my sight."

"Oh? A yellow tongue, you say? Then how do you explain that this pig's tongue has a larger and more learned vocabulary than your whore-mongering mind could get together in a hundred years?"

"I'm no whoremonger. But what I do know is that last St. David's

Day you went to that house in Schemmergasse and sent for those two silk-spinner girls. Sixteen tuns of wine you drank, you and your herd of unwashed students."

"That is not true."

"Oh, yes, it is true. And the way you all lay with the women, I'm surprised to find you still fit and well. One would have thought your instrument of pleasure ought to have rotted and dropped off long ago."

"What would you know about instruments of pleasure, you bloated tub of dye? You can't even distinguish between a fart and a sigh."

"Between wine and piss I can."

"Ha! Prove it. As long as someone doesn't tell you it's wine—talking of which, shall we have another one?"

"Why not? Let's have another one."

"What's all that?" asked a bewildered Jacob.

Richmodis stared grimly down at the candlelit cellar. "That? That's my father and uncle."

"What are they doing?"

"They call it learned disputations, though the only thing in dispute is who can finish his glass quickest."

"Do they do it often?"

"Whenever they can find a suitable topic." Richmodis sighed. "Come on, we'd better go down and join them. They'd have difficulty getting up the steps."

"But it's early!" exclaimed Jacob incredulously.

She gave him a scornful look. "So what? I just thank the Holy Apostles they don't drink in their sleep."

Shaking his head, Jacob followed her, taking care not to slip on the greasy steps. At the bottom they found themselves in something that was more like a cave than a cellar, though surprisingly spacious. What was immediately obvious was that it was a well-filled wine store. There was a constant drip of moisture from the ceiling and a slightly foul smell from the latrine, which Jacob had noticed next to the cellar. "Dungeon" was the word that occurred to Jacob, though one he would not have minded being locked up in.

Even stranger, however, were the two men sitting on the floor, a candle between them, earthenware jugs in their hands, continuing their debate as if Jacob and Richmodis were simply two further casks that would form the basis of some future dispute. They were around fifty. One was short and fat, with no neck at all, a bright red face, and a few remaining hairs, the color of which had gradually faded to somewhere between brown and nothing. His fingers were grotesquely twisted, recalling trees that had been struck by lightning. A thin, wavy beard, obviously attempting to emulate Jacob's shock of hair, stuck out in all directions. Despite the cool temperature, sweat was streaming from his every pore.

The other was the exact opposite. Emerging from the plain habit was a long scrawny neck on top of which a round head, equipped with a dangerously long, pointed nose and chin, which always seemed to be on the attack, was nodding back and forth all the time. Apart from the arched brows he was completely bald. From the sum total of his physical attributes, he ought to have been frighteningly ugly, but strangely enough he wasn't. His little eyes glinted with intelligence and high spirits, and the corners of his mouth were turned up in an expression of permanent amusement. Jacob was immediately drawn to him.

And both were talking and moaning, moaning and talking.

"Silence!" shouted Richmodis.

It was as if St. Augustine had performed a miracle. They shut their mouths and looked at each other in bewilderment. The fat one grimaced, as if he had a headache.

"Why are you shouting, Richmodis, my child?" he asked.

"Jacob," she said, without taking her eyes off the man, "this is my dearly beloved father, Goddert von Weiden. Beside him you see my uncle, the learned dean and physician, Dr. Jaspar Rodenkirchen, master of the seven liberal arts and professor of canon law at the Franciscan College. Both must have been sitting in this cellar since around midday yesterday, and they ask me why I'm shouting."

"I quite agree with my daughter," said Goddert von Weiden, in a voice as solemn as if he were laying a foundation stone. "Our behavior has been unchristian in the extreme. If you hadn't gone and filled your cellar with wine, I could lead a life that was more pleasing in the sight of God."

"Your birth wasn't pleasing in the sight of God," Jaspar teased him with a wink in Jacob's direction. After a certain amount of toing and froing Richmodis and Jacob had managed to lure the two disputants out of the cellar. They continued their disputation as they made their way up to the surface, but turned out to be less drunk than Richmodis had feared. Now they were sitting under the oppressively low beams of the downstairs room, around a table with an elaborately woven cloth showing St. Francis preaching.

"You're wearing my coat," Goddert remarked.

Jacob felt weary and worn out. The pain in his shoulder was almost unbearable. He would have been quite happy to take off Goddert's coat, but by now his arm was stiff and almost useless.

"He's wearing your coat because he needs help." Richmodis came out of the back room and placed a yeast cake on the table.

"Just the thing!" exclaimed Jaspar.

"Neither of you deserve it. Do you realize, Father, since early yesterday I've been looking after the house, seeing to the customers, dyeing the cloth, and slaving away from morning to night, not to mention having to invent the most ridiculous stories to stop the men pestering me?"

"Including that one?" asked Goddert warily, pointing at Jacob.

"Of course not!" She gave Jacob a look full of warmth and started to tear off pieces of the loaf and hand them around.

"Jacob gave me a whistle," she said with unmistakable pride.

"And what did you give him in return?" Jaspar giggled.

"Father's old clothes."

Goddert von Weiden went even redder in the face, if that was possible, but instead of the expected lecture, he just cleared his throat and bit off a piece of his cake.

Jacob was totally baffled. "Weren't you telling me he chased you all around the house crying blue murder?" he said in a low voice to Richmodis.

"I did," she replied with an impenetrable smile.

"But he—"

She leaned down and said softly, "I was pulling your leg. He's the most kindhearted of men. Only you must never tell him or he might start getting too full of himself."

"Hey!" shouted Goddert, cheeks bulging. "Stop that whispering."

"Why shouldn't they?" Jaspar snapped. "Just because no woman wants to whisper in your ear anymore."

"I have them whispering in my ear all the time, blockhead. The only whispers you'll get will be in the confessional."

"If I waited for women to come from you with something to confess, I might as well close my confessional down."

"You'd never do that. You'd have nowhere left to indulge your lascivious desires."

"Do not blaspheme the sacrament of confession, Waldensian!"

"Waldensian? Me a Waldensian?"

"And a lying one, too."

"Ridiculous. Accusing an honest craftsman of heresy! Anyway, the Waldenses are—"

"I know, I know."

"You know nothing. You're just not interested in ecclesiastical matters. Though I can well understand your dislike of the Waldenses. They want to ban people like you from saying mass and accepting presents."

"What do you mean, people like me?"

"Unworthy priests who commit fornication."

"The Waldenses never said anything like that, you simpleton, and I wouldn't care if they did. Have you got rheumatism of the brain or something, trying to argue about the Waldenses with a scholar? Don't you know they deny purgatory and their lay brothers preach against the veneration of saints?"

"They do not."

"Oh, yes, they do. You won't be able to pray to St. Francis when your back hurts, and when you're dead there won't be any requiem mass for your soul, no prayers, nothing. That's what your Waldenses want, only they don't even stick to their own rules."

"You're joking! They unmarried, every one of them, and—"

"And?"

"And they do nothing that is not according to the pure teaching of Christ."

"They don't? Then why were three of them put on trial in Aachen this summer?"

"Certainly not for going to that house in Schemmergasse."

"I did not go to that house in Schemmergasse."

"Pull the other one."

"And I'll tell you another thing, you son of an aardvark sow. They are heretics and were quite rightly placed under ban at the Synod of Verona."

"The Synod of Verona was a joke, a bad joke. It was only called because the pope was worried about losing his income from indulgences."

"The ban was promulgated jointly by God's representative on earth, Pope Lucius III, and the emperor, Frederick Barbarossa, because, as you seem to know, astonishingly enough, your tatterdemalion Waldenses in their sandals are against indulgences. But I ask you, what will happen if we have no more indulgences? Do you want to deprive people of the God-given opportunity of buying their way out of the consequences of their minor transgressions? And I have to tell you, Goddert, there's a disturbing tendency to overemphasize the poverty of the clergy. I sometimes worry we are turning into a nation of Cathars and Albigensians. Do you realize that our magnificent cathedral, which will tower over the Christian world, was only possible through indulgences?"

"Oh, you can keep your indulgences. That may be all well and good, but it can't be right to condemn to death preachers who are against the death penalty themselves."

"The Waldenses are only against it so they can spread their heretical beliefs unpunished."

"Not at all. It's the pure Christian faith they preach. I would even go so far as to say Christ himself is speaking through them."

"Don't let anyone else hear you say that."

"I don't care who hears me. I'm not saying I'm a Waldensian myself, but their insistence on the sacraments of penance, communion, and baptism seems to me more in keeping with the teachings of Christ than the outrageously dissolute behavior of the mendicant orders—or your expensive wine cellar."

"What have you against my wine cellar?"

"Nothing. Shall we have another?"

"Enough!" Richmodis brought the flat of her hand down on the table.

"And what's your opinion on this subject?" Goddert, who was obviously looking for allies, inquired of Jacob.

"I'm not interested in politics," said Jacob in a weak voice. He could not repress a groan as he felt another vicious stab of pain in his shoulder.

"See what you're doing?" said Richmodis angrily. "He needs help and here you two are, arguing like a pair of tinkers. Nobody's having another drink here. Not even you, Father."

"What do you say to that?" Goddert wrung his hands in despair. "Other children talk respectfully to their parents. Well, then, Jaspar, you're the physician, do something."

Jaspar Rodenkirchen gave Jacob a severe look from under his knitted brows.

"Pain?" he asked.

Jacob nodded. "In my shoulder. It's getting worse all the time."

"What happened?"

"I ran into a wall."

"Makes sense. Can you move your arm?"

Jacob tried, but the only result was a further wave of pain.

"Right." Jaspar stood up. "Richmodis, help him get his coat and jerkin off. I need to take a look at it."

"With pleasure." Richmodis grinned and immediately started fiddling with Jacob's clothes.

"Can I help?" asked Goddert, making an attempt to get up.

"Better not. We want to make him better, not kill him."

Not kill him? thought Jacob as he took off the coat with Richmodis's help. Don't worry, there are others who want to take care of that. Laboriously he managed to peel off his jerkin.

Jaspar gave his shoulder and arm a close examination. "Hm," he said. His fingers felt Jacob's shoulder blade and explored the back of his neck and his collarbone. "Hm, hm."

He examined his armpit, then the shoulder again. "Hm."

"Is it serious?" asked Richmodis with concern.

"Leprosy's serious. Come here a minute, Richmodis."

Jacob saw him whisper something to her, but couldn't hear anything. She nodded and went back to him. "Would you have any objection," she asked with a coquettish smile, "if I embraced you?"

"Er—" Jacob gave Goddert a questioning look, but he just shrugged his shoulders. "No, of course not."

Richmodis grinned. Jacob felt her soft arms around him. She held him tight and pressed him so close he could hardly breathe. She was warm. He felt the first stirrings of arousal and forgot the pain for a moment. He didn't notice that his injured arm had been left out of the embrace, hardly noticed even when Jaspar grasped his hand.

Richmodis looked at him.

Her lips parted slightly and Jacob—

"Aaaarrrrgggghhhh!"

For a second everything went black. He felt like being sick. Without warning, Jaspar had almost torn his arm out, while Richmodis pulled with all her might in the opposite direction. Now she let go. His knees almost gave way, but he managed to stop himself and staggered over to the bench.

"What was all that about?" he panted.

"Move your arm," said Jaspar calmly.

"I think I deserve some explan— What's this?" Jacob rubbed his shoulder and stretched out his arm. It still hurt, but nothing like as much as before.

"What did you do?" he asked, uncertain.

"Nothing. I just put the joint back in place. It was slightly out. Not completely, the pain would have been too much to bear, but it wasn't quite the way the good Lord intended. Do you feel better now?"

Jacob nodded. The feeling of wretchedness had vanished. With his arm, his mind was back in working order, too. "Thank you," he said.

"Don't mention it," bellowed Goddert in his genial manner.

"What have you got to do with it?" cried Jaspar in annoyance. "If you'd helped, we'd have been burying him now."

Richmodis slapped the table again. "Do you think you could stop quarreling for a moment? Jacob has something to tell us."

Goddert raised his hand. "I do have a question."

"What?"

"Who is this Jacob, actually?"

"Correct," Jaspar broke in. "That's a damned good question. Whom have I been treating?"

"He's a—" But Richmodis got no further. Jacob had raised his hand and was astonished when all three fell silent.

He told them his story.

FROM THE LIFE OF A FOX

It was a quiet year.

The emperor issued an unpopular edict against the autonomy of cathedral cities, especially Cologne. The archbishop of Cologne confirmed the consecration of the Church of the Maccabees. A preaching order took over a building in Stolkgasse and a priest was convicted of murder. Otherwise nothing much happened.

Jacob was born.

He very quickly lost count of the number of his birthdays. There was nothing unusual in that. Very few knew exactly how old they were. His parents were peasants, taciturn folk who farmed a hide of land on the estates of the cathedral chapter in Worringen, a village outside Cologne. Their annual rent was two pfennigs. They weren't married, since that would have required a further payment of six pfennigs, which they could ill afford.

Jacob's earliest memory was of a hollow in the clay floor. He was put there when his parents and older brothers and sisters were out in the fields, or doing their labor on the home farm. Over the edge he could see the fire in the middle of the floor and steam rising from the large earthenware pot above it. At first he was too small to get out of the hollow on his own, but as he grew bigger, he kept on going off. When they found him in the plowed field or among the pigs, they would put him back in, until there was no point and, anyway, the hollow was occupied by his successor.

He didn't know how many brothers and sisters he had either. His mother used to talk of a blasted army, but she smiled as she did so. She had problems counting, especially since some died soon after birth and she was constantly pregnant. His father beat her for that, but he also beat her when she refused to let him have his way with her. Jacob could never remember her rebelling against this treatment. She always tried to smile, while the look in her eyes became sadder and sadder.

That was the way things were.

Just when he could walk and therefore, according to his father, also work, several of his brothers and sisters all died of some fever. He did not have the impression his father was particularly sorry. His mother cried, but that was probably more for the pain she herself had had to endure. Then she apologized to God for succumbing to such unrestrained grief and stared into space. A priest came and the bodies were removed.

That didn't make the helpings at mealtimes any bigger. They ate gruel and gruel and gruel. By this time Jacob had learned that there were much better-off peasants with farms belonging to the chapter estates. They got on well with the steward and some even had good Sunday clothes. His father, who, day in, day out, wore the same homespun, moaned about them at every opportunity, calling them crawling lickspittles. It made no difference to his fortunes. Jacob did not know why his father was poor. In fact, he knew nothing except that he wanted to get away and see the world.

He must have been three or four when his mother took him to Cologne one day. She had to deliver some hose she had made to order for the cathedral chapter and Jacob went on and on at her until he was allowed to go, too. One of the steward's men happened to be going and took the pair of them in his cart, which was at least better than having to walk.

And that was how he came to fall in love for the first time.

It was a chilly May day, but the whole city was thronging the streets, while thousands of burghers in their finery were streaming out of the gates bearing flowers and branches. The people had come, they were told, to see Isabella of England, who was to stay in the city before going on her way to marry the emperor, Frederick II. The archbishop of Cologne was accompanying her to Worms, where the wedding was to take place. To the glory of the city, which for the archbishop was basically the same as his own, he had arranged for her to stay in Cologne for six weeks. The citizens were beside themselves. Isabella in Cologne! The emperor's bride was said to be more beautiful than the sun, more delectable than the morning dew! Arnold, the prior of St. Gereon, was overwhelmed to be allowed to welcome her in his house for the duration of her stay and shower her with luxury. Arnold, whose pride was only exceeded by his garrulousness, went on to everyone about it. His boasting became so outrageous that the archbishop considered withdrawing the privilege, at which Arnold quieted down somewhat and awaited Isabella's arrival with the same quivering impatience as all the other inhabitants of the city.

Jacob's mother decided to delay their return to the village so they could watch Isabella enter the city. She laughed and joked; suddenly her eyes, usually so sad, were sparkling with life. Babbling away, they gradually pushed their way through the crush lining the route until they were right at the front. Jacob was in a fever of anticipation at the promised marvel that was sending the crowd delirious: the incomparable Isabella.

And she came.

What a spectacle! Some ingenious mind had hit on the idea of making ships that appeared to float on dry ground, pulled by horses hidden beneath silk cloths. In them were clerics playing sweet melodies on fiddles, harps, hurdy-gurdies, tin whistles, and shawms, while alongside soldiers in armor rode on gaily caparisoned horses and children in white with lilies in their hair danced along in front of the bride waving garlands.

At last Isabella herself came, riding in state on a strawberry roan with a magnificent white mane and tail, followed by the archbishop and Petrus de Viena, the emperor's lord advocate. Four youths with wreaths in their hair, wearing gold blouses and purple hose, the black eagle embroidered on their chests, protected the fair princess from the sun with a canopy covered in tassels and bows. Beneath this second sky, veiled in mystery, almost a being from another world, she seemed closer to the Blessed Virgin than any woman before, indeed, almost outshone the Mother of God, so that the crowd, in blasphemous ecstasy, fell to their knees and some, forgetting the dividing line between truth and the wiles of the Devil, started to pray. And the noble ladies on their balconies, so beautiful and yet, even unveiled, not nearly so beautiful, tormented by their own vanity, masking their jealousy beneath tones of humble but false deference, ravaged by uncertainty and envy, demanded to see her face, to see at last the face of the English saint, princess, lady, whore, strumpet, destroying angel—her face, her face, her face!

With the whole crowd going wild in its desire to see her, Isabella lifted up her tiny white hands and, in a simple movement, removed both hat and veil, and the mystery was revealed.

And Jacob knew there was a God in heaven.

He sensed it in his small body. He was filled with love and reverence for true beauty, which came to him as a refreshing draught, a blessing from the Almighty. He was aware of his beating heart and fevered brow, felt the bliss only a boy in love can feel.

They stood there, gaping. Jacob's mother forgot the steward's man with the cart and when they went to find him, hours later, he was gone. They had to walk. It was a long way to their village for little Jacob, who fell into a gentle sleep as they sat under an oak tree in the night, his heart full of Isabella and the hope that after all there was a God who loved mankind.

It was late the following afternoon that they reached the farm.

His father beat his mother till she collapsed. What did she think she was doing, he screamed at her, staying away for so long? She did not reply. There were no words for this world, nor for the world to come, toward which she had turned her eyes.

A few days passed. Jacob's mother died.

She passed away without her smile and Jacob's father stood there, stone-faced.

From that day on life on the farm was one long hell. The following year the fever returned and carried off more of Jacob's brothers and sisters. The youngest suffered an even worse fate when the handle of the pot over the fire broke, sending a flood of boiling water over the floor and into the hollow. This time the priest did not come. He sent a message to say he had important business to deal with and would come, if possible, at the next full moon. Jacob's father didn't wait that long, and another small grave appeared behind the house. After that he stopped talking to other people and refused to have anything to do with them. Jacob heard other children say he had the evil eye and had probably turned various people into pigs in order to increase his livestock. Suddenly Jacob too was regarded with suspicion. Red hair was not a sign of a good Christian. They started throwing stones at him and he had no idea why.

One day a wandering journeyman, with the latest news from Cologne, knocked on the door, looking for a bed for the night. Whether it was his total isolation from other company, or the fact that he went more and more in fear of his life because he was supposed to dabble in the black arts, his father offered the journeyman lodging for a few days. In return for the bed and the hard, black peasant bread, the man talked all the time of what was going on in the world and his father listened, in silence as always, just shaking his head now and then.

Jacob listened, too, breathless and with shining eyes. The dark room was suddenly alive with strange figures and happenings, and he greedily absorbed every word, without understanding the least of what was said. But he felt once more the fascination of a strange and exciting world in which everything seemed to be of the utmost complexity.

Thus they learned that the old archbishop had died and been succeeded by Conrad von Hochstaden. The most fantastic stories were circulating about him. If their guest was to be believed, this Conrad was something of a villain, violent and dangerous, quite willing to engineer an opportune accident. Before his election as archbishop he was provost of St. Mary's-by-the-Steps. At some point he must have decided that was not enough for a man of his ability and assigned the office of provost of the cathedral chapter to himself, even though the post was already occupied. He suggested to the old provost he should vacate his house as quickly as possible, which the latter refused to do. Conrad solved the embarrassing situation by pulling strings to get the old provost excommunicated.

It was a scandal. The whole city was up in arms.

The inevitable ensued. Conrad was summoned to Rome to appear before the Curia. But the Romans had reckoned without Conrad. Hochstaden only appeared where he wanted to appear. The response was immediate. The pope's representatives arrived in Cologne to restore the old provost to his post. He, however, did not dare enter the cathedral, where Conrad was lording it with a couple of unpleasant-looking thugs, explaining to all and sundry he would challenge anyone who refused to recognize his authority. So the provost sent a proxy for the papal legates to install in office, saying he would deal with the matter himself once Conrad had given in and crawled back to that den of iniquity known as St. Mary's.

All hell was let loose. Foaming with rage, Conrad dragged the legates out of the cathedral by the hair. Then he set off at the head of his gang for the provost's house, where they removed everything that wasn't actually nailed down, smashed the rest to bits, and took the terrified old man prisoner.

Enough, the pope decided, was enough. One of his flock was defying the power of the Holy Roman Church and some of its most distinguished servants. Very soon, Conrad found himself excommunicated. The interdict was pronounced and Conrad would doubtless have come to a sorry end had not events taken a completely absurd turn.

Conrad was elected archbishop.

Had he had the time, Conrad would probably have laughed himself silly. As it was, he was all sweetness and light, released the provost from captivity, dusted him down, and apologized to him. What had their disagreement been about? Provost of the cathedral chapter? The old man was provost of the chapter.

So the good burghers of Cologne had a bully as archbishop. But Conrad was not stupid. He knew that the citizens had more than once made their opinion of their archiepiscopal lords crystal clear. Just under two hundred years ago they had thrown Archbishop Anno out because he had commandeered a ship for his guest, the bishop of Münster. Christ

Almighty, what was a ship and a bit of cargo that had been thrown into the Rhine so that Münster would not have to sit among flax and cheese! But Anno had been forced to flee, slipping out by a tunnel like a rat, otherwise the citizens would probably have killed him.

And then Philip von Heinsberg, who had left the city, only to find they had immediately started building a wall behind his back. Fine to have a wall, but shouldn't the bastards have asked first?

Finally Engelbert von Berg. He had been stabbed in the back by his own nephew. The nephew didn't come from Cologne, true, but that was irrelevant. Engelbert had been the city's lord and master, and that was why he had been killed. The citizens of Cologne had blood on their hands, sacred blood!

And Conrad's predecessor? He had made debts. Of course he had! What was money in the fight against the Devil? What in Christ's name was it that made the Cologne merchants insist on repayment of their loans, as if the archbishop were a common debtor, at the same time denouncing him to the pope as a libertine who committed fornication with the wives of German knights and squandered their money on feasting and orgies?

Impudent, ungrateful rabble!

But the city was also the leading trading power in the empire and enjoyed privileges that made it as good as a free imperial city, such as the right to levy dues and mint coins. To make an enemy of the city would only bring problems. Better to acknowledge their rights.

For the moment at least.

The journeyman had also heard that the people in Cologne did not really trust Conrad. Everyone knew that the new archbishop's cleverness was only surpassed by his unscrupulousness. For the moment he appeared as meek as a little lamb, though in the opinion of the citizens he was anything but meek and bore no resemblance whatsoever to a harmless grass-eater. Things were bound to get lively at some point, that was for sure.

Conrad was simply too crafty.

For the moment, though, no one had any complaints. On the contrary. He had opened two ale houses, the Medehuys in Old Market Square and the Middes in Follerstraße. That had meant a beer tax, but as long as they had plenty to drink, the burghers of Cologne were not too worried about taxes. No one had forgotten that terrible time, in 1225, when Archbishop Engelbert had briefly forbidden the brewing of beer.

The journeyman had been in the Medehuys and it had been to his taste. He went into raptures about the beer, praising every bubble in the foaming head. The way he talked about the effect of drinking this, for him unknown, liquid made Jacob feel like a dusty mug.

He listened, fascinated.

And with every word the tattered journeyman uttered, stuffing pieces of bread into his mouth so greedily he bit his own fingers, Jacob's dreams took him farther and farther away from the farm and his father, and into the city, even if he had no idea what a provost, a papal legate, or an archbishop was. In his mind's eye he kept on seeing Isabella's pure, white face, kept on reliving that one day he had spent in Cologne, and more than ever the city came to represent the true life his mother had told him about when the warmth of her smile still brightened his life.

His father cursed Cologne. Otherwise he said nothing.

The journeyman left and Jacob was slaving away in the fields once more. Another brother died, leaving only him and an elder brother. Their father drove them like draft oxen. The weeks passed with agonizing slowness, one day the same as the next. Summer came, and still he saw the image of Isabella, still Cologne called. He was infected with love and the longing for a different world.

One very hot, very restless night, he got up quietly from his bed of straw, took a hunk of bread, and went out, away from their shack, across their fields until he could no longer see the small, squat hovel.

Then he started to run.

After a while he had to rest. The cathedral estates lay far behind him, the sun was about to rise above the horizon. Hungrily he bit off a piece of bread, decided to stretch out for a while, and fell asleep in the middle of the meadow.

It was the humming of the bees that woke him.

He leaped up, rubbing his eyes to clear them. At first he had no idea where he was, nor how he came to be there. The sun was right overhead; nowhere was there any sign of human habitation, just gently rolling meadows with bushes and tall shrubs. Only a few steps away was the edge of a wood.

Then he remembered. He had run away.

Suddenly he felt small and shabby. He hardly dared look up; he felt God's eye resting on him with the weight of a death sentence. You have deserted your father and brother, the farm, everything, said God. You are a coward and a traitor, Jacob. You don't deserve to live. Repent.

Turn back.

For a moment he hesitated. Isabella. The city. Pulsating with life like the heart in his chest. Then he picked up what was left of the bread, turned around dejectedly, and tried to work out which direction he had come from. After casting around for a while, he found the path that led back to the farms. He had run quite a way, he realized, and set off as fast as his legs would carry him.

It was late afternoon when, with a heavy heart, but ready to take his deserved punishment like a man, he came around the hedge bordering the land his father leased. Their hovel could be seen from here and, despite his fear, he was almost glad to be back. He would think up some explanation, perhaps he'd even tell the truth. His father wouldn't kill him; after all, he needed him in the fields. Perhaps he'd have to go hungry for a day, but he'd survive. Or perhaps he'd have to herd the pigs when it was his brother's turn. He could live with that, too. Or he'd have to—

His musing came to a sudden halt.

There, some way in front of him, where his home was, a column of dirty brown smoke rose up into the blue sky.

At first he thought his father must be burning some rubbish. It must be a big fire he'd lit. Too big. There was no reason for such a big fire, nothing he could think of, anyway. He looked again.

Their hovel had disappeared.

Jacob felt his limbs go numb and a lock seemed to snap shut in his mind. He felt he couldn't breathe. His reason pointed out that there ought to be a shack there and demanded that reality go back to the former, accustomed version immediately.

The column of smoke stayed.

Jacob dropped the bread. With a cry he set off running, stumbling over the furrows, waving his hands around wildly, until he was close enough to the dark smoke to see clearly the charred beams that were the remains of his home.

His eyes burned. His mind refused to comprehend, but gradually the terrible truth crept into his mind like a spider.

He went closer.

And closer still.

One more step.

And saw—

—saw—

"What?" Richmodis asked softly.

Jacob stared into space. He felt he had fallen backward through time. With difficulty he forced himself to return to the present.

"Yes, what?" Jaspar Rodenkirchen leaned forward. "What was it you saw?"

Jacob was silent.

"Nothing," he said eventually.

"Nothing? What do you mean, nothing?" exclaimed Goddert, clearly dissatisfied with the answer.

Jacob shrugged his shoulders. "Nothing. There was nothing there. Just charred wood and smoking lumps of peat."

"What then? What did you do next?"

"What I had intended to do anyway. I went to Cologne."

"And your father? Your brother? What about—"

Jaspar interrupted him. "One moment. Our young friend has presumably not come here to tell us the whole story of his life, although I have to admit I find it very moving."

Jacob didn't know what to say. He had not intended to tell them everything. He hardly knew these people, but they had been hanging on his every word, as if it had been a sermon about the Last Judgment. And it was just the story of any little boy.

A little boy I used to know. That thought suddenly appeared in Jacob's mind. Was that really me? He felt as if he had been telling the story of someone else, without really knowing why.

"I went to Cologne," he repeated pensively.

Richmodis placed her hand on his arm. "You don't have to tell us any more."

"Why not?" bellowed Goddert. "It's a truly beautiful and interesting story. You don't often hear stories like that nowadays. And paying a doctor with a story seems to me a highly original idea."

Jaspar nodded. "There's no disputing that. Though once again you can see no farther than the ruby-red tip of your nose. Or do you imagine I could buy wine with stories?"

"Of course you could," said Jacob.

"I could?" Jaspar's nose and chin went on the attack together. "Then you know more than I do. How can you do that?"

"You can. I used to have a friend in Cologne, Bram, an old whistle player who lived in a house in Spielmannsgasse, where all the musicians and players live. He was also a storyteller," Jacob went on. "He would stand at some corner or other and play his whistle, until he had enough people watching. Then he'd start talking about far-off countries, legendary kingdoms, and enchanted castles, about fair princesses and fearless knights, journeys across storm-tossed oceans, combats with giants and sea monsters, and about the world's end."

"Nobody's ever been to the world's end," snorted Goddert.

"Maybe. But Bram earned quite a lot of money with his descriptions of it."

"I remember Bram," said Jaspar, frowning. "He claimed to have been a crusader."

Jacob nodded. "Yes. He was on the last Crusade. You should have heard him telling his stories in Haymarket. Everyone listened, even the great merchants, the Hirzelins and Hardefusts, the Quattermarts, Lyskirchner, or Kleingedancks, stopped their horses to listen. Patricians and clerics, monks and nuns, even the suffragan of Great St. Martin's, the one who's always fulminating against the works of the Devil. And Bram knew how to tell a story! The merchants laughed at him, claiming his descriptions were completely devoid of truth, but they listened spellbound. And they all gave him something: money, wine, fruit. God knows, we had a good life in those first years."

"I always say those mountebanks don't do too badly," Goddert declared.

"Bram took me in when I finally reached Cologne after several days wandering around. I can't have been particularly pleasing to the eye. A scrawny, red-haired thing with big eyes and an even bigger appetite."

"A little fox-cub." Jaspar grinned.

"It was Bram who called me Fox. Strangely enough, not because of my hair. He thought there was something of the sly fox in the way I kept on at him until he decided I could be of use to him."

"And were you?"

Jacob shrugged. "I don't know."

"Where is he now?" asked Richmodis. "I can't remember ever having heard of this Bram."

"He's dead. Died years ago. Toward the end he was so ill I went out and played the whistle by myself. Bram taught me everything he knew. He even had a few clever conjuring tricks."

"That's right!" exclaimed Richmodis eagerly, giving her father's beard a tug. "Jacob will pull a whistle out of your ear."

"Ouch. Stop that. You wouldn't get a whistle in a respectable person's ear."

"Oh, yes, you would," Jaspar broke in, "if there's no brain behind it. I'd say you could pull enough whistles out of your ears to supply Mainz and Aachen as well as Cologne."

"It didn't bring much in." Jacob hurried on with his story before the two of them could start another of their disputations. "I played my whistle and tried to tell Bram's stories, but people didn't stop and gather around."

"Even though you play so well," said Richmodis with a look of outraged astonishment.

"Half the people in Cologne can play the whistle."

"But you play better," she insisted.

Jacob gave her a grateful smile. "I'll teach you. I promised and I'll keep my promise."

"And now?" Goddert demanded. "Do you still live in the house in Spielmannsgasse?"

Jacob, somewhat embarrassed, stared at his piece of yeast cake. "No. After Bram died I didn't have enough money. And I had problems with a gang of beggars. So I left Cologne and tried Aachen. But I had trouble there, too. The last few years I've just been traveling around. I find it difficult to stay in one place for any length of time."

"So what brought you back to Cologne?"

"I don't know. The past? I had a piece of luck when I inherited the lean-to by the Wall. Soon after that I met Maria. She had a real roof over her head, and at first we got on so well I promised Tilman to let him have the shack, because I thought I'd soon be moving in with Maria and her brothel keeper. Well, I was wrong."

"So now?"

"So now I play my whistle. Not very often, though I do make new ones to sell. Occasionally I find work down at the harbor. And then sometimes—"

"And then sometimes you steal what you need," Jaspar said. He gave Jacob a long look. "But that's not the story you were going to tell us. Or, if my instinct does not deceive me, will have to tell us if you're to get out of the mess you've obviously got yourself into. With God's help, of course. Right. You've kept us entertained, Jacob, I'm not ungrateful, and even in Goddert's tub of a body there beats a true Christian heart. How can we help you—provided, that is, that you haven't killed someone?"

Jacob felt their eyes on him. He thought about leaving. The image of Maria had come into his mind, Tilman's grotesquely contorted body. As if he only had to tell what he had seen to condemn his audience to death. All of them sitting there, Richmodis, Jaspar, Goddert. As if nothing could protect them from the short, swift bolts from the miniature crossbow once they had heard his secret. He could not sacrifice more people for the truth.

Run away, then. Once again.

Richmodis seemed to guess his thoughts. "Don't you trust us?" she asked.

It was a trick. Richmodis knew it and Jacob knew it. The decision was no longer his alone. It would reflect on the trustworthiness of these who had looked after him. She had him trapped.

Jaspar gave Richmodis a quick glance. "Half a story is no story," he said slowly. Then he raised his eyebrows, as if expecting the worst. "But, of course, if you don't trust us ..."

"Yes," growled Goddert, "if there's a lack of trust, you can't do anything about it."

Jacob took a deep breath and looked at them, one after the other. "Oh, I do," he said through clenched teeth, "I do trust you."

Richmodis gave a little smile of victory. Jaspar and Goddert grinned at each other.

"More than you're going to like," Jacob whispered.

RHEINGASSE

There were a dozen men gathered around the table, burly men with horny hands and weather-beaten faces. They stared at the tall figure of Urquhart with a mixture of fear, uncertainty, and respect. Matthias leaned against the door, arms crossed, as Urquhart gave the servants his instructions. After a while he went out, reassured to a certain extent. The horses for him and Johann were ready.

"I don't think that was a particularly good idea," said Johann as a groom helped him into the saddle. Like Matthias, he was wearing a long black cloak as a sign of mourning.

"It's the only idea that makes sense," replied Matthias.

Johann dismissed the groom with a wave of the hand and waited until he was out of earshot. "Urquhart is an ungodly murderer," he said irritably. "That we use him is no reason to bring him into the house. Apart from that, I consider it highly dangerous."

"I know." Matthias leaped into the saddle and patted his mount's muscular neck. The horse whinnied. "So what could we have done, in your considered opinion? Arrange a meeting outside the town? Find some quiet spot in the country and recruit twelve volunteers from the surrounding farms? We'd have wasted a whole day. Or do nothing and hope the red-headed bastard will keep his filthy trap shut?"

"That would be risky," Johann reluctantly agreed.

"Precisely. After Gerhard's funeral I'll have a word with Lorenzo and ask him to let us have a few soldiers."

"Urquhart mustn't speak—"

"Don't worry, he won't. Lorenzo will tell his men the same story that Urquhart's telling the servants—some rascally redhead relieved the Overstolzes of a gold guilder—and place them at the main gates. Our fox might just have the idea of leaving town."

"Does Lorenzo have the authority?"

"I selected him because of that, Johann. Anyway, he'll try. After all, he has to earn all the money we pay him."

"Hm, well, all right," growled Johann. "We must tell the others."

They set their horses going at a slow walk and rode out through the great gate into Rheingasse. The street was crowded, but the people immediately made way when they saw the two patricians in their dark clothes. Many mumbled a quick prayer. The news of Gerhard's death had reached the farthest corners of the city and everyone knew where the two horsemen were headed.

"Theoderich will call a meeting," said Matthias, guiding his horse between two apathetic beggars, "but I suspect there will be a full turnout at the funeral."

"You never know," muttered Johann.

"You're right. For example, I saw Daniel this morning behind the stables. Do you think he slept there?"

"I have no idea what Daniel was up to behind the stables," said Johann testily. He obviously regretted having brought up the subject with his remark.

Matthias frowned. "You ought to keep an eye on him," he said, the reproach all too evident in his voice.

"Ought I?" Johann's lips turned down in a mocking grin. "And who keeps an eye on your children? I've heard Gertrude say she might just as well have married an ice floe on the Rhine, for all the difference it would have made. Do you show the same warmth toward your children?"

Matthias glowered at him. He knew that among the extensive Overstolz clan he enjoyed the dubious reputation of being without feeling or pity. "That is irrelevant," he said icily.

"No," said Johann, sighing, "it's never relevant, is it? We all know Daniel still hasn't got over losing the office of magistrate. He was one of the youngest. I can reprimand him, but I can't condemn him for the bitterness he feels."

"Always the same old story." Matthias gave a scornful snort. "Have you forgotten, we bought the post for Daniel. And wasn't I a magistrate, too? Didn't Conrad get rid of me in the same insulting way as he did Daniel? Do you see me in the ale houses, in low company, drinking like a fish, swearing, and molesting respectable women?"

Johann did not reply. He had no desire to pursue the subject any further. It had been the sole topic of conversation since the archbishop had relieved almost all the magistrates as well as one of the burgomasters of their posts the previous year. As a result, both Matthias and Daniel had had to accept that their political careers were finished. There were far fewer patricians in the new council, and those who were patricians had to work together with tradesmen and shopkeepers.

"I recently had the pleasure of reading what our friend Gottfried Hagen had to say about the archbishop's new council," said Johann, in an attempt to change the subject. *"And though it be a sin, still I would hate the asses that have been put at the head of the holy city of Cologne. You can put an ass inside a lion's skin, it will still bray like an ass."*

Matthias gave a sour grin.

"And he goes on: *They tax rich and poor more than ever and share their ill-gotten gains with the bishop. When they must pronounce judgment, they first ask the bishop what judgment would be acceptable to him, so they do not lose his favor. They are always guided by the wishes expressed by the bishop and nothing happens against his will."*

"Gottfried's right, of course, but if he goes on writing things like that, he'll end up on the gallows. Bloody fools and arselickers! A magistrate who decides in favor of the noble houses exposes himself to the most vitriolic attacks."

"It will all change," said Johann confidently.

They had left the crowded marketplaces behind them. Once they were past the archbishop's palace, behind which part of the new cathedral chancel could be seen, they would be able to get on more quickly.

"Certainly," Matthias agreed, "everything will change. I just hope it changes in our favor, that's all."

"Why are you so concerned? We'll find your redhead, don't worry. Anyway, who'll believe a beggar?"

"That's what I said, too. But in the first place, Urquhart thinks there are certain people who would be quite happy to listen to the biggest scoundrel in the city, and in the second, I'm concerned about our alliance. I'm sorry that it has to be your son who causes me most concern. After Kuno, that is."

Johann felt his heart sink.

"You know it yourself, Johann," Matthias added.

Johann nodded gloomily. "Daniel will obey me. I promise."

Matthias looked at him. Then he attempted a placatory smile. "Don't misunderstand me, Johann. How you bring up your son is your own business. But we're engaged in a hazardous venture. You and I see things clearly. Hatred hasn't clouded our judgment. Heinrich is just a coward, I can live with that. But Daniel and Kuno have a tendency to extreme emotional outbursts and their dislike of each other is growing stronger by the hour."

"I know."

"We must keep the two of them apart as much as we can."

"That will hardly be possible. Look."

Matthias followed the direction Johann's finger was pointing. They were in Marzellenstraße now, not far from Gerhard Morart's large house. Old and young, rich and poor had come to pay their last respects to the architect. They included an array of patricians such as was seldom seen, expressing the general admiration for a man who wanted to build the perfect church and whom God, in His mercy, had taken up to the paradise he deserved.

Kuno was among them.

And coming down Marzellenstraße from the other side was Daniel, a self-satisfied smirk on his lips.

Trouble was not very far away.

SEVERINSTRAßE

Jacob was exhausted.

He stood at the window watching Richmodis take her unwilling father, complaining all the time and dragging his feet, back to their house. Goddert had been fired up by Jacob's story. Horrified and outraged at what he had heard, he was all for setting off in pursuit of the demon at once, of informing the magistrates and constables, no, better the governor and the executioner or, no, why not go straight to the archbishop, who could summon a posse of clerics to crush the Devil beneath the weight of their prayers.

"We're not going to crush anything today," was all Jaspar had said.

"And why not?" snapped Goddert. "Are you too scared?"

"No, too sensible. You can pray till the roof falls on your head, I'm going to use mine."

"Huh! You couldn't even use your head for a tonsure! If this poor, oppressed soul here"—he pointed at Jacob with a dramatic gesture—"is being pursued by the Devil or one of his demons, then we must call on the Lord without delay, if not just for his sake, then for the sake of Gerhard Morart."

"That is based on the assumption that the poor oppressed soul here is right. Who says it was the Devil? Or that Jacob is telling the truth? Were you there?"

"Were you there when they cut down poor Archbishop Engelbert? You still can't deny he was murdered."

"What I can't deny is that you're a stupid ass, Goddert. Gerhard

Morart, God rest his soul, fell from a great height and broke every bone in his body, which does not prove conclusively it was the Devil. Engelbert's body, on the other hand, had precisely forty-seven wounds—"

"More than three hundred it was!"

"—as Caesarius von Heisterbach wrote in his *Vita, passio et miracula beati Engelberti Coloniensis Archiepiscopi*. Wounds that he could hardly have inflicted on himself. And his murderer wasn't the Devil, but Friedrich von Isenburg."

"He was a devil!"

"He was Engelbert's nephew, pea brain! I have to admit, though, that Engelbert wasn't poor. He was a robber and bully, like our Conrad. It was not without reason that the pope excommunicated him."

"That just shows your lack of respect toward your superiors in the Church. You'd also have to admit that Engelbert led the crusade against the Waldenses and Albigensians—"

"Because he liked fighting."

"To do penance, you mudslinger!"

"Nonsense. He couldn't tell the difference between a penance and a pig."

"Better than you, he could!"

And so on and so on.

Like a herd of stampeding horses, the disputation was leaving the original topic farther and farther behind. Jacob's brain was numb with exhaustion.

Richmodis stroked his hair. "Don't let Jaspar fool you," she said softly. "He argues for the fun of it, but when things get serious his mind's as sharp as a razor."

"I hope so." Jacob sighed. "I can't stand much more of that kind of conversation."

She looked at him with a sympathetic, almost tender look in her eyes. Jacob felt a sudden fear she might go and he would never see her again.

"I'll come and see you as soon as I can," she said, as if she could read his thoughts. They were probably written all over his face.

"Do you believe me?" Jacob asked.

She thought for a moment. "Yes, I think I do."

"Let's have a drink," Goddert shouted, the formula that brought their disputations to a conclusion.

Richmodis jumped up, before her uncle had the chance to give his standard response. "No! No more drinks. We're going home, if you know where that is."

"But—"

"No buts."

Goddert accepted his lot, though with bad grace, muttering incomprehensibly to himself. He'd probably soon be sleeping off the drink. The way he waddled down the street reminded Jacob of the dancing bears you sometimes saw in Old Market Square. Beside him Richmodis looked like his trainer. The wind was toying with her brown hair.

"A pretty child, isn't she?" Jaspar's voice came from behind him.

"She has a pretty nose," Jacob replied. He turned away from the window, went over to the tiled stove and slumped onto the bench. Maria had been pretty, too. She could have been beautiful. Could have become beautiful if she hadn't— Jacob shook his head. He must put these thoughts out of his mind.

Jaspar observed him in silence.

"You don't believe me," Jacob said.

"Well, now." Jaspar massaged his nose. "There are whole worlds between believing and disbelieving. I believe you when you say you saw something. But was it really there?"

"It was there."

"Perhaps you got hold of the wrong end of the stick."

"Then the wrong end of the stick killed Gerhard Morart. Killed Maria and Tilman. Almost killed me. What more do you want?"

Jaspar frowned. "The truth."

"That is the truth."

"Is it? I would say it's what you saw. Nowadays the truth tends to be trumpeted abroad all too quickly, especially when it concerns the Devil. Was it the Devil?"

Jacob looked him up and down. "If you don't believe me," he said calmly, "why don't you throw me out?"

Jaspar seemed both irritated and amused at the same time. "I don't know."

"Good." Jacob stood up. "Or not good. Whatever. Thank you for your time."

"You're going?"

"Yes."

"I think that would be unwise."

"Why?"

Jaspar came over and stood so close to Jacob the tips of their noses were almost touching. There was a glint in his eyes. "Because you have a soused herring in your head where you should have a brain. Because if you leave now it will prove God created a fool who deserves all he gets. Are you so simple-minded you can't understand anything besides yes or no, black or white, day or night? Don't be ridiculous. Why do you think I've spent so long listening to you, instead of handing you over to the archbishop's justices, as was probably my duty, given the numerous petty crimes you've doubtless committed? You have the brazen cheek to come into my house, go moaning on at me, then stand on your measly little pride. If I were the kind of man who swallows every so-called truth whole I'd be no use to you whatsoever. Quite the contrary. A fool trying to protect a fool. Saints preserve us! Just because I don't say I believe you doesn't mean I think you're lying. Oh, dear, is that too complicated? Are all those 'nots' too much for the poor fish inside your skull? Go and find someone else who'd invite a beggar and a thief in to listen to his life story."

Jaspar came even closer and bared his teeth. "But if you go, don't even think of coming back. Do you understand, you self-pitying apology for a clown?"

Jacob felt the fury rise up inside him. He looked for a devastating reply. "Yes," he heard himself say like a good little boy.

Jaspar nodded with a grim smile. "That's right. Now sit back down on that bench."

Jacob looked around, as if he might find his bravado somewhere in the room. Then he gave up. His anger was replaced by a feeling that was not unlike having his head plunged into a bucket of ice-cold water. He went back to the bench by the stove and sat down.

"So you don't believe me?" he asked warily.

"Not necessarily."

"Do you think I'm lying, then?"

"Ah!" Jaspar made a bizarre-looking jump. "Our friend is learning the art of dialectics. May even be trying to engage me in a Socratic dialogue. No, I do not think you're lying."

"But that doesn't make sense," moaned Jacob, completely at a loss.

Jaspar sighed. "No Socrates after all." He sat down beside Jacob and clasped his hands behind his bald head. "Right. There are two men who have never done each other any harm. One night the archangel appears to one of them and announces that the other will hit him over the head with a rock and kill him. Terrified, the man picks up a rock and hurls it at the other so as to beat him to it. But his aim is poor and the other, seeing himself attacked, picks up the stone and strikes the first man dead in self-defense, of course, thus fulfilling the archangel's prophecy. Did the archangel speak the truth?"

Jacob thought for a while. "Who would doubt the words of an archangel?" he said. "But I still don't see what you're getting at."

"The truth. The archangel told the man the other would kill him. He didn't say the other *intended* to kill him. But the first man took what he thought was the truth as the truth. Looked at in this light, it was his misinterpretation of the archangel's prophecy, that is something that was not the truth, that led to it being fulfilled, that is the truth. If, on the other hand, he had ignored the warning, then nothing would have happened. But in that case the archangel would have lied, which, as you quite rightly point out, is *de facto* impossible. Leaving us with a dilemma. Do you follow me so far?"

"I—I'm trying. Yes, I think so."

"Good," said Jaspar. "So where is the truth in the story?"

Jacob thought. Hard. It was like a fairground inside his head. Stalls being opened, music blaring, peasants dancing across the floor with thunderous steps, bawling and shouting.

"So?" asked Jaspar.

"The archangel alone is in possession of the truth," Jacob declared.

"Is he? Did he tell the truth, then?"

"Of course. What he said came true."

"Only because the man didn't understand the truth. But if he didn't understand it, then the archangel may well have intended the truth, but he didn't tell the truth."

"That's impossible."

"Exactly. Every divine prophecy is clear, or are we to assume an archangel lacks the intellectual capacity to communicate with an ordinary mortal?"

"Perhaps the archangel intended the man to misunderstand?" Jacob proposed hesitantly.

"Possible. But then he would have told a deliberate lie to provoke the misunderstanding. Where does that leave the truth?"

"Just a minute," Jacob exclaimed. The fairground inside his head was threatening to degenerate into complete pandemonium. "The truth is that the archangel told the truth. The man *was* hit over the head and killed."

"But you've just said yourself he was killed because the archangel told a deliberate lie."

Jacob slumped back down. "Oh, yes," he admitted sheepishly.

"But an archangel always tells the truth, yes?"

"I—"

"So where is it, this truth?"

"Couldn't we talk about something else?"

"No."

"The truth is nowhere in your story, dammit."

"Really?"

"I don't know. Why are you telling me all this?"

Jaspar smiled. "Because you are like the man the archangel appeared to. You judge by appearances as well. You don't think. It's possible you might have told the truth, and everything happened as you said. But can you be sure?"

Jacob was silent for a long time. "Tell me where the truth is," he begged.

"The truth? It's simple. There was no archangel. The man imagined it. That solves our dilemma."

Jacob stared at him, openmouthed. "A bloody clever conjuring trick."

"Thank you."

"Don't mention it. Does that mean I dreamed it all, too?"

Jaspar shrugged his shoulders. "Who knows. You see how difficult it is to get at the truth. To see the truth, you must first doubt it. Put another way, in a desperate situation you have two alternatives. Headlong flight, as so far—"

"Or?"

"Or you use your head." Jaspar stood up. "But do not forget," he said, a severe expression on his face, "that I still have no proof that you're really telling the truth." Then a smile tugged at the corners of his mouth. "But I like you. At least I'm willing to try to find out. In the meantime you can stay here. Just think of yourself as my servant. And now you'd better get a few hours' sleep. You look a little pale about the gills."

Jacob let out a slow breath. "How did you mean that?"

"What?"

"That about using my head. What do you think I should do instead of running away?"

Jaspar spread his hands out. "Isn't it obvious? Go on the attack."

MEMENTO MORI

Matthias stood by the bier with Gerhard's body, immersed in his memories.

He had gotten on well with the architect. Not that they had been quite what you would call friends. Matthias would not have sacrificed a friend. That would have been impossible anyway since, basically, he had no friends. But there was a characteristic he had shared with Gerhard, an exceptional clarity of mind combined with the ability to plan months and years ahead. Too few people saw time as something to be planned. The mystics even denied its very existence because an ever-rolling stream of time made possible what they condemned as heresy: progress, poison to the minds of the logicians with their Roscelin of Compiègne, Peter Abelard, Roger Bacon, Anselm, and the like. Most people saw time as a gift from God, to be consumed rather than exploited, parceled up into lauds and vespers, prime, terce, sext and none, matins and compline, rising, eating, working, eating, sleeping.

Time seen as the stage for human activity prompted the question of what a man could achieve in the course of his allotted span, if anything. The mystic's concept of stasis was countered by the ideas of beginning and completion. But to complete something you had to live long enough, and did man ever live long enough to complete the things he began? A question that brought cries of "Heresy!" and "Criticizing God!" from traditionalists. It was the lot of man to suffer in silence, not to create. When the mystics talked of a crusade, they meant a crusade against the humanists as well. Christendom was more and more splitting up into enemy camps and Gerhard Morart, whose ambition had been to create something impossible to complete, had been pulled this way and that.

Matthias found the argument interesting, too. Did not he also, as he built up the Overstolz empire, place one stone upon another? It was not without reason that one of the mocking names for merchants was "sellers of time." It also expressed an undercurrent of unease. They certainly never stood still.

The two men had often discussed the relationship between idea and execution, whether the concept of a new cathedral was incomplete without its physical realization and whether it was important to see your ideas carried through to completion. It was in this latter point that their views diverged. Matthias's rational approach, which, as he well knew, came from a lack of imagination, led to a single-minded pursuit of immediate profit. Gerhard, on the other hand, saw reason simply as the best method of giving ideas that were clearly impracticable a basis of probability. In the final analysis, Gerhard had been a passionate visionary, inspired with the idea of creating something completely new, of introducing a revolutionary style into architecture that would fill the massive, earthbound buildings of his time, dominated by stone and shade, with pure light, soaring, slender, sublime—and above all, with no restriction on size. There was to be nothing castlelike about his vision of the heavenly city, the new Jerusalem, where God sat in state with His angels. Castles were the home of the Devil.

That was indeed something new. But however much they respected and admired him, some of his fellow citizens felt Gerhard's enjoyment of the role of creator was all too plain to see. It was hardly surprising that the simple folk began to assume he had magic powers and rumors spread that he had called up Satan in the dead of night. There were many among the mendicant orders in particular who would have liked to see him tried for heresy and burned at the stake, together with Conrad von Hochstaden and Albertus Magnus. Had not Joachim of Fiore, whom the Franciscans held in high regard, prophesied the dawn of a new age for 1260, the age of a truly poor church? Was that colossal monument to human pride being built in Cologne an expression of that poverty? For many, Joachim's prophecy represented the absolute truth, therefore the new cathedral, that most ambitious of enterprises, could only be the work of the Devil.

But then the pope and the emperor would have had to be burned along with Gerhard, since they supported the cathedral. It would be unwise, however, to criticize their decision publicly, if one wanted to avoid being beheaded, drowned, hung, drawn and quartered, or boiled in oil. The Holy Father had described the cathedral as a holy work and it was best to leave holy works be.

So the critics of the new cathedral in Cologne contented themselves with general sermons on dens of iniquity and vanity, which was nothing new, but not a risk, either. Soon Gerhard's supposed pact had become merely part of the local folklore.

Gerhard's real genius, however, lay less in conceiving a building such as the new cathedral, the perfect church, than in actually getting it built. His plans were not the product of visionary euphoria but of logical reasoning. Gerhard saw himself as a scientist pursuing goals that were absolutely unscientific. He marked out the space for the freest unfolding of the spirit with compass and measuring line; in his attempt to give it universal validity he submitted his divine inspiration to the unfeeling plumb line, transposed the exhilaration of heavenward soaring into a pinnacle of measurable height. And with every inch the cathedral grew, he became ever

more painfully aware how small man was in the sight of God and how pitiful his attempt to rise above himself.

This contradictory nature of his work had brought Gerhard to the brink
of despair. He might succeed in completing the impossible church, but not
in imbuing it with meaning. Even as it rose up, it was a self-contradiction.
It only worked in the mind; none of the goals that had instigated the idea
of the building would ever be achieved.

Archbishop Conrad had laid not a foundation stone, but a gravestone
to his hopes.

Despite all this, there had never been the slightest suggestion Gerhard
was contemplating asking to be released from his contract. Deeply unhappy
within himself, he had accepted the worldly nature of his commission, giving his passion for art and architecture free rein. There was no lack of money.
The pope was happy to sign letters of indulgence, wealthy princes and clerics
donated considerable sums in addition to offerings from the Church in Rome.
In the meantime the archbishop's *petitores* were abroad everywhere, tireless in
their pursuit of contributions. Only a few years ago Conrad had asked Henry
III of England to commend the collectors to his people; the proceeds had been
unparalleled.

Gerhard built as if his life depended on it. And it did.

When he finally realized he would never see his building completed,
not even the chancel, he threw himself into his work with even greater
determination. It was his church, his idea. And there was still the power
of logic. The completed cathedral existed—on parchment. The impossible
cathedral had been alive inside his head, without the constraints of time
and space, as long as he had been alive.

Matthias gave a pitying shake of the head. "You were right," he said
softly to the corpse, "you achieved none of your goals."

Gerhard was wearing a costly shroud. He had had it made some
time ago and had obtained permission from Conrad to place it, just for a
moment, on the bones of the Three Kings, whose relics had been brought
to the city less than a hundred years ago. To be accompanied by the Wise
Men on his last journey was Gerhard's deepest wish.

"—as he walked along the planks he was looking up at the heavens," one of them was proclaiming.

"Surely he must have seen the Holy Spirit," the other cried, "his face was transfigured."

"God was telling him, 'Come, I will take you up into My Kingdom.'"

"Whatever it was he saw, he did not keep his eye on the walkway—"

"Alas, alas."

"—and although, in my attempt to save him, I called out—"

"So did I, so did I!"

"My lord, I cried, watch your step—"

"—or you will fall—"

"—go no farther. But it was too late. I saw him fall, fall like a withered apple from the tree—"

"He fell and his bones were shattered."

"—and break in two like a dry stick."

The crowd was holding its breath. Matthias leaned against the doorpost watching the performance with interest. The shorter of the two, a chubby fellow, had worked himself up into a frenzy.

"And when we went to the aid of our fallen brother," he declaimed, "to offer him our spiritual assistance, he opened his eyes, one last time—"

"—and confessed—"

"—confessed his sins, yes. 'May the Lord forgive me my trespasses,' he said, 'as I forgive those who have trespassed against me—'"

"'—that I may be received into God's grace—'"

"'Amen!' and died."

"'—and be assured of eternal peace,' he said, and—"

"And died!"

"In the name of the Lord, yes. And died."

"Amen, amen."

The people were moved. Some made the sign of the cross. The two monks looked at each other, visibly pleased with themselves.

"Tell us again, reverend brothers," screeched a woman, pulling a pair of grubby children to the front. "The children didn't hear."

Memento mori.

Matthias watched as the Dominican monks drew the sheet over Gerhard's head and sewed it up. Each one did one stitch, while their quiet singing and praying filled the room. The air was heavy with incense. The body was blessed with incense and sprinkled with holy water.

Guda, Gerhard's widow, was sitting beside the body, deep in prayer. The previous evening she had washed the body, the priests had anointed it, and then, together with the family and neighbors, kept watch through the night, praying for Gerhard's soul.

Why am I not praying for him? Matthias wondered. I had no quarrel with him.

Because I can't, he concluded dispassionately.

He looked around. There were not many gathered in the half-lit room. The street outside was teeming with people who wanted to bid their last farewell or were simply curious to see the funeral procession. Inside, on the other hand, only clerics, family, friends, and nobles were allowed. He knew them all, apart from a few monks. From the Overstolzes, Gertrude and Johann's wife, Hadewig, had hurried over the previous evening to support Guda in her hour of need, to join with her in prayer. Johann and Theoderich were behind him, staring blankly at the winding sheet the body was sewn up in, while Daniel was looking up at the ceiling, a bored expression on his face. Various members of the stonemason's guild had hastily drummed up a quorum. Two of Gerhard's sons and a daughter, all in holy orders, were kneeling beside Guda. Other noble families had sent representatives.

Kuno was the only member of the Kone family present. Stone-faced, he ignored the others. Matthias watched him from beneath knitted brows.

Suddenly he noticed two strangers who came in, sank to their knees by the bier, crossed themselves, and nodded deferentially to Guda, before going out again. From their habits they must belong to one of the numerous mendicant orders. They had only stayed a few moments, but Matthias thought he knew who they were. He slipped unobtrusively away from the mourners and quickly followed them. They were standing outside the house, gesticulating and speaking to the people.

The monk with the louder voice raised his hands to heaven and opened his eyes wide. "O Lord," he wailed, "how painful it is for me to bear witness to the death of Thy son Gerhard again and again. I would have given my life to save him, yet Thy will be done. But still, to see him fall while my brother here, Andreas von Helmerode, and I were sitting in pious contemplation beside one of the chapels, O Holy Mother of God, sweet vessel of grace and mercy, it was as if I were being tortured by a thousand red-hot knives. But is it our place to lament if it has pleased the Lord to take brother Gerhard to his bosom? Should we not be joyful and give thanks for the moment when, leaving this unimportant earthly existence behind, he was born anew? For, dear brothers and sisters, what is death but our true birth? What should we feel in the face of death but joyous anticipation that we, too, will soon appear before our Judge to be blessed with His infinite mercy. True, the cathedral has lost its guiding hand, but others will come and they will be imbued with Gerhard's spirit. This is not a moment for vanity, not a moment to turn our thoughts to material things, to stones and towers, colored glass and mosaics. Yes, we saw Gerhard fall, saw him plunge from the highest point of the scaffolding at a moment when he was communing with God. You call it an accident? I call it Divine Providence and grace!"

"What sins did Gerhard confess to?" a man in the crowd shouted.

The monk went red as a beetroot and clenched his fist. "How dare you ask!" he roared. "May God send His lightning down upon you and shrivel you up, body and soul."

"You should be praying instead of asking questions," the second monk broke in, making the sign of the cross again, "praying all the time. Do you want to meet the poor soul in your dreams, accusing you of not having supported it with all your heart? Recite the Creed, sing the *Te deum*. Remember, at this very moment the dead man is on his way to appear before his heavenly Judge, weighed down with his sins, humbly offering up his remorse. But woe betide the sinner who stumbles, for the Devil's fiendish crew lies in wait for the lamb along the path it must take to its Merciful Shepherd. Stinking filth, demonic obscenities, the wolves of darkness!" He made a grand gesture, as if to damn Cologne and all the surrounding villages. "Verily I say unto you, all of you, each and every one, will have to take that path, and you will long to have the prayers of the whole of Christendom to keep you safe from the clutches of the Evil One, who will try to drag you down to the darkest depths of hell where Leviathan writhes in transports of satanic delight on its red-hot grill, crushing human souls in its count-less claws. Remember, we all must die! It opens its gaping maw, and its teeth are terrible round about! Its eyes are like the eyelids of the morning! Out of its mouth go burning lamps, and sparks of fire leap out! Out of its nostrils goeth smoke, as out of a seething cauldron! Its breath kindleth coals and a flame goeth out of its mouth! There is not its like upon earth."

The terrifying image the monk had neatly borrowed from the Book of Job had its effect. Many of those around turned pale, some putting their heads in their hands and groaning, "Lord, forgive us our sins."

"Forgive us our sins, is it? Then pray. Did not the angels, when they were taking Saint Martin to the world above, have such terrible struggles with the Powers of Darkness, that even the heavenly choirs fell silent? Pray! Pray!"

"Yes, pray, pray." The crowd took up his words, heads were bowed, hands clasped, some sank to their knees, sobbing and trembling.

The fatter of the two monks gave the other a meaningful look and jerked his head in the direction of the corner of the street. Time to leave. The pair of them slowly made their way out of the kneeling crowd, then gradually quickened their pace.

Urquhart's witnesses.

Matthias gathered up the skirts of his cloak, pushed his way through the crowd, and hurried after them. "Reverend Brothers!" he called out.

The monks stopped and turned, their eyes full of suspicion. When they saw he was a patrician, they immediately bowed their heads and adopted a deferential posture. "How can we be of service?" asked the fat monk.

"You were the only ones who saw Gerhard fall?" Matthias asked.

"Definitely."

"Then there is just one thing I would ask of you. Speak in praise of Gerhard wherever you go."

"Well, er—"

"You are itinerant monks?"

"Yes." The taller raised his chin and a smug look appeared on his face. "It is the Lord's will that we preach His Word all over the land. We say mass in the villages and hamlets, but sometimes we come to the towns and cities."

"A magnificent city, this Cologne, a holy city," added the other in hushed tones, moving his head this way and that, as if he could not see enough of it.

Matthias smiled. "Yes, of course. Tell people what you saw at the cathedral. People everywhere. They say there are some"—he leaned forward and put on a conspiratorial air—"who would drag Gerhard's name through the mud."

"Is that possible?" gasped the fat monk.

"I'm afraid it is. They bear false witness against you and claim it was not an accident."

A wary glint appeared in the monk's eyes. "But?"

"But murder. Perhaps even the Devil."

"Absolute nonsense, of course." The monk drew out the words.

"And a great sin to make such a claim," the other added. "A good thing such lies are without foundation, since we can testify to what really happened."

Matthias nodded. "A real blessing, Brother. Let us thank the Lord that He led you to the right place at the right time. I can rely on you, then?"

The two nodded alacritously.

"Most certainly."

"We will announce it wherever we go."

"Provided God watches over us and supplies our modest needs."

"Which He does not always do."

"Brother! Who would criticize the Creator? If He does not always do so, then I am sure it is for the good of our souls. We will go on our way in humility—"

"And hunger. Sometimes."

They looked at him, smiling. Matthias took out a coin.

"The Lord be with you," the fat monk murmured unctuously. The coin vanished into the depths of his grubby habit. "And now you must excuse us. Our Christian duty calls."

"Of course, reverend Brothers."

They grinned their excuses once more and took off. Matthias watched them until they had disappeared around the corner. He hadn't realized Urquhart would send the two to the funeral. Not a bad idea. The people had certainly swallowed their account of Gerhard's death. That would make things more difficult for the redhead.

But not difficult enough.

Matthias shivered at the thought of the damage he might do. They had to find him.

He hurried back to Gerhard's house. The funeral procession was just starting. The bells of the old cathedral had begun to ring out the death knell. The bier was preceded by monks, deacons and acolytes, the provost of the cathedral chapter, and the suffragan in their vestments, with the processional crucifix, holy water basin, thurible, and candles, even though it was broad daylight. The body was carried by members of the stonemasons' guild, followed by Guda, the family, and friends. Nuns and lay sisters carrying candles sang psalms and said prayers. One of the nuns pushed another aside to get nearer the body, a routine happening at the funeral of important persons. Those who prayed most for the salvation of the dignitary would have a better chance at the Last Judgment.

Gerhard's body would lie in state in the cathedral for three days. Monks would sit beside him, reciting the *Kyrie* and perhaps, even though it was forbidden, one of the pagan songs from the old religion, all the time waving the thurible to mask the inevitable smell. Now, in the cooler days of September, it wasn't so bad, but three days was still three days.

First, however, there was the requiem mass to get through. That meant listening to interminable sermons, then enduring visions of the end of the world and the Day of Judgment called up by the power of the *Dies irae*, when the trumpet shall sound and even death will look on in amazement. Since the Franciscans had made this poem—its author was said to have carved the words in stone—part of the mass, it struck fear and terror into the hearts of the faithful with apocalyptic visions, to comfort them in the end with a reminder of the mercy of Jesus.

Matthias took his place in the procession and concentrated on business matters.

At that moment the quarrel blew up.

Whatever Daniel, who unfortunately was walking beside Kuno, may have said, he suddenly slumped to the ground as if felled by an axe. Kuno had punched him. And he was pulling him back to his feet, his face contorted with rage, preparing to hit him again.

Daniel's nose was bleeding. He ducked and butted Kuno in the stomach. With a yelp, Kuno stumbled backward, gasping for breath. Then he kicked Daniel in the groin, which had the desired effect.

The front half of the procession was continuing on its way, as if nothing had happened; the rear half halted.

Daniel drew his sword. With two strides, Matthias was beside him and knocked it out of his hand. Immediately Kuno attacked. Johann quickly came up from behind and held him, while Matthias immobilized Daniel.

"Let him go," shouted Kuno.

"That's enough," Johann barked.

"No. Let him use his sword. Let everyone see what a gang of murderers he's in."

"Imbecile," hissed Daniel. "You want my sword? You can have it. Right between the eyes would be best, if you ask me."

Matthias gave him a few quick slaps on the face. "Not another word, do you hear?"

"But he started it. I—"

"You will keep your mouth shut," growled Matthias, quivering with rage. "Remember this is a funeral, not an ale house, and try not to bring any more dishonor on the name of Overstolz. Or shall we bury the two of you along with Gerhard?"

"He—"

"I don't give a damn what he did." He turned to Kuno. "And you, off you go. Don't let me see you till the funeral's over. We'll talk about this later."

"I don't take orders from you," Kuno retorted, beside himself. He wriggled out of Johann's grasp. "And certainly not from that bastard, that ruffian, that killer, that—"

"Oh, yes, you do," said Johann calmly. "And you obey them, otherwise I'll see you get a public whipping. And don't go talking about killers."

The people behind, clerics, patricians, and burghers, were crowding round, full of curiosity.

"I warn you," said Johann.

The two faced each other, panting. Kuno was white as a sheet while Daniel's features were contorted with hatred and loathing.

"Traitor!" said Daniel hoarsely. Without so much as a glance at Kuno, he wiped the blood from his upper lip, picked up his sword, and rejoined the procession, limping.

Kuno watched him go. Then he became aware of all the eyes on him. He straightened up, turned his back on the crowd, and not without a certain dignity, strode away in the opposite direction.

"He loved him, too much," muttered Johann.

"Yes, he loved Gerhard," said Matthias out loud, turning to the people around. "And Daniel loved him, too. Love made them blind and each thought he was closest to him. Thus love can engender hatred and turn friends into enemies. Forgive them. Now let us go and pay our last respects to Gerhard."

Strangely, the crowd seemed happy with the explanation he had quickly cobbled together. As if Daniel had ever felt anything like love for Gerhard! They all set off again together.

Johann moved next to him. "Well lied," he said.

"Sweet bleeding Jesus!" Matthias exclaimed, contrary to his usual dislike of strong language. "If Kuno goes on like this, we'll all be saying our last prayers."

Johann was silent for a while. Eventually he said, "He will not go on like that."

"It's easy enough to say that! And what about your mad son who almost split the other madman's head open? These things have got to stop, Johann."

"They will stop."

Matthias muttered a few more curses. The procession was slowly approaching the cathedral. The sound of the bells made their whole bodies vibrate.

They will stop—

Matthias could not let the matter rest. "What do you mean by that?"

"I spoke with Mother yesterday evening. We discussed Kuno. She suggested I read the Bible."

"Blithildis!?" said Matthias. "What's wrong with her? She usually gives rather more practical advice than that. I can't believe she's getting soft in her old age. After all, it was her idea to—"

"Shh." Johann placed a finger to his lips.

"Sorry," Matthias mumbled.

"She recommended the Psalms because there's a passage she felt fit the situation. How well do you know your Bible?"

"I know my account books better."

"As was to be expected. Psalm one hundred and nine, verse eight."

Matthias's brow furrowed. "No idea."

"Neither had I. So I went and looked it up to see what Mother's advice was."

"And?"

Johann gave a deep sigh. "It is very clear: *Let his days be few—*"

Matthias let out a low whistle. "That's what she thinks, is it?"

"*—and let another take his office.*"

HAYMARKET

Urquhart was standing under the lime trees, watching the market. He knew that his instructions had been too much for the servants' simple minds. He had positioned them around the city on the chain principle. It was a strategy they used in the Scottish Highlands to communicate over long distances. They were divided into pairs and each kept an area under observation, just within view of the next pair. They carried a torch with them, and when they saw the enemy, one of them held it aloft so that the flame and the inevitable greasy black smoke could be seen from a distance. Sword in hand, the other would approach the enemy, assuming there were not too many, then retreat in order to lure them toward his other comrades. They in their turn would light their torches, that being the signal to close up. Carried out competently, this maneuver allowed a scattered group of warriors slowly to surround an enemy, who would keep on chasing after a different man until they realized too late they had fallen into a trap.

Accordingly Urquhart had divided the servants up into pairs. Since, in the city, they could not rely on keeping the next pair in sight, the aim was to drive the redhead, once he had been spotted, toward the other pairs, until they had him trapped. A simple plan, one would have thought.

Matthias's servants had stared at him openmouthed. He had had to explain the principle several times. By the time they had understood it, they had forgotten the color of Jacob's hair or what he looked like. Urquhart repeated his explanations patiently, but he found their stupidity infuriating. If, as appeared to be the case, Jacob had at least a modicum of common sense, he would make himself unrecognizable. His only hope was that Jacob would make a mistake.

At the moment one pair was keeping Haymarket under observation, one Old Market Square, and a third the area around the cathedral site. Six men for at most one-tenth of the city. There was no other way. He had to station most of his men in the crowded parts of the city. Three other pairs were patrolling the area between St. Severin's and the Brook, from the Church of the Apostles past New Market Square as far as St. Cecilia's and the district around St. Ursula's and Eigelstein Gate.

Urquhart put them out of his mind. He hoped Matthias's contact would be able to post soldiers at the city gates.

His only reassurance at the moment was the tiny crossbow he could feel under his cloak. He strolled across Haymarket, studying faces. The market was in full swing. He walked along the meat stalls, submitting each man he passed to a few seconds of highly concentrated scrutiny. He worked to a set scheme, which allowed him to register the essential details, categorize and assess them before acting or proceeding to the next. It was a skill acquired through years of practice; he could not have explained how he went about it. Urquhart was far from being vain, but there was hardly anyone he had come across who was capable of seeing patterns as he could; very few could even think logically. People perceived things as if through a haze, and the haze was called religion.

This worked to his advantage. Urquhart believed in nothing. Neither in God, nor the Devil. He didn't even believe in the value of his own or any other existence.

Perhaps, he thought, as his eyes captured another face, analyzed and released it, this architect would have been a man he could have talked to, a man with whom he could have shared a jug of wine and a few jokes about their fellow men. What he had seen of the cathedral under construction had inspired his respect. If it did actually represent the overall plan, he had a logical structure before him. For the ring of chapels around the apse, that steeply soaring, straining caricature of perfection, was cold. Its mathematical precision took the life out of any inspiration.

Capture, analyze, release.

A little farther on was the part of the market where offal was sold: liver, heart, and tripe, kidneys and sweetbreads. He elbowed his way through and watched the butchers as they weighed handfuls of pale white or blue-and-red-veined collops, strings, and folds, and passed them to the customer. One rummaged around in a mass of undefined entrails and pulled out a long, tangled intestine. The pile started to move, pieces slithering over each other like skinned snakes, bodies still warm and twitching. He saw the butcher's arm plunge back into the mass, again and again, presumably the pieces on offer were too long, too short, too thick, or too thin. Again and again the man plunged his hand into the moist pile and pulled something out—

The world turned red.

He saw a man in armor, an iron claw descending and pulling something out of the body of a child, something warm, gleaming, sticky. The child was still alive. It must be making the high-pitched, unearthly shrill sound, and all about him—

His head was pounding.

Urquhart closed his eyes and pressed his fists to the sides of his head. The image faded.

"What's wrong? Don't you feel well?"

He blinked. He was at the market. It was just the entrails of dead animals.

"Do you need help?"

He turned to face the woman and looked at her, without really registering her features. A nun. Concerned.

Urquhart forced his lips into a smile. Then he realized he was recovering quickly. A different man's strange memory of a different life had almost gone.

"It's all right, thank you, reverend Sister," he murmured, bowing his head in acknowledgment.

"You're quite sure?"

"A slight headache, that's all. The unexpected blessing of your Christian sympathy has worked miracles. I thank you."

She blushed. "The Lord be with you."

"And with you, Sister."

She made the sign of the cross and hurried off. Urquhart watched her go and wondered what had happened. It was a long time since he had had one of these attacks. Why now?

And what was it he had seen?

He no longer knew. The horror had sunk beneath the black waves of oblivion.

Almost automatically his eye went back to capturing the features of the people going about their business, analyzing them, releasing them, going on to the next. Swiftly, precisely, coldly.

DEUS LO VOLT!

It was already getting dark by the time Jacob woke up. He rolled over on the pile of dry twigs that formed his mattress and found himself staring into the yellow gleam of a cat's eyes. "What are you doing here?" he asked. "Are you going to set me on fire?"

It frequently happened in these tiny wooden houses. Cats would lie on the still-warm ashes in the fireplace and when they were driven off there would still be some glowing embers caught in their fur. Then they ran up to the loft, which was full of kindling, pine shavings, and other combustible material, and in no time at all the house was in flames.

The cat objected to the insinuation. It mewled, turned its backside toward him, and released a substantial jet of urine. Jacob stretched, wondering how long he had slept. After Jaspar had driven him to despair with the story about the archangel, he had crawled up to the loft, collapsed onto a pile of kindling, and fallen asleep on the spot. He must have slept through the whole day.

But he was still alive, that was the important thing.

At the memory of what he had been through during the last twenty-four hours he felt a tremor of fear. But it was bearable, as was the pain in his shoulder. Jacob felt revitalized. He also felt a strong desire to do something. Jaspar would probably be downstairs. He found the trapdoor, ran his fingers through his hair to make himself reasonably presentable, and clambered down the ladder.

In the room a massive, good-natured-looking man was sitting by the fire chewing at a joint of fatty ham. For a moment Jacob felt like running away. But the man didn't look as if he was in league with murderers and devils. Cautiously Jacob stepped a little closer and nodded.

"And a very good day to you, too," said the man, his mouth full, so that the words were scarcely comprehensible.

Jacob sat down carefully on the bench and looked him up and down. "I'm called Jacob," he said.

The man nodded, grunted, and continued to tear at the piece of ham.

"Jacob the Fox. That's what they call me. Jaspar probably mentioned me?"

A further grunt was the response. Impossible to say whether it expressed agreement or appreciation of the food. Clearly not a great conversationalist.

"Right," said Jacob, crossing his legs, "your turn."

"Rolof."

"What?"

" 'm called Rolof. Servant."

"Aha. Jaspar's servant."

"Mmm." Rolof took a deep breath and let out a colossal burp.

"And? Where is he? Jaspar, I mean."

Rolof seemed to have understood that a conversation was unavoidable, even if the idea of continuing to gnaw the ham joint was more attractive.

He licked the fat from his lips. "St. Mary Magdalene's. Sermon. Epistle to the Hebrews, yes? At least that's what he said."

"St. Mary Magdalene's? The little church opposite St. Severin's?"

"Mmm. 's dean there. Little church? Yes, but lovely. Not a great big lump like St. Severin's."

"Er, Rolof," said Jacob, shifting along the bench toward him, "that joint of ham you've got there, er, could you imagine, I mean, assuming you don't think you really need the whole of that huge piece, you know it could give you a horrible stomachache, my uncle, for example, he ate an enormous piece like that, all by himself, it wasn't so long ago, and it killed him, his body stank of ham for days on end, it made even the grave-diggers throw up into his grave, and it probably meant he didn't go to heaven, either, all because of the ham, now you wouldn't want that, would you?"

Rolof froze. He sat there motionless for a long time. Then he looked at Jacob. "No," he said slowly.

"I thought so." Jacob gave a jovial laugh and put his arm around Rolof's shoulder. "Now I would be willing to take some off you. Let's say half."

Rolof nodded, gave him a friendly grin, and continued to work at the smoked meat with his huge jaws. That was all.

Jacob started to grow uneasy. "Rolof?"

"Mmm."

"You want to go to heaven, don't you?"

"Mmm."

"You understood what I said?"

"Yes. You said, when I die, I'll stink of smoked ham. Great, yes? Everyone'll know Rolof was rich man, lots of ham to eat, yes?"

"Unbelievable!" muttered Jacob and retreated into his corner.

After a while Rolof leaned toward him and bared his teeth. "You hungry?"

"What a question to ask! Of course I'm hungry."

"There." He was actually holding half the joint out to Jacob. His heart missed a beat, then he grabbed it and took such an enthusiastic bite the fat came spurting out. How long was it since he had eaten something like this? Not since Bram had died, if at all.

It tasted salty. Rancid. Delicious!

Rolof leaned back, a smug expression on his face, and began to lick his fingers. "Jaspar says Rolof has one big advantage," he grunted. "Rolof looks thick as two short planks, yes?"

Jacob stopped chewing and gave him a cautious glance. He didn't quite know what to say. Any comment could be the wrong thing.

"But," Rolof went on with a sly look, "Rolof's not. You want ham, yes? Make up tall story. Not a fox, an ass, yes? In a fox's skin. Could've asked."

"I did ask," Jacob protested.

Rolof laughed. "Did lie. Your story's rubbish. Impossible." He raised his index finger and beamed. "No uncle. Jaspar says you've not got anyone, never had. But no uncle, no ham story, yes?" He rubbed his belly, satisfied with his demonstration of intellectual superiority. Soon after, his snores were making the beams shake.

"I suspect you're supposed to be keeping an eye on me." Jacob giggled and returned to his piece of paradise.

At last Jaspar came, putting an end to the tranquility of the tiny, crooked room. He seemed irritated and gave the bench a sharp kick. Rolof awoke with a start. Then Jaspar's eye fell on Jacob. He raised his brows, as if seeing him for the first time, scratched his bald head, and pulled at the end of his nose. "Oh, yes," he said, cleared his throat, and disappeared.

"Oho," said Rolof. "Better I go, yes? Every time Jaspar talks of Hebrews—oh! oh!"

"What's all this about the Hebrews?" Jacob asked, getting up to see where Jaspar had gone. He heard the sound of the trapdoor in the backyard. Obviously Jaspar felt in need of a visit to his wine cellar.

Rolof looked all around, lumbered over to Jacob, and whispered confidentially, "Jaspar Rodenkirchen, people can't understand him." He made a dismissive gesture. "Too clever. Can talk till his teeth fall out, yes? Because—the Hebrews—I know nothing about it, only it says something about peace and brotherly love, entertaining strangers and good things like that. At least I think so, but he always gets furious, in a rage, like an animal, bleeeh, bleeeh."

"Yes, because those are the only words you can understand," growled Jaspar, coming in with a well-filled jug in his arm. "Bleeeh, bleeeh. For Rolof that's a whole sentence with subject, object, and predicate. That's why he can understand pigs. What do the pigs say, Rolof? What do they say? 'Eat me, eat me,' isn't that what they say? Incredible the way he can understand pigs. Not even St. Francis could speak their language so perfectly."

"Comes from all that ham," Jacob whispered to Rolof.

The servant roared with laughter until he was left gasping for breath. Then he stood there, apparently unsure what to do next. He decided to try yawning. It worked. "Late," he observed.

"Oh, excellent," Jaspar mocked. "We've learned to distinguish between morning and evening! What an intellectual achievement. The world will tremble at the power of your mind."

"Yes." Rolof nodded, completely unabashed. "Going to bed."

He yawned again, then climbed the stairs. They heard him singing, some unmelodious plaint that suddenly broke off, to be followed by the familiar snore, proving that for every unpleasant noise there is an even more unpleasant one.

Jaspar placed two mugs on the table, filled them, and invited Jacob to drink. They emptied them in one draught, Jacob greedily, Jaspar with the unhurried calm of the experienced drinker.

"So," he said, and put his mug on the table, refilled it, drank, put it down again, refilled it, emptied it, put it down again, and looked at Jacob as if he saw things rather more clearly than a few minutes ago. "How did you sleep, my little fox-cub?"

Jacob felt odd. The stuff was going to his head. "Like a fox-cub," he said.

"Marvelous. My house a fox's earth. How's the arm?"

"Better."

"Better? That's good."

They were silent for a while. Jacob wondered whether he ought to bring up his problem, although he would have preferred to be able to forget everything.

The silence began to weigh on him. "You gave a sermon on the Hebrews?" he asked, more out of politeness than anything.

Jaspar gave him a surprised look. "How on earth—oh, of course, Rolof. Yes, I told him what I was going to preach on. Sometimes I really don't know whether he has the brain of a piglet or the sly duplicity of my cat. But he's a good servant—when he's not sleeping or eating. Yes, I preached on Hebrews and some of my fine parishioners did not like it."

He snapped his jaws shut. His fury was almost tangible. Jacob stared at his mug. They could go on like this, drinking and saying nothing, but the idea didn't appeal to him much. He suddenly felt the need to know more about Jaspar.

"Why not?" he asked.

"Why not?" Jaspar grunted, pouring himself some more wine. "Because they're unrepentant hypocrites through and through, our good Christian ladies and gentlemen, and because that unspeakable whoreson Alexander is preaching a crusade and they're delighted, instead of being outraged. As if the so-called holy city of Cologne didn't have good reason to mistrust the promptings of the Roman snake that calls himself pope. The people of Cologne of all places."

"Why Cologne of all places?"

Jaspar rolled his eyes. "O Lord! See Thy son Jacob, he lives within the walls of *Colonia Claudia Ara Agrippinensium*, but what does he know of it? Nothing. Or have you heard of the lost children? Anno Domini 1212?"

Jacob shook his head.

"Just as I thought. But you do know what a crusade is?"

"Yes. A just war to win back the Holy Land from the heathen."

"Amazing! The words just roll off his tongue! Learned off by heart so he doesn't need to think about it. *Sancta simplicitas!* Now, if you were to ask me, I would say a crusade is a mockery of the teaching of Augustine, put about by another blockhead known as Urban II. God, what am I doing talking to you about crusades and Augustine? I must be out of my mind."

"Perhaps." Jacob was starting to get angry. "No, definitely. You're out of your mind and I'm an imbecile. How is it possible I'm talking to the venerable Jaspar Rodenkirchen, dean, physician, and goodness knows what else? To know nothing is unforgivable, of course."

"What's unforgivable is to have an empty head."

"Oh, right. It's all my fault. I've been surrounded by sages all my life. I only had to ask. Everyone was just waiting for the opportunity to fill my head with knowledge. Wasn't I stupid? Unforgivable, as you say."

Angrily he grabbed the jug, poured himself some wine, and gulped it down. Jaspar watched him in amazement.

"What's all this? The poor don't need to be ashamed of their ignorance, I know that. No one expects a philosophical treatise from you. Blessed are the poor in spirit, for they—"

"I am not poor in spirit! And when I don't know something, it doesn't bother me until someone insists on rubbing my nose in it, at the same time spouting platitudes such as 'use your head.' How can I, reverend sir, when there's obviously nothing in it? At the moment I don't even know what to do to survive the next few days. I'm an ignorant fox, yes, or more likely a wretched little squirrel, but I will not accept insults. Not even from you, however many times you boast about wanting to help me."

His mouthful of wine went down the wrong way; he coughed and gasped for breath. Jaspar looked on, then stretched over and gave him a thump on the back.

"So you really want to know about the Crusades?"

"Yes," Jacob panted, "why not?"

"A history lesson. Might be a little dry."

"Doesn't matter."

"Hm. Right then. I'll have to go back a little. Pour yourself more wine. There's still some in the jug?"

"Should be enough."

"Good. You've heard of the Holy Roman Empire, I suppose?"

"Of course."

Jaspar shook his head. "There's no 'of course' about it. To be precise, it's a divided empire; holy or not, it has disintegrated over the centuries. On the one hand there's the East Roman empire with Byzantium as its center and the West Roman with Rome. If you think things are pretty turbulent now, let me tell you they were much worse when the old empire finally collapsed, about two hundred years ago. The pope inveighed against the supposed depravity of the kings and emperors. The old story. When the spiritual and secular powers are at each other's throats they like to use our Lord Jesus Christ as a figurehead. The king got them to elect an antipope. Suddenly there were two popes. God had two representatives on earth who couldn't stand each other and always proclaimed something different from their opposite number. One spoke of the dunghill of Rome, the other of the king's whore. All very edifying. The Roman pope excommunicated the king. Unfortunately that was only valid for the West Roman empire. There was also the East Roman, with an emperor in Byzantium who didn't give two hoots for Rome. He was a rather dubious character anyway, who had got to the throne by a bloody intrigue, which had really irritated the Vatican. So what did the pope do in his righteous anger? What do you think?"

Jacob shrugged his shoulders. "Difficult to say."

"What would you have done as the pope of Rome?"

"I would have excommunicated the other one as well."

"Very good, Fox. That was exactly what the pope did. Not that the Byzantine emperor cared. He didn't care about much. Not even about the Seljuks who were at the gates—"

"Seljuks?"

"Sorry. Seljuks, Pechenegs, all Turkish tribes that Mohammed had united with the Arabs. So their empire stretched from Khorasan across Iran and the Caucasus, over Mesopotamia, Syria, and Palestine as far as the Hejaz. A huge area. And now the infidels wanted Byzantium as well. Given the conflict of interest within Christendom, the most they were likely to be faced with was a few toothless quotations from the Bible. The emperor of Byzantium was as false-hearted as he was weak, which was probably a good thing because it made him easier to depose. There was the usual palace revolution and a remarkable young man by the name of Alexios came to power. Once he was firmly established, he took stock and the result was not encouraging. Many parts of the empire had fallen into the hands of the Turks and the rest threatened to follow suit."

Jaspar licked his lips and had a drink.

"In addition to which," he went on, "Alexios had problems with Rome. The excommunication had been passed on to him like foot-and-mouth disease. No hope of help from the West. So Alexios tackled the Seljuks, Pechenegs, and what have you on his own, drove them back and managed to negotiate a peace, a pretty flimsy affair, but still. For the benefit of Christendom, he announced, though basically all he was interested in was regaining his territory. He couldn't have cared less about the fact that the holy places—Palestine, the Holy Sepulcher, Jerusalem, Antioch, where St. Peter had lived—were under Seljuk rule, which was what the pope was so concerned about. All the horror stories about the ungodly Turks who slaughtered Christian pilgrims by the thousand, cooked and ate them, were products of the overheated imagination of deranged hermits. The Christians in the occupied territories had the advantage of Islamic law, the most tolerant there is, if you ask me. They were allowed to practice their religion and had very few complaints, certainly not enough to send a call for help to the West. Is this all beyond you, or would you like to hear the rest?"

"Of course. Go on."

Jaspar smiled. "You're not so muddleheaded as that mat of red hair would suggest. Right then. Back in Rome things were improving. Both the pope and the antipope died and a new one was elected. He called himself Urban II and if I said before he was a blockhead, that was only half the story. He certainly wasn't stupid, but his indolence was nothing short of blasphemous. He simply had no desire to quarrel with anyone at all. The first thing he did was to lift the excommunication from Alexios, fighting with his back to the wall in far-off Byzantium, and conclude a treaty of friendship with him. Two crooks who deserved each other, ha! Alexios immediately tried to think up ways of winkling a few pious warriors out of his new friend, to help him win back some of the occupied territory, Anatolia in particular. But there were limits to this friendship, since Urban just wasn't interested in war. He ran his church and that was that. Alexios was unhappy with that. What was the point of an ally who did nothing? So he sent an embassy of twelve ambassadors to Piacenza, where Urban was holding a council, and they went on at great length about the sufferings of the Christians under the yoke of Islam, wailed and gnashed their teeth at the siege of the Holy City, and made a great to-do about pilgrims on their way to Palestine being hung by the feet and chopped into little pieces while still alive and God knows what other nonsense. All hugely exaggerated and full of oriental rhetoric, which they learned down there. But effective. Urban promised help. Promising was one thing Urban was good at."

"And? Did he send help?"

"Urban? Not straightaway." Jaspar giggled. "As I said, he was a cleric through and through, and preferred to spend his time in the usual ecclesiastical pursuits. Canonizations, witch trials, that kind of thing. But at least he'd promised. Alexios was rubbing his hands at the prospect of a hundred well-armed knights, and Urban would certainly have sent them, sooner or later—if he hadn't had that blasted dream."

Jacob, who was listening fascinated, went to fill his mug, but there was nothing to fill it with.

"Oh," said Jaspar and teetered off toward the back of the room.

"I'm not bothered," Jacob called out after him.

"But I am."

"You can't just stop like that."

"Why not?" Jaspar's voice was already coming from outside. "The story took hundreds of years to become history, but you can't wait."

"I want to know what happened next. And you still haven't told me about the lost children."

Jaspar was trying to open the trapdoor in the yard. "Well, if you insist, come out here."

Jacob jumped up and went out into the dark yard. Jaspar had lit a candle and indicated he should go down first. Cautiously they negotiated the slippery steps. Jacob was plunged into the damp, musty smell once more and a strange feeling of timelessness came over him. The darkness in front echoed with the drip of water. Then candlelight filled the immediate surroundings. Jaspar was standing beside him.

"Could you imagine spending the rest of your life here?" he asked. "Not out of choice, but if you had to?"

"Not even by choice."

Jaspar gave a dry laugh. "And yet this is paradise. What do we know about the Crusades anyway?" He went over to a barrel and drew off two or three pints. As he followed him, Jacob seemed to be floating. He wasn't used to the stuff. He spun around, arms outstretched, and felt himself sink to the ground like a feather.

Jaspar gave him a searching look and placed the candle on the ground in front of him. Then he sat down opposite and filled the mugs. "This is a better place to talk about the Crusades," he said, taking a draught.

Jacob followed suit. "Agreed."

"No, you misunderstand. This cellar is a hole in the ground. It's unhealthy and oppressive. It's my penitential chamber."

"Nice penance." Jacob grinned.

"I could just as easily drink up there, in the warm. But that's what I don't do. To sit in a cozy, well-heated room talking about injustice and suffering seems to me tantamount to mocking those who really suffer. You want to know what Urban dreamed? He claimed the Lord appeared to him and commanded him to take up arms in the name of the Cross against the heathen and unbelievers. In November of the year of our Lord 1095 he preached the Crusade at the Council of Clermont, beseeching rich and poor to wipe out the Turks in a massive campaign, a holy, just war the like of which had never been seen. And everyone who was there—and there were lots, too many—burghers, merchants, clerics, and soldiers, tore their clothes into crosses, screaming *Deus lo volt! Deus lo volt!*

He was silent for a while. Jacob didn't ask what the war-cry meant. He could guess.

"So off they went, kings and princes, knights and squires, thieves and beggars, priests and bishops, the riffraff from the streets, swindlers, murderers, anyone who could ride or walk. They set off rejoicing to fight for the Lord, bribed by the unparalleled remission of their sins, if only they would take up the sword and journey to the Holy Land. And they kept on crying *Deus lo volt!*, as if God could have wanted them to massacre the unbelievers in their own land, steeping their hands in the blood of the Jews of Mainz, Worms, Speyer, and other cities, to indulge in mindless, wholesale slaughter, beheading, burning, disemboweling innocent men, women, and children, laying waste to the countryside, plundering, the scourge of even the Christians they claimed to be going to liberate."

Jaspar spat on the ground. "God willed that? The stories your Bram told about the Crusades were a load of crap. I heard them and nothing could be further from the truth, even if he did put it over well. Bram was no crusader. He'd got to know a few of those who came back with no arms, no legs, or no wits left. Hungary and Byzantium, Istria and Constantinople, everything was razed to the ground. I read what a chronicler from Mainz wrote, before they butchered him, too: *Why did the sky not go black? Why did the stars not extinguish their light? And the sun and the moon, why did they not go dark in the vault of heaven when, on one day, eleven hundred holy people were murdered and slaughtered, so many infants and children who had not yet sinned, so many poor, innocent souls?* They beseeched the Almighty to help them, but the Almighty happened to be somewhere else, or perhaps He thought they deserved it. And all that happened while they were still here, in our towns and cities."

He shook his head. "Then they went off to the Holy Land, in the name of the Lord. The scum, the foot soldiers, the bands of marauders, never arrived. They either died of starvation, were killed, or simply dropped dead on the way. But the great armies of knights did get there. They besieged Jerusalem. For five weeks! They sweated themselves silly in their armor, they must have stunk like pigs, they were foul and festering, but they held on. Then they entered the city. It is said that on that day our men waded up to their horses' fetlocks, to their knees in Saracen blood. What was their new Christian kingdom founded on? On murder! On torture and mutilation! On rape and pillage! Those are your Christians, my son. That is the

Christianity we're so proud of. Brotherly love!" He spat contemptuously. "And what is it Paul says to the Hebrews? A few boring injunctions: *Let brotherly love continue. Be not forgetful to entertain strangers, for thereby some have entertained angels unawares. Remember them that are in bonds, as bound with them; and them which suffer adversity, as being yourselves also in the body.*"

Jacob waved his mug as he tried not to lose his balance. "But that was all a long time ago," he said, the sounds merging into one long word.

"No!" Jaspar shook his head violently. "No, the Saracens reconquered Jerusalem. There was one Crusade after another, especially after even a saint like Bernard of Clairvaux placed himself at the service of the butchers. You know Bernard?"

"Not as such—"

"Of course not. Again there were letters of indulgence, sold like quack remedies, papal bulls sanctioned murder and more murder. And the knights! Life in a castle can get pretty boring when there's no call for your skills, so they put their armor on and went out crying *Deus lo volt!* again. But it was no use. They couldn't repeat the pathetic success of the first Crusade. Lured by the promise of fabulous treasure, they went to the Holy Land to be defeated and die, fighting for power among themselves, with the Church trying to consolidate its leading role. Honorable reasons, as you can see. And then the Crusade came to Cologne. Or rather, its vile breath blew through the streets and touched a boy named Nicholas and one or two other ten-year-olds. This Nicholas stood up in the streets and called on all the children to follow him to Jerusalem and defeat the Saracens by the power of faith alone. They intended to part the Mediterranean as Moses had parted the Red Sea, this infantile horde, and even priests and pilgrims didn't think it beneath them to join it, not to mention maids and servants. God knows how they managed to cross the Alps, the youngest not even six years old, but by the time they reached Genoa most were dead and they were reduced to a pitiful handful. And what happened? What happened, eh?"

Jaspar's fist hammered on the stone floor. "Nothing! Nothing at all! The sea didn't give a shit for them. Part? What, me? I need a prophet for that, or at least a Bernard of Clairvaux. There they stood, the lost children, exhausted, robbed of everything they had, weeping and wailing. In St. Denis there was another such lost child, Stephen. He'd not yet grown a beard, but they still followed him by the thousand and they marched to Marseilles. *Suffer the little children to come unto me*, said the Lord, but in Marseilles it was two merchants who said that. They packed the children on ships and sold them as slaves to the very men they had set out to conquer, Egyptians and Algerians. Now do you wonder why the people of Cologne of all places have good reason to be suspicious of Crusades?"

Jaspar's voice had started to go around and around Jacob, like a dog yapping at his heels. He put his mug down. It fell over. "They should have just boxed the children around the ears," he babbled.

"They should have. But they didn't. Do you know what the pope said? *These children shame us. For while they hasten to win back the Holy Land, we lie asleep.* That is what he said. But one year later, when the disaster was there for all to see, they hanged Nicholas's father in Cologne. Suddenly it was all his fault; he had sent his son off out of a desire for glory. Suddenly everyone thought it had been madness. Funny, isn't it? And now? Conrad von Hochstaden has announced a sermon against the unbelievers for the day after tomorrow. He's going to deliver it in one of the chapels of his new cathedral. In Rome recently a new Crusade was proclaimed against the Tartars. Does anything strike you?"

Jacob was finding thinking difficult. Did anything strike him? "No," he decided.

Jaspar reached over and grabbed him by the jerkin. "Yes! It's starting again. I talk of brotherly love and the Christian life, and they talk of Crusades. God knows, I'm not overendowed with morality, I drink, I swear, and, yes, as Goddert quite rightly pointed out, I fornicate, and I think the Waldenses should be punished, and a few other heretical curs along with them—but a Crusade can't be God's will. It's too cruel. It makes a mockery of the cross on which Christ died. He damn well didn't die so we could start a bloodbath in Jerusalem, or anywhere else in the world for that matter."

Jacob stared at him. Jaspar's chin was slowly merging with his forehead, while a second nose had appeared. He burped.

Then Jaspar's face dropped from view to be gradually replaced by the patterns of shadow on the cellar ceiling. Incapable of thinking of anything but sleep, Jacob slid to the floor.

Jaspar's hand tugged at his breeches. "Hey, just a minute, Fox-cub, I've just remembered. There's something I wanted to ask. You forgot to mention it this morning."

"I know nothing about politics," mumbled Jacob, eyes closed.

"Forget politics. Jacob? Hey, Fox-cub?"

"Mmm?"

"What did he say?"

"What did wh-who say?"

"Gerhard, dammit. What did he say to you? His last words?"

"Last—?" What had Gerhard said? Who was this Gerhard?

Then he remembered. "He—said—"

"Yes?"

For a while there was silence.

Then Jacob began to snore gently.

RHEINGASSE

The mood was as gloomy as the evening.

Almost the whole group was gathered around the wide black table. Of the Overstolzes, Johann, Matthias, Daniel, and Theoderich were there, plus Heinrich von Mainz. Kuno represented the Kones, since his brothers, Bruno and Hermann, had been exiled. It would have been fatal for them to let themselves be seen in Cologne.

Blithildis Overstolz was sitting a little to one side. She looked as if she were sleeping. Only the slight trembling of her fingers showed that she was wide awake and alert.

There was nothing on the table, no wine, no fruit.

Johann looked around the assembled company. "Good," he said, "we're all here. Seven who share a secret plan. Plus two banished men whose fate is in our hands." He paused. "That is not many when you remember our goal and in whose interest we are acting. Each one of us has sworn an oath committing him to absolute, unconditional silence and obedience as far as our cause is concerned. One would have thought such a handful of loyal comrades would be like a coat of chain mail, each link so interwoven, no one can tear it apart. United we stand." His eyes went around the table and rested on Kuno, who was sitting with bowed head. "Clearly I was wrong. Can you tell me why, Kuno?"

Kuno turned toward him without meeting his gaze. "Ask Daniel," he replied in a low voice.

"I'll ask Daniel soon enough. For the moment the question is, why did you knock him down at Gerhard's funeral? Apart from the danger to us all that represented, it was an act of sacrilege."

"Sacrilege?" Kuno leaped up. "You can talk of sacrilege? You who had Gerhard murdered?"

Daniel stared daggers, but he remained silent.

"Sit down," said Johann calmly. "If you are going to talk of Gerhard's murderers, then remember you are as much a murderer as we are."

"You made the decision, not me."

"No. We took certain measures to attain certain goals that we, and many of our class, hope to achieve. You too, Kuno. You leaped at the chance of freeing your brothers from their banishment—without expressing any scruples about the action we all deemed unavoidable. Do you really think you can pick and choose as far as responsibility is concerned? Accept what seems reasonable to you and leave us to bear the rest because it's not to your taste? You didn't bat an eyelid at the idea of ordering a death, indeed, you were one of the first to agree. But now you seem to want to distinguish between one death and another, you accept one but not the other, though both are grievous sins. Are you less of a sinner than the rest of us because you didn't reckon with the death of a man you loved and therefore refuse to accept responsibility for it? As I said, you cannot pick and choose when all these actions flow from one and the same decision, which you made along with the others. You may not have wanted Gerhard's death, but you must accept responsibility for it, whether you like it or not. If you reject it, then you reject us and place yourself outside our group. We will be compelled to regard you as someone we cannot trust."

Kuno had gone pale. He started to speak, then shook his head and sat down.

"And now to you, Daniel," Johann went on in the same flat tone. "You knew how hurt Kuno was. Kuno Kone has no parents; Gerhard was father and friend to him. What did you say to him during the funeral?"

"I told him he was a coward. Is that reason to attack me?"

"That's not true," Kuno screamed at him. "You accused Gerhard and me of—of unnatural lusts."

"You're crazy."

"Crazy. What would you call it if someone asked you—" He broke off. His chin began to tremble.

"What did you say to Kuno?" Johann repeated his question.

Daniel's lips quivered with contempt. He looked at Kuno, eyes half closed, and leaned back. "I asked him what he had done with his strong perfume, since he was on his way to sleep with a dead man for the next three nights."

There was shocked silence in the room. All eyes turned away from Daniel. He frowned and folded his arms defiantly.

"Daniel," said Matthias softly, "if it were up to me, I would beat you till the flesh dropped from your bones."

Daniel stared at the ceiling.

"Yes, well—" said Johann. He placed his fingertips together. "Things are not going as well as they might. We have gone as close as we can to attracting attention to ourselves by putting some of our servants at Urquhart's disposal. The redhead still hasn't been found. Urquhart's idea of getting his witnesses to perform outside Gerhard's house was a neat tactical stroke, but we still can't rest easy. This Jacob could be passing on what he knows at any moment. We'll have to keep our eyes open, too. This situation has unfortunately made further deaths necessary—"

"A whore and a beggar," muttered Daniel dismissively.

"You shouldn't talk like that about whores," Theoderich remarked. "If my information is correct, you make pretty frequent use of their services."

"—and will also result in the death of the redhead." Johann could scarcely control his irritation. "We have to live with it, and we will have to

atone for it. I pray the Lord no more deaths will prove necessary and that
Urquhart can proceed to his main task without further damage. So much
for the position at the moment."

"Yes." Heinrich von Mainz sighed. "Bad enough."

Blithildis's head shot up. "Bad? Oh, no."

Those few words were enough to bring deathly silence to the room.
The men stared at the table, unmoving.

"It was a bad day," the old woman whispered, "when our men had
to go down on their knees before Conrad, in front of twenty thousand
people, to beg forgiveness for their just and godly deeds. It was bad when
those among us who refused to serve a corrupt, criminal archbishop
left the city as free men to be brought back and beheaded like common
thieves. Twenty-four patricians in Conrad's prison, at the mercy of his
greed and hard heart, and so many outlawed and scattered abroad over
the face of the earth, like the peoples after Babel, can there be worse? Bad,
too, are the faintheartedness and shoddy doubts of the moralists, who
look for any excuse not to act, the fear of the rabbits pretending to be
lions who squeak and quail at the sight of a toothless cur. But worst of
all are secret alliances where they raise their fists, shout out watchwords,
and pledge their lives to a noble end, and then turn into a pack of whining
women, ready to betray everything they swore to fight for body and soul.
Men who wear a sword yet cannot kill a rat, those are the worst."

She raised two bony hands in solemn entreaty.

"What we are doing is right. The deaths are regrettable. Every minute
that is left to me will be a prayer for those unfortunate souls. How should I
not suffer with them, I who have already tasted of death's profound peace?
The brother of sleep lies with me, one last, sweet lover before I enter into
the glory of light and give back the gift of life to the Creator. And yet, my
every heartbeat hammers out defiance of those who would destroy us, the
whores of the Baphomet and the Great Beast, my every breath pants for
justice and revenge for our dead and our exiles. Who among you will tell
me my longing is vain, that I must depart this life grieving and unfulfilled,
that I have hoped and prayed to no avail? If there is one among you who

will tell me that, let him stand before me. I will see him. Blind old woman that I am, I will know him."

Her hands sank limply to her lap. In their wake her words left the silence of the grave, the speechlessness of shame and self-knowledge.

She bowed her head and spoke no more.

Johann cleared his throat. "We will not abandon our plan," he declared. "The oath is still valid. I think everyone knows the part he has to play. Kuno—"

Kuno continued staring into space.

"—I think it would be better if you did not take part in our future discussions. That is all, gentlemen."

Without a further word, Johann stood up and left the room.

NOTTURNO

"I can't get to sleep."

Richmodis sighed. She turned over onto her side and peered through the darkness to Goddert's bed. The blanket rose over his body like a miniature Ararat. All that was lacking was a tiny ark.

"What's the matter?" she asked gently.

"I can't stop thinking about that fellow," Goddert muttered.

"Jacob?"

"He saw the Devil. I don't like the idea of the Devil sitting up there on the cathedral spitting down on us."

Richmodis thought for a moment. Then she got up, shuffled across the room on bare feet to Goddert, and took his hand. "What if it wasn't the Devil?" she said.

"Not the Devil?" Goddert gave a growl. "It could only be the Devil, he must just've taken on human form. The way he often does. What times do we live in when Satan comes to fetch the soul of an architect building a cathedral?"

"Hmm. Father?"

"What?"

"Skip all this about the Devil, all right? Just tell me what's on your mind."

Goddert scratched his sparse beard. "Well," he said cautiously.

"Well?"

"He told us a lot of things, didn't he, that red-haired lad? We ought to help him, don't you agree?"

"Certainly."

"You don't think he was lying? What I mean is, if he isn't a liar, then Christian charity demands we should help him. But I'm still not sure whether we can trust him. He could be a rogue. I say that just for the sake of argument."

"Correct. He could be."

"How should I put it?" Goddert wheezed. "I've got a soft heart, and when you gave him something to keep him warm, you probably got that from me. There's nothing wrong with that, as such—"

"But?"

Goddert put his hands behind his head. The bed frame creaked under his weight. "Well."

Richmodis smiled and gave his beard a little tug. "You know what I think, Father? Your soft heart tells you to help him. But if you help him, that means you believe him, which means you trust him. And unfortunately there's no good reason to tell someone you trust not to see your daughter. Only you don't want to lose her. A nice dilemma, eh?"

"Stuff and nonsense," Goddert snorted. "Balderdash. Don't get ideas above your head, missy. That's neither here nor there. I didn't say it and I didn't think it. A beggar, a good-for-nothing, and you from a respectable family. The thought never entered my head."

"Ha! You're jealous, like all fathers."

"Me? Jealous? Pull the other one. Why aren't you sleeping? Off you go to your bed. Get a move on."

"I will do what I think fit."

Offended, Goddert pushed out his lower lip, pulled his blanket tighter around him, and turned to the wall. "Jealous!" he muttered. "Did you ever hear such childish prattle?"

Richmodis gave him a kiss and got back into her warm bed.

After a while the night watchman cried the tenth hour. She heard the clatter of hooves as he passed beneath their window. It was a comforting noise. She drew up her knees and snuggled deeper under the blanket.

"Richmodis?"

Aha.

"Do you like the lad?"

She giggled, thumbed her nose mentally at Goddert, and wrapped her arms tightly around her.

Τhe tenth hour had passed.

Johann was kneeling at the little altar, trying to pray. He looked over to the wide bed where Hadewig would normally be sleeping. Today she was keeping the death watch with Guda Morart. His wife knew nothing of the alliance, none of their wives knew. She had no idea that he, who had received Gerhard in his house, as had the Kones and many other patrician families, had given his approval to his murder. She did not even know he had been murdered.

But for how long?

Johann suddenly realized that from the moment they had sealed their alliance, the men had distanced themselves more and more from their families. They had become outsiders in their own homes. He wished he could discuss the affair with Hadewig. He loved her, she loved him, and yet he was alone.

He asked himself what price they would have to pay. Not the price of earthly justice—if everything went well, they would never be found out—but the one their own self-respect would demand. Something inside them would die a little with every excuse they allowed themselves to get away with for their sin against life, the justifications with which they absolved themselves, at the same time recognizing them for the self-deceptions they were. What would be left of them when it was all over?

What would be left of him?

Johann thought of Urquhart out there. He knew as good as nothing about him, no more than the count of Jülich, who had sent him to them. He appeared like a deep red shadow against the gold-leaf background of an age in which things seemed nearer and more familiar the farther apart they were. Tears of courtly love beside streams of blood, the sophistication of the court side by side with the crudity of peasant life, dependent on each other, determining each other. The terrible and the beautiful, two sides of a magic mirror. People passed through from one world to the other—and were still in the same world.

In which world did Urquhart live? Was he hell or did he carry hell within him? People were familiar with death. The passion with which executions were carried out corresponded precisely to the passion that led to murder. But it was the coldness inside Urquhart that both fascinated and repelled Johann because he could find no reason for it, not even the blood money. How many had murdered and slaughtered in the name of their faith? But they did it out of religious fervor, others out of cruelty or the perverse pleasure they took in the sufferings of their victims; there were the robbers who did it for gain, those who hated, and those who loved too much.

And then there were the hired killers, mindless and cruel.

But Urquhart was not mindless. The look in his eyes spoke of cold intelligence. A look so sharp you could cut yourself on it! He had a high, handsome forehead, a soft, cultured voice, almost gentle, with a tone of mild mockery.

Why did he kill?

Johann shook his head. Pointless reflections. He had seen Urquhart just once that morning, when Matthias had brought him to the house, and had spoken briefly to him. Why was he so desperate to find out what made him tick?

Fear, he thought. Fear of asking how far away I am from what Urquhart is. Whether the difference is one of kind or just one of degree.

Fear of finding out how one becomes like him.

Johann raised his right hand to cross himself.

He couldn't.

T he two night watchmen turned their horses out of Saxengasse into Haymarket. They had just called midnight. In an hour the

Franciscans, Benedictines, and Carmelites would be getting up for matins, to greet the new day with psalms and listen to readings from the Church fathers. Most of them with their eyes closed and snoring.

"Getting cold," one said with a yawn.

"You should be glad," said his comrade. "When it gets cold the thieves stay in the warm, the down-and-outs freeze to death, and the streets are quiet."

The house entrances passed, solid blocks of darkness.

"Did you hear they found two dead bodies this morning? A whore in Berlich with a bolt through her eye and a man by the Duck Ponds, he had one through the back of his neck. Odd little things they were. Like a crossbow bolt, only somehow too small."

"So what? Scum."

"Still." He shivered. "It's odd."

"I'm quite happy if they start cutting each other's throats. Peace and quiet for us."

"Sure, but who goes shooting these funny little bolts nobody's ever seen before? The canon of St. Margaret's mentioned the Devil. A possibility, don't you think? Whatever, my parents are so scared they've shoved the table up against the door."

"What's the point?" The other man gave a harsh laugh. "Let the Devil come. We'll keep our eyes open."

The other grunted some kind of agreement. They rode on in silence, across Haymarket and down past the malt mill. The horse in front snorted. The man stroked its mane, muttering quiet words to calm it down, then resumed his sleepy posture, slumped slightly forward.

Urquhart watched them pass.

They had ridden so close by him he could have stretched out a hand to pat the horse's flanks. His fingers touched the polished wood of his tiny crossbow. It was almost a caress.

Then he set off to check the churches where the homeless slept in the doorways.

13 September

✠

PLANS

"Now I know what we've got to do," said Jaspar, his cheeks bulging with currant porridge.

Jacob was clasping his head.

"What's the matter?" asked Jaspar. "Ill again?"

"Drunk."

"Stuff and nonsense. The drink was yesterday. Look outside. The sun's shining, the Lord has sent us a new day and phenomenal new thoughts into my head, since nothing will grow on top." He waved his finger impatiently over Jacob's bowl. "What's wrong? I get the maid to make us some sweet porridge that would have the emperor himself licking his lips and you sit looking at it as if the currants had legs."

"It's my stomach that feels as if it had legs." Jacob groaned. There was a thumping above his head. Rolof was working in the loft and he was doing it noisily. Too noisily for Jacob's state of health.

"The youth of today!" Jaspar shook his head. "Go out, if you must, and stick your head under the pump."

"I didn't see one."

"Where do you mean? In the yard? My house does not have the luxury appointments of Goddert von Weiden's. Just past St. Severin's there's—

ach, nonsense Rodenkirchen, you jackass. You mustn't be seen outside with that burning bush of yours. I'll go and see if I can find a habit for you."

He scraped up the last of his porridge, licked his fingers with relish, and smacked his lips. "Excellent. Come on, eat up."

"I can't."

"You must, otherwise you're out on the street." He grinned smugly. "And that would be a pity when I've thought up such a splendid plan."

Jacob took his bowl resignedly and set about it. Jaspar was right. The stuff not only tasted good, it did him good. "What plan?" he asked from behind two hands sticky with porridge.

"Simple. There were two witnesses, you say, who spoke of an accident. Assuming you've got the story right, they must be lying. But what do they get out of it? They could make a lot more of a lovely, dramatic murder, so why go for a common or garden-variety little slip? What do you think?"

"I don't. My head won't start working again till I've managed to force this unaccustomed treat down me."

"But it sticks out like a sore thumb. Even Goddert would see something so patently obvious."

"Right then." Jacob pushed the bowl away and tried to think. "They lied, without any clear advantage to themselves. Unless, of course, they killed him."

"Getting warm. But if I've got it right, you only saw one man on the scaffolding—we'll assume it wasn't the Devil. Where was the second witness?"

"There was no one else there."

"Exactly. And our oh-so-willing witnesses didn't kill anyone, either. But they're in league with the murderer. Why? Because he's paying them. They were waiting nearby to be on the spot as quickly as possible, ready to tell their story before the body was cold. And what does that tell us about the murderer, Fox-cub?"

Jacob thought for a moment. "He prepared his crime?" he conjectured.

Jaspar gave a little whistle of applause. "Not bad for a thick head. But I'd go even further and say that also he could *afford* Gerhard's death. Bribery costs money. Of course, they might just have owed him a favor, but it makes no difference. Either way, the witnesses were bought. Now to my simple priest's mind, a knave will be open to other pieces of knavery. A man who sells his word for money has also sold his honor, prostituted his soul. He can be bought again. For the highest offer." He grinned. "How about making these so-called witnesses one ourselves?"

"With money? I'd have to rob a church first."

"I wouldn't be entirely happy with that," said Jaspar drily. "I was thinking more of a pretend offer."

Jacob nodded. "Of course. I go out and start asking for the witnesses to Gerhard's accident. How long do you think I'd last?"

Jaspar rolled his eyes and sent up a short prayer. "Don't act more stupid than you really are," he said. "Do you think I've forgotten? Gerhard's death will have been reported to the magistrates and they will certainly have taken a statement from the witnesses. Now it so happens that one of the magistrates, since Conrad got rid of the old lot, is a friend of mine. Bodo's his name. He's master of the guild of brewers, so you can see we have a common interest. I'll ask him where we can find the pair."

"The magistrates," Jacob mused. That was good. "How soon can you see this Bodo?"

Jaspar spread his hands. "As soon as I want. Now if you like. He doesn't live far away."

"Good. Give me a habit or a hat, something to hide my hair. Then we can be off."

"Keep your hair on, Fox-cub. You're not going at all. You're going to be so good as to chop the firewood in my yard."

"But—"

"No buts. I do something for you, you do something for me."

"I'll do anything for you, but you've got to take me with you, d'you hear? Disguised and in your company, I wouldn't be in any danger. After all, it's a magistrate we'll be talking to."

"I hear you." Jaspar sighed. "And I can see you doing something silly behind my back. I'll send Rolof to fetch Richmodis, to give you a good reason not to do something silly."

"I—" Did Jaspar say Richmodis? "All right."

"You see?" Jaspar rubbed his hands. "Aren't you lucky? Old Uncle Jaspar does the spadework for you and scatters the seeds of reason. You may thank me. If it leads to anything, you can still come along." He placed his finger on the end of his nose. "Just a minute. There was something else. Something I needed to know? Damn, we don't get any younger. No matter. I'll be away for an hour or two. Don't do anything stupid while I'm gone."

Jacob was thinking of Richmodis. "Of course not." Then something occurred to him. "Tell Richmodis to bring her whistle."

Jaspar turned at the bottom of the stair, a severe expression on his face. "Didn't I say something about chopping wood?"

"No problem. She'll be the one playing."

"But she doesn't know how."

"That's why she needs to learn."

Muttering something incomprehensible in Latin, Jaspar went to find Rolof.

JASPAR

That morning Bodo Schuif, master brewer, did not look like a man who meant to spend the day tending his tuns of mash. As Jaspar arrived he was wearing his best coat and about to leave.

"Nevertheless," he said, putting his arm around Jaspar's shoulders, "there's still time for a jar, don't you think, Rodenkirchen?"

"You would have to assure me that beer, consumed after large quantities of red wine, has a purgative effect, promotes the digestion, and will not impair the harmonious functioning of my organs and bodily fluids."

"Consider yourself assured."

"Then lead me to it."

The brewer gave the maid a sign. Before long two foaming mugs were standing on the table and in no time at all the two men had white mustaches.

"And where is your good lady?" asked Jaspar casually.

Schuif gave a drawn-out, rumbling burp. "At the market. I told her I wanted crayfish pie today, no one makes a better. Do you fancy a bite yourself?"

Jaspar's mouth watered. "I'm afraid not," he said reluctantly. "It looks as if I'll be occupied with urgent business."

"Me too." Schuif sighed. "There's always urgent bloody business. Since I was elected magistrate I seem to be spending more time in the Town Hall than anywhere else. There's another meeting this morning. Why, I don't know, there's nothing important to be dealt with. Recently it's the wife who's been looking after the business. She's almost better at it than me, the Lord be praised."

He laughed and took a deep pull at his beer. "D'you know," he said when he'd wiped the foam from his mouth, "the ones who give us the most trouble are those louts who call themselves the noble houses. Instead of the council of magistrates doing what it's supposed to do and administering justice, we spend all our time squabbling with the few patricians left on it. Conrad cleared out the cesspit that was the old council and replaced it with honest traders and craftsmen, but there's still a few patricians among us. I ask you, what do they want, these noble gentlemen? Behave as if they'd lost all their influence when what really gets up their noses is seeing ordinary burghers getting their sweaty hands on their supposed privileges."

"No, they can't stand that."

"You know how I feel about it. I'm not petty-minded. Each to his own, I say. But the magistrates are responsible for the administration of justice and the running of the city. That means for Cologne. The whole of Cologne. Where would we be if those who represent everyone, the poor and needy as well, only came from the patrician families?"

"'Would we be'? That's the way things used to be."

"Yes, and praise and thanks be to Jesus Christ that our lord archbishop took the shovel to that pile of dung! A bloody scandal, the way things used to be done! The guilds weren't entirely free of blame, I have to admit. We let the patricians infiltrate us, even elected some guildmasters, all for the sake of profit. But that was all. Was it our fault the noble families increased their influence along with their wealth? They got everywhere, like blasted mildew. Conrad was right to kick up a fuss about them using their positions to protect criminals and help them evade his jurisdiction."

Jaspar grinned. Bodo was so proud of being a magistrate, he never tired of trotting out the well-known facts again and again. Since becoming a magistrate he had tried to moderate his rough language, not always with success. No wonder the patricians, who had studied and seen the world, reacted to people like Bodo as if they had the itch. Despite the fact that, according to the statutes, anyone who was sound of mind and body, born within wedlock, and not convicted of any crime could become a magistrate, previously only representatives of the noble houses had occupied the magistrates' seats. If the patricians had had their way, people like Bodo would have got a kick in the seat of the pants rather than a seat on the council. A brewer as magistrate was a slap in the eye for the old families, especially as it came from Conrad von Hochstaden.

"Well?" asked Schuif with a frown.

"You're right, as always, Bodo."

"That's not what I mean. Do you like my magic potion? You're keeping so quiet about it I almost take it as an insult."

"Sorry." Jaspar emptied his mug demonstratively. The beer was sweet and stuck to his teeth, almost a meal in itself.

"That's better." Schuif smiled. He stood up and smoothed out his coat. "And now I must be off. That is—" He frowned and gave Jaspar a questioning look. "Did you come for a reason?"

"Oh, nothing special. I was interested in poor Gerhard's tragic accident."

Schuif nodded fiercely. "Yes. Terrible, now the building's coming on so well. Could it be God didn't want him to finish the perfect church? I have a theory of my own there."

"Huh!" Jaspar made a dismissive gesture. "Gerhard could have lived to be a hundred and not seen it finished."

"Don't say that. There are miracles—"

"There are architects. I've nothing against miracles, but Gerhard Morart was a human being like you and me."

Schuif rested his knuckles on the table and leaned down to Jaspar conspiratorially. "Yes, perhaps we need a different word for it. You're right, miracles are generally attributed to saints. Perhaps we should be talking of the Devil?"

"Not again." Jaspar groaned.

"What do you mean, not again? And why not, anyway? If you ask me, Gerhard had dealings with the Arch-fiend. My wife says he jumped off that scaffolding."

Jaspar leaned back, shaking his head. "Your wife should stick to crayfish pie. Do you really believe that?"

"Anything's possible," said Schuif, wagging his finger at Jaspar.

"If anything's possible," Jaspar countered, "what do you think of another theory, namely that Gerhard didn't jump, but—"

"But what?"

Jaspar bit his lip. Better keep quiet about that. Instead he asked, "Have you spoken to the witnesses?"

"Yes, we questioned them."

"Reliable?"

"I'd say so. Two respectable monks, preachers who happened to be staying in Cologne. Benedictines, if I'm not mistaken."

"Aha," said Jaspar. "Then they'll be staying with their fellow Benedictines?"

"No, they're lodging at St. Gereon's, if you must know. Why do you want to know, anyway?"

"There's a lot more I want to know. I'd be interested in their names."

"Well, why not? One was called—just a moment—Justus? Brother Justus or Justinius? Can't quite remember. The other's an Andreas von Helmerode. I can't for the life of me think why you want to know all this, but then you always were a mystery. My wife says with all your questions you'll eat your way right through history. And when you come out the other side, you'll see it's just the same."

"As I said, just curiosity." Jaspar stood up. "Thanks for the beer. Perhaps you'll come around for a jug of wine sometime?"

"Love to. When my official duties give me time."

"I have a suggestion. Make time."

Schuif furrowed his brow, obviously trying to work this out. Jaspar patted him on the shoulder and hurried out without a further word.

When he entered the pilgrim's hostel of St. Gereon it was full of bustle. This was nothing unusual. Cologne attracted large numbers of pilgrims, which was hardly surprising given the presence of important relics such as the bones of the Three Kings.

St. Gereon itself boasted the bones of its patron saint, as well as those of St. Gregorius Marcus and his followers. Not long ago the fourth-century Roman atrium, on which the site was based, had been converted into imposing cloisters and the hostel had been opened the previous year. St. Gereon was a beautiful building and Jaspar took a little time to wander around the cloisters.

A monk came hurrying toward him, a bundle of scrolls under his arm. "Excuse me," Jaspar called out.

The monk started and crossed himself, dropping half his scrolls in the process. Jaspar bent down to pick them up.

"No!" The monk pushed him away and grabbed the scrolls.

"I was just trying to help."

"Of course. It was my fault. Brother—?"

"Jaspar Rodenkirchen, physician and dean of St. Mary Magdalene's."

"Brother Jaspar, these scrolls must only be touched by those authorized."

"Of whom you are one, I assume?"

"Precisely. Can I be of assistance?"

"Perhaps you can. I'm looking for the two monks who were witnesses when God called Gerhard Morart to Him. One was called Andreas von Helmerode and the other's name could have been Justus—"

"Justinius von Singen!" The monk nodded eagerly. "We have the honor of entertaining them under our unworthy roof. They saw him when he was called to his Maker, but I must say, I think it was a damned shame he had to die."

"Brother!" exclaimed Jaspar in horrified tones.

Shocked at his unconscious blasphemy, the monk was going to cross himself again, but restrained himself just in time. "God's will be done," he said.

"On earth as it is in heaven." Jaspar nodded, a severe look on his face. "I don't want to keep you from your important business any longer, Brother, so if you could just tell me where I can find Andreas and Justinius—"

"I will send a novice to fetch them."

The monk turned and passed through an archway. A short while later Jaspar saw a spotty boy in a novice's habit shoot out and disappear into the building opposite. After a time he reappeared, followed by two monks who clearly belonged to the mendicant orders.

"There's the man who wants to speak to you," he muttered shyly, head bowed. He stumbled backward along the cloisters for a few yards, then turned and ran off full tilt.

"Andreas von Helmerode? Justinius von Singen?"

The pair looked at each other uncertainly. "I am Justinius," said the shorter, fatter of the two. "But who are you?"

Jaspar slapped his forehead. "You must excuse me for forgetting to introduce myself. I am dean of St. Mary Magdalene's. A good friend of Gerhard Morart. They say you saw the tragic accident from quite close to—"

The suspicion vanished from the monks' faces. They had answered this kind of question often enough. Justinius came closer and spread his arms wide. "Like a bird he was in the sight of the Lord," he declaimed. "As his body approached the earth, from which it came and to which it will return, his spirit rose in glory to be united with the All Highest. As Saint Paul says in his letter to the Philippians, *Seek those things which are above, where Christ sitteth on the right hand of God.*"

Jaspar nodded and smiled. "Beautifully put," he said. "Though is it not in Colossians where we find those comforting words, while in Philippians it says, *For our conversation is in heaven?*"

The smile froze on the fat monk's lips. "Yes, that is possible. For the ways of the Lord are unfathomable and Holy Writ more often than not perverted by irresponsible translators, to the confusion of honest seekers after truth."

Andreas hastened to back him up. "It doesn't affect the sense of the words."

"No indeed, and it is a comfort to me," said Jaspar, going over to a window from which the monastery's magnificent orchard could be seen, "to know that you were with Gerhard when he died. Reports say you even heard his confession?"

"Oh, certainly."

"And gave him extreme unction?"

Andreas gave him a funny look. "How could we have given him extreme unction since we didn't have the oil with us? Had we known—"

"Which we didn't," Justinius interjected.

"Now I find that surprising," said Jaspar softly.

"You do?"

"Yes, since you both knew very well that Gerhard Morart was to die at that time on that evening, as the murderer had told you."

It was as if the two had looked back at the destruction of Sodom and Gomorrah.

"What is more," Jaspar went on, unmoved, "you also knew beforehand what you were to say afterward. Is that not so?"

"You are—you—" gasped Justinius.

"You must be mistaken, Brother," Andreas quickly broke in. "I am sure you have good reason to make these accusations, these, yes, vile accusations, but you've got the wrong persons. We are but two humble servants in the vineyard of the Lord. And you are not an inquisitor."

"Yes, yes, I know. And you are committed to the ideal of Saint Benedict."

"Absolutely!"

"Absolutely," repeated Justinius, wiping the sweat from his brow.

Jaspar smiled and started to walk up and down. "We all subscribe to Benedict's interpretation of the poverty of Christ and His disciples," he said, "and we are quite right to do so. But it sometimes seems to me that the hunger that accompanies it—and I mean the hunger for everything: life, whores, roast pork—causes certain rumblings in our pious bellies. I'm sure you know what I mean. Being a mendicant entails accepting alms—"

"But not for one's personal possession," insisted Justinius.

"Of course not. You have taken on the ideal of poverty and devoted your whole lives to the praise of the Lord and the well-being of Christendom. Nevertheless, could it not be that someone came and offered special alms for, let us say, a special service?"

"'Special services' can cover a multitude of sins," said Justinius, cautiously if not inappropriately.

"It can?" Jaspar brought his perambulation to an end right in front of the two monks. "Then let me be more specific. I'm talking of the 'alms' you were paid to present Gerhard's murder as an accident."

"Outrageous!" roared Andreas.

"Blasphemy!" screeched Justinius.

"I have not blasphemed God," said Jaspar calmly.

"You blaspheme Him by blaspheming His servants."

"Is not the opposite rather the case? Is it not His servants who blaspheme Him by telling lies?"

Justinius opened his mouth, pumped his lungs full of air and swallowed. "I see no point in continuing this discussion," he said between clenched teeth. "Never before have I been so offended, so insulted, so . . . so humiliated!"

He turned on his heel and left in high dudgeon. Andreas flashed Jaspar a quick glance and made to follow.

"One hundred gold marks," Jaspar said, more to himself.

Andreas was rooted to the spot. Jaspar turned to face him, his index finger on the tip of his nose. "Was it that much?"

"I've no idea what you're talking about," replied Andreas sullenly, but with an undertone of uncertainty.

"I'm talking about money, reverend Brother. Since you are obviously unwilling to help me formulate my offer, I can only guess."

"What offer?"

"Twice what Gerhard's murderer paid you."

"I don't know who you're talking about," insisted Andreas, but stayed where he was.

"We both know whom I'm talking about, the tall man with long hair. Tell me, have the pair of you thought how you are going to justify your paid lie on Judgment Day? The Devil and his minions are looking over our shoulders, Brother, every day. Counting every syllable missed out during the anthems, every minute slept during the sermon. Now just imagine: not only do I absolve you of your grievous sin, as my office permits me, within certain limits, but you come out of the affair both purified and enriched."

Andreas was staring. His fingers clenched. "God will reward me," he said, not very convincingly.

"I know, Brother," said Jaspar soothingly, patting Andreas on the cheek. "But God will be unhappy, to say the least, with the fact that you have shielded a murderer and accepted bloodstained money. Money can be washed clean, of course, but can you wash your soul clean? Is not our first reward that purgatory of which Saint Paul says it is a fire that shall try every man's work, of what sort it is? Does not Boniface tell us of the terrible pits of scorching fire we must pass through on our way to the heavenly kingdom to decide who will arrive purified on the other side and who will descend into the sunless abyss? Do you want to burn eternally for your sins, Andreas, when I am offering you the chance of atonement and a reward into the bargain?"

Andreas looked to the side as he considered this. "How much will my remorse be worth?" he asked.

"How much were you given?"

"Ten gold marks."

"Only ten?" Jaspar said in amazement. "You sold your souls too cheaply. What do you say to twenty?"

Now Andreas looked at him. "Each?"

"Hmm. All right, it's a promise. But for that I want the truth."

"The money first."

"Not so fast." Jaspar jerked his thumb in the direction Justinius had gone. "What about your friend?"

"Justinius? For twenty gold marks he'd admit to the murder of the eleven thousand virgins."

Jaspar smiled. "Better and better. And just so there's no misunderstanding: I want the truth. Then a statement to the city council so that no more innocent people are killed. Your stupid lie has had unfortunate consequences. I give you my word that I will purify your soul and"—he gave Andreas a wink—"your purse."

Andreas looked around nervously. Monks and pilgrims kept passing, though none came too close. But the curiosity on the faces of the monks, especially the younger brethren, was unmistakable. They were always curious, about everyone and everything.

"Not here and not now," he decided.

"Where then?"

"After mass Justinius and I were going to the bathhouse opposite Little St. Martin's for, er, for a good wash."

The bathhouse opposite Little St. Martin's had a number of facilities on offer, none of which contributed to the purification of the soul. Jaspar was well aware of this. Too often his weak flesh drew him to the establishment, where every attempt was made to reward it for its weakness.

"When shall I be there?" he asked.

"Ah." Andreas's lips curved in a slight smile. "First we need a period of quiet contemplation to thank God for the invigorating effects of hot water and massage—I mean foot baths. Come around midday, and bring the money. We'll be undisturbed there."

"A good idea, Brother," said Jaspar. "May I give you a piece of advice?"

"If you wish."

"Don't think you're cleverer than you are."

THE TOWN HALL

The bells of the old cathedral were striking ten.

With all the dignity he could muster, Bodo entered the great meeting room of the *house where the citizens meet*, as it was carved in Latin above the door. He threw back his shoulders and went to join the group who were talking together in low voices.

"Ah, Herr Schuif," said one. "And what's your opinion?"

"About what?" asked Bodo.

"About the murders in Berlich and by the Duck Ponds?"

"Not exactly the most shining examples of Christian living," said another, "but men and women all the same."

"My initial opinion," said Bodo, "is that they're dead. Are there suspects?"

"There are always people willing to accuse others," replied the first. "But we have to be careful. I remember the old council had a man broken on the wheel who had been accused of being a werewolf. Afterward it turned out his only crime was staying alive too long for his heirs."

Knowing laughter and conspiratorial looks were the response.

"Things are not always as they seem," remarked the first magistrate.

"And do not always seem the way they are," the second added with a sage nod.

"Quite right." Bodo saw his chance to impress. "Take the case of Gerhard Morart. I had a very interesting talk with an old friend this morning. He was asking me about the names of those two witnesses. You know, the two mendicants who saw him fall. An accident, say some. He jumped, possessed by the Devil, others think more probable." He lowered his voice to a whisper. "But my old friend was hinting at a third possibility, although propriety or perhaps caution prevented him from saying right out what he thought."

"And what," drawled the first magistrate, "might he have been hinting at?"

"I didn't press him. It was only going over his words later that it struck me. I think what he was suggesting was that at least Gerhard was not responsible for his own death."

"Who was, then? The Devil?"

"No. At least not directly."

"Don't keep us on tenterhooks."

"Well." Bodo cocked his head self-importantly. "What if someone pushed him...?"

"Murder?" The other magistrate laughed out loud and shook his head. "Is your friend right in the head? Two upright men in holy orders tell us it was an accident, they even heard his confession—"

"And we questioned the two for a long time," added the second. "If someone had pushed Gerhard, then presumably they would have seen it and told us."

"I know. Nevertheless."

"Somewhat far-fetched, Herr Schuif. Did your friend really talk of murder?"

Bodo hesitated. "Not as such," he admitted.

"But you suspect that's what he had in mind?"

"I know Jaspar. He likes to talk in riddles. Often I can't understand him. This time, though—"

The other cut him short. "This time we will proceed to the meeting, where we have more important matters to discuss." He seemed to have lost interest.

Bodo shrugged his shoulders. They set off up the stairs to the council chamber on the first floor. On the half-landing he felt a hand on his shoulder. He slowed down.

It was the second magistrate. "You must excuse me if I sounded so suspicious," he whispered as they continued slowly up the stairs. "It's a delicate matter. Certain ... persons are of the same opinion as your friend. Keep that to yourself. For various reasons it doesn't seem opportune to discuss it in public. What did you say your friend was called?"

"Jaspar Rodenkirchen," Bodo replied, getting excited. "And you really think—"

"What I think is neither here nor there. Let us say one must make the truth known at the right time and in the right place. This Jaspar, would you trust his judgment?"

"I should say so! He's a physician and dean of St. Mary Magdalene's, master of arts and so on and so forth."

"And you think he intends to question the witnesses again?"

"He said that."

"Hmm. I understand. I just hope he and the others are wrong, but my hopes have no legal status and my wishes are less objective than a thorough investigation. May Gerhard's soul find peace, and may the murderers—if your friend is right—suffer unimaginable torments. But justice is a matter for the magistrates. I'd advise your friend not to take things into his own hands. Tell him to confide in us."

They had reached the council chamber. "After you," said the other magistrate with a friendly smile to Bodo.

Bodo gave a dignified nod and entered the chamber.

The other watched him go in. Then he turned on his heel, ran down the steps two at a time, and disappeared down Judengasse.

LAST WORDS

"Middle finger," said Jacob.

"She'll never learn to play, will she?" said Rolof.

"If I'd wanted your opinion, you old polecat, I'd have grunted," Richmodis said with a laugh.

"Don't talk to Rolof like that," growled Goddert from the corner where he was refilling his mug with wine. He had insisted on coming. "Polecats are God's creatures, too."

Jacob took her middle finger and gently placed it on the correct hole. They had been practicing playing the whistle ever since Jaspar had left. Unfortunately Richmodis's talent in that direction fell far short of her other merits. "I just can't get the change from here to there," she complained.

"From where to where?" Jacob asked.

"From there—to there."

"You can do it if you try. Now blow."

Richmodis placed the whistle to her lips and took a deep breath. The result could hardly be classified as music. Sweet as a snake bite, thought Jacob.

"Told you," muttered Rolof. "She'll never learn."

"Oh, yes, she will," retorted Goddert. "She needs a bit of practice, that's all."

"My fingers feel as if they're going to break off." Richmodis slapped the whistle down on the table, pouted, and looked at Jacob from beneath her long eyelashes. "I save your life and you torture me."

"Torture?" said Jacob, baffled. "But you wanted to—"

"Feminine logic." Goddert giggled. "I get it all the time at home."

"Oh, Jacob," she breathed, "you play us something."

"You'll never learn like that."

"I do want to learn, but I need"—she gave him a sugary smile that made his heart melt—"inspiration. Just once, please. Play a dance tune so this fat lump can get some exercise. Then I'll practice day and night, promise."

"You will?" Jacob grinned. "How can I resist that argument?"

He picked up his whistle and started to play a fast peasant dance. Richmodis immediately jumped up and tugged and pulled at Rolof until he lumbered around the room with her, still mumbling and grumbling. Then he started to enjoy it, and the lumbering turned into a stamping that made the floor creak and tremble. Richmodis spun around and around him. Jacob watched her hair fly and played faster and faster, beating out the rhythm with his foot on the floor. Goddert decided to join in and thumped the table with his fist.

The door opened.

Jaspar Rodenkirchen came in, stared goggle-eyed at the goings-on, and went out again.

"Oh, dear," said Rolof.

Jacob put down his whistle.

Richmodis pulled a face, put her hands to her mouth, and called out, "Uncle Jaspar."

Jaspar came back in with a sigh of relief.

"What was wrong?" asked Goddert cautiously.

"What was wrong?" Jaspar scratched his bald pate. "I was in the wrong house. Must have gone next door. There were four lunatics trying to pull it down. You're all nice and quiet, thank God. And Jacob's chopped the wood, haven't you, Fox-cub?"

"Oh, the wood! Err—"

"And my old friend Goddert's drinking water from the well. Let's see, Goddert, you crimson crayfish. What's this? Wine? Where did you get that?"

Goddert squirmed. "Erm, you know—"

"No, I do not know."

"The cellar was open and I thought, well, someone might go and steal the wine. I was worried, you see—"

"Oh, now I do see. And I thought you'd repeated the miracle at Cana. Could that be my wine cellar you're talking about, and therefore my wine?"

"Your wine?" said Goddert with an astonished glance at the jug. "How could that be, my dear Jaspar, when Saint Benedict's Rule says that monks must not own anything, not even the habit that clothes their nakedness?"

"Outrageous! You drink my wine and then dare to quote Saint Benedict at me!"

"And you? Begrudge an old friend his last glass."

"What?" Jaspar exclaimed in horror. "Things are that bad?"

"Well, no. But if I were to die, this jug of wine might be my last comfort. Would you deny me it?"

"You're not going to die. You're much too busy ruining me."

"I could have a stroke, now, at this very moment."

"Impossible."

"No, it's not. What proof do you have?"

"You're right, none at all."

"May a thunderbolt strike you, you heartless wretch. Just imagine they came to, let's say, arrest me—unjustly, of course—for some crime and burned me at the stake. Wouldn't you be prostrate with grief?"

"You wouldn't burn. You consist of nothing but wine and fat. It'd make a stench, but no fire."

"How can you be so unfeeling?"

"I'm not unfeeling."

"You are. You're miserly. All this fuss about a few mugfuls. I'm ashamed of you. Your stupid wine sticks in my throat now. Why don't you follow the example of Ensfried? You know, the priest who was asked for alms on the way to mass, and as he had no money with him, he went into a dark corner of St. Mary's, took off his breeches, and gave them to the beggar. And he even tried to keep his work of Christian charity a secret and didn't take off his fur cloak when he was sitting by the fire—"

"Rubbish. Your Ensfried was an invention of some pious chronicler. Are you asking me to give you my breeches?"

"Lord preserve us from the sight of your nakedness!"

"I'll tell you something, Goddert. You can drink till you burst, for all I care, but I'd like to be asked first before you go stomping down there to draw yourself a jug. I think I've earned that much consideration."

"Right then. I'm asking. Shall we have another?"

"Let's have another." Jaspar, back in a good mood, smacked his lips. "And while Goddert's fetching another mug from where he found his, perhaps I will condescend to tell you what I've achieved this morning."

"Why only two mugs?" asked Richmodis in a sharp tone.

"Because only seasoned drinkers are allowed wine before sext, and Jacob needs a clear head anyway."

"Did you manage to track down the witnesses?" asked Jacob excitedly. At the same time he felt the return of the fear he had forgotten for the last few hours.

"Hm," said Jaspar. "Do you really want to hear?"

"Please."

"You scratch my back. Now if you'd chopped the wood—"

"I'll chop up a whole forest if you like, but don't keep me on tenterhooks like this." I have to know whether I was seeing things, Jacob thought. It all seemed so long ago now, so unreal, that he had suddenly started to have doubts whether he had actually seen the fiendish figure with the long hair.

But Maria and Tilman were dead. Or had he dreamed that, too?

Imperturbable, Jaspar waited until Goddert returned with his mug, took a long draught, and licked his lips. "Aah, I needed that. You were right, Jacob, I've not only found the witnesses, I've spoken to them."

"And?"

"Two mendicants, Justinius von Singen and Andreas von Helmerode. The one behaves as if butter wouldn't melt in his mouth, the other is more open to temptation, especially when it takes the form of filthy lucre. He's willing to recant."

"So they were definitely bribed."

"Yes."

"Well, then!" Jacob leaned back and let out a deep breath.

"We have a rendezvous with this pretty pair. This time you're coming, too. I'll get you a fine habit with a hood you can wear to the bathhouse."

"Why to the bathhouse?"

"Oh, did I forget to mention it? We're to meet them in the bathhouse opposite Little St. Martin's."

"Monks in the bathhouse?"

"That—er"—Jaspar cleared his throat—"does happen, people say. What's that got to do with it anyway? Aren't you going to thank me for everything I've done for you? What I can't do, of course, is supply the forty gold marks it will cost to persuade Andreas and Justinius to change their minds and give evidence to the city council."

"They won't do that anyway," Richmodis broke in. "They might tell you they were bribed, but not the magistrates. That would be to admit they lied before."

"So what, you prattling baggage? What can happen to them? They haven't killed anyone; they just have to admit they saw someone and describe him. They can always say they kept silent out of fear, because they thought the Devil was involved. Now they come along, all sackcloth and ashes. They'll probably be expelled from the city, but with forty gold marks in their pockets, that's no great hardship."

"Except they aren't going to get them."

"No. But if they tell us who Gerhard's murderer is, we'll make it public anyway and their lives won't be worth a brass farthing. Unless they go to the magistrates for protection. Then they'll have no choice but to tell the truth, money or no money."

"When are we to see them?" asked Jacob.

"There's still a good two hours," replied Jaspar coolly.

"Two hours," Goddert muttered. "We ought to offer up a prayer to the Virgin—"

"Yes, Goddert, you do that. You do the praying while I do the thinking." He looked at Jacob, his brow furrowed. Then his expression brightened. "Oh, yes. Now I remember what I wanted to ask you this morning. You still haven't told me."

"What?"

"Gerhard's last words."

True! How could he have forgotten something so important?

"Well?"

Jacob thought. "It is wrong."

"What's wrong?" asked Richmodis, puzzled.

"That's what Gerhard said. 'It is wrong.' Those were his last words, 'It is wrong.' I don't find them at all puzzling. If someone pushed me off the top of a cathedral, I would have said it was wrong."

Rolof gave a snort of laughter and immediately fell silent again.

"'It is wrong,'" mused Jaspar, ignoring him. "You think he was referring to his murder?"

"What else?"

Jaspar shook his head vigorously. "I don't think so."

Goddert wagged his index finger. "Yes. There's always something mystical, something sublime about last words."

"No, there isn't, Goddert," Jaspar snapped irritatedly. "All this last words stuff is a load of nonsense. Do you think someone who's lying there with every bone in his body smashed is going to go to the trouble of thinking up some original curtain line? As if any ass turns into a poet just because he's about to depart the stage."

"Many a man has been inspired when the soul is freed from the prison of the flesh. Saint Francis of Assisi even spoke in verse." Goddert puffed himself up and declaimed,

"Praise be to Thee, my Lord, through our sister, the death of the body,
For no living man can escape her:
Woe unto those who die in mortal sin;
Blessed are those she finds in Thy most holy will.
For the second death cannot harm them."

"My God, listen to Goddert! And I always thought he'd never learned anything," exclaimed Jaspar in amazement. "You're still wrong, though. The great man wrote those lines long before he died, but only revealed them on his deathbed. Very spiritual but not particularly spontaneous."

"Then take Archbishop Anno. Didn't he see the destruction of Cologne on his deathbed?"

"Anno had a fever, took several weeks to die. Plenty of time to rehearse his last words."

"But he called on Peter and all the saints to protect Cologne."

"Probably because he believed the Virgin had vouchsafed him such a terrible vision as a punishment for the way he'd treated the citizens."

"Anno was a saint. He loved the people of Cologne with all his heart!"

"You'll have known him, of course—he only died two hundred years ago, while all I've done is read his *Life*. As for being a saint, I don't doubt his miracles, but if you ask me, I'd say he had more eyes put out than he healed. No wonder he prayed for the city on his deathbed, but more out of fear of purgatory than for the welfare of the city."

"If I was a cleric, I'd accuse you of blasphemous talk. I sometimes wonder which of us follows the teachings of the Church more closely, you in your habit or a hardworking dyer like me."

"You aren't a hardworking dyer, you're an old drunkard with a hard-working daughter. As to your mania for last words, let me remind you of

Saint Clare of Assisi. She died just seven years ago saying, 'Father, into Thy hands I commend my spirit'—very pious, but not particularly original or mystical."

"And what about all the saints who suffered and died for their faith," cried Goddert, who had gone bright red, "and still found words of defiance for their tormentors or had visions of the future?"

"Were you there? Most of them will have said 'ouch.' Last words are bandied about like relics. Three months ago Conrad sent the king of France a casket supposedly containing the bones of Saint Berga. If it goes on like this, we'll have to add another nought to the eleven thousand virgins to explain the miraculous appearance of holy bones."

Goddert drew a deep breath to reply, but instead gave a muffled growl and emptied his mug of wine.

"And now we have another set of broken bones," said Jaspar, looking around at them pensively. "What was going on inside Gerhard? He's dying and he knows it. Would he say 'It is wrong' about his own death? No one would dream of calling God wrong when He decides to call someone to Him, even if a murderer does have a hand in it."

"But what is it that's wrong, then?" asked Jacob, confused. "If Gerhard wasn't talking about himself, it's beginning to sound like one of Goddert's mystical utterances after all."

Goddert nodded vigorously.

"Not mystical," said Jaspar. He rested his long chin in his hands. "Peter Abelard said that words do not veil reality, but reveal it. What reality did Gerhard want to reveal? Or, to put it another way, why did he have to die?"

"A rival?" Goddert suggested tentatively. "There are many who would like to be in charge of building the cathedral."

"Hmm. There's a young man called Arnold. A good stonemason. I believe the cathedral chapter has had its eye on him for some time."

"I certainly had no intention of accusing the chapter of anything untoward," Goddert declared hastily. "I just thought—"

"Why not?"

Goddert stared at him, openmouthed. This time his horrified incredulity seemed genuine. "Jaspar! How could even the shadow of suspicion fall on the cathedral canons? After all, they are the ones who instigated this holy work."

"You mean the cathedral? That's not a holy work."

Goddert went even redder. "What? How can you say something like that? You're always carping and criticizing."

"No, I'm not. I just happen to know that Conrad laid the foundation stone on the spot set aside for his tomb, which poses the question of whose glory is this temple being built to, the Lord's or Conrad's?"

Goddert slapped his hand on the table. "You just have to drag everything through the mud."

"All right." Jaspar raised his hands in appeasement. "May the Lord preserve your simple faith. Anyway, you'll be pleased to know I've come to the same conclusion as you. The chapter had nothing to do with Gerhard's death. The cathedral was an expression of its power, too, and who better than Gerhard to realize it? Arnold will probably succeed to the position, but just because he's a capable young stonemason, not for any dubious reasons." He sighed. "Which brings us back to the question of what Gerhard meant when he said, 'It is wrong.'"

"Perhaps he was referring to the future," suggested Jacob.

"The future?" echoed Goddert.

"Yes. To something that's going to happen. Something so important it was worth using his last breath for. Perhaps he knew some secret and it weighed on his conscience. So much so that someone expected Gerhard to tell the whole world what he thought was wrong."

"And reveal a dark secret that was other people's secret, too. Excellent, Fox-cub." Jaspar could hardly contain himself. "Gerhard Morart knew something he shouldn't have. He had become a danger. He was killed so he would take the secret, his murderer's secret, to the grave with him."

Richmodis swallowed and looked at Jaspar. "Then it's not just the murder of an architect?"

"No. There's something else. Something that's still to happen."

"Lord preserve us," said Goddert in a hoarse voice. "I daren't imagine what's behind it. If they're willing to kill Gerhard Morart to keep it secret, then it's not going to be some petty crime."

"Another murder, yes?" said Rolof impassively.

Everyone turned to look at him, but Rolof was fully occupied with a pear.

"That can't be my Rolof," mocked Jaspar. "Someone must have been speaking through him."

"But he could still have been speaking the truth," cried Richmodis.

"You must go and see your magistrate friend," Goddert insisted. "You must tell him everything."

"No," Jaspar decided, "not yet."

"But there's no point in making inquiries ourselves. It's too dangerous."

"Then go home, you old coward. You're the one who was determined to help Jacob. We can't go to the magistrates before we've got these supposed witnesses on our side. That reminds me. Do you happen to have forty gold marks?"

"Of course, Jaspar," Goddert declared. "Forty thousand, if you want. I'm the richest man in Cologne, aren't I?"

"All right, all right."

"That's not a bad idea at all, Uncle Jaspar," said Richmodis. "Tell the magistrates. It's the only way of protecting Jacob and it'll still allow us to talk to the witnesses."

"They wouldn't believe us, child," Jaspar insisted. Whenever he called her child he was being serious. "We have no proof, and Jacob is not exactly what you'd call a pillar of society. And anyway, what do you think the magistrates would do, now the old wolves have been replaced by a herd of sheep? Conrad's puppets wherever you look. Whatever you think of the so-called noble houses—arrogant, corrupt, cruel—there's too few left on the council. Only this morning Bodo was boasting about his important position again. I like the old fellow, but he's just as spineless and brainless as most of the tradesmen who fell for Conrad's sweet talk when he got nowhere with the patricians."

"There are still some patricians."

"But they've lost influence. Perhaps it's a good thing, but you can have too much of a good thing. Even the Overstolzes provide just one magistrate. That's all that's left of their power and authority."

"That's right," agreed Goddert. "I heard his name mentioned recently. What was he called?"

Jaspar sighed. "Theoderich. But that's irrelevant."

RHEINGASSE

"Bodo Schuif," said Theoderich. "But that's irrelevant."

"Bodo Schuif," mused Matthias, and he slowly strode up and down the room. "That's that ignorant ass of a brewer. And he believes the murder theory?"

"Bodo will believe anything until someone comes to persuade him of the opposite. He's not a danger. The one we have to concentrate on is this Jaspar Rodenkirchen."

"You think he's been talking to the redhead?"

"There's a strong presumption."

"What do you know about him?"

Theoderich Overstolz shrugged his shoulders. "There wasn't much time. I did what I could. Jaspar Rodenkirchen is dean of St. Mary Magdalene's; also claims to be a physician and Master of the Seven Arts. Lives diagonally opposite St. Severin's. A braggart, if you ask me, whom God has blessed with remarkable ugliness, but loved by his congregation."

Matthias looked at him, brows furrowed. "We can't afford to keep on killing people. A whore I don't care about, but a dean—"

"Forget the dean. We can let him live. What I mean is we might get at the redhead through him."

"Too late. The fox has put the dean in the picture, therefore both represent a risk." Matthias was rocking back and forth on his feet. He was nervous and getting irritated because he couldn't think what to do.

"Let's discuss it with Urquhart," suggested Theoderich.

"Yes," said Matthias reflectively.

"And I agree with Johann," said Theoderich, taking a handful of grapes from a bowl and stuffing some in his mouth. "It wasn't particularly clever to bring Urquhart into the house. We can ignore the redhead. The important thing is that no one connects the murderer with us.

Matthias shook his head irascibly. "I've told you a hundred times, when I brought him here he was wearing the habit of a Friar Minor. He was unrecognizable; can't you get that into your thick skull? We've got other problems. We must stop this talk of murder spreading and putting people on the alert. No one'll pay much attention to whores and down-and-outs getting killed; those kinds of things happen. But how are we going to carry out our plan if respected burghers start deciding their lives aren't safe in Cologne, dammit? And then this problem with Gerhard's last words."

"Gerhard fell off the cathedral," said Theoderich matter-of-factly, chewing his grapes. "There were no last words."

With a few quick steps Matthias was beside him and dashed the grapes out of his hand. He grabbed Theoderich by the collar. "Urquhart said this Fox, or whatever he calls himself, put his ear to Gerhard's lips, you idiot," he snarled. "What if he could still speak? Perhaps he said, yes, one of my murderers is called Theoderich Overstolz, you all know him, he's a magistrate. And Jacob tells the dean, and the dean works on Urquhart's witnesses, and tomorrow they come to fetch you—and me as well. And they'll drag your blind old aunt Blithildis to the place of execution and tie her between two horses, before they hand you over to the executioner."

Theoderich took a deep breath. "You're right," he croaked.

"Good." Matthias straightened up and wiped his hand on his breeches.

"Matthias, we're starting to quarrel among ourselves."

"Don't be such a baby."

"That's not what I'm getting at. Our alliance is in crisis and I can't see things improving. It's dangerous. Remember Daniel and Kuno. Even you and Johann don't always agree."

Matthias brooded for a few moment. "You're right," he said softly. "So close to our goal and we threaten to split apart." He drew himself up. "Back to this dean. You talked to Bodo—what do you think he'll do?"

"Try to find the witnesses."

"Hmm. The witnesses."

"We haven't much time. It's past ten and I don't know where Urquhart is—"

"But I do. He's distributed the servants around the city. His own section is the market district. It won't take me long to find him. There, you see, Theoderich, things aren't as bad as they seem. Now we know where the Fox is most likely to be hiding, we know who's protecting him, and we know they're tracking down the witnesses."

Matthias smiled to himself. "That should give Urquhart something to work on."

THE BATHHOUSE

"Aaaaah!" Justinius von Singen sighed.

The girl laughed and poured another stream of warm water over him. She was pretty and well worth the sin.

"O Lord, I thank you," murmured Justinius, half blissfully, half remorsefully, as his right hand felt the breasts of his ministering angel and his left slipped down her stomach and under the water. At the same time he watched the girl sitting at the edge of the pool, playing her harp and singing to her instrument. She was in the bloom of youth, a veritable goddess, and her thin white dress revealed more than it concealed.

Drunk with joy, Justinius hummed to the music, out of tune, while his eyes wandered from the beautiful harper up to the galleries above the bathers, where men, young and old, some very old, were standing. They occasionally threw down coins and wreaths of flowers and the girls would jump up and, laughing, spread out their dresses to catch them, at the same time revealing their hidden charms. The music, the singing, the murmur of conversation, the splash of water all merged into a timeless stream in which rational thought was swallowed up as he abandoned himself to the siren voice of lust.

Justinius burped and laid his head on the girl's shoulder.

Little St. Martin's bathhouse was crowded at that hour. Clerics were there, though they tended to slip in quietly, for the attendants were as experienced in the arts of love as in giving hot and cold baths, massaging, beating the bathers with bundles of twigs, or rubbing them down with brushes made of cardoon bristles, which left them feeling as if liquid fire were running through their veins. At one time there had probably been a curtain separating the men's from the women's section, but all that remained were three iron rings in the ceiling.

Now the copper tubs and great brick basins were open to all. Decorated trays floated on the water, loaded with jugs of wine and various delicacies. Justinius had one right by his belly with a chicken on it roasted to such a crisp golden brown that it was a delight to the eye.

The girl giggled even more and pushed his hand away.

"Oooooh," said Justinius, winking at Andreas, who was sitting on the other side of the basin, taking no notice of anything.

Justinius frowned. Then he sent a huge wave of water splashing over Andreas. "Hey! Why so gloomy?"

"What?" Andreas shook his head. "I'm not gloomy. I just can't stop thinking about that man who came to see us this morning."

"Oh, him again." Justinius sighed. "Don't I keep telling you not to worry so much? I agreed with you, didn't I, that we should accept his generous offer and get out of Cologne as quickly as possible?"

"He wants us to make a statement to the council," Andreas reminded him. "That makes a quick getaway impossible."

"The council can go hang itself. We tell the man what we know, take the money, and before the council can get off their fat arses we'll be spending it on a life of luxury in Aachen." He leaned forward and grinned. "I've heard Aachen's fantastic. Have you been there? What else would you expect from the city where they crown the kings?" He put his head to one side and shrugged. "On the other hand, they say nothing can compare with

Cologne, so I can understand your feelings." He nestled his head against the girl's shoulder, groaning with pleasure.

Andreas pursed his lips. "I hope you're right."

"I'm always right. The big fellow with the long hair gave us something and we did what he asked. Now someone else wants to give us something, so we do what he asks. What's wrong with that?"

"I don't know. How did he find out we had anything to do with Blondie?"

"What does it matter? This Jaspar will be here soon. We'll go into one of the side rooms, do the deal, take the money, tell him what happened and what we know—God knows, I'm an honest man, Andreas—and take ourselves off to some other place where you can get plenty of meat on your dagger. By the time Blondie's realized we've let something slip, we'll be over the hills and far away."

"I hope you're right," Andreas repeated, a little less tensed up.

"Of course I am. Look around. This is the life! And we'll live forever, God forgive my sinful tongue."

The girl laughed. "Here everything's forgiven," she said, pouring another bowl of water over him.

Justinius shook himself luxuriously and pulled himself up onto the side. "What manly passion our Creator has implanted in us," he cried. "Keep yourself in readiness for me, my rose, pearl of this holy city. I will betake myself to the massage couch and when I return you will feel the sword of my desire, O blessed body of the Whore of Babylon."

Andreas gave him a scornful look. "You should have another look at the scriptures some time," he said. "That was a load of nonsense."

Justinius gave a roar of laughter. "Life is a load of nonsense."

"Yes," said Andreas, sighing, "for once you might just be right."

Still laughing, Justinius went to the back of the room and pushed aside a curtain, revealing a small candle-lit cubicle with a wooden table covered in towels and blankets, a tub of steaming water, and some jugs filled with fragrant oil. One could have a massage from the owner and his assistants, or from the girls as long as the curtain remained closed.

Grunting and groaning, Justinius pulled himself onto the table, pressed his belly flat on the soft blankets, and closed his eyes. He had paid for the full treatment. First a good kneading from a pair of strong male hands, then he would roll over on his back and take on the sweet burden of sin in whatever shapely form it should appear. The owner of the bathhouse was discreet and showed a sure touch in his selection of companions for his customers. The surprise was all part of the fun.

Justinius began to hum softly.

The curtain rustled and he heard the masseur come in. No point in turning over yet. There was a scraping noise. The man was pulling one of the jugs of oil closer.

"Give me a good going over." He giggled, not opening his eyes. "I want to erupt like a volcano."

The man laughed softly and placed his hands on Justinius's back. They were pleasantly warm. With powerful yet gentle movements he spread the oil over his shoulders and started to loosen the muscles with rhythmic kneading. Justinius gave a groan of pleasure.

"You like it?" asked the masseur quietly.

"Oh, yes. You do it perfectly."

"Thank you."

"Although—but don't take this personally—you lack the charms of the priestess who will succeed you in this temple and spoil me in a quite different and more delightful way."

"Of course."

The hands moved across his shoulder blades to his spine, parting and coming together again as they slowly made their way down to his waist. Justinius felt the warmth begin to spread over his whole body.

"This is going to be something"—he grinned in anticipation—"a fitting farewell to the holy city."

"All in good time," said the masseur. "Aren't you a monk?"

"Yes." Justinius frowned. What was the point of a question like that in a place like this? "There are worse sins," he quickly added, at the same time wondering why he felt the need to excuse himself to this fellow.

On the other hand, God could see everything. Even in a closed cubicle of a bathhouse in Cologne.

"There's no need to worry," said the masseur softly. His thumbs glided up Justinius's ribs to his armpits. "There have been saints who were fond of women, if you know what I mean. Abstinence is a modern invention. You don't have to pretend with me. I knew some students, years ago. Their only reason for studying was to gain a well-endowed benefice and well-endowed women. There was a song—"

The tips of his fingers squeezed the fat at the base of Justinius's neck, released it, then moved lower down. "It's a confession the wandering scholars used to sing—presumably they granted themselves absolution. *Light are the elements forming my matter*, they sang, *Like a dry leaf, the storm winds scatter.* And *My breast is pierced by women's beauty. My hand can't touch? Let the heart do duty.*"

"Sounds like a good song," said Justinius, though with a frisson of unease somewhere at the back of his mind. He had the feeling he knew this masseur.

"*Greedier for love I am, than God's grace to win. Dead my soul, so all I care is to save my skin,*" the man continued. The movements of his hands followed the rhythm of the poem. Or was it the other way around? "*The hardest thing of all, I say, is to tame our nature. Who can keep out lustful thoughts near a lovely creature? We are young, impossible to obey this hard law. Our bodies too are young, they know omnia vincit amor.*"

"Quite right," agreed Justinius, if slightly doubtfully.

"And what does it say in the *Romance of the Rose*? *Marriage is a hateful tie. Nature is not so stupid as to put Mariette in the world for Robichon alone, or Robichon for Mariette, or Agnes or Perette. There is no doubt, dear child, that she made everyone for everyone.* How true! Then *Follow nature without hesitation. I forgive you all your sins as long as you are in harmony with nature. Be swifter than the squirrel, tuck up your skirts to enjoy the wind, or, if you prefer, go naked* and so on and so forth. And all these supposed blasphemers who wrote such verses ended their lives as good Christians. The Archpoet sang the praises of Frederick Barbarossa, Hugo Primas taught in Paris and Orleans, and Serlo of Wilton mended his ways in England and died a pious Cistercian, Walter of Chatillon as a canon, all of them men who enjoyed life to the full and cared little for the Church's rules."

"How comforting," muttered Justinius. What was the point of all this? All the names and things the fellow knew? Much too well-educated for a bathhouse assistant. And then the voice. He knew that voice. But from where?

"Listen," said Justinius, "I—"

"But"—the pleasantly powerful hands continued without pause—"how many died in misery? A chaste, God-fearing man like Tristan, burning with such love and fleshly desire he fell sick and died. Even if he was united with his beloved after death, how he suffered for it."

Who was this Tristan, dammit? Justinius von Singen was no monk, he was a swindler, a charlatan in a monk's habit who could churn out standard portions of the Bible, usually mixing them up. What was it this bastard wanted of him?

Suddenly he felt afraid. "I want you to stop," he gabbled.

As if he had not heard, the masseur continued to knead his flesh, digging the tips of his fingers into Justinius's ribs.

"And fair Isolde, promised to King Mark of Cornwall"—he continued his lecture—"where did love lead her? Did it protect her against the deceived king, who wondered whether to burn her or abandon her to the lepers? And when he finally relented and let her go, what was left for her? Brokenhearted for her Tristan, she lay beside a rotting carcass, Justinius. What an end to love!"

"What do you want?" panted Justinius, trying to get up.

The fingers flitted up and down his spine.

"For there are no secrets on earth, everything comes to light, and in the light everything looks shabby, and the light is the punishment, and the punishment is—pain."

"Please, I—"

Something cracked.

Justinius gave a yelp of pain. His head was pressed down, then the hands continued their gentle, pleasant massaging.

"And now we'll see," said that terribly familiar voice, "who can bear pain. And who can't."

Again it was like a lance thrust between Justinius's bones. He screamed and tried to get up, but the merciless iron grip forced him down onto the bed, his face in the towels.

His tormentor laughed. "You see, Justinius, that's the advantage of these bathhouses. The audible expressions of pleasure go unheard in such a discreet establishment. And all that music out there. You can scream as much as you like."

"What have I done to you?" Justinius whimpered.

"Done?" The hands gently grasped his shoulders and massaged the muscles. "Betrayed me, that's what you've done, reverend Brother. I paid you well to be witnesses, but you obviously prefer to collaborate with the dean of St. Mary Magdalene's."

So that's what it was. That was the voice. "Please—" Justinius begged.

"Now, now. I don't want to hurt you. I just want the truth."

The truth? "It was—it was nothing," Justinius groaned. "This dean came along. I don't know what he wanted, we talked about various things, but not about Gerhard—"

The sentence ended in a further scream. Justinius's fingers gripped the edge of the bed.

"Interesting, human anatomy," the voice went on calmly. "Didn't you know how fragile a shoulder blade is?"

The tears were running down Justinius's cheeks. Tears of pain.

"Will you tell me the truth now?"

Justinius tried to speak, but all that came out was a moan. In a futile attempt to escape he tried to pull himself to the top of the bed. The hands gripped him and pulled him back.

"Come now, Justinius, relax. How can two old friends have a sensible conversation if you're all tensed up like that?"

"He—" Justinius swallowed. "He knew about you. And he knew you killed Gerhard and that's the truth, in the name of God I swear it."

"That's more like it." As if to reward him, the hands made soothing circular movements over his shoulders. "But he made you an offer, didn't he?"

"Double."

"Not more?"

"No," Justinius cried, "as God is my witness, no."

"And you accepted?"

"No, of course not, we—"

The sound of breaking bones was sickening. He almost fainted from the pain.

"Justinius? Are you still there? Sorry, but a good massage can get a bit rough. Did you accept his offer?"

Justinius let out an unintelligible babble. The saliva was running down his chin.

"Clearer, please."

"Yes. Yes!"

"When and where are you to meet the dean?"

"Here," Justinius whispered. "Please don't hurt me anymore— Our Father, who art in heaven—"

"Oh, you know a prayer? Your piety shames me. I asked you when."

"Soon—he should be here any minute. Please, I beg you, no more pain, please—"

The other leaned down close. Justinius could feel something soft on his back. Hair. Long blond hair. "Don't worry, Justinius," said Urquhart softly, "you won't feel any more pain."

The fingers reached his neck.

Justinius couldn't hear the last dull crack.

𝕬ndreas von Helmerode leaned back in the water. He felt a profound disquiet. On the one hand, he wished he could take things as calmly as Justinius, who was at this moment doubtless lying on the bed in his cubicle and nothing would disturb him.

On the other hand, he was the one who had had to get them out of a jam more than once. As soon as money was mentioned, Justinius threw caution to the winds.

Perhaps it was time to turn respectable. The swindling and living on their wits had gone on for long enough, going around as false priests, exploiting the grief of simple people mourning their loved ones, the faith of those too eager to believe. The stranger's offer had been a godsend, and one of the easiest things they'd had to do—just lie. Thanks to his own foresight they had not squandered everything. There was some money laid by, including some from the blond stranger. In fact, there was enough. Better to stop while they could.

The harpist smiled at him. Her voice rose in a sweet trill that went right through him.

It was high time that bald dean put in an appearance. Then take the money and run. To Aachen or anywhere. "Away from Cologne, that's the main thing," Andreas muttered to himself. He took hold of one of his feet and started to pull off some hard skin.

Someone slipped into the water beside him.

Andreas paid no attention. He studied his toes, then threw the harpist a winning smile, but she had turned to someone else. Serves you right, thought Andreas, if you go around with a long face all the time.

He slid down until he was completely underwater. Warm. Pleasant. Invigorating. What a hopeless miseryguts he was. He should go and chat up that pretty girl playing the harp. He put his hands on the bottom to push himself up.

He couldn't.

To his astonishment he realized someone was pushing him down. For a moment he thought it was just a joke. Then he was seized with panic and started to thrash his legs.

A hand grasped his throat.

It was all over very quickly.

Urquhart closed Andreas's eyes and mouth under the water, then pulled him up. Now he was sitting there as if he were sleeping. No one had noticed anything, they were all too preoccupied and the men in the gallery had eyes for the fair sex alone.

Without a further glance at the dead body, Urquhart got out of the water. Despite his great height and physique, he went unnoticed. He had a slightly hunched gait he adopted on such occasions, the gait of the downtrodden and dispossessed. If he wanted, he could dominate a packed room with his physical presence alone. If not, he was almost invisible, a nobody.

He picked up a towel, dried himself, went to the room where the bathers' clothes were kept, dressed, and strolled out into the street.

Bright light greeted him. The sun was shining.

Unnaturally bright.

He put his hand over his eyes, but the brightness remained. And in the brightness he saw the child again and the iron claw plunging into the twitching, writhing body—

No! He could not allow these attacks to continue. Not now, not ever.

Urquhart filled his lungs to the bursting point with air and let his breath out in a slow, controlled exhalation. Then he held his right hand out in front of him. After a few seconds it started to tremble slightly.

Again he took a deep breath and let it out slowly. This time his hand did not tremble.

His eyes scoured the street. If they were keeping to his instructions, two of Matthias's servants ought to be somewhere nearby. After a while they came along the street, chattering away. He raised his hand in the agreed signal and went to meet them.

Jacob the Fox might cover his red mop, but they would recognize the dean. According to the description Matthias had given him an hour ago, there could only be one face like that. Jaspar Rodenkirchen would come alone or with the Fox, not suspecting that he was expected. One way or another he would fall into the trap. Then they would stay hard on his heels, unobserved.

The servants would, that is.

He himself had other plans. If Jaspar brought the Fox with him, all the better. If the dean came alone, Jacob was sure to be where Urquhart was about to go.

THE TRAP

"I've been thinking about your friend a bit," said Jaspar as they went down Severinstraße together.

"What friend?" Jacob asked. He pulled the hood of Jaspar's old habit farther down over his face. During the last couple of days he'd worn more coats and cloaks than in his whole life before. Despite the disguise, he felt horribly exposed.

"The one who wants to get you," replied Jaspar. "Word has got around that there is someone in Cologne using strange little arrows, and we two know who it is. But what kind of weapon is it?"

"A crossbow. Didn't I tell you?"

"You did. With that power of penetration it has to be a crossbow. Only the bolts are too small for every known type of crossbow."

Too small? Jacob thought. True, the bolts were too small. But he knew nothing about weapons.

"Tell me again, Fox-cub, what he was carrying while he was chasing you."

"What we've been talking about all the time."

"Yes, but how was he holding it?"

"Holding it?"

"God in heaven! Just describe how he was holding it."

Jacob frowned, then stretched out his right hand. "Like that, I think. More or less."

"In his right hand?" Jaspar clicked his tongue. "Not with both hands?"

"No."

"You're sure?"

Jacob tried to picture in his mind again what he had seen when he had turned around in the narrow alley and looked his pursuer in the face. "Yes," he said, "absolutely sure."

"Interesting." Jaspar smiled. "There is no crossbow you can hold in one hand while running after someone at the same time."

"But it was a crossbow," Jacob insisted.

"Of course it was." Jaspar seemed very pleased with himself.

"All right, you fount of knowledge," said Jacob, sighing, "what is it you know this time that no one else knows?"

"Oh," said Jaspar, putting on a humble expression, "I know that I know nothing. A man in ancient Greece said that. It appeals to me. Now Platonic forms, would you like to hear—"

"Oh, no, not another of your lectures!" Jacob protested.

"You're not interested in learning? Your loss. But I know a lot about the Crusades as well. You may have noticed. I've read eyewitness accounts and heard the stories of various poor wretches who made it back home. I know the odd secret of the Orient—Al Khwarizmi's algebra, Rhazes's medical writings, Avicenna's *Canon medicinae*, Alfarabius's powerful philosophy—although I can't remember as much as I should and I'd like to know more. But the key secret of the Muslims is well known to me. It's called progress. In many ways they're a good bit ahead of us."

In unison, the bells of St. George's, St Jacob's, and the church of the Carmelites struck the first hour of the afternoon. Jaspar quickened his step. "Come on, we'd better hurry up before those scoundrels change their minds. Now: weapons. The crusaders discovered that the infidels were decidedly inventive in that respect. Rolling siege towers, castles bristling with lances on the backs of elephants, and catapults that not only send their projectiles into the enemy camp, but actually hit what they're meant to hit. And among all these reports there was one I heard years ago about single-handed crossbows. Very light, a work of art almost, and extremely elastic. With small bolts. You can't shoot as far with them as with the big ones, but you're quicker on the draw and can keep the other hand free for your sword. The Saracens' sharpshooters, the man told me, are incredibly accurate with them, even when they're charging the enemy on horseback or on foot. Before you know it, you have one of those little bolts sticking out of your chest. Not a pleasant experience."

It certainly made Jacob think as he trotted along beside Jaspar. "So the murderer's a crusader," he said. "How does that help us?"

"Was." Jaspar corrected him. "Was a crusader. If he was, then he'll have brought it back with him. A fairly recent invention, by all accounts. As far as I know, the first examples appeared during the last Crusade under Louis IX. He started out from France in 1248 and went via Cyprus to Egypt, where he took Damietta at the mouth of the Nile. I'll spare you the horrors of the campaign. Suffice it to say that Louis was captured, but, incredibly, released for a large ransom. The Crusade ended in the Kingdom of Jerusalem, but not the city, and the army was wiped out at Acre on the coast. A total disaster. Most of those who did make it home never got over the experience. They felt they had failed, felt guilty for not having managed to carry out God's will, whatever they thought that was, not to mention the constant massacres, less an expression of Christian liberation than a perversion of human nature."

He paused for breath. "I have to say that some of the crusaders, however much I condemn their deeds, were motivated by a vision. But most of them were unscrupulous adventurers and they had no idea of what actually awaited them. They wallowed in dreams of immeasurable riches and generous remission of sins. Others, brave knights, experienced in warfare but blinded by the legends of the Holy Grail, probably imagined it would be like a grand tournament."

Jaspar shook his head. "I don't know why I'm going on like this, we haven't the time. The point is, it was in connection with that Crusade that I heard about the tiny crossbow. Some poor devil who had lost his legs at the siege of Acre rambled on about it during confession. And I didn't know whether to believe him. He was already a bit—" Jaspar tapped his forehead.

"When did this Crusade end?" Jacob asked.

"Six years ago. So it would fit in with this monster going about his business in Cologne. We know a little more about him."

"So? What help is it to know him?"

"Knowledge always helps. Can't you get that into that empty water-tub you have for a brain?" said Jaspar as they walked along by the Brook. "He is a former crusader who has committed murders. And will commit a further murder, if we assume that the main action is still to come. The basic question, it seems to me, is: is he acting on his own initiative or on someone else's behalf? Gerhard's death shocked Cologne. If that's only the prelude, then it's more than just an old crusader running amok, especially considering how well planned the whole thing was. So we assume the man's being paid. Well paid, probably. They'll have chosen him carefully."

"Who're they?"

"How should I know? Someone with money and influence, I suspect. Someone willing to pay for a silent, invisible executioner, who probably still has an exceptionally difficult task to perform. He buys himself witnesses and on the same evening as the murder manages to get rid of the only two people you told about it. So we have a mind capable of logical planning, rare enough nowadays with the followers of Saint Bernard railing against reason and trying to stop the wheel of time. He's intelligent, quick, and skillful, probably very strong physically, and an expert shot into the bargain. Now most crusaders were complete blockheads, ergo our murderer must have belonged to the elite."

"So why does he go around murdering? The Crusade is over. If he's so clever, why doesn't he just go home?"

"That," said Jaspar, "is a good question."

They had reached the street of Little St. Martin's. The church was some way down on the left and opposite it, according to Jaspar, the bathhouse where they were to meet Justinius von Singen and Andreas von Helmerode. Jacob had never been in a bathhouse, but at the moment all that interested him was the false witnesses. If he and Jaspar managed to persuade them to change sides, as he fervently hoped they would, and make a statement to the council, then his nightmare might be over and the long-haired monster consigned to the jaws of hell out of which it had crawled. If only—

"Wait," Jaspar said softly and stopped.

Jacob stumbled on for a step, then turned to face him. "What is it? Why are we stopping?"

Silently Jaspar pointed to an obviously excited gathering outside the bathhouse. A gang of children came running from that direction. As they went past, Jaspar grabbed one by the sleeve.

"Lemme go," the urchin shouted. Jaspar's bald pate and long nose seemed to fill him with fear.

"Right away, my son, if you tell us what's happening down there."

"Two men's been done in. Lemme go, I didn't do nothin'. Lemme go."

"Stop shouting," hissed Jaspar and let go of his sleeve. The boy chased after the others as if the Devil were at his heels.

Grasping Jacob by the arm, Jaspar swung around. "We've got to get away."

"But—" Away? Jacob felt his heart sink and looked back.

"Keep walking," Jaspar commanded. "Behave normally. Don't hurry."

"What's wrong?" asked Jacob, already filled with dread.

"Once again our murderer has been quicker. We stroll along discussing how clever he is, idiots that we are, like lambs to the slaughter, my bald head shining in the sun for all to see."

Jacob looked back again. Four men, burly types in the dress of house servants, had emerged from the throng and were following them.

"We're being followed?" asked Jaspar, not turning his head.

"Four," said Jacob dully.

"Perhaps we're in luck," said Jaspar. Jacob took another quick glance behind and saw the men quicken their step. Now they were almost running, "They didn't count on us turning back like that. Once we're past the malt mill we'll split up. You go off to the left, get among the crowds in Haymarket. I'll take the opposite direction."

"But where will we—"

"Do you understand, dammit?"

"Yes."

"I'll find you somewhere. Now!"

Before Jacob could say anything, Jaspar gave him a push and ran off to the right, through a courtyard toward St. Mary's. As he spun around, Jacob saw the four men abandon all pretense and set off after them, bawling and shouting.

He dived in among the people thronging the market stalls.

SEVERINSTRAßE

Rolof swore.

He cursed Jaspar's cook because she had been ill for days and there was no decent food to eat, and he cursed the maid because she hadn't

cooked enough currant porridge that morning before going to stay with
her parents out in the country for a week. He cursed the fact that he was the
one who had to chop firewood, do the shopping, and clean the house, all
on his own, and finally he cursed Jaspar Rodenkirchen, because it had to be
someone's fault. And as he unloaded the big handcart and carried the tub
of soused herrings, the sack of peas, the half ounce of ginger, the brown
sugar, and the butter into the back, he cursed Jacob, who had eaten some
of the porridge he had had to go without, then Richmodis and Goddert,
adding, for good measure, the archbishop, the king, and the pope. After
that, he couldn't think of anyone else and he didn't have the nerve to curse
saints.

That didn't mean that Rolof didn't love them all, especially Jaspar,
Richmodis, and Goddert. Cursing was just his natural reaction to work.

Exhausted by the unloading and the cursing, he wiped the sweat from
his brow and rubbed his belly. His eye fell on the handcart, which he had
tipped up and leaned against the wall. One of the wheels was squeaking.
He wondered whether to do something about it. That would mean more
work. More work would mean more cursing, but Rolof regarded the mouth
as a place where things went in rather than came out. He looked up at the
sun and thought long and hard about what he should do. After a while he
came to the conclusion he should do nothing, at least for the moment.
With a brief prayer of thanks to the Lord for vouchsafing this insight, he
went indoors and sank onto the fireside bench.

Just a moment! Jaspar had mentioned the wood in the yard. Didn't it
need chopping?

Jacob hadn't chopped any, even though he was supposed to. Surely if
it had been that important, Jaspar would have insisted. But he hadn't. So
why should Rolof have to do it? Anyway, he thought it was a waste of fine
wood to burn it while the sun was shining and filling the house with natural warmth. No need to bother, then.

But if there was?

You can't chop wood in your sleep, Rolof thought. Hey, that was a
good idea! Get some sleep. He stretched, yawned, and was about to head
for the stairs, when there was a knock at the door.

"One thing after another," he grumbled. Still yawning, he waddled over to the door and opened it.

"The Lord be with you," said the man with a friendly smile. "Is Jaspar at home?"

Rolof blinked and looked the man up and down. Up meant putting his head right back. The man was tall. He was wearing the black habit of the Dominicans.

"Does he know you?" asked Rolof.

The man raised his bushy brows in astonishment. "But of course. Jaspar and I studied at college together. I haven't seen him and his bald head for ages. May I come in?"

Rolof hesitated. "Jaspar's not here, yes?"

"Oh, what a pity. No one at all at home?"

Rolof pondered this. "Yes, there is," he said slowly. "Me. I think."

"Perhaps I could wait, then? You see, I'm just passing through and I'm pretty weary. In a couple of hours I'll have to be going, to say mass in a village outside. It'd be such a shame if I couldn't at least say hello to the old rogue."

He beamed at Rolof, who scratched his chin. Didn't Jaspar say hospitality was an important duty? Perhaps because it was connected with drinking, and drinking was good. And the man was in holy orders, even if he didn't appear to have a tonsure. But then what did Rolof know of holy orders?

Rolof shrugged his shoulders. "Of course, Father," he said, with all the politeness he could muster, stepped aside, and lowered his head respectfully.

"I thank you." The man stepped inside and looked around with interest.

"Er, there." Rolof pointed to the fireplace, where the fire was crackling. "Sit by the fire. I'll see if there's any wine—"

"No, no." The man sat down and folded his arms. "Please don't go to any trouble, my son. Sit down here. We can enjoy a cozy chat."

"A chat?" Rolof echoed with a skeptical look.

"Why not? I've heard there have been all sorts of goings-on in Cologne. I haven't been able to get the exact details, unfortunately, but someone did say the architect in charge of the cathedral fell to his death. Is that true?"

Rolof stared at him and then at the fire. "Yes," he replied.

"How dreadful. Such great plans and then this!" The stranger shook his head. "But the ways of the Lord are unfathomable. How did it happen?"

Rolof slumped back on the bench. A cozy chat was beyond him. That Gerhard had not fallen but had been pushed, that much he had understood; also that something terrible was going to happen. Strange, the way he'd heard himself say someone else was going to be murdered. That had exhausted him and he hadn't said anything else. But what should he say now?

The stranger leaned forward and gave him an encouraging nod. "Speak, my son. It would do my heart good to hear you, even if what you have to say will also sadden it. I did hear"—he looked around then, coming closer and lowering his voice as if there were someone else in the room—"not everyone agrees about the way he came to die."

"It was the Devil," Rolof blurted out.

"Aha! The Devil. Who says that?"

"The—" Rolof halted. "The man," he said cautiously.

"Which man?"

"Who was here."

"Oh, him. I see. The redhead, you mean?"

Rolof looked at the stranger, racking his brains as to what he should say. If only Jaspar would come back. Slowly, his lips pressed tightly together, he nodded.

The stranger seemed very satisfied. "I thought so. I know that redhead. A very fertile imagination he's got. A liar, did you know that? Who did he tell all this nonsense to, my dear—what was your name?"

"Rolof."

"My dear Rolof, the Lord looks down on you and sees a devout servant. But the Lord looks down in anger on those who out of vanity would slander others. Unburden your heart and tell me what this redhead—is his name not Jacob? Jacob the Fox he calls himself in his presumptuous pride, as if he were cunning and wise—said to you about poor Gerhard Morart."

"Yes, well—" Rolof shifted uneasily on the bench. "Came yesterday, yes? Just Jaspar and Goddert here, drinking as usual. And Richmodis. She's sweet." Rolof gave an ecstatic smile. "Nose like a tree in the wind."

"Beautifully put, my friend. I hope it's a compliment to the young lady."

"Richmodis's sweet. The redhead told us some strange things. Don't know if I should—" He bit his lip and was silent. Keep your stupid trap shut, Rolof, he told himself.

The stranger was no longer smiling. "Who else did he tell?"

"Else?"

"Who else? Apart from those you've told me about?"

"Don't know."

"When is Jaspar coming back?"

"Don't know."

"And Jacob? Jacob the Fox?"

"Don't know."

The stranger looked at him appraisingly. Then he relaxed and leaned back, a beatific smile on his face. "Is not the world a fine place, Rolof? I think I will have that mug of wine, if you wouldn't mind. Blessed are they that know nothing."

"Blessed are they that know nothing," muttered Rolof glumly.

JACOB

Their pursuers had obviously split up as well. When Jacob reached the meat stalls and looked around he could see only two. He skidded through the mud and headed for the maze of alleys behind the iron market. That was his only hope of getting away. He knew every nook and cranny there and would have the advantage over the men chasing him.

They were getting closer. It was incredibly cramped. Swearing under his breath, he jumped over a large dog and suddenly came face-to-face with a portly matron who completely filled the gap between the cheese and the vegetable stalls. She regarded him with a baleful gleam in her eye, obviously not intending to budge an inch. Behind him he heard furious barking that ended with a yelp before turning into a whimper. Then he heard the all-too-familiar cry, "Stop, thief! The one in the habit! Don't let him get away."

Jacob spun around. The two men and the dog were a tangle of limbs and black paws. The men were just getting up again, pointing at him.

"Thief!" The woman joined in, swung an immense radish, and hit Jacob over the head with it, setting off a magnificent display of stars. He pulled the radish out of her hand, threw it at his pursuers, at the same time performing a neat sidestep, which landed him among piles of yellow cheeses. For a moment he found himself staring into the horrified face of the cheesemonger, then he rolled over and pushed him out of the way.

"Thief!" screeched the woman behind him. "He took my radish. My lovely radish."

Jacob didn't wait to see if the two men were plowing through the cheeses after him, he zigzagged between the shiny wares of the ironmongers and into the tangle of narrow streets separating the market from the Rhine. He heard footsteps splatting through the mud behind. They were still on his trail. No point in hiding while they still had him in view. In front the street widened out. He would have to dive off to the left or the right. Then he saw a pile of empty barrels carefully stacked on top of each other, ready to be sent out. Behind them a man was checking them off against a scroll. Jacob dashed around the back of the pile just as his pursuers entered the street, faces twisted with rage.

"Sorry," said Jacob. He gave the man with the scroll a firm push, sending him, arms flailing and with a despairing yell, staggering against the barrels and dislodging them. With a hollow rumble, the whole stack, at first slowly, then faster and faster, started to roll toward the two men. Jacob saw their eyes open wide with horror, then there was a sickening thud. One was felled immediately, the other was twirled around before he managed to escape back along the alley. Jacob didn't stop to enjoy the spectacle, but took the opportunity to give them the slip. He dived into Salzgasse and sped along to the fish market.

There he stopped, panting.

Where now? Who were these people chasing him and Jaspar anyway? What had they to do with the man with the long hair? And where was he?

All a mistake. The idea flashed through his mind. They've nothing to do with it, nothing at all. A double murder in the bathhouse and two people who'd suddenly turned away. They'd drawn suspicion upon themselves. Maybe people even thought they were the murderers.

Who said the dead men were Justinius von Singen and Andreas von Helmerode? Jaspar had jumped to the wrong conclusion. And ruined their only chance.

"Thief! There he is!"

Or perhaps not? No time to think. One of the two had obviously managed to escape the avalanche of barrels and was running out of Salzgasse toward him. He was pointing at Jacob, but he was looking at something beyond him. Quickly Jacob turned around and saw three more men in similar dress staring at him.

"Curses," he muttered.

They fanned out to the left and right. He couldn't go back, and in front the fish stalls were packed close together. He couldn't get away by running along them, the men were too near.

It had to be fish!

"I don't like fish." He moaned. Then, accepting the unavoidable, he dived into the crowd, elbowing people aside and heading straight for the biggest stall, setting off shouts of protest in his wake. The long table, piled high with eels, herring, mackerel, catfish, and crayfish loomed up, a menacing, stinking, slippery nightmare. The men and women behind it, busy selling their wares, stared at him in disbelief as it gradually dawned on them that he had no intention of stopping. Just in time, they dropped the fish they were holding and hastily jumped aside, putting their hands up to protect themselves.

Jacob leaped.

Beneath him he saw the pile of eels like a tangle of snakes, the jagged red sea of crayfish, the silvery waves of herring. The stall seemed to go on forever, as if some fiend kept adding on another bit, with different kinds of sea creatures waiting to enfold him in their slimy embrace. He stretched out his arms and prayed for wings, but it didn't stop him dropping down toward an ocean without water, moist, twitching bodies, gaping mouths and claws, spidery legs, a sticky, shiny mass of slithering obscenity into which Jacob was falling, down and down, desperately flailing his arms, to land in a pile of octopuses.

At first all he could see was tentacles. They grabbed him, their suckers attaching themselves to his clothes. Then he saw the chaos his dash for freedom had created. The three pursuers, once they had overcome their initial amazement, had tried to follow him, but this time the stallholders had been ready and blocked their path. Two of the men couldn't stop in time. They crashed into the furious fishmongers and all went sprawling across the counter in a welter of flying fish. The stall began to wobble dangerously. With shrieks and cries women leaped out of the way, trying to fend off the sea creatures flying toward them. The pile of eels turned into a whirlpool in which one of the pursuers disappeared head first, while the stall tilted more and more, raining crayfish on the other. Finally the great long counter toppled over, burying fishmongers, customers, and pursuers beneath it. Jacob saw several carp skimming across the ground toward him. He rolled out of the octopus tangle, went sprawling on the slippery surface, then managed to get to his feet. No one was paying him any attention, even though he was the one who had triggered off the mêlée. It all happened so quickly, and everyone was trying to get themselves to safety.

Then he saw his first two pursuers coming around the collapsed stall. He set off running again, retching from the smell of fish, past Great St. Martin's and through the rest of the fish stalls. The others kept on his heels, but the distance between them was gradually increasing. He had to do something to shake them off before reinforcements appeared from the opposite direction again. Panting, he sped along between the city wall on the Rhine embankment and the cathedral building site and turned into Dranckgasse. That took him out of sight of his pursuers for a moment, even if it must be obvious to them which direction he had taken. Somehow he had to become invisible. He had to—

A covered wagon drawn by two shaggy oxen was rumbling along the street, the carter dozing in the sun. There was a slight gap between the two parts of the canvas cover, but it was impossible to tell what load the cart was carrying. Only one way to find out: jump in. Jacob gathered his strength for one more leap and dived into the blackness between the two sheets.

His head cracked against something hard. With a groan, he rolled onto his back then sat up.

Barrels!

Head throbbing, he crawled to the back of the cart and cautiously peeped out between the canvas sheets. The two men appeared by the Wall at the end of the street. They seemed confused and were jabbering and gesticulating at each other, clearly arguing about what to do next.

Then one pointed to the wagon.

"What has the Devil got against me?" Jacob sighed. Hurriedly he looked around for somewhere to hide. Nothing, apart from the barrels, and they filled the front of the cart with nowhere he could squeeze into between them.

Suddenly there was a terrible screech from the axles and Jacob was thrown to one side as the wagon slowly turned left, to the accompaniment of a bizarre series of noises. They must be going through Priest Gate. That meant they were out of sight of his pursuers, at least for a few seconds. Quickly Jacob crawled to the back and dropped out under the canvas, catching his foot on the planks and bashing his head again. He could dimly hear footsteps approaching. His head was spinning.

"The cart went in there," shouted a voice.

"And what if he's not in it?" asked a second, out of breath.

"Where else would he be, stupid?"

They were coming and Jacob the Fox was lying in the street, gift-wrapped. If only he could think clearly. He scrambled to his feet and, half staggering, half running, caught up with the cart. Then he dropped to the ground and crawled underneath, only narrowly avoiding the iron-clad wheels, pulled himself onto the broad central shaft, drew up his legs, and stuck his fingers through the gaps between the planks above him. He was clinging to the underneath of the cart like a bat. As long as they didn't check there, he was invisible.

The steps came around the corner and up to the cart. Turning his aching head to one side, he saw two pairs of legs.

"Hey, you! Carter! Stop!"

"Whaaat?"

"Stop, goddammit!"

The wagon came to an abrupt halt. Jacob held on even tighter so as not to be thrown off the shaft by the jolt.

"What d'you want?" he heard the carter demand gruffly.

"A look in your cart."

"Why?"

"You're hiding a thief in the back."

"A thief?" The carter laughed uproariously. "Don't you think I'd know if I was, you blockhead? It's wine I've got."

"If you've got nothing to hide, then let us check," insisted the other.

"If you must," grumbled the carter, jumping down. Jacob saw the legs of the three of them go right around the cart, then he heard the cover being pulled back. There was more clatter and the cart swayed as one of his pursuers jumped up and walked around on the planks, bent double.

"Anything?" his partner called up.

"Barrels," came the surly reply. "What's in the barrels?"

"Thieves," cackled the carter. "Pickled thieves, one to a barrel."

"Ha, ha, very funny," snapped the one in the cart. The planks creaked under his feet. He was coming closer to the part above Jacob. Too late he remembered that his fingers were sticking out slightly through the gaps. The next moment the man trod on them. Everything went black and red. Jacob bit his tongue to stop himself crying out. Get off, he prayed, please get off.

"Come on, get down," said the man on the ground. "He's not there. I told you so."

The other turned on his heel a little, scraping the skin off Jacob's fingers. The sweat was pouring off him. Scarcely conscious, he gritted his teeth.

"There's a stink of fish here."

"You're imagining it. We all stink of fish. Now won't you get down?"

"All right then."

Wonderful! The relief! The boot had gone. Trembling, Jacob slowly let out his breath.

"And what was it your thief stole?" asked the carter, now full of curiosity, as the man jumped down.

"That's none of your business."

"Now just a minute. If I stop and let you search my cart, the least you could do is tell me why."

"He stole a guilder from our master, Matthias Overstolz," the other explained. "Right there in the street! Right outside his house in Rheingasse!"

"Unbelievable."

Jacob couldn't believe his ears. Stolen a guilder? Him? When, for Christ's sake?

"A redheaded bastard. Tell us if you see him. We'll be keeping up our patrol around here for a while yet."

"All that for just one guilder?"

"Herr Overstolz doesn't like being robbed."

"No, and he doesn't like us shooting our mouths off either," said the other, adding to the carter, "Off you go now."

Muttering something incomprehensible, the carter climbed back into his seat.

"Matthias will be furious," said one of the pursuers softly.

"Not to mention his odd friend," replied the other.

"The long-haired Dominican?"

"Mmm."

The cart started with a shudder, almost throwing Jacob off the shaft. He just managed to stop himself from falling. He heard something splatter onto the muddy ground, then another. Contorting his neck, he managed to look down.

Octopuses!

They were dropping off his habit. Christ Almighty, they must have stowed away when he landed on the fish stall. Now he was done for.

But this time fate was kind to him. No one shouted, "Hey, you! Stop!" No one looked under the cart, a glint of triumph in their eyes. The voices grew fainter. They were going away.

Jacob clung on as tightly as his throbbing fingers would allow. Better stay with the cart for a while before jumping off. It rumbled slowly along Pfaffenstraße, then turned into Minoritenstraße. Jacob was bumped and jolted until he felt none of his bones were left in their original place. Steeling himself against the pain, he put up with it all along Breite Straße with its stones and potholes, stops and starts, until they were opposite the Church of the Holy Apostles. There he decided to jump off.

He tried to pull his fingers out of the gaps between the planks.

He couldn't.

He tried again. Still no luck. He was stuck. That's impossible, he thought, I must be dreaming.

He gave a sharp tug to try to free his hands. The only result was a suppressed yelp of pain. He was stuck.

"Stop."

Once more, swaying and creaking, the cart stopped. Jacob watched the iron-studded boots and leg-armor of soldiers go around the cart, heard the canvas being thrown back once more. They must have reached the city gate.

The soldiers muttered to each other. Jacob held his breath. Another pair of legs appeared in his field of vision. The shoes below the richly embroidered robe were decorated with buckles at the side. They were in the form of lilies and glistened purple in the sunlight.

After what seemed an eternity, the canvas cover was replaced.

"Nothing, Your Excellency."

"Just barrels."

A rumble of acquiescence came from the owner of the purple buckles. The soldiers stepped back and the carter barked his "Gee-up." Totally bewildered, Jacob lay back on the shaft as the cart rattled through the Frisian Gate, taking him out of Cologne and into the unknown.

RICHMODIS

At the same time on the Brook Goddert was grumbling to Richmodis. "Huh, and that Jacob of yours will be lying in Little St. Martin's bathhouse indulging in God knows what dissipation." His gnarled fingers were having difficulty tying a knot.

"You just get on with your parcels," Richmodis snapped.

They had left at the same time as Jaspar and Jacob to return to their house on the Brook. It was high time they got back to their dyeing. Goddert seemed a different person. He no longer complained about being unable to work because of his arthritis, but set to as in the old days, though with a somewhat morose doggedness. Richmodis knew why. He felt useless and stupid. His hands were deformed, his brain hopelessly condemned to defeat by Jaspar's razor-sharp mind. She was all he had. But Richmodis needed him less and less, while he needed her more and more. There was no one left to look up to him.

They made up parcels of the blue cloth in silence. Goddert had decided to deliver them himself. He'd have to go around half the city, which meant he'd be late getting back, but he had obstinately refused all help. "You shut up," he muttered. "If people knew how my daughter treats me."

"No worse than the way you treat me." She let the parcel she was doing sink to her lap and brushed the sweat-soaked hair out of her eyes. "Look, Father—"

"Other children treat their parents with respect."

"I respect you."

"No, you don't."

She went over to him and wrapped her arms around his tub of a body.

"I respect you for every pound you weigh." She laughed. "Can you imagine how much that adds up to?"

Goddert stiffened and turned his head away.

"Father," said Richmodis, sighing.

"All right."

"I don't know what's the matter with you. I like this Jacob, and that's all. What's wrong with that?"

Goddert scratched his beard. At last he turned and looked her in the eye. "Nothing. There are other lads I would have chosen for you, but—"

"Well?"

"Why can't our family be like any other? The father chooses the husband, that's the way things are."

"For goodness sake!" Richmodis looked up to heaven. "What makes you think I see anything in that stray fox other than a creature who's been done an injustice? I feel sorry for him. Did I ever say I felt anything more?"

"Hmmm."

"Anyway," she said, giving his beard a good tug with both hands, "I do what I want."

"Yes, that's what you keep on saying," Goddert exclaimed. "That's exactly what I'm talking about."

"So? Where's the problem?"

"The problem is, you can't fool me."

"You like him, too."

"Yes, certainly—"

"And you married my mother against your father's wishes."

"I did what?" Goddert was taken by surprise.

Richmodis shrugged her shoulders. "At least you're always bragging about not bowing and scraping to anyone and always getting your own way."

"But that's not the same thing," he growled, without being able entirely to repress a grin.

"Oh, yes, it is."

"You're a girl."

"Thanks for reminding me. I'd almost forgotten."

"Little minx."

"Pigheaded old jackass."

Goddert gasped and wagged his finger at her. "I'll teach you manners this evening."

"I can hardly wait."

"Bah!"

She thumbed her nose at Goddert, then helped him finish tying up his parcels. "You'll be back by dinnertime, won't you?"

"Hard to say. There's quite a pile of stuff."

"Look, Father, please. If it's too heavy, leave it. You're not as young as you were."

"It won't be too heavy."

"You don't have anything to prove. Least of all to me."

"But it won't be too heavy for me."

"Fine." She shook her head and gave him a kiss. "Off we go, then."

"What do you mean 'we'?"

"I'm popping over to Jaspar's. They might be back already. Anyway, I thought the old toper might like a bit of fruit." She took a basket and filled it with pears. They left together. Goddert, small, bent under the weight of his burden, waddled off in the direction of Mauritiussteinweg. Richmodis watched him go, wondering how to get across to him that she preferred him as an arthritic lazybones.

She'd have to have a word with Jaspar about it.

Eventually she set off, strolling to Severinstraße with her basket on her arm. She was still a long way off when she saw the handcart leaned up against the wall of Jaspar's house. Rolof had obviously been doing some work. Who would he have been cursing today?

She knocked and went in.

Rolof was on the bench by the fireside. His greedy eyes immediately fell on the pears. "For me?" he asked, smiling all over his face.

"Not for you, greedy guts, I—"

She halted and looked at the man at the other end of the bench, who stood up when she came in. He was unusually tall, and a torrent of silky blond hair fell down over his black monk's habit to his waist. His forehead was high, his nose straight and slender, and his teeth, when he smiled, perfectly regular. His eyes, under brows the width of a man's finger, glowed amber flecked with gold.

Behind them was something else. An abyss.

She looked at him and knew who he was.

Jacob's description had been sketchy, but there was no possible doubt. For a moment she wondered whether it would be a good idea to run away. The Dominican, or rather, the man pretending to be a Dominican, came toward her. Involuntarily she took a step back. He stopped.

"Forgive me if I was too entranced by your beauty." His voice was soft and cultured. "Would you do me the pleasure of telling me your name?"

Richmodis bit her lip.

"That's Richmodis." Rolof grinned. "Didn't I say she was sweet?"

"Truly, my son, you did." He kept his eyes fixed on her. "Richmodis, an enchanting name, though the songs of the troubadours would better express such comeliness than any name. Are you a—relative of my old friend Jaspar?"

"Yes," she said, putting her basket down on the table. A thousand thoughts flashed through her mind at once. Perhaps the best thing would be to behave naturally. "And no," she added quickly. "More a kind of friend, if you like"—she paused—"reverend Father."

"Nonsense." Rolof laughed, snatching a pear before she could stop him. "She's his niece, yes? Cheeky young hussy, but nice."

"Rolof! Who asked your opinion?"

Rolof, who was already biting into the pear, froze, a puzzled look on his face. "Sorry, sorry," he muttered with a timid glance at the stranger. But the stranger's eyes were for Richmodis alone, and an odd change came over them, as if a plan were forming behind them.

"His niece," he said.

"Uh-huh." She threw her head back, shaking her locks. With pounding heart, but her chin raised defiantly, now she went up to him, scrutinizing him. "Reverend Brother or not," she said pointedly, "I still think it is impolite not to tell me your name, when I have revealed mine. Is it not good manners to introduce yourself when you enter a strange house?"

The man's eyebrows shot up in amusement. "Quite right. I must apologize."

"Your name, then," she demanded.

The blow to her face came so quickly she was speechless with astonishment. The next lifted her off her feet. Arms wide, she flew over a stool, crashed into the wall, and sank to the ground.

Rolof bellowed. Through a haze, Richmodis saw him throw the pear away and fling himself on her attacker.

Then everything went black.

THE RHINE WHARF

The cranes groaned under the weight, and in the tread wheels operating the cranes, the laborers groaned. It was the sixth ship to be unloaded that day. The goods consisted entirely of bales of cloth from Holland, heavy as lead.

Leaning against a stack of crates, Matthias checked the list of wares that had arrived, ticking off those he intended to purchase. The right of staple, he thought to himself with satisfaction, was rapidly becoming one of the pillars of the Cologne economy. It had been granted a little over a year ago, and now no merchant, whether from Hungary, Poland, Bohemia, Bavaria in the east, Flanders or Brabant in the north, or from the Upper Rhine, could take his goods through Cologne without first offering them for sale in the market for three days. The privilege also applied to goods that arrived by land.

To Matthias's mind it was a privilege for which the city had had to wait far too long. They had been pursuing it, like the Devil a lost soul, for over a hundred years. Since the channel of the Middle Rhine, which started at Cologne, was relatively shallow, merchants taking their goods upstream had no option but to transfer them to smaller ships there. Was it not then logical to take the opportunity to offer them for sale? Far be it from the citizens to assume this natural feature gave them any rights. After all, it would be tantamount to blasphemy to think that God had made the channel shallower just to divert a stream of gold into the pockets of the merchants.

But then the Church, of all institutions, had promoted the worldly interests of the merchants and patricians. It was Conrad von Hochstaden, always mindful of the needs of his flock, to whom the city owed the privilege! A neat stroke that appealed not to their hearts, but to their purses. The good thing about the right of staple was that during those three days only Cologne merchants had the right to buy. What was more, they could inspect the goods and, if they were found unsatisfactory, tip them into the Rhine. The result was that only the freshest fish and best wines were served in Cologne and the most desirable wares never reached the southern German territories.

There was just one thing about it that stuck in Matthias's throat. The feeling of being under an obligation to Conrad. It was a paradoxical situation that could only be dealt with by cold reason, cutting out the emotions. His ice-cold reason was one of the few things Matthias thanked the Creator for. At least now and then, when he had time.

His index finger slid smoothly down the list, stopping at one item, a consignment of brocade. "Inspect and buy," he said.

His chief clerk beside him gave a respectful nod and hurried over to where the ships' owners were shouting instructions to the stevedores and waiting to start negotiations. Matthias added up a few figures in his head and decided it was a good day. Good enough to consider the purchase of a few barrels of fine wine newly arrived from Spain.

"Matthias!"

He stared out at the river, feeling his good mood evaporate. "What do you want?" he asked coldly.

Kuno Kone came up from behind, slowly walked around, and planted himself in front of him. "I would like a word with you, if you would be so kind."

Matthias hesitated, one eye still on the barrels of wine. Then he lost interest in them and shrugged his shoulders. "I can't think what there is to talk about," he said irritably.

"I can. You have excluded me from your discussions."

"That was Johann, not me."

"Yes, you, too," Kuno insisted. "You agree with Johann that I might betray our plan. What an unworthy suspicion!"

"Unworthy? Oh, we're unworthy now, are we?" The corners of Matthias's mouth turned down in scorn. "You won't get anywhere with me with hackneyed phrases like that. What would have been your reaction if I'd knocked, say, Johann or Theoderich down?"

"I—I would have taken a less heavy-handed approach."

"Aha, less heavy-handed!" Matthias gave a harsh laugh. "You're a sentimental clod, Kuno. I'm not suggesting you're going to betray us, but your brain is softened by emotion, and that's even worse. With the best of intentions you can produce the worst of results. That's why you've been excluded. There's no more to say."

"There is!" Kuno shook his head vigorously. "I'm willing to ignore the hurt and the insults, but have you forgotten it's my brothers who are living in exile, banished and outlawed?"

"Of course not."

"They were magistrates too, just like—Daniel." He had great difficulty pronouncing the name. "Bruno and Hermann would die for our alliance, they—"

"No one is going to die for an alliance whose sole function is to represent his interests."

"But they believe in the alliance, and they believe in me. Who's going to keep them informed, if not me?"

"You should have thought of that before."

"It's never too late for remorse, Matthias."

Matthias, still staring at the river, slowly shook his head. "Too late for you," he said.

"Matthias! Trust me. Please. I have to know how things stand. What about the redhead? Has Urquhart—"

"Leave me in peace."

"And what shall I tell my brothers?"

Matthias stared at him from beneath furrowed brows. "As far as I'm concerned, you can tell them they have a weakling for a brother who lacks self-control. They can always complain to me, once they're allowed back in Cologne. For the time being—"

He broke off. One of the servants he had assigned to Urquhart was coming into the customs yard.

"Matthias, I beg you—" Kuno pleaded.

Matthias silenced him with a gesture, tensely waiting for the messenger. The man was completely out of breath. Without a word, he took a parchment roll tied with a leather thong out of his doublet and handed it to Matthias.

"What's this?"

"Your friend, the Dominican with the fair hair," the servant panted.

"Yes? And? Out with it!"

"He gave it to me, sir."

"Without saying anything? Pull yourself together, man. Where did you meet him?"

"He met me, sir. We were checking the area around St. Cecilia's when he suddenly appeared. He was pushing a large handcart, fully loaded, with a blanket over it, all I know is—no, just a minute, I was to tell you the cart was full of life and that it was, was—how did he put it, for God's sake?— oh yes, it was of the utmost importance that you read the letter, and, and—"

He halted. From the expression of despair on his face, it was clear he had lost the thread of Urquhart's words.

"Remember," Matthias barked at him, "or it'll be the last thing you forget."

"—and lose no time at all." As the words came rushing out, the servant heaved a sigh of relief.

Impatiently Matthias tore the scroll out of his hand, untied the thong, and started to read. Out of the corner of his eye he saw Kuno edging closer. Lowering the letter, he gave him an icy stare. "It's about time you left."

"You can't simply send me away like that," wailed Kuno. "I promise to make up for my mistake—"

"Go!"

Breathing heavily, Kuno stared at him for a moment, as if undecided whether to fall to his knees or strike Matthias down. Then he angrily gathered his cloak around him, turned on his heel without a further word, and stalked off. Matthias watched him until he had disappeared through the gate.

The servant was hopping nervously from one foot to the other. "There's something else, sir—"

"Out with it, then."

With a nervous start, the man began his tale, but went about it in such a stuttering, roundabout way, Matthias at first had no idea what he was trying to tell him. Finally he realized they had allowed the redhead and the dean to escape.

He stared at the parchment. "You all deserve a good thrashing," he said. A thin smile appeared on his lips. "However, the news is not entirely bad and I've better things to do at the moment. Get back to your post before I change my mind."

The servant made a clumsy bow and ran off.

Matthias waved his chief clerk over and gave him a series of instructions. Then he left the wharf and hurried up Rheingasse, past the Overstolz mansion to the modest building where Johann performed his miracles of accounting. He flew up the stairs, two at a time, and burst into Johann's office.

"The dean and the redhead have got away," he cried, slapping the scroll down on the table, right under Johann's nose.

Johann looked up. He seemed worn out. "I know," he said dully. "And I can add that we have two further deaths to—how shall I put it?—to cheer? To deplore?"

"What!? Who?"

"Urquhart's witnesses. Things get around. Someone has disturbed the discreet activities at the Little St. Martin bathhouse. For the moment they've arrested the owner and his assistants. Some whores also fell under suspicion." Johann snorted. "But they say the whores have been freed. No one could explain how they managed to break three ribs of one of their customers, plus his shoulder blade and neck."

"And the other?" asked Matthias, fascinated.

Johann shrugged his shoulders. "They can't decide whether he drowned or suffocated."

"Well, well, well."

Johann stood up and went to the window. "Matthias, I can't say I feel happy about all this. I thought Urquhart was going to be our instrument, but I'm starting to feel like the butcher who took on a wolf as his assistant. You understand what I'm saying?"

"Of course." Matthias went over and held up the scroll in front of his face. "But before you start worrying about Urquhart, you should read his message."

With a dubious look, Johann took the scroll. He read it, read it again, then shook his head in disbelief. "He's taken a hostage?"

"Yes. And we've got a safe hiding place."

"Not in the house again!"

Matthias made a calming gesture. "No, not in the house. I was thinking of the old warehouse by the river. No one ever goes there. Everything will be over by tomorrow, God—or the Devil, if you prefer—willing. Then he can do what he likes with his hostage, and with all the foxes and deans he can find. The important thing is that they all hold their tongues until then."

"Tomorrow," whispered Johann.

Matthias grasped his arm, squeezing it hard. "We're so close to success, Johann, we mustn't lose heart now. Tomorrow, yes, tomorrow! Let's keep our minds fixed on tomorrow."

Johann kept looking out of the window. Life outside was so peaceful, so orderly, everything in its place. What would things be like after tomorrow?

"Send one of the servants to show him the way," he said.

"The servants are too woolly headed," Matthias snapped. "The one who came to tell me they'd lost Jaspar and the Fox, for example, forgot to mention the two dead bodies in the bathhouse. I'd prefer to see Urquhart myself."

"Too risky. It was bad enough bringing him to the house."

"I—"

"Don't worry, I wouldn't have thought of a better idea. Send one of the servants to go with him, no, better get him just to tell Urquhart the way—and hand over a supply of leather straps," he added with a humorless smile. "Hostages are best when they're tightly tied to one's interests."

"He'll make sure of that." Matthias grinned.

"I hope so." Johann ran his fingers through his hair, then went back to his desk. "With all this to worry about, the work's just piling up," he moaned.

"Perhaps. But it's worth it."

"Yes, you're right, of course. See the necessary steps are taken. I'll inform the others."

In the doorway Matthias turned around. "By the way, Kuno wants to come back," he said hesitantly.

Johann looked up. "Did he tell you that?"

"Yes. Just now."

"And what did you say?"

"I sent him away. Although—" Matthias frowned. "Perhaps it would be better to send him straight to hell."

"I didn't hear that," said Johann grimly.

"No? Oh, well," said Matthias, "a time and place for everything, eh, Johann? A time and a place for everything."

THE LIVING DEAD

Thrrummp!

A hole in the road. Full of water.

Jacob would have liked to be able to feel his body all over. He had the suspicion his breastbone had slipped down to somewhere near his pelvis. For the time being, however, he had to abandon his efforts to free his fingers from the grip of the planks above. As long as the cart was still moving, there was nothing for it but to wait patiently and pray to some saint or other who had been in a similar situation.

He was sopping wet. Windmills were whirling inside his head. No saint had ever been through anything like this. They were grilled over a low flame, boiled in extra-virgin olive oil, cut up with red-hot pincers, or pulled in all directions at once by four horses. None had ever gone to heaven via a cart shaft. It was ridiculous.

Jacob stared at the planks. By now he knew every line and curve of the grain. His imagination turned them into rivers through a dark forest, into unmade roads like this one, pitted and fissured; the panorama of wormholes became a hellish, crater-pocked landscape and the knothole a mysterious land beyond human knowledge. You didn't realize what there was in a simple piece of wood until you were forced to stare at it from close proximity.

After what seemed like an eternity he heard the carter shout, "Whoa." As far as he could tell from his admittedly restricted viewpoint, there was nothing around that suggested human habitation. He saw the carter's legs as he jumped down. They moved away, parted. There was a splash as a stream of urine hit the ground.

Jacob tried once more to free his fingers from the planks. He went about it systematically this time, one by one, instead of trying to pull them all out at once. He began with the little finger of his left hand, twisting and jiggling it, freeing it little by little until it was released. One out of ten! At least it was a start. If he could get one out there was hope he might eventually be able to resume an upright posture.

He just had to keep on twisting and jiggling.

The relieved carter came back, climbed up into his seat, and urged the horses on. He would have to make do with just the little finger for the moment.

Some time later Jacob saw walls along the side of the road. Once he briefly heard voices. Then, with a repeat of the nerve-jangling noises, the cart turned off to the right onto a flat area, where it halted. Clearly it was likely to be a longer stop this time, since the carter had disappeared into a building a few yards away.

Patiently Jacob set to work. Now that he no longer had to brace himself against the swaying and shuddering of the cart, it turned out that things weren't as bad as he thought. The remaining fingers of his left hand did cling rather obstinately to the planks, but once they were free, the right hand slipped out by itself and Jacob fell off the shaft onto the dusty ground.

With a sigh of relief, he lay there, trying to recover. Then he examined his hands. His knuckles hurt and were bleeding, but he didn't care. He had escaped and that was the only thing that mattered.

Only—escaped to *where*?

Like a little mouse, silent and on all fours, he crept out from under the cart and surveyed the terrain. His first impression was of a spacious courtyard or, rather, a gently rising square ending a little way ahead in an ivy-covered wall with closely planted trees behind. On the right was a long row of low buildings, not dissimilar to a monastery dormitory, with a wide entrance leading into a still larger open space. Beyond it the squat tower of a small church could be seen, also surrounded by trees. From the closest building, where the carter had gone, Jacob could hear the faint sound of voices.

He walked around the cart and saw a wall with a gate, through which they had evidently come.

A gate that two men were just closing.

He quickly pulled the hood back over his head. He couldn't make out what kind of building this was. It didn't seem to be a monastery, nor a village or hamlet, and the walls were too low for a castle compound. The men wore cloaks and hoods, but they weren't monks. His preferred option was to run away, but that was no longer possible. The two men could turn at any moment. Better to take the bull by the horns.

Assuming a dignified priestly posture, he went over to one of the cloaked figures and tapped him on the shoulder. "Excuse me," he said.

The man turned around.

Jacob recoiled in horror. He was staring at a decaying skull without nose or lips. Where the left eye should have been was a hole gleaming with yellow pus. The other was regarding him expressionlessly.

Unable to repress his retching, he took another step back.

The being stretched out something toward him that had perhaps once been a hand and came closer. Unarticulated grunts came from its throat. Now the other man had joined them. A tangle of beard covered his face, which was unmarked, apart from a few weeping patches. With a suspicious look, he watched Jacob as he staggered back, unable to take his eyes off the horrifying figure. Then he burst out into harsh laughter.

Slowly they came toward him.

Jacob turned and ran toward the church, where a few men and women were standing, talking quietly among themselves. As he approached they looked up at him.

Ravaged faces. Missing limbs.

At that moment the door of the building where the carter had gone opened. A man whose legs ended at his knees crawled out to see what was going on. Laboriously he struggled in Jacob's direction. The two from the gate were catching up with him while the group by the church prepared to encircle him. Desperately Jacob searched for an escape, but wherever he looked the place was bounded by walls. He was trapped. They had surrounded him, were ready to fall on him, tear him to pieces, transform him into one of them. Jacob's head was ringing. He stumbled and fell to his knees.

One of the men opened a hole of a mouth with spittle dribbling out, and squatted down. "Can we help you?" he asked politely.

Help? Jacob blinked and looked around. Regarded dispassionately, one could hardly say they had surrounded him. On the contrary, they were observing him timidly and keeping their distance.

Again the bearded man from the gate laughed. "Hannes always gives them a fright the first time," he roared. It didn't sound at all threatening, just amused and friendly. The strange grunts were still coming from the faceless man's chest, but now Jacob realized he was laughing, too, the laughter of a man with no mouth, probably no tongue.

The bell inside Jacob's head stopped ringing. "Where am I?" he asked, getting back to his feet. He could feel his heart beating at the top of his chest, just below his throat.

The two men exchanged puzzled glances, then looked at Jacob again. "You're in Melaten. How can you not know the leper colony, since you came here yourself?"

Melaten! The leper colony! The largest in Cologne, to the west of the city, on the road to Aachen. He had escaped—to a leper colony!

The living dead, they called them. To contract leprosy meant to be taken away from your family and friends, no longer be part of their lives. The laws were inexorable. There was even a rite, with obsequies, eulogy, and last blessing, in which the congregation said farewell to lepers as to someone who had died. After that they began their lives in the leper community, away from society. Any contact with healthy people—in church, at the market, the inn, the mill, the communal oven—was forbidden on pain of punishment. They were not allowed to wash in flowing water. If they wanted to buy something, they were not allowed to touch it until they had bought it. If they should happen to speak with a healthy person, they had to keep downwind of them. They were only allowed to go out of the colony with the permission of the hospice master, only allowed to visit the city on a few days of the year to beg, clearly identifiable in their jacket and breeches, white cloak down to their knees, white gloves, and large hat, and carrying their wooden rattle so people could hear them coming.

Lepers died twice. They were the dead who were still waiting for death. Excluded from society and left with nothing but their hope of heaven. Those who could afford it bought a place in a leper house like Melaten, one of the largest in the German Empire, others built primitive shacks on designated land or lived a vagrant life.

The immense pity everyone felt for them was only outweighed by their revulsion.

Jacob shivered. He pulled his habit around him and clasped his arms tightly. "Excuse me, but—" He shot a quick glance at the gate.

"Did you come with the cart?" asked the man.

"Yes, I—"

"Saint Dionysus be praised! You must be the priest they were going to send. Follow me, Father, he's in the last house. Though whether he's still alive or not, I don't know."

Now they thought he was a priest! Was he going to have to give someone the last rites? "I—I really ought to be going," he stammered.

The man shook his head. "It won't take long, Father. Who else is there to pray for him?"

"Pray? But I'm—no, wait." Jacob rubbed his eyes and thought. He was wearing a habit, therefore he was a monk. Would they let him go if he admitted he wasn't?

He'd think of a way out of the situation. Somehow. "Good," he said, "let's go."

"No!" It was a well-known voice that rang out.

Jacob spun around. "Jaspar!" he exclaimed, as much in bewilderment as relief.

"I'll do that," said Jaspar, as if their meeting was expected. "Got here before me, did you? Have you been cadging a lift again? No matter. You wait here. My novice," he explained to the man. "A bit timid, unfortunately, and not quite right in the head, either. Always forgetting things, sometimes even his own name."

"A bit old for a novice, isn't he?" said the man hesitantly, with a side glance at Jacob.

"Yes. It's his low intelligence. He'll never rise any higher."

Jacob's chin sank. "Hey, Jaspar, what's all this?"

"You just keep your mouth shut and wait for me, d'you hear? Stay here till I get back, don't run away and don't talk to people."

"But—"

"No buts. Sit over there by that wall."

Speechless, Jacob watched him go with the man and a few others across to the buildings, entering the last one. The lepers remaining outside went about their business, leaving Jacob by himself. With a shake of the head, he sat down against the church wall and examined his scraped fingers again.

It was quite a long time before Jaspar returned. The man was still with him. "I'm glad his sufferings are at an end," Jacob heard him say.

"The grace of the Lord is immeasurable and His ways a mystery to us" was Jaspar's devout reply. "Peace be unto his soul. Spend the night in prayer for him. He partakes of eternal life, but his way will be hard and full of danger. The Powers of Darkness lie in wait for him on his way to heavenly bliss, like robbers trying to steal his soul."

"We will pray, I promise. In the meantime may I invite you to a mug of wine in our inn?"

"Thank you for the kind thought, but my novice and I have a long walk ahead of us. To the leper house on Judenbüchel." Jaspar put on a mournful expression. "The same story. It's a tragedy."

"The Lord is calling many to appear before Him at the moment."

"He calls them to join the heavenly choirs in praising Him."

"Surely. By the way, I heard there have been some strange deaths in the city."

Jacob went over to join them. "I—" he said.

"Didn't I tell you to keep your mouth shut?" snapped Jaspar, then went on to the man, "If you would like to do me a favor, you could let me have a couple of white cloaks, pairs of gloves, and hats. There was a fire in the washhouse and they're a bit short of them in the Judenbüchel house at the moment. Some of them need to go into the city tomorrow. Oh, and two rattles. If you can spare them, of course."

"Wait here," said the man. "I'll see what we can do."

Jaspar, a self-satisfied smile on his face, watched him disappear between the buildings.

"What's all this about me not being right in the head?" hissed Jacob.

In his inimitable way, Jaspar raised his brows. "Well, I had to find some way or other of extricating you from the mess you'd got yourself into. Or would you rather have given the dying man the last rites?"

"Of course not."

"You see? It's best if they think you're a simpleton. After all, you did come here underneath the cart of the man who regularly delivers the wine to Melaten. He might be a bit annoyed when he hears about it."

"More than annoyed," said Jacob. "He was told I'm a thief."

"Who told him? The men who stopped the cart?"

"Uh-huh."

"Now that is interesting. What are you supposed to have stolen?"

"One guilder."

"Oh, what a naughty fox-cub you are!"

"Forget the jokes. I'm supposed to have—"

Jaspar shook his head and put his finger to his lips. "We'll talk later. Here's our friend."

The man, who turned out to be the hospice master himself, came carrying some clothes tied up in a bundle and two rattles.

"Too kind," said Jaspar with an extravagant bow. His nose and chin looked as if they might get stuck in the ground. Jacob hesitated, then quickly followed his example.

"Not at all," replied the man. "It's we who have to thank you, Father."

"You will get the clothes back."

"No hurry. And they've just been washed, so you needn't worry about touching them."

"Once more, thank you."

"God be with you in your difficult task."

They said farewell and left the hospice through the orchard. There was a narrow gate there that was open all day. That was the way Jaspar had come in.

Jacob was relieved to be out of the leper colony, though at the same time he was ashamed of his fear and would gladly have stayed awhile. He somehow felt he had run away again instead of facing up to something important, bringing unhappy memories to the surface. He kept looking back as they made their way along the road to Cologne. He sensed he would not forget his involuntary visit that quickly. Then, suddenly, he felt strong and full of life again. The lepers had lost everything. He still had a chance of winning.

Jaspar seemed to have guessed his thoughts. "The disease bothers them less than it does healthy people," he said. "If you're incurably ill and dead for the world, what's to stop you laughing at yourself? They have no hope or, to be more precise, one should say they are free from hope. A huge difference. Paradoxically, losing everything can mean you lose despondency and despair as well."

"Have you been there before?" asked Jacob.

Jaspar nodded. "Several times."

"Were you never afraid of becoming infected?"

"No. It's all rather exaggerated. Although no one will admit it, in fact you have to have damn bad luck to catch it. You only saw the sick people, but there are two living in Melaten with their spouses, and they're not infected."

"I thought the lepers were forbidden to come into contact with healthy people."

"They are, unless an uninfected person joins them of their own free will. Other people go to Melaten as well, the carter with the wine, for example, and the washerwomen. And you know the man with the bells who goes around begging for them, he's dealing with them all the time. But you hardly ever hear of people like that catching the disease, and if they do, it's only after many years. No, the lepers are not a real danger. They are a warning to the arrogant. Leprosy doesn't distinguish between rich and poor; anyone can catch it. A just punishment God visited on those accursed crusaders, to bring back together with all the treasures they stole from the East." He glanced at Jacob and grinned. "Good old Hannes gave you quite a fright, didn't he?"

"Hannes is the one with no face?"

"The worst case in Melaten. It's odd that he's alive. Still alive, I mean."

"Still laughing, too," said Jacob. "But tell me, how did you find me? What happened to you after we split up?"

Jaspar made fluttering movements with his fingers. "I got away," he laughed. "I think the men hadn't actually been ordered to capture us, just to stick to us until our crazy crusader could dispatch us in some quiet corner. It's probably a bit different with you, but they can't just kidnap or even kill me in the middle of the street. What they hadn't counted on was that we would smell a rat and run off. They were suddenly afraid they'd lose sight of us and be blamed for it later, so they dropped their pretense and took chase. They didn't send the most intelligent specimens of humanity after us, thank God. Unseen by them, I went straight into St. Mary's. It never occurred to the idiots I'd hide in the first church I came to. It was obvious they wouldn't stop to think until they got to Highgate. Then they'd retrace their steps. So I went straight out by the side door and back to Haymarket, hoping I'd find you there. No problem! That clout on the head with the radish was quite spectacular. I couldn't join up with you, but I saw everything from a distance. When I realized you were safe for the moment under the cart, I strolled along a good way behind. It wasn't going that fast and I assumed it would have to stop somewhere. Then when I saw it turn into the gate at Melaten I had to get a move on, but I was too late, they'd already closed the door. Fortunately I know Melaten and I know the little gate at the back." He nodded smugly. "So that's how I saved you. You can write me a thank-you letter—oh, no, of course you can't. And all the time I was trotting along behind, I kept wondering, why doesn't the Fox jump off? To be honest, I still don't understand."

"Because the Fox was trapped," said Jacob sourly. "He'd got his paws stuck in between the planks."

"And couldn't get them out?" Jaspar laughed out loud. "That story would get me a drink in any inn in Cologne."

"I think I'd prefer it if you kept it to yourself."

"If the men who were after you only knew! But they know nothing. I imagine they haven't been told what it's all about. They'll have just been given some cock-and-bull story why we have to be caught."

"They knew damn well why they were chasing me," said Jacob.

"You? Oh, yes, you've stolen one guilder, you rascal. Who from, if I might inquire?"

"Matthias Overstolz."

Jaspar stopped and stared. "From him? But why him, for God's sake?"

"I didn't steal it," Jacob protested. "He gave it to me. Yesterday morning. And now I'm supposed to have stolen it."

"One moment," said Jaspar. He seemed confused. "Why would Matthias Overstolz give you a guilder?"

"I was standing outside their house in Rheingasse, trying to wrap my jerkin around my head. Haven't I told you this?"

"No," said Jaspar, frowning. "Who knows what else you've forgotten to tell me."

They walked along in silence for a while. The sun was low in the sky, making the fields and meadows all around glow with an almost unnatural intensity.

"Fox-cub, are you telling me the truth?"

"Why do you ask?"

"Jacob," he said, "we only met yesterday. I have great but not unbounded trust in you. So just reassure me. Is everything you have told me so far the truth?"

"Yes, dammit, it is."

"Good." Jaspar nodded. "Then presumably we know the name of at least one of those who ordered Gerhard's death."

"Matthias Overstolz?" asked Jacob, dumbfounded.

"And not only him," Jaspar went on. "Suddenly everything's clear. I've been racking my brains to think how our meeting with the witnesses could have got out. I'm afraid I let too much slip to Bodo, and of course he couldn't wait to tell his fellow magistrates about it. And one of his fellow magistrates—"

"—is Theoderich Overstolz." This is terrible, thought Jacob. One of the most powerful Cologne families wants me dead. "But what have the Overstolzes to do with all this?"

Jaspar shrugged his shoulders. "Didn't you say yourself something big must be going on? Gerhard probably got wind of it. They won't get their hands dirty themselves, even though Matthias Overstolz's dislike of you may well be personal by now."

"Why on earth should it be?"

"Isn't it obvious? You've made him look a fool. How do you think he felt when he realized he'd given a guilder to you of all people, the man they're desperately trying to find? Matthias has the reputation of relying on cold logic alone. Some people say he only goes to church because his calculations admit the possibility there might be a God after all. He could have thought up any crime he liked to tell his servants—I'm assuming they're Overstolz servants—why they had to catch you. But no, he accuses you of having stolen one measly guilder. If there's not a desire for vengeance behind that, I don't know what vengeance is."

Jacob took a deep breath. "In other words I'm dead."

"You look alive and kicking to me," replied Jaspar cheerfully.

"Yes. For the moment."

Jaspar subjected the bridge of his nose to a good rubbing. "Let's assume it's all politics," he said. "If a patrician family starts killing architects and liquidating everyone who happens to get a whisper of it, I hardly dare to think what they're really up to. We should be proud, Fox-cub. We may all finish on the wrong end of a crossbow bolt, but at least we can't complain we've fallen into the hands of some third-rate rogues. However, far be it from me to oppose the will of the Lord, but I prefer my body as it is, without an extra hole; yours, too, I might add. So let's get down to some hard thinking about how to save our skins."

"By putting pressure on the Overstolzes?" suggested Jacob.

"Good idea. Let's play it through. You've got two names and a strong suspicion. Great. You yourself—forgive me for pointing this out—are a wily scoundrel and petty thief, but you present yourself, hand on heart, to the council of magistrates, to prove that the Overstolzes pushed Gerhard Morart off the scaffolding. Matthias Overstolz is a fiend, you say. He is guilty of the most heinous crimes, you say, though he didn't actually commit one of them himself and you don't actually know what the other one is. And then there's this fellow with long hair. I don't actually know who he is, but, all in all, I have this funny feeling in the pit of my stomach and I suggest that is reason enough for you, my noble lords, to pack Cologne's leading merchant family off to prison."

"Aren't there a couple of them there already?"

"Yes, but it was the archbishop who put them in, not the dean of St.

Mary Magdalene's, not to mention some pilfering miscreant. And what if Matthias and Theoderich are only two of a much larger band, members of some powerful conspiracy? You might go and tell the burgomaster all you know and find he's in on the plot!"

Jacob's shoulders sagged. "What is there we can do, then?" he asked despondently.

"What I advised yesterday," Jaspar replied. "Attack. We'll never discover the truth if we limit ourselves to what we already know. Gilbert of Tournai said that before me, by the way. Our only chance is to find out what they plan to do so we can be one step ahead at the decisive moment. Yesterday that was my advice to you. Now we're both involved."

He looked up in the sky to watch a flight of geese on their way south for the winter. "If it's not too late already," he muttered.

RICHMODIS

It was the regular jolting and squeaking that brought her around. Her first feeling was that she was about to suffocate. She tried to move but couldn't, even though she was painfully aware of some limbs while she couldn't feel others at all. She tried to work out what was causing the pain and gradually realized someone had trussed her up from top to toe with straps that bit into her and forced her body into an unnatural position.

She tried to shout, but there was something large and soft stuck in her mouth. No wonder she was fighting for air. She could hear faint cries, horses whinnying, street noises. She was lying on something sloping in complete darkness. She felt the panic rising. Again she tried to move. Something was planted firmly on her shoulder.

"Keep still," said a soft voice, "or I'll have to kill you."

She shuddered. She didn't dare move again. The last thing she could remember was Rolof throwing himself at the tall stranger, a stranger she had recognized without ever having seen him before. Jacob had told them about him. He was the man who had murdered Gerhard. He had knocked her down.

Scarcely able to breathe, she lay there trying to conquer her fear. She was close to hysteria, but if she let herself go, he might carry out his threat.

At last the jolting stopped. She was pulled off the slope she was lying on and fell to the ground. She had a soft landing from the mass of blankets she was wrapped in, which were now unwound. She must have looked like a huge parcel, unrecognizable as a human being.

The man bent over her. His gleaming mane fell around her; she felt as if she were inside a weeping willow. Then he pulled her up and undid some of the straps. At last she could stretch, but it was agonizingly painful as the blood began to circulate through her numb limbs. The man pulled the gag from her mouth and she lay on her back panting, afraid and yet grateful for the fresh air. At least she wasn't going to die of suffocation.

She lifted up her head and looked around, trying to work out where she was. Rough masonry walls, huge beams, and the ceiling black with soot. A little light came in through a narrow slit. She saw Jaspar's handcart.

She'd been brought here in the handcart. Where on earth was Rolof, then?

Motionless, the stranger watched her. Cautiously she tried to stretch her arms, but she was still bound hand and foot, incapable of moving.

"Where am I?" she asked in a weak voice.

Without a word, he came over to her and lifted her up until she was standing on her feet, legs trembling. Then he picked her up effortlessly and carried her over to one of the massive pillars supporting the roof.

"Please tell me where you've brought me," she begged.

He leaned her against the pillar and started to tie her up, so tight she was almost part of it.

She felt a glimmer of hope. If he was going to all this trouble, he couldn't intend to kill her. At least not immediately. It looked as if he was going to leave her here and was making sure she couldn't escape. He must have something else in mind for her. Whether it would be better or worse than being killed was another question entirely.

He pulled the straps tighter and Richmodis gave an involuntary groan. He calmly stood in front of her, scrutinizing his handiwork thoroughly. Again Richmodis was filled with nameless fear at the void behind his eyes. What she saw was an empty shell, a handsome mask. She wondered how God could have created such a being.

Jacob had not ruled out the possibility it was the Devil. Could he have been right?

That means you must be in hell, she thought. What nonsense. Whoever heard of someone being taken down to hell in a handcart?

She tried again to get him to speak. "Where is Rolof?" she asked. The stranger raised his eyebrows slightly, turned away with a shrug of the shoulders, and went to one of the heavy doors.

"Why have you brought me here?" she cried in desperation.

He stopped and turned to face her. "I'd given up hope of hearing an intelligent question from you," he said, coming back to her. "It's not a particularly intelligent age we live in, don't you agree? With whom can an educated person discuss anything new nowadays? The scholars at the universities have let themselves be made into lackeys of the popes, who themselves just slavishly follow Saint Bernard's decree that there can be nothing new and that life on earth is of no significance. Fine, if that's what he thinks, we can always open up the way to a better world."

His fingers stroked her cheek. With a shudder, she turned her head aside, the only movement she was capable of.

He smiled. "I am not going to tell you where you are, nor what I intend to do with you."

"Who are you?"

"Now then." He wagged his finger playfully at her. "You had promised to ask intelligent questions. That is not an intelligent question."

"You killed Gerhard Morart."

"I killed him?" The stranger raised his brows in mock amazement. "I can remember having given him a push. Is it my fault he had made the scaffolding so narrow?"

"And you killed that girl, the girl in Berlich," she said. "Why do you do things like that?"

"She was in the way when I took aim."

"Who will be the next one in your way?" she whispered.

"That's enough questions, Richmodis." He spread his hands wide. "I can't know everything. Life's little surprises come all unexpected. As far as I'm concerned, you can live to be a hundred."

She couldn't repress a cough. A stab of pain went through her lungs. "And what do I have to do to earn that?"

"Nothing." He winked at her, as if they were old friends, and brought out the gag again. "You must excuse me if I can't continue our little conversation. I have to go. I have important business to see to and need a little rest. A holy work"—he laughed—"as someone might put it who was foolish enough to believe in God."

It was strange, but for all that she hated and loathed him, for all the fear she had of him, the idea that he might leave her alone in this cold, terrible place seemed even worse.

"Who says God does not exist?" she asked hastily.

He paused and gave her a thoughtful look. "An intelligent question. Prove He exists."

"No. You prove He doesn't exist."

She had listened to enough of this kind of discussion between Goddert and Jaspar. Suddenly a disputation seemed the one possible bridge to the stranger.

He came closer. So close she could feel his breath on her face.

"Prove to me that God doesn't exist," Richmodis repeated, her voice quavering.

"I could do that," he said quietly, "but you wouldn't like it."

"Just because I'm a woman?" she hissed. "Gerhard's murderer is not usually so softhearted."

A frown appeared on his forehead. "There's nothing personal about this," he said. Oddly enough, it sounded as if he meant it.

"There isn't? That's all right, then, I suppose."

"What I am doing, I am doing for a purpose. I don't take pleasure in killing people, but it doesn't bother me either. I have accepted a commission in the course of which the deaths of several people became necessary, that's all."

"That's not everything by a long shot, from what I hear."

"Remember what killed the cat, Richmodis. I'm going now."

"Why do you make people suffer so much?"

He shook his head. "It is not my fault if people suffer. I bear no responsibility for their deaths. How many people die in whatever manner doesn't concern me. It doesn't make any difference. The world is pointless and it will stay that way, with or without humans."

Fury welled up inside her. "How can you be so cynical? Every human life is sacred; every human being was created by God for a purpose."

"God does not exist."

"Then prove it."

"No."

"Because you can't."

"Because I don't want to."

"Prove it!"

"Why?" The look he gave her was almost pitying. "I know He doesn't exist, but you have no right to demand I prove He doesn't. If you insist on thinking I won't because I can't, I can live with that. You can believe what you like as far as I'm concerned."

He lifted up the gag.

I'm losing him, thought Richmodis. I must learn as much as I can about him. There must be a spark of feeling somewhere inside him. "What did they do to you to make you like this?" she asked, surprised at her own question.

The expression froze on his face.

For a brief moment Richmodis thought she had managed to get through to him. Then suddenly he smiled again. "Nice try," he said with a mixture of mockery and admiration, then quickly stuffed the gag between her teeth, turned, and headed for the door, his cloak swirling. "Unfortunately not quite good enough. Don't worry, I'll be back. I might even let you go. You're safe here. Now neither the Fox nor your uncle will dare go around spreading stories about a supposed murder."

The hinges creaked as he opened the door. Richmodis had a brief view of a courtyard with a wall beyond.

"Behave yourself, like a well-brought-up girl should." In the fading light of the late afternoon he was just a shadow, a figment of the imagination, a bad dream. "And if you need proof of the complete absence of Divine Providence and the pointlessness of human existence, just think of me. One of millions."

The door slammed shut behind him. She was alone with the rats.

Urquhart slumped back against the wall of the abandoned warehouse and closed his eyes. The images were threatening to return. He felt himself being dragged down into the red whirlpool of memories from which waves of sound rose up toward him, those strangely shrill tones he would never have thought a human being capable of producing.

No! That is not me, he told himself. They are someone else's memories. I have no history.

His muscles relaxed.

The servant who had described the way to the old warehouse had also given him a message that told him that Jaspar and the Fox had es-caped from Little St. Martin's. Urquhart had expected it. He congratulated himself on the success of his visit to Severinstraße. It didn't matter that they had got away. Not in the least. They could call off the search for them.

He considered briefly whether it would not be better to kill the woman now. He was going to kill her anyway, when it was all over, so why not now? No, it made better sense to keep her alive for the moment. He would need her to entice Jaspar and the Fox into his trap. And anyone else who had heard their story. He would arrange to hand over the hostage tomorrow evening. Once he had them all there, he could kill them one by one and set the building on fire. A few charred skeletons would be found. An accident, that would be all.

Assuming it would be of any importance after what was due to happen on the morrow.

He observed the long shadows of the battlements in the courtyard. They were creeping toward the building as if they were about to grasp it. The black fingers of fate, quite poetic! Perhaps he should write poems. By now he had accumulated so much wealth that he could devote the rest of his life to the only worthwhile occupation—enjoyment. Without regret or remorse, without limits, without purpose or plan, without feelings of guilt, without a single thought for the past or future. His pleasures would be boundless, his indulgence endless, and the images would fade for good and never return. Perhaps he would set himself up as a scholar and build a palace of wisdom with a court that could become the Santiago de Compostella of philosophical inquiry, to which the greatest intellects of Christendom would make pilgrimage. He would encourage bold speculation and then amuse himself royally at the expense of the fools who sought the meaning of life. He would encourage them and then drop them at the decisive moment. He would prove that God did not exist, nor anything similar to Him, that the world was just a black abyss in which nothing was worth aiming for apart from the enjoyment of the moment, with no regard for morality, obligation, or virtue. He would even demonstrate the meaninglessness of this ridiculous nominalism since there was no reality at all behind general concepts, no good, no evil, nothing.

The ruler of nothingness! A delightful idea.

He had this one last commission to complete, here in Cologne, then he would give up killing and devote himself to enjoyment. His mind was made up.

Urquhart pushed himself away from the wall and left the tumbledown courtyard. Matthias and he had agreed to meet every two hours between now and the early morning, in case something unexpected should crop up. That would leave him plenty of opportunity to check on the girl. Perhaps he would even feel like a conversation.

THE MESSAGE

They put on the leper's clothes before they reached the city wall, out of sight of the guards on the gate. Jacob was still afraid of infection, but Jaspar assured him there was no danger. They took up their rattles and approached the city gate. It was worth a try. Although lepers were only officially allowed in Cologne on certain days of the year, the regulation was not very strictly applied as long as the beggars had their distinctive dress and rattles.

Today the guards seemed to be in a charitable mood and let them pass. They went through Cock Gate, making plenty of noise. No one who saw them bothered to give them a second look, so no one noticed that the white cloaks covered habits instead of knee breeches, nor that the two fatally ill men were the picture of health.

Jacob had had his doubts. "A pretty conspicuous disguise."

"And therefore an especially good one," Jaspar had replied. "The best of all. The ideal way not to attract attention is to behave in as conspicuous a way as possible."

"I don't understand."

"By all the saints! Have you been basking in the light of my wisdom for two whole days with no result at all? Anyone who is after us will assume we will be creeping around the city like thieves in the night. They'll be on the lookout for two little mice scurrying along, heads bowed. That we might attract attention to ourselves would never occur to them."

"Not to the servants, but perhaps to the Shadow."

"Even he's not omniscient."

As they walked through the city, not particularly hurrying, the sun was going down and everything in the streets merging into a uniform gray. Jaspar kept having to grab Jacob's coat. "Don't run."

"We've got plenty of time, have we?"

"Yes, but only one life. Lepers don't run."

An east wind came up, blowing leaves and rubbish along the street. They crossed New Market Square, where the cattle market was just finishing, strolled along to Sternengasse, and from there toward Highgate. Their only problem was trying to avoid the charitable attentions of a few good Christians who wanted to give them money or food. They muttered something about a vow that forbade them from accepting alms in the street. However nonsensical they were, vows were looked on as inviolable. No one questioned a vow.

As they turned into Severinstraße, the first raindrops began to fall and it became noticeably colder. "Can't we go a bit quicker now?" Jacob urged. "There's hardly anyone left out in the street."

"This is precisely the place where we have to hobble along like two lepers with one foot in the grave," said Jaspar, unmoved. "If they're still looking for us, they'll have posted someone near my house. No one will find anything odd about lepers begging at the door, but seeing them having a race would arouse suspicion in even the dullest mind."

Sulkily Jacob bowed to fate and pulled his hat down over his face. The rain got heavier. By the time they reached Jaspar's house, they were soaked through.

"What now?" asked Jacob.

"Now? We knock and beg for alms. Rolof opens the door and lets us in—"

"You of all people come up with a stupid idea like that?" Jacob broke in. "No sensible person would let a leper into his house."

"But Rolof is not a sensible person, everyone knows that. Don't try to beat me at my own game. At least we've made it this far. Once we're inside we'll get rid of these clothes, then I challenge anyone to prove they saw two lepers go in."

He knocked loudly on the door several times.

"No one in," said Jacob.

"Impossible." Jaspar shook his head in bewilderment and thumped the door with his fist. The house echoed with the sound. "Rolof's always in at this time."

"Perhaps he's asleep."

"Not impossible," agreed Jaspar, annoyed. "I think you're right, Fox-cub, he's taking a nap. Just you wait!" With that Jaspar hammered on the door with both fists, as if he were trying to make a hole in it. Jacob looked around nervously. That wasn't the normal behavior of a leper anymore. Jaspar seemed suddenly to come to the same conclusion. He stopped hammering and started looking worried.

"What if they're waiting for us inside?" whispered Jacob.

"That's what I was trying to establish by knocking," Jaspar growled.

"Without success."

"Huh! Anyway, these servants are thick as two short planks. They won't even give us a good look. They'll be too scared."

"But what if—"

"If your long-haired friend's there, we run for it."

Jacob was hopping nervously from one foot to the other. He swung his rattle a bit for good measure. Then he grabbed Jaspar by the arm. "I think we should get away while the going's good."

Jaspar raised an eyebrow at him. "Oh, yes? And go where?"

"I—" That was the question. Where? "No idea. To Richmodis and Goddert's place, perhaps?"

"Oh, brilliant!" Jaspar mocked. "What a genius! He's too cowardly to go in himself, but he's quite happy to put Richmodis in danger."

"All right, all right." Jacob turned away, his face red with shame. "A stupid idea, I agree."

"It was. But we all say stupid things sometimes. Come on, let's just go in and get it over with."

Jaspar pushed open the door and they went in. It was dark in the room, just a few embers glowing in the fireplace.

"He hasn't even kept the fire up, the useless lump!"

Jacob peered into the gloom. "You can't see anything."

"We'll soon see something. Where's the candlestick?"

Jaspar stomped across the room to a shelf opposite the fireplace, while Jacob tried to make something of the dark shapes. The table, a stool, the bench by the fire.

A shadow, massive, motionless.

"Jaspar—"

"Don't interrupt. Now where's that blasted candlestick?"

"There's someone here."

"What?" There was a clatter. A spark flared up, then another, and the room was gradually bathed in soft, golden candlelight. It fell on the fireside bench and on Rolof.

"God in heaven!" Jaspar whispered. Hesitantly they went over to him. Jacob felt he wanted to be sick. He also wanted to look away but found he couldn't.

"Whatever have they done to him?"

Rolof's eyes were staring at the ceiling. His nose had been smashed in. But that was a mere detail compared to the way the murderer had arranged the body. A long hank of thick dark hair cascaded down from his wide-open mouth onto his chest and curled up over his fat belly. Which had been—

"They've slit him open," Jacob gasped.

Jaspar was grinding his teeth. "Yes."

"But why? What had he done to them, goddammit? He was no danger to them. He . . ." His voice failed. With sudden realization, he pulled the hair out of Rolof's mouth. "Richmodis," he croaked.

Jaspar pointed to Rolof's forehead. "Look." It sounded almost matter-of-fact, as if he were drawing attention to some interesting object. Except that his finger was trembling.

Jacob leaned forward. "What on earth is that?"

There were smears on Rolof's forehead. Symbols joining up to make a complicated pattern.

"Writing," replied Jaspar. "That's why he did that to him. The murderer needed blood to write."

"And what—"

"A message." He sank down on the bench beside Rolof and put his head in his hands.

Jacob shuddered. He was afraid to hear the truth, although by now he suspected it. "Out with it," he said hoarsely. "What is the message?"

"*She's alive. Silence.*"

RHEINGASSE

Johann rested his chin on his hand and stared across the table, uncertain what to reply.

After Matthias had sent the servant to tell Urquhart the way to the old warehouse, Johann had tried to call an immediate meeting of the group, a vain hope on a busy weekday. At least Theoderich, a somewhat tipsy Daniel, and Heinrich von Mainz had turned up. In a few short sentences he told them about the hostage. Their reactions varied. While Heinrich, as usual, had no clear opinion, Theoderich looked unhappy. Johann could understand that. They had set off an avalanche. The situation was beginning to get out of control. Now it was Urquhart who was making the rules, while the original purity of their goal was being increasingly tarnished by crude necessity. The means were becoming an end.

Daniel, on the other hand, was delighted; he could not praise Urquhart's astute move highly enough. Johann felt disgusted at his own son. Of course Daniel was right. Though only from a coldly rational standpoint. More and more, Johann was asking himself whether they had not in fact become slaves to a barbaric attitude that was pushing them in the wrong direction.

After that he had tried to work for an hour but couldn't keep his mind on it. Eventually he gave up and went home to pray and to go up and see the old woman to let her know what was happening and to take reassurance from her steadfastness of purpose.

The old woman was asleep.

He had stood at the window for a long time, staring out into the rain that had started. Evening was approaching and with it the time of the family meal, but he did not feel in the least hungry. Feeling weary, he asked Hadewig to leave him to his own devices for a while and had withdrawn to his study, hoping the night would pass quickly, even though he viewed the coming day with horror.

He had not been alone for long.

It was Kuno. The young patrician begged to be allowed to attend their meetings again.

Johann was silent, trying to hide his uncertainty behind a blank expression. Deep down inside he could understand Kuno better than ever. But they had gone too far. They could not go back now, and that was Kuno's fatal mistake. Wanting to reverse everything, even if he did claim to support the cause wholeheartedly again.

Johann clasped his hands and slowly shook his head. "No," he declared.

"What are you afraid of?" asked Kuno.

"Your unwillingness to accept the logical consequences of your decisions," Johann replied. "You volunteer to take part in a struggle, but you want to fight it without weapons. You want to defeat your enemy, but at the same time spare him. Wars are won on the field of battle, not inside your head. I wouldn't put it past you to destroy us all just because you thought you could save someone else."

"That is not—" Kuno objected.

Johann raised his hand and cut him short. "I'm saying this because I think you are far too sentimental. Not that I've anything against feelings, but we should never have let you join the alliance. We had no choice, I suppose. None of us had. Now, though, I do have a choice. To trust you or to exercise caution."

"And you don't trust me?"

"No. You'd be lying if you tried to tell me you'd gotten over Gerhard's death and given it your approval."

"I never claimed I did! It's just that I believe in our cause, as I always have done."

"No, you don't."

Kuno started to say something, then hesitated.

"Well?" asked Johann.

"All I do know," said Kuno in deliberate tones, "is that people who have done us no harm have had to die. We feel an injustice has been done to the members of our families who have lost their lives or their freedom, not because they harmed anyone, simply because they wanted to protect their rights. Yes, it's true I agreed to a plan, the consequences of which

I reject, and I am well aware there is something contradictory in that."
He leaned forward, looking Johann calmly in the eye. "But you, too, Johann
Overstolz, subscribed to that plan. Has it not occurred to you by now that
you cannot combat injustice by acting unjustly yourself?"

Johann nodded. "It has. And I respect what you have to say, Kuno. But
you have just provided conclusive proof that we cannot rely on you. My
answer is no, we will not take you back."

Kuno's face was expressionless as he stared back at Johann. Then he
stood up and left the room without a further word.

H e was both unhappy and relieved. If Johann would not make peace
with him, then none of the others would. Blinded by Blithildis's
hatred, Johann and Matthias had abandoned all their principles. But this
final decision from Johann set him free. Not free from guilt for having voted
for the alliance and thus unwittingly contributing to Gerhard's death. No
one could ever absolve him from that. But he no longer had any obligation
toward the unholy alliance.

He had broken with them.

On the landing he turned to look back at the closed door to Johann's
study. He bore the old man no malice. Presumably Johann had to act as he
had. It no longer interested him.

"Well, well, well, what have we here?"

Kuno looked down. Daniel was leaning against the wall at the foot of
the stairs, grinning like the cat that had eaten the cream.

For a moment Kuno was tempted to hurl a few well-aimed insults at him
in revenge for the shame Daniel had brought on him at Gerhard's funeral. But
his pride won the day. He was beyond that, too. Without hurrying, he went
down the stairs until he was standing eye to eye with the young Overstolz. A
cloud of alcohol fumes enveloped him. Daniel was roaring drunk.

"It's the friend of bold young men." The tip of Daniel's tongue flick-
ered in and out between his teeth. "Want to join in again, do we? Well, we
won't let you."

Kuno looked at him, full of loathing. "You're a disgrace to your family," he said softly. He made to walk on, but Daniel grabbed him by the arm.

"Let go of me," said Kuno, barely able to control himself.

"Why? Suddenly decided we don't like to be touched by men's hands, have we?" Daniel wrinkled his nose in contempt and let go of Kuno's arm as if he had the pox. "Huh, who cares about you and your sniveling? You make me sick. Still whining about the deaths?" He bared his teeth. "Better save a few tears, crybaby, they won't be the last."

Kuno turned away. They won't be the last— "What do you mean?" he asked, still not looking at Daniel.

"What do I mean?" Daniel spat on the floor and stabbed him in the ribs with his index finger. "Wouldn't that be too heavy a burden for such a sensitive flower that wilts at the slightest hard decision? I couldn't do that to you, Kuno, I know how much it makes you suffer. Or should I?" He minced around Kuno until he was peering up at him. "Aaaah! A steely gaze! Have we a man after all? I'm impressed, Kuno. You put the fear of God into me, you really do."

Suddenly he tripped and stumbled against the banister.

"You're not even capable of supporting the burden of your own body," said Kuno contemptuously, "never mind burdening me."

"Oh, yes?" Daniel grinned. "Aren't you burdened enough with your worm-eaten Gerhard Morart? Ooooh, poor Gerhard, poor, poor Gerhard. Fell off the scaffolding. What bad luck. And you're to blame." He staggered over to Kuno and stood in front of him, swaying. "That's not the only thing you're to blame for. You're to blame for everything. You really want to know who's next on the list? Go to the old warehouse."

"What are you talking about, you beer-swilling Overstolz sot?"

"Hah!" Daniel made a theatrical gesture, almost losing his balance in the process. "I ought to kill you for that, on the spot. But then you wouldn't suffer anymore. Yes, my dear, tenderhearted friend, Urquhart has taken a young thing away from her nearest and dearest. Now he's got them all where he wants them, the Fox, the dean—"

"The dean? Who's that?"

"No, no, Kunikins, you don't have to know everything. Just enough to get your arse in a lather."

"You've no idea what you're talking about."

"A lovely girl, so I heard. Urquhart told Matthias she's the niece of the dean the Fox holed up with—"

"What fox?"

"The one who saw how your beloved master Gerhard learned to fly, the one—"

"Yes? Go on."

Daniel's eyes focused. All at once he seemed almost sober. "What are you after, Kuno?" he asked, emphasizing each single word.

"What am I after?"

"There's something wrong. Why are you suddenly all ears?"

"Just listening to you, my friend."

"Get out, you loathsome—"

"You can save your breath," said Kuno calmly, "I'm going." He turned on his heel and hurried out of the house into Rheingasse.

"—loathsome worm, slimy beast, excrescence on the backside of humanity—" Daniel screamed as he left.

Kuno ignored him completely. At last he knew what he must do.

Daniel leaned against the newel post, breathing heavily, as the door closed behind Kuno. Above him the door to Johann's study opened. "What's all the noise about, Daniel?"

He looked up and shrugged his shoulders. "Nothing. Kuno was being insolent, that's all."

Johann looked down at him angrily. "Kuno may be a fool and a danger, but never insolent."

"Father—"

"No! I don't want to hear your shouting here. Do it in your own home, where your wife's been waiting far too long for you, but not here. Understood?"

Daniel ground his teeth. "Understood."

"I didn't hear. Louder."

"All right! Understood. Understood!"

Daniel gave a howl of fury, strode unsteadily across the hall, and flung the door open. Outside the rain was splattering on the mud.

That was a mistake, he thought. You should have kept your mouth shut. You'd better sort it out.

SEVERINSTRAßE

"We can't stay here," Jacob declared.

They had laid Rolof on the bench and closed his eyes. They couldn't do any more for him at the moment. Jaspar's usual affability had given way to seething anger. Despite being pursued himself, he had so far treated the affair with a kind of academic interest. Now he was directly involved. His house had been broken into, his family put under threat, his servant brutally murdered. And there was another change in him. Beneath his quivering fury was uncertainty. For the first time he seemed to feel fear.

That did not stop him from kneeling down beside Rolof's body and accompanying him on his journey to a better world with silent prayers. Jacob stood there, not sure what he could say to the Lord. He hardly knew any prayers, so he asked Him to look mercifully on Rolof's soul, repeated the request several times, and then felt enough was enough.

"We've got to go," he said urgently.

Jaspar continued to pray.

"Do you understand?"

"Why?" Jaspar growled.

"Why? God, they know everything about us."

"So what?"

"Are we going to wait for them to come back and send us to join Rolof?"

"In the first place," said Jaspar irritatedly, as he got up, "I presume it wasn't a them but a him, that is, Gerhard's murderer. In the second place, why should he come back? He's got a hostage. He doesn't need to bother with us anymore. None of us is going to say a blind word."

"Are you absolutely sure?" asked Jacob uncertainly.

Jaspar was silent. Somehow his silence seemed to last too long.

"All right." Jacob sat down on one of the stools. "I'm sorry I came to your house. I blame myself for what's happened to Richmodis and I'm sad about Rolof. And I feel terrible that something might happen to you or Goddert. I'm very sorry, dammit! But it's happened now and I can't do anything to change it. It was your decision to help me. If you want, I'll go and try to find Richmodis. If you never want to set eyes on me again, I can understand that. Only, however much I have to be grateful to you for, don't blame me because you decided to help me."

Jaspar frowned. "When did I ever blame you for anything?"

"Not out loud, Jaspar, but you thought it. You see me as responsible for all this. In a way I am. But you had a free choice. Nobody forced you. Don't think I'm being ungrateful, I just want you to be open with me. Throw me out, if you like, but don't pretend you want to help me, while inside you're beginning to hate me."

"Who's saying I hate you?"

"No one is. But at the moment you're thinking, if I hadn't met this goddamn good-for-nothing—or, if you like, if I hadn't helped him—Rolof would still be alive and no one would be in danger. You're weighing my life against those of Rolof and Richmodis, and I come off worse. You don't have to tell me, I know. But I also know this may be your last opportunity to decide, and I don't want you deceiving yourself and me. I can live—and die—with anything, apart from the contempt of a Good Samaritan who's standing by me, not for my sake, but for his own self-respect." He lowered his voice. "I don't need anyone to tell me my life is worth less than that of others. Send me away, if you want. But leave me my pride."

Jaspar put his head on one side and squinted at Jacob. "You think this is the right moment to tell me all this?"

"Yes."

"Hmmm." He sat down facing Jacob and massaged the bridge of his nose. For a while all that could be heard was the drumming of the raindrops on the shutters.

"You're right, I did see you as responsible. I was thinking, what right has he to live, when my servant had to die for his sake and Richmodis is God-knows-where, assuming she's still alive. He should be feeling so guilty he wished the earth would open and swallow him up. And he has the cheek to ask whether I'm sure my suspicions are correct. He doesn't deserve to live! How can God allow worthwhile people to suffer because of a piece of scum?"

He paused.

"But I had forgotten, just for a moment, that no life is worthless. What is worse, I was trying to wriggle out of the responsibility. It's easier to condemn you than to admit I'm responsible for everything myself."

Jaspar hesitated. Then he raised his head and looked Jacob in the eye. "I thank you for the lesson, Fox-cub. Will you continue to accept my help?"

Jacob looked at him and suddenly couldn't repress a laugh.

"What now?" asked Jaspar indignantly.

"Nothing. It's just that—you have an unusual expression when you apologize."

"Unusual?"

"A bit like—"

"Like what?"

"There was this capon—"

"Impudent brat!" snorted Jaspar. "That's what you get when for once in your life you admit a mistake."

"Perhaps that's why. Once in your life."

Jaspar stared at him angrily. Then he had to laugh and for a while they both cackled away. It was nervous, overwrought, hysterical laughter, but it did them good all the same.

"Poor Rolof," said Jaspar at last.

Jacob nodded.

"Well?" Jaspar's brow furrowed like a plowed field. "I still think we should go onto the attack."

"Attack who? How? When Richmodis—"

Jaspar leaned forward. "Richmodis has disappeared. We won't help her by sitting around doing nothing, and certainly not Rolof. I also don't think we can trust the man who abducted her. He intends to kill us all. But do you know what I think? I think we're already making things a bit awkward for him."

"How?" Jacob asked skeptically. "So far people on our side have done nothing but get killed."

"True. But why then did he take Richmodis hostage instead of just killing her? In that case I'm convinced he's telling the truth. She's alive. What I mean is, why did he take her hostage?"

"Because it suited him. He can do as he likes with us."

"No, goddammit! Because he had no choice! Don't you see? All his attempts to get those who know about Gerhard's murder out of the way have failed. Even if he were to kill Richmodis and the two of us, and Goddert into the bargain, he still wouldn't know who else we'd told. He's losing already. He's lost track of the number of people who might be in the know. So he's had to find a way of silencing us all at once; he's had to go on the defensive. He's made mistakes. Perhaps we can get him to make another."

"We can't." Jacob waved the suggestion away. "We don't know his name, nor where to find him."

"We know he was a crusader."

"Thousands were. Thousands and thousands."

"Yes, I know. But this one is special. Probably a noble, a former knight or cleric, since he can write. Though I'm not too keen on his taste in ink. Studied in Paris."

"How do you make that out?"

Jaspar pulled a face. "From Rolof, unfortunately. I told you, our murderer is starting to make mistakes. Over the years each university developed its own style of writing. The Bolognese, the English, the Parisian, to name but a few. The letters on Rolof's forehead are pure Paris school."

"So what? You're forgetting the patricians. Whatever we find out about him, they're the ones we're up against."

"Or not. Why did they hire a murderer, eh? To do the work they don't want to—or can't—do themselves. Including murder, abduction, and torture. I can even imagine they might have given him a free hand to a certain extent."

"Still," objected Jacob, "what does it help, knowing about him?"

"Know your opponent, you know his plan."

"And who was it said that?"

"Me. Well, no, the Roman emperor Julius Caesar. But it could have been me. Doesn't matter anyway."

Jacob sighed. "That's all well and good, but I can't think of a way to find out anything about him."

"Of course you can't. You're the Fox while I'm a—what did you call me?"

"Capon."

"A capon, yes, a capon who's wide awake and doesn't intend to get slaughtered. A capon who intends to win this battle. And he will."

"I suspect the capon's got it wrong there," said Jacob.

"No, that's not what he's got."

"What has he got then?"

"An idea!"

KUNO

The old warehouse . . .

Kuno was sitting in his dining room, trying to work out which warehouse Daniel had been talking about. He may have been half drunk, but on that point he was presumably to be trusted. A woman was being held prisoner there. Who she was Kuno did not know. Much of what Daniel had thoughtlessly let slip was a mystery to him. The inference, however, was crystal clear. People were once more under threat because of the accursed alliance, the redhead they called the Fox and a woman, perhaps others.

The woman was in the old warehouse. But which warehouse?

He leaned back and feverishly racked his brains.

He knew quite a lot about the Overstolz's properties. His parents had been frequent guests of Johann Overstolz. And of his mother, Blithildis, the old despot, as people called her behind her back, for she had come to dominate the Overstolz household more and more. There was something uncanny about the blind old woman. Years ago she had mistakenly been declared dead. For three days she had given no sign of life, then had woken up, helpless, tied to a chair. She, even more than old Gottschalk Overstolz, was the one who pulled the strings in the most powerful patrician family of Cologne, and Kuno knew that it was only hatred that kept her alive. Hatred of all who had harmed the house of Overstolz without having been made to pay for it.

Since the death of his father two years ago—long after his mother— Kuno had lived in the large family residence with his brothers, Bruno and Hermann, and their wives. It had been a short period of happiness before the fateful blow struck.

His brothers' wives, Margarethe and Elizabeth, were now living with their relatives, out of fear of reprisals from the Cologne authorities. Bruno and Hermann were in hiding at the court of the count of Jülich, leaving Kuno alone in the family house.

He felt lonely. He suspected his initial enthusiasm for the alliance was a result of his loneliness. But then he remembered that he had always been alone. His father had not thought much of him; he felt his son was too soft and did not really understand him. His mother had died too early. He got on better with his brothers, but without there being any real warmth between them. His only genuine friends had been Gerhard Morart and his wife Guda, old friends of the family who, after the commission for the cathedral from Conrad von Hochstaden, had been welcome guests in the houses of all the great families. At some point or other Kuno had realized that Gerhard, probably without being aware of it, had supplanted his father and taken over his role. Kuno loved the old man, and suddenly strange rumors started to appear, the significance of which Kuno did not fully understand. Were they figments of a diseased imagination or did they correspond to a truth he refused to admit to himself? The rumors were spread by Daniel . . .

Kuno rubbed his eyes and forced his mind back to the question of the warehouse.

Why did nobody take him seriously? All his life he had never been more than an appendage. He lacked the determination of his brothers, who had become involved in political life from an early age, the business sense of his father, everything. Yet he was the only one left in Cologne.

The loneliest of all.

The warehouse! The warehouse!

He knew all the Overstolz warehouses. Most of them, anyway. Almost all were old, depending on how you defined old, of course. What did Daniel mean? Mean by "old," that is?

Daniel was a rebel, a self-centered rebel without a cause. A late follower of the Goliards, with their love of wine, women, and song, but without their poverty, despising tradition simply because it was tradition. What would "old" mean to someone like that?

Old in the sense of a ruin?

Too old.

Old and abandoned!

Kuno clicked his fingers. That was it. It was an abandoned warehouse Daniel had been talking about, one that was no longer in use.

He couldn't ask questions about it, but that probably wasn't necessary. He knew of several old, abandoned warehouses belonging to the Overstolzes. They were all by the Wall, opposite the river island of Rheinau. Mournful, tumbledown sheds that were not even let out because the Overstolzes would rather allow them to decay than pay tax on the rent.

A good idea to have a look around there.

Kuno smiled. At last there was something meaningful he could do.

THE MADMAN

The impressive, if gloomy, shape of St. Pantaleon rose up before them as, leaning into the wind, they turned into Walengasse. The rain had gotten inside Jacob's hood and was running down his neck. During the last hour it had become bitterly cold. He was looking forward to getting into the monastery as he would have looked forward to any dry place.

They had left the lepers' outfits behind; they might do more harm than good now. If Jaspar was right and they were no longer being pursued, there was no point in disguise. Jacob insisted on covering his hair, so was still wearing Jaspar's old habit. He had tucked his hands up the sleeves, which would have made him look as if he were wrapped in devout contemplation were it not for the unchristian pace they were hurrying along at. Jaspar, on the other hand, was striding along, fists pumping the air like a peasant. His hood had slipped down, leaving the rain to beat a tattoo on his bald pate, and with every step he seemed to be trying to stamp his way through the soft mud to hell.

They met no one. God knows, it was no fun being out in the city in the pouring rain.

On their way they had briefly looked in at the house on the Brook. Goddert wasn't there. At first they had been worried, but there was no indication that anything had happened to him. If the murderer already had Richmodis, what was the point of taking Goddert, too?

So they had continued on their way to Walengasse, while Jaspar explained to Jacob what he hoped to learn there.

"You remember I mentioned a cripple who told me about the tiny crossbows? The man with no legs. St. Pantaleon has a large hospice and he's been living there for several years. I've seen him two or three times without speaking to him. I've no idea if we'll get any sense out of him; even when I talked to him before he wasn't quite right in the head. If my theory's correct and our murderer was a crusader, then they'll have fought in the same battles. An educated man with hair down to his waist will have stood out among the dregs of humanity their armies were mostly made up of."

"What? Among thousands of men?"

"The armies were always commanded by a small group of kings, counts, and bishops. I'm assuming he was one of them."

"A bold assumption."

"I know it sounds harebrained, but it's worth a try all the same."

"Anything's better than sitting around doing nothing," Jacob agreed. By now they had reached St. Pantaleon. Above the door in the solid wall an oil lamp was swinging in the wind, knocking against the stone at irregular intervals.

Shoulders hunched, they squeezed in under the narrow projecting roof and knocked. It wasn't long before a tiny window was pushed up. Watery eyes twitched uneasily to and fro under bushy brows.

"It's after vespers," an old man's voice croaked.

"True, reverend Brother," said Jaspar. "I would not have been so bold as to ask for admittance at this late hour, if I and Brother Jacob here were not engaged on a mission of Christian charity to thwart a devilish attempt to ensnare innocent people body and soul."

"And who are you?"

"Jaspar Rodenkirchen, dean of St. Mary Magdalene's. Also physician and Master of Arts."

The fluttering of the pupils became even more hectic. "I must ask the abbot."

"We quite understand," Jaspar assured him, "and respect the prudence of venerable old age. The only thing we would ask is that you do so as quickly as you can since it has pleased the Lord to make the heavens shed tears at the sins of the ungodly."

"Wait here." The flap slid down.

"Senile bloody half-wit," growled Jaspar. "I know Saint Benedict, talking about monks, said, 'Become a fool for Christ's sake,' but he didn't mean they should ignore the gift of reason." In fury he strode up and down along the wall. "'I must ask the abbot, I must ask the abbot.' And who's the abbot to ask? Does God have to decide every time whether a door is to be opened or closed? Will these monks never learn to think?"

It was quite some time before the door creaked open and they hurried inside.

A monk who was indeed very old and bent indicated the tall man at his side who was regarding them with a benevolent gaze. He and Jaspar grasped each other by the shoulders and exchanged a brief kiss.

"What can I do for you at this late hour, Brother Jaspar?" the abbot asked.

"A small matter. It is very important I speak to someone in the hospice." Jaspar smiled. "If it is no trouble, of course."

Clasping his arms behind his back, the abbot assumed a lofty expression. He looked as if he were giving the matter earnest consideration. "You're late," he said skeptically.

"I know."

"Did you not say something to Brother Laurence here about the machinations of the Devil? As you will know, the monks in this monastery fear the Devil at all times, but experience tells us that he is at his most dangerous after dark. That is why we have to subject guests who arrive this late to particular scrutiny. You must not interpret our cautiousness as suspicion, but—"

"Not in the least," Jaspar broke in. "To be precise, the Devil I was talking about is the fiend that comes from the past to torment our innermost souls. Old wounds reopen. But often it is the old wounds that lead us to new weapons, if you get my meaning?"

The abbot clearly did not, but he nodded affably.

"Furthermore," Jaspar went on, "this fiend manifests itself in madness and speaks out of the mouths of those whose spirits are confused. I do not mean to suggest you are housing this fiend here. The balm of your care, I have heard, soothes the sufferings of those poor souls whose minds rave in a confusion of tongues."

"We have established a special section for that kind of case," said the abbot, not without pride.

"Yes, it is praised far and wide. Your reputation for compassion is only exceeded by the fame of your learning. Or was it the other way around? I know that the brothers here have astonishing expertise in that area. But to get to the nub of my request, there is in that section a poor soul whose name, I believe, is Hieronymus and who may be able to help us track down this foul fiend."

The abbot pricked up his ears. "What am I to understand by that?"

"The precise details," said Jaspar mysteriously, "must remain a secret. It is an extremely delicate matter involving some very important personages."

"Here in Cologne?" the abbot whispered.

"In this very city. The poor man I am looking for lost both his legs at Acre."

"Yes, that's Hieronymus."

"Excellent. We have to speak to him."

"Hmm, that will not be easy. He'll be asleep. Hieronymus has been sleeping a lot recently. I think he will soon go to his eternal rest."

"All the more important we speak to him before that," declared Jaspar. "It will not take long, and if Hieronymus has nothing to tell us, he can go straight back to sleep."

Jacob shivered. They were standing in the cloisters around the inner courtyard and the wind was blowing in through the narrow arched windows, tearing at the flames of the torches in the iron rings.

Again the abbot thought long and hard.

"Very well," he said eventually, "I would not want to stand in the way of a holy work. Our reputation for good works has always imbued our monastery with a—let us say an aura of mystical greatness which gives it a radiance we must strive to keep shining untarnished."

"It will shine ever more brightly, I promise you."

"You would be willing, er, to bear witness to that?"

"Wherever I can."

"So be it. We humbly praise Thee, Lord. Brother Laurence will take you to Hieronymus. But do not keep him from his divine repose for too long, I beg you. The grace of the Lord is about him."

The abbot dismissed them with a wave of the hand and they followed the old monk as he shuffled around the cloisters. After a while they turned down an unlit corridor at the end of which Laurence pushed open a door.

In the semidark they saw a room full of wooden beds with men, or what was left of them, asleep on them. The abbey looked after the sick men without charge, solely for God's mercy and grace, as long as they came with a recommendation from the city council. That kept the situation in St. Pantaleon within bounds. Really bad cases, those who were raving or dangerous, were locked up in the towers of the city walls, with windows facing out toward the countryside, so that those who lived nearby were not disturbed by the shouting and screaming. The worst were kept in chains. The straw in their cells was changed four times a year, when the barber also came to shave their beards and heads, generally with the help of strong men. Some families sold their lunatic members to showmen who made large wooden cages, known as loony boxes, for them outside the city gates. For a few coppers people could observe their drooling, grimacing, and frequent fits for as long as they could stand it.

Compared to these, the poor souls in St. Pantaleon were relatively well off, even if they were bound to their beds with leather straps and ate out of iron pans. The monks regarded them as material to study the boundary between madness and possession by the Devil, something that was of the greatest importance for the spiritual welfare of their patients. The treatment consisted of benedictions and other ecclesiastical rites; occasionally it was even successful.

A monk with a candle came hurrying up to them. He had obviously been sleeping. He was rubbing his eyes and stretching his neck.

"What's this?" he mumbled. "Oh, it's you, Brother Laurence."

"What were you doing, Henricus?" the old monk asked irascibly.

"Preparing myself for compline."

"You were sleeping."

"I wasn't. I was deep in meditation—"

"You were sleeping. I must report it to the abbot."

The monk looked over the old monk's shoulders at the two visitors and rolled his eyes. "Of course, Brother Laurence, you must tell the abbot. Is that why you're here?"

"Take these two gentlemen to Hieronymus. They wish to talk to him."

"He's probably asleep."

"Then wake him up."

Jaspar gave the monk a friendly nod. The monk shrugged his shoulders and turned. "Come with me."

They followed him between the beds. Most of the patients were sleeping or staring into space. One was muttering a litany of animal names. When Jacob looked back, he saw the old man disappear into the corridor, shaking his head.

Hieronymus was not asleep. He was sitting on his bed, his little finger boring into his left ear, an activity which seemed to demand his full attention, for he ignored the new arrivals. A threadbare jute blanket covered him up to his waist. Where the outlines of his legs should have been it lay flat on the bed.

"Hieronymus," said the monk in a friendly voice, stroking his hair, "someone's come to see you. Look."

A toothless, twisted face covered in white stubble squinted up at them. "Not now," he said.

"Why not? It's a long time since you had a visitor."

Hieronymus dug his finger farther into his ear. "Leave me in peace."

"But Hieronymus, we haven't prayed to Saint Paul yet today. Saint Paul won't like that. And now you refuse to receive your visitors."

"No! Wait! Wait!" Hieronymus suddenly shouted. "I've got him. He's trapped. Think you can get away from me, do you? I've got you now."

Henricus gave them a significant glance.

"What's he doing?" whispered Jaspar.

"He's convinced someone moved into his ear some time ago. With all his furniture and everything. And he makes a fire in the winter, Hieronymus says, and complains of earache."

"Why doesn't he just let him stay there?"

Henricus lowered his voice. "Because the creature in his ear keeps telling him evil things. So he says. We've checked up in various books. It's obviously a manifestation of the Devil, any child could see that. On the other hand, the Devil taking up residence in someone's ear is new."

"He resides in hell, and that's what I would call earache." Jaspar bent down and gently pulled Hieronymus's finger out of his ear. "We need your help," he said softly.

"Help?" Hieronymus seemed so confused he forgot the squatter in his ear for the moment.

"You're a brave man, Hieronymus. You fought for the Cross. Do you remember?"

Hieronymus gave Jaspar a suspicious look and pressed his lips together. Then he nodded vigorously.

"I knew it." Jaspar grinned. "A hero. Fought with the bravest of the brave. Truly impressive."

"Side by side," declared Hieronymus.

"Do you remember all the proud knights?"

"Wasn't a knight," said Hieronymus in a tone of regret. "Had to go on foot. I like going on foot, even now. Not like the knights. Always up on some nag, loaded down with iron. But there's nothing inside the iron."

"What does he mean, he likes going on foot?" Jacob asked in surprise.

"Well"—Henricus shrugged—"he likes it."

"But he hasn't got—"

"Quiet back there," Jaspar hissed. "My friend Hieronymus and I have matters to discuss."

"There's nothing inside the armor." Hieronymus giggled. "I looked inside some. It was lying in the sand."

"But you remember the knights, the noble lords?"

"Of course. I like going on foot."

"Yes, I know. They all liked going on foot in those days, didn't they. You got as far as Acre."

Hieronymus twitched. "Acre," he whispered. "As far as Acre. Cursed city."

"Hieronymus can remember everything if he wants," said Henricus proudly.

"That's not the impression he gives me," said Jacob doubtfully.

"That's enough!" Jaspar stretched out his arm and pointed to the other side of the room. "Off you go and lie down, or dance or whatever, but get away from here. Off you go."

Jacob didn't dare object. Henricus even looked delighted, thanked Jaspar, and went to lie down. Soon he began snoring quietly. Jacob watched him enviously, leaned against the doorpost, and pondered.

After a while he saw Hieronymus start to gesticulate wildly. His fingers made the most bizarre shapes in the air. Some gave Jacob the uncomfortable feeling he was describing methods of torture.

Then he gave a whimpering cry and buried his head in his hands. Jaspar put his arm around his shoulders and talked comfortingly to him.

Hieronymus brayed with laughter and started gesticulating again.

Jacob listened to the wind moaning around the monastery walls.

After what seemed an eternity Jaspar came back and woke Henricus to let them out. In silence he led them around the cloisters to the main gate.

"Don't forget compline," said Jaspar with a smile.

"Huh!" Henricus snorted. "When did I ever forget it? What did the old loony tell you, by the way?"

"He told us the monks in this monastery are too inquisitive."

"He did?" said Henricus in amazement. "Ah, well."

They left him and hurried through the mud back to the Brook.

"And?" asked Jacob. With the wind whistling around his ears, he had to speak loudly. "Did you get anything out of him?"

"Yes and no."

"What is that supposed to mean? Yes or no?"

"Hieronymus's memory has its gaps, but he does remember the crossbows. And he remembered that they got hold of one or two. He mentioned the names of a surprising number of knights and counts, he even met King Louis—well, not met exactly, heard him speak. All in all he can remember quite a lot. Then he talked about the war and what they did with the infidels after the capture of Damietta."

"What did they do?"

Jaspar shook his head. "Just be glad you don't know. They gathered all the children together, and the young girls. It would be a huge exaggeration to say they simply killed them. They did other things it's better not to talk about. A knight with hair down to his waist he couldn't remember, however."

"So we've been wasting our time?"

Jaspar gave him a disapproving look. "Nothing's a waste of time, remember that."

KUNO

Beneath the city walls, between Three Kings Gate in the south and Neckelskaulen Gate was an area of old stone buildings that had been originally used to store fish. The stone kept the heat out. Several of the buildings belonged to the Overstolz family, but were no longer in use. They backed onto the Wall and several had narrow passages through to the riverside.

Kuno scurried along the inside of the Wall. The wind came funneling down Bayenstraße while the water seemed to be coming from all sides, from above, below, behind, in front. Perhaps it was the start of a new flood. So far it had been fine, despite the advanced season, but this night was bringing a turn in the weather. It was no longer warm rain, a summer storm that cleared the sultry air for a few hours. There was the icy cold of northern seas on the wind, a harbinger of frosts to come. The Rhine would freeze over in the winter and they would be able to walk over to Deutz on the eastern bank again.

Odd, thought Kuno, why should that come into my mind just now? It would be nice to go across to Deutz once more. And I'd like to see the snow on the battlements and turrets again, on the walls and steep roofs of the churches, chapels, and abbeys, on the trees in the orchards and on

Haymarket, with the people stepping gingerly between the stalls, so as not to slip and get laughed at.

He shook himself in the rain like a dog. On his left was the first of the dreary line of old warehouses. He had more important things to do than wallow in memories.

Some of the warehouses by Three Kings Gate had a courtyard in front and a surrounding wall, often with a rotting but heavy wooden gate almost impossible for one man to open on his own. Kuno decided to investigate the other buildings first. There were more than he had thought and the very first he came to turned out to be locked. He tried to look in through the windows, but they were too high and he had to climb. The walls were greasy from the rain and he slipped several times before he managed to get up to one. All he could see inside was impenetrable darkness.

"Anyone there?"

His echoing voice and the howling of the storm combined in a ghostly chorale. He pulled himself up through the opening, dropped down into the warehouse, and lit the torch he carried in his belt. He looked around. A few rats scattered in panic, but otherwise there was no sign of life.

The idea of climbing back up through the window did not appeal to him. The door was barred on the inside by a beam, but he pushed it aside and came out into Bayenstraße. Miserably he contemplated the row of mute, black facades. The rain sweeping across was so heavy he could not even see Bayen Tower. He still had them all to check and already he was soaked to the skin.

What if Daniel had been lying? He was probably sitting in the warmth, enjoying a glass of wine, and laughing himself silly.

If, if . . .

Head down, he ran to the next warehouse. It was easier getting in this time since there was no door, just some rusty hinges hanging down. But there was no one there either.

By the time he reached the first of the buildings with a wall and courtyard he had no idea how long he had been searching. He'd have to climb again. His fingers were aching, but there was nothing for it, the gate was shut tight. Finding a reasonable handhold, he clambered up another wall, but there was no one in the yard or the building. A ladder led to the upper floor. The rungs creaked ominously as he mounted it. The first thing he saw was more rats, but it was lighter there as the room had five wide windows looking out over the Rhine. At some point it must have been an office. All that was left were a few planks lying around. The water was dripping in through a hole in the roof. He pushed his sopping-wet hair out of his eyes and looked down at the river. It seemed like some gray, shaggy beast, swirling and writhing in its attempt to escape from its narrow bed, kept there by the force of Divine Providence alone.

If it kept raining like this, they'd have to hang him out to dry in the morning.

Back on the ground floor, he noticed the narrow door in the back wall leading to the riverbank. It, too, was barred on the inside. He opened it and went out onto the wharves. The wind whipped his coat around his legs. He saw the cargo ships, tugging at their moorings, bringing stone from the Drachenfels for the new cathedral. Between there and Three Kings Gate he could just make out two more entrances in the wall, but they were bound to be barred. Cursing, he went back in and climbed out of the yard in the same laborious manner he had come in. In Bayenstraße, panting and wheezing, he was close to giving up.

He looked around. The night watchmen patrolled here every hour. Their lantern was not to be seen. On to the next, then.

A pleasant surprise at last. Two worm-eaten planks were all that was left of the gate to the next yard. One wall less to climb over. Quickly he went in. Seeing nothing in the yard, he went to the door and pushed at it. It wasn't barred and opened much more easily than he expected, so that he almost lost his balance and fell over. Steadying himself, he took out his torch as the door swung silently shut behind him. Once the tar was burning well he took a few steps forward.

In front of him was a large handcart. It didn't look as if it belonged in this abandoned ruin and there were blankets strewn all over the floor. It made such a bizarre sight that he stood staring and it was a while before he sensed another noise apart from the howling of the wind. A faint whimpering, like a child or an injured animal. Hesitantly, he raised his torch higher and went around the cart. In the flickering light he saw a massive pillar. And another. And another.

The fourth pillar had eyes staring at him.

The girl had been tied to the stone with a large number of leather straps. She certainly wouldn't be able to move a muscle. She had been gagged but not blindfolded. A mass of dark hair fell down over her forehead and onto her shoulders.

Despite the picture of misery she presented, Kuno let out a laugh of triumph. He rammed the torch firmly between the planks of the handcart, hurried back to the pillar, and untied the piece of cloth around her mouth. She spat out the gag herself.

"Oh, God!" she panted, then filled her lungs with air and coughed. "I thought I was going to suffocate."

"What are you called?" Kuno asked in excitement.

"What?" She shook her head as if to clear it.

"That's all right." Kuno stroked her cheek reassuringly and took out his dagger. Quickly he began to cut through the straps tying her to the pillar. "Don't worry, I've come to get you out. I'm a friend."

"A friend?"

Her knees gave way, but Kuno caught her in time. She was still tied up with straps. Working calmly with his knife, he freed her legs, then her arms. She immediately tried to get to her feet and gave a loud groan. Her limbs must be completely numb.

"Wait, I'll help you."

"No."

Gritting her teeth, she pulled herself up by the pillar. "I have to do this myself. Who are you, anyway?"

"My name is Kuno."

Quivering, she stood up and started to massage her wrists. She gave way at the knees again but managed to stop herself from falling.

"Did Jacob send you?" she asked, breathless. "Or Jaspar?"

"Jaspar?" Kuno echoed. Daniel had mentioned a dean and— "You mean the Fox?"

"Yes." She staggered toward him and clutched him. "Where are they?"

"I don't know. I really don't know. I don't even know your name."

"Richmodis. But then—"

"Do you think you can walk?"

"Just about."

"Wait." There were some poles leaned against one of the walls. "You need something to support yourself with."

She saw what he was looking at and shook her head. "They're no use, Kuno. They're too heavy. I'll manage."

"You're sure?"

"I'm sure. But how did you—"

"Later. We must get away from here."

He hurried to the door. She was stumbling, but determined to keep up with him. "Where are we going?" she asked.

"I'll take you to my house," he said with a grin of satisfaction. "It's just a short walk and the weather's perfect, quite delightful. Take my arm."

She smiled and Kuno opened the door.

Daniel was standing outside.

GODDERT

Goddert von Weiden felt as though he had been chopped up into pieces, then roughly sewn back together again. He hadn't worked so hard for years. The bells were about to ring nine and he still wasn't home. And as if that wasn't enough, he was sopping wet. True, you could object that for the last two hours he had not so much been working as sitting drinking dark beer with one of his more generous customers. But they'd talked business, oh, yes, indeed.

You're an old fool, Goddert told himself as he splashed his way through the mud toward the Brook. Who goes out in weather like this? He didn't even meet a pig or dog. With every new torrent that poured over him he felt his rheumatism get worse and thought longingly of a warm fire and the contents of Jaspar's cellar. Even the sound of his steps, the squelch as he pulled his feet out of the mud, seemed to mock him. Left, right, left, right—old, fool, old, fool.

Then he remembered Jacob and shook his head. Richmodis was right. What was he trying to prove? That the world would come to a standstill without Goddert von Weiden? Even more stupid was to try to compete with the younger man. No one else was interested and, anyway, he could only lose and make himself look ridiculous. No fool like an old fool.

He decided to apologize to Richmodis. He felt a flush of pride. Where was there a man big enough to ask his own daughter to forgive him? Then she'd tell him all the latest news about the strange story Jacob had got himself involved in, and he'd stretch out his feet in front of a roaring fire and thank God for the roof over his head.

His footsteps had stopped beating out "old fool."

With rasping breath he plodded up the Brook to his house. The shutters were closed, no light could be seen through the gaps. Was Richmodis asleep already?

He went in. It was dark inside. "Richmodis?" he shouted, then clapped his hand to his lips. What a peasant he was. To wake the poor child. Then he remembered how busy he'd been all day. He'd earned some supper. And the fire was cold. What kind of way to behave was that, going to bed before your father had come home from a hard day's work? She could at least have put a jug of wine out for him.

"Richmodis?"

He lit an oil lamp, then, grunting and groaning, went up to the bedroom. He stared in astonishment. She wasn't there! She wasn't home at all.

Of course she isn't, you nincompoop, he told himself. She said she was going to see Jaspar, though what she really meant was that redhead. She'd still be sitting there, unable to tear herself away, while Jaspar kept refilling the glasses.

A cozy little party. A party without Goddert von Weiden?

Never!

Nodding sagely, he went back down, put out the lamp, and set off again.

THE WAREHOUSE

The man stood facing them with drawn sword. She had seen him before. His name was Daniel Overstolz. He had been a magistrate before Conrad von Hochstaden had broken the power of the patricians and redistributed the offices. Since then Daniel had the reputation in the city of being a philanderer who would chase after any skirt and was too fond of the bottle. He was seen often enough riding through the street with his cronies. The women liked him for his good looks and cheerful disposition, though he was also said to be heartless and not particularly intelligent.

He wasn't good-looking at the moment. His hair was plastered all over his head and his face oddly puffy and twisted.

"Judas," he hissed.

Kuno took her arm and stepped back. "Take it easy, Daniel. You've got it wrong."

Daniel Overstolz followed them and they fell back again. "Oh, yes?" sneered Daniel. "I've got it wrong, have I? Where were you off to with your little tart, then?"

"Daniel, please, there's no point in us fighting."

"Oh. Please, is it? I'm flattered. Not long ago you were at my throat, now you're dripping with politeness and respect. Who do you think you are, you bastard? You think yourself so superior, don't you, you sanctimonious prig. Traitor! What gives you the right to destroy our alliance and send us all to the gallows?"

Kuno raised his hands in appeasement. "That's not it," he said urgently. "Don't you see, the alliance is already broken. We've done too many things that are wrong. That wasn't what we agreed. That wasn't what we were supposed to be fighting for."

Daniel stared at him, a grim look on his face, then at Richmodis. Without knowing what it was all about, she nodded. "Kuno's right, we—"

"You'll keep your mouth shut, you damn whore," he screamed at her. With a couple of strides he was beside her and pulled her away from Kuno by the hair. She tried to resist, but her aching legs gave way and she fell to the ground. Horrified, Kuno jumped to her aid. The next moment the point of Daniel's sword was at his chest.

"Not a step closer, rat."

"Daniel," said Kuno. His voice was trembling, but he kept himself under control. "We have to talk about this. You were a magistrate yourself—"

"*Was* a magistrate. Yes."

"You dispensed justice. Have you forgotten? You were a good judge; people admired and respected you because you weren't corrupt. You despised violence and sought the truth. You would never have shed the blood of innocent people."

Richmodis stood up, trembling. Daniel was still holding her hair, but he didn't move.

Cautiously, Kuno raised his hand and slowly pushed the sword to one side. Then he took a step toward them. His eyes were shining.

"Think back, Daniel. Think how important justice was to you. We all subscribed to a common goal because we believed in a higher justice. I still believe in it. Our goal was good, but it led to evil the moment innocent people were sacrificed for it. Look into your heart, Daniel. You lost your position, but not your self-respect. I know what loss means. I lost my parents and my only friend; in our blindness we sacrificed him. I blame myself as much as the rest of you. I know how you feel; I can understand the fury, the disappointment, the longing for revenge. Revenge is sweet, but forgiveness is sweeter, Daniel, far sweeter. Please help me to put an end to this madness."

"Don't move."

"All right, Daniel, all right."

Daniel twisted Richmodis's head around so she was facing him. "A fine speech. What do you think? I'd like to hear your opinion."

She looked into his eyes, fear tightening her throat. "Yes," she whispered. "Kuno's right. You should listen to him. I don't know what this is all about, but I'm sure you're not bad. I believe what you really want is peace."

"Do you hear?" said Kuno, hope in his voice.

Daniel still had not moved. Then he nodded deliberately. "It's nice that you believe in me. It's truly wonderful to know." He grinned. "That means it will be an even greater pleasure to send you both to hell." He broke out into wild laughter and raised his sword. "Good-bye, fools. For your information, Kuno, I took whatever bribes I could. I wasn't interested in justice, but I had power, d'you understand, Kuno, power. That's what it was all about, power. And now I have the power to chop off your head, then rape this whore here before I send her after you and—urrrrgh!"

Like lightning, Richmodis had bent down and slammed her elbow into Daniel's stomach. He doubled up. Kuno hit him on the back of the neck, sending him tumbling to the ground.

"Run!" Kuno shouted.

Daniel's sword came up and stabbed Kuno in the leg. He groaned and staggered back, his hand feeling for his dagger.

When Daniel got to his feet, his face was twisted in a mask that had nothing human about it. He growled like a wolf. As his blade came slashing down, Kuno just managed to avoid it, but tripped and fell.

Richmodis looked around in desperation. Her eye fell on the heavy poles by the pillar.

"Run, for God's sake," Kuno shouted, rolling over to one side as Daniel's sword came crashing down on the stones in a shower of sparks. The next moment he had his dagger in his hand.

"Bastard!" panted Daniel.

She couldn't just run away. There seemed to be a thousand knives pricking at her as she hurried over to the pillar and grabbed one of the poles. It was heavy and splintery.

Kuno was defending himself desperately. He got back to his feet, warding off Daniel's blows with his dagger. The blood was running down his thigh.

An angry hissing came from Daniel's throat. He fell on his opponent again. The storeroom echoed with the clash of iron and Kuno's dagger flew out of his hand in a high arc. Daniel laughed and plunged his sword in Kuno's side. When he pulled it out, it was red with blood.

Kuno stared at him in disbelief. Then he fell to his knees.

"Farewell, Kuno dear," Daniel panted, his sword uplifted for the final blow.

"Daniel!" Richmodis shouted, raising her improvised club.

Daniel turned and understood—too late. The club came swinging down and smashed into his face, the impact sending him flying over Kuno. He landed on his back with a thud and the sword fell out of his hand.

Richmodis dropped the pole, grabbed the sword, and raised it above her head.

"No!" Kuno groaned. "Don't!"

He was holding one hand to his side. The other was stretched out toward Richmodis. "No. We must—get away. Leave him—"

Breathing heavily, the sword still raised, Richmodis stood over Daniel, who was covering his face with his hands and whimpering.

"Yes," she said hoarsely.

"You'll have to—support me. Give—give me the sword." Kuno was deathly pale. Richmodis tried to pull him up. He pushed himself off the ground and managed to get his arm around her shoulders.

"Where's your house?"

He shook his head. "We can't go there. Not now. If Urquhart finds out—"

"Don't talk," said Richmodis grimly. "Try to keep going for a while."

She grasped him firmly and together they staggered out into the storm.

GODDERT

Goddert pulled his cloak tight around his shoulders and walked as fast as his short legs would carry him. He had nothing against rain, but this was too much of a good thing. Was the time at hand? The apocalypse?

For a brief moment he thought he could see the night watchman's lantern in the distance by St. Severin's Gate; then another squall came, blurring everything.

"Urgghhh," said Goddert, giving precise expression to his opinion of the meteorological situation as he shook himself and knocked on Jaspar's door. "What are you up to in there? I need a drink."

No answer. That really was the limit. His late wife's brother was not inviting him in. He gave the door a vindictive thump. It swung open.

Goddert peered in. It was pitch dark in here as well, just a faint glow from the ashes in the fireplace. Where the hell were they all? And why hadn't he brought a lantern? Just like an old fool.

He felt his way in and tried to think where Jaspar kept his candles. Since he was here, he might as well have a drink. Someone who had been out in this awful weather twice now could hardly be expected to go home unfortified. Jaspar surely wouldn't object to him having one for the road, however much he kept saying he preferred to be asked.

Throwing his wet cloak into a corner, he felt his way along the table to the bench by the fire. He needed to sit down. By this time his eyes had become more used to the darkness. Was that a candlestick on the table? He grasped it, carried it over to the fireplace, and tried to light the wick from the embers. After a couple of attempts, he succeeded. Pleased with himself, he took the candlestick back to the table to leave it there while he went to look for something to drink.

He saw Rolof.

He froze.

"Our Father, who art in heaven," he whispered.

He began to tremble uncontrollably. The candlestick fell to the floor and the candle went out. Stumbling, he backed toward the door. "Richmodis," he moaned, "Jaspar, Rolof. Oh, God, what shall I do, oh, Lord, what—"

A heavy hand was placed on his shoulder. "Nothing," said a voice.

THE WAREHOUSE

Daniel was crawling nowhere on all fours. Every direction was the same. There was a flicker of light in front of his eyes, but the light came from inside his head. Otherwise he couldn't see anything at all.

He felt his face. His nose and forehead hurt horribly. His fingers touched something wet and sticky. A terrible thought came into his head.

The whore had knocked his eyes out.

It brought him to his feet. With a howl of rage he set off running blindly, tripped over something, and fell flat on his face. Once more he pulled himself up. Someone was whimpering. He tried to work out where the noise was coming from until he realized he was making it himself. Both hands stretched out in front; he cautiously stepped forward without the slightest idea where he was heading. His fingers encountered masonry. After a while they came to a corner. He would keep feeling his way, he decided, until he found the door. Then across the courtyard and along the house walls—

Suddenly his fingers felt a different texture. Cloth.

Cloth that was moving.

Daniel shrank back against the wall. "Kuno?" he whispered.

Someone took a step toward him.

"Can't you see I'm defenseless?" Daniel panted. "You wouldn't—I mean—that witch blinded me, Kuno, look, she smashed my eyeballs. Oh, God, Kuno, I'm begging for mercy. I'm begging you now. I'm blind, do you hear, blind—"

"Don't exaggerate. You're not blind. It would help if you opened your eyes."

Daniel froze. Then he blinked. His lids were stuck together with blood, but suddenly he could see again. In the gloom of the warehouse he could make out the silhouette of a very tall man in front of him. "You're not Kuno."

"No. I am your obedient servant. I see that my charming guest has flown the coop. I presume you didn't help her on her way?"

"Urquhart?" Daniel exclaimed in surprise.

"That remains to be seen." There was a note of caution in the voice. "More important is, who are you? What I do with you depends on who you are, so your answer had better be good. One I find convincing."

"Is Daniel Overstolz convincing enough?"

"Worth considering. If you're telling the truth, I will be Urquhart. If not, then your executioner."

"This is outrageous!" Daniel felt his old arrogance return. "My father is Johann Overstolz, one of the most powerful men in Cologne. We pay you for your services, not for your insolence."

There was a brief silence, broken by the sound of a slap as Daniel's head jerked to one side.

"What—?" he gasped.

"The next will come from the other side," said Urquhart calmly. "Then from this side again. We can keep it up until dawn, if you like. I have time until then, as you well know. It's obvious you're an Overstolz. Only rich merchant scum that bought its patent of nobility and never held a scholarly book in its hand would show itself up with such empty-headed yapping. What are you doing here?"

"When I tell my father—"

"No, I will tell your father. I will tell your father that my bargaining counter has escaped, leaving behind his son, who appears to have taken a beating. From the young lady herself? Do you think he'll enjoy hearing that? Will he be proud? Or perhaps you aren't his son at all? We can easily find that out."

Daniel felt the other grasp his collar and pull him toward him. "Quickly now. I need to speak with Matthias."

"But Matthias was going to meet you every two hours—"

"That would be too late, blockhead. Where is he now?"

"I don't know," wailed Daniel.

"Then your father will know. If he is your father."

He let go of Daniel, shoving him back against the wall. Daniel coughed and spluttered. "It's not my fault," he muttered.

"No, of course not." Urquhart smiled. "Nothing's ever anyone's fault, is it? Now tell me what happened. And get on with it."

WAITING

Goddert yelped. He shook the hand off and took a leap he would not have believed himself capable of.

"Good Lord above!" he exclaimed. "Did you give me a surprise!"

"Sorry." Jaspar regarded his hand as if it were a poisonous spider. With a shrug of the shoulders he picked up the candlestick and disappeared into the darkness. They heard him rummaging around for a while, then saw him again as the candle lit up.

"Where have you been?" Goddert was babbling and Jacob could see that his nerves were in tatters. Rolof was still stretched out on the bench as if he were sleeping through everything as usual.

"Goddert, there's something we have to tell you—" Jacob said.

"Tell me? And what about that?" Goddert's trembling finger pointed at Rolof.

"He's dead."

"Christ almighty, I can see that!"

"That's not important for the moment, Goddert—"

"Not important?" Distraught, Goddert ran over to Rolof and back again. He dug his fingers into his shaggy beard and looked around wildly. "And where's Richmodis?" he croaked.

"That's what I've been trying to tell you. Do me a favor and sit down, will you?"

Goddert went paler than he already was and sank down on a stool. Jacob felt like simply running away. It was his fault everything had turned out like this. He brought misfortune to everyone. What could they say to Goddert?

"You, too, Fox-cub," ordered Jaspar.

Abashed, he sat down opposite Goddert and tried to look him in the face.

"Nothing's happened to Richmodis?" Goddert asked, like a child.

"I don't know." Jaspar shook his head. "I don't know. No idea, Goddert. She's been kidnapped."

"Kidnapped?"

"Gerhard's murderer, at least that's what we suspect, has taken her away somewhere. If we can believe him, she's alive, and at the moment I believe him."

"Kidnapped," whispered Goddert, with a blank stare.

"We have to—"

"What's been happening?" whined Goddert. "Everything was fine yesterday. Who would want to kidnap my child? She's never done anyone any harm, she—"

Jaspar and Jacob exchanged glances. Then, gently, they told him what had happened since they had last seen him. But Goddert only seemed to be taking half of it in. His eyes kept being drawn to Rolof's body. Eventually it became clear he wasn't listening at all. He just kept moaning, "Richmodis."

"There's no point," Jaspar said quietly to Jacob. "The shock's been too much for him."

"What are we to do with him?" whispered Jacob.

"With whom? With Goddert or Rolof?"

"Both."

"Goddert we'll take home—at least there he won't have to see poor Rolof all the time. That's the best we can do for him for the moment. As for Rolof? I don't like having a body that's been slit open and written on with his own blood lying about the house. Looks suspiciously like heathen rites. I think for the time being we should get him out of the way, however much it pains me not to give poor Rolof a proper burial. Let's get Goddert home first. You'll stay with him and I'll come back and"—he cleared his throat—"clear up."

They took Goddert by the arm and led him out unresisting. His eyes were blinded by tears. The fury of the storm had increased and several times they almost ended up together in the mire. It was something of a miracle that Goddert was able to put one foot in front of the other. He was rapidly succumbing to apathy. Jacob remembered how he himself had staggered along the Duck Ponds two days ago after he had found Maria's body, ready to accept any lie, provided it was better than the reality, shattered and yet strangely uninvolved, an interested observer of his own wretchedness.

He felt immensely sorry for the old man.

At last the houses on the Brook appeared through the slanting curtain of rain. They hurried on, heads well down between their shoulders. Goddert was whimpering to himself.

Jacob clenched his teeth. Then he saw something and stopped in his tracks.

There was a jerk as Jaspar took another stride. Goddert slipped out of their grasp and went sprawling, splashing mud in all directions.

"For God's sake, Fox-cub, what's all that about?"

"Look." Jacob pointed.

Jaspar squinted. There was a faint gleam of light between the shutters of Goddert's house.

Light.

"Goddert," said Jacob, speaking slowly and clearly, "did you leave anything burning when you went out?"

From the ground Goddert gave Jacob an uncomprehending look. "No."

"Not a candle, an oil lamp, fire in the grate?"

"Definitely not. Why do you ask?"

"Sorry, I'd forgotten the Lord didn't bless you with the gift of long sight. It looks as if you have visitors. Were you expecting any?"

"I'm not expecting anyone at all. You must be wrong." Then his face was transformed. "But perhaps—perhaps Richmodis is back!"

He scrambled to his feet and set off for the house. Jaspar grabbed hold of him. "Nonsense, Goddert. Face up to the facts. She's been kidnapped."

"No," Goddert shouted. "It's Richmodis! She's come back. My little girl! Don't you see, Jaspar, it's all been a terrible mistake and she's back. Let go of me!"

"For Christ's sake, Goddert."

"No. Let go." His strength suddenly seemed to have returned. He pulled himself free and set off running toward the house.

"The fool!" Jaspar swore. "Goddert, stay here. You've no idea who's in there," he shouted.

"Richmodis!"

They slithered along behind him, but Goddert was too quick for them. They saw him fling open the door and disappear inside, then heard his cry.

"Oh, Lord," groaned Jaspar.

A few steps brought them to the house. They clattered into the room and came to an abrupt halt. Jaspar's chin dropped. "Richmodis," he gasped.

Goddert was pressing her to him, as if he could hold her so close nothing in the world would ever take her away again. The tears were running down his cheeks. Richmodis was patting his rounded back. Her hair was disheveled and dripping wet. She gently prized his arms away from her and stroked his face. "Are you all right, Father?"

Goddert was laughing and crying at the same time. "Who cares how I am? Holy Virgin, I thank you. Oh, God, I thought I'd never see you again!" His head swung around to Jaspar and Jacob. "Ha! Didn't I tell you? My little girl!"

Jaspar grinned. He went over and, throwing his arms wide, hugged the pair of them. "Goddert," he said solemnly, "you can say what you like about your mental capacity, but that of your stomach is far superior to mine."

They laughed and held one another tight. Jacob stood by the door observing a happiness that, for a moment, blotted out everything else. Then he felt sadness welling up inside him and turned away.

"That's enough," said Richmodis. "Come and look in the back room."

They followed her. A man was lying on the massive kitchen table. His face was terribly pale, his clothes soaked in blood in several places. As they entered he laboriously raised his head.

Jaspar was beside him immediately. "What happened?"

"Sword wounds. One in the leg, the other in the side. I was just going to bandage them."

"We must wash them first. Get me some wine, vinegar, and water. Cloths as well. Quickly."

"I'll fetch the wine," said Goddert.

"I want it to wash him with, Goddert, to wash him! Understood?"

Goddert gave him a withering look and hurried off. Richmodis brought some cloths. With an expressionless look on his face, Jasper examined the man, felt his body, checked his pulse, and wiped the sweat from his brow.

"How do you feel?" he asked.

The man groaned and tried to sit up. Jaspar gently pushed him back down. "Don't move. We have to bandage your ribs first. Tell me your name."

"Kuno Kone," the man whispered.

Jaspar paused for a second. "Kone? The merchant house?"

Kuno nodded.

"Well, well, well. Curiouser and curiouser."

Jacob looked down at the man, feeling superfluous. He was about to say something, but Goddert shoved him to one side and put a brimming pail of water and two jugs on the floor beside the table. Jaspar sniffed them.

"That smells of vinegar," he declared and picked up the other. "This's probably wine. But it's best to be sure." He put the jug to his lips and took a long draught.

"Hey," Goddert protested. "To wash him, you said."

"Firstly," said Jaspar, licking his lips, "anything I use to wash our friend here must have my specific approval, and secondly you can let me have a knife instead of stupid comments. I'll have to cut his clothes away."

Grumbling to himself, Goddert went to find a knife as Richmodis returned with another pile of rags. They all ignored Jacob.

"Can I do anything?" he asked hesitantly.

Jaspar looked up for a moment. "Play your whistle," he said.

Jacob stared in astonishment. "Do what?"

"Don't you understand German? Play your whistle. Until we've got him bandaged up."

Breathing heavily, Kuno seemed about to protest.

"And you can keep your trap shut," Jaspar commanded. "We'll talk later. Goddert, the knife. Richmodis, soak that cloth in vinegar. Well, Jacob? Haven't you any whistles left? I thought they grew on you, like monkeys on a tree. Come on. I want music if I've got to work at this hour of the night."

Jacob felt inside the habit. The last thing he would have thought of was his whistle. It was still there. It had survived the fishmarket and the horrific journey under the cart. He took it out from his belt, twisting and turning it in his fingers, at a loss for what to play.

At that moment Richmodis looked up at him. And smiled.

It was that brief, warm smile.

Jacob started with the merriest tune he knew. And as Jaspar silently cut away Kuno's clothes and then, with Richmodis's help, washed him, carefully cleaning the wounds, and Goddert obediently brought fresh water and wrung out the cloths, the music gradually seemed to bring warmth to the room. With each silvery note peace and strength came flooding in, each arpeggio, each refrain drove the specter of fear a little further away. The faces of the others lost their careworn look and Jacob was fired with the joy of making music as he had not been for a long time. His whistle was a weapon combating despair; it rang out in their hopeless situation as if they had reason to celebrate, scorned danger with mocking trills, dismissed their terrors with a wave of its magic wand, rejoicing and pouring out the song of creation in cascade after cascade, calling up images of glittering stars and showers of pearls, exotic cities with minarets and slim towers of jasper, stories of fantasy and adventure, just as old Bram had taught him, Bram who, though perhaps not a crusader, had been a sorcerer who could conjure joy out of thin air. Jacob helped them recover something of the vitality they felt they had lost in the storm, smoothed the turbulent waves of confusion and revived their spirits until the blood surged through their veins and Goddert broke out into cheerful laughter.

With a guilty start, he let the whistle sink from his lips. The mood immediately cooled a little, but the icy despair had gone.

A satisfied look on his face, Jaspar washed his hands. "Good. He's sleeping. I could do with a drink. What do you say, Goddert"—he looked at Richmodis and then Jacob—"What does everyone say, shall we have a mug of wine?"

"A mug of wine!"

They filled the mugs and went into the front room, telling one another what had happened. Jaspar pretended he was too exhausted to talk and left it to Jacob to put the others in the picture. But Jacob was well aware of the real purpose behind it. Jaspar had sensed his feeling of isolation and, like a good friend, was drawing him into the group.

When they had finished, they sat in silence for a while, each occupied with their own thoughts.

"Let's be under no illusion," said Jaspar eventually. "The situation's worse than ever."

"Why?" asked Goddert in astonishment. "Richmodis is here and we can't bring poor Rolof back to life. It was God's will."

"Do stop prattling on about God's will, for God's sake," Jaspar snapped. "I find it remarkable the way God is made responsible for everything."

"Jaspar's right," said Jacob. "If the man who kidnapped Richmodis—and he's obviously the same man that I saw on the cathedral—if he finds out she's escaped, he'll come looking for us. He's got nothing that gives him a hold over us anymore. It's back to square one. He has to kill us if he wants to make sure we won't talk. Sooner or later—"

"Sooner or later he'll come here," said Jaspar.

"But he doesn't know where we live," said Goddert, a quiver in his voice.

"He found my house, even though I didn't send a written invitation with a map. Anyway, he talked to Rolof and it's easy to squeeze things out of him."

"*Was* easy," said Richmodis quietly.

"Yes." Jaspar's face was filled with remorse. "Stupid of me. Which reminds me, I really ought to go back and do something about the body. You never know, my housekeeper might take it into her head to get better and do some tidying up. I can already hear her shrieks rousing all the neighbors. And with these women's imagination the next thing you'll hear will be: Jaspar Rodenkirchen's put the evil eye on his servant."

"Then be quick about it," said Goddert.

"I can't, you dimwit."

"Huh! Coward. I'll go." He emptied his mug and struck the table with his fist.

Jaspar looked at him in exasperation. "And what would be the point of that? Do you always think with your belly? What's the first place the murderer will look for us? He might imagine we're stupid enough to meet at my place, but I certainly don't intend to prove him right." He thought for a moment. "Perhaps he'll go to Kuno's house first. If Daniel's told him everything, he'll be in danger as much as we are. I would have suggested we hide in my church, but I'm afraid Kuno wouldn't make it that far. Like it or not, we've got to stay here."

"We could carry him," suggested Jacob.

"Not even if we carry him."

"It would be pointless anyway," said Richmodis. "If he knows your house, he'll know your church."

"True. Have you any weapons in the house, Goddert?"

Goddert started. "You mean to fight?" he asked, horrified.

"I might have to, mean to or not. Or Jacob might, or Richmodis. Or"—Jaspar bared his teeth in a fearsome grin—"you might! Coward indeed!"

"Just the usual, the armor and two spears."

"No sword?"

"Yes," said Richmodis. "We've got one. It's under the chest by the window. We took it off Daniel."

"Well, that's something at least."

"No, it's nothing. How do you think you're going to fight such a superior opponent?" asked Goddert.

"Didn't Richmodis put up a fight?" asked Jacob angrily.

Jaspar grinned. "Listen to our fox bark, Goddert. Do you mean to do nothing to save your fat skin? Has the woad got to your brain, that you've forgotten how to fight? Even Abelard could handle a sword, and he was a cleric."

"Abelard was a philanderer. He became a cleric when his philandering was cut off."

"Go on, joke about it. He was still more of a man than fat Goddert who won't fight to save his life. *A superior opponent!* Perhaps that's what David should have said when the Philistines pitched their camp in Ephesdammim. Six cubits and a span was Goliath's height, and he had a helmet of brass on his head and was armed with a coat of mail, the weight of which was five thousand shekels of brass. And David? No armor, just five smooth stones and a sling."

"That was man against man," growled Goddert. "Everything was open and aboveboard. The Philistines had no secrets. David knew his opponent, while we're fighting against a shadow, a phantom with powerful forces behind him."

"Yes, yes, Goddert, times have changed. Isn't the Evil One cunning?" He massaged the bridge of his nose. "But what he does not know is the size of the reception party, if he does in fact find us. They've lost sight of Jacob and me. I suspect he'll be looking for Kuno, first and foremost. He seems to be the only one who really knows something and is clearly prepared to spill the beans. Assuming he wakes up again, that is," he added, lowering his voice.

He stood up. "Goddert," he said in resolute tones, "you go and shut up the house. Make sure the fiend can't get in anywhere. Bolt and bar everything, as if you were shutting out the whole world. Then he's welcome to come."

Richmodis rested her chin on her hands and gave him a doubtful look. "I saw his eyes," she said.

Jaspar frowned. "Uh-huh. And what did they say?"

"That there are no closed doors for him." She hesitated. "Apart from one."

"Which one?"

"The one inside him."

RHEINGASSE

"The plan has failed," said Johann firmly. "We must abandon it."

"No!" Matthias replied sharply.

The argument had been going back and forth for some time now. After Daniel had returned, wounded and scarcely able to stand, they had hastily called a meeting. None of them could get to sleep that night anyway. They agreed to meet in Rheingasse, on the first floor, where it had all begun. Only Blithildis was absent. It was not that she objected to being carried there in her chair at that time of night; she simply could not understand the fuss. For her there was no doubt that everything would go ahead as she had planned.

Johann, on the other hand, was having more and more doubts.

"Everything's getting out of hand," Theoderich agreed. "When I heard we had a hostage, I thought for a moment Urquhart had things back under control. Now we're up the creek without a paddle."

"We've not achieved anything," said Heinrich von Mainz gloomily, "not a single thing."

Matthias leaped up. "That is not true. I can't believe what I'm hearing. Are you suggesting we give up now, so close to success? We're almost there."

"And what are these great achievements, pray?" asked Johann with bitter scorn.

"We—"

"We got rid of Gerhard Morart," said Theoderich, "that's all. The rest has been a shambles. It would have been better if Urquhart had simply left the redhead alone."

"If he'd left him alone half the city would know by now." Matthias started to pace up and down angrily.

"Nobody would have believed a good-for-nothing like that."

"That isn't true. We don't know what Gerhard whispered to him. We had no choice."

"Correct me if my arithmetic is wrong," said Johann deliberately, "but with the Fox, the dean, and his niece, that's at least three who represent a danger to us. Plus all those we don't know about. Each one of them had—still has—plenty of opportunity to hawk their knowledge around the city. Then there's that Bodo Schuif. The dean let slip something that made him think."

"Bodo's an imbecile," Theoderich declared.

"Not enough of an imbecile to dismiss it as the ramblings of a drunken priest. Are we going to kill Bodo as well?"

"If it's unavoidable," said Matthias.

"But that still wouldn't solve the problem, Matthias. It's too late to silence people. We must give up. Go and tell Urquhart to clear out of the city. With any luck that'll be the end of it. No one knows we were behind the murders. They can't prove we had anything to do with it and with Urquhart gone there's no murderer. We must abandon the plan as long as there's still time."

"Abandon it?" Matthias snorted. "The same whining and wailing all the time. What difference would that make? You can't undo Gerhard's murder, but you can create the risk they might be able to prove we ordered it. All honor to your high-mindedness, Johann, but in the light of what we have already done, what happens tomorrow is completely irrelevant."

"It has nothing to do with high-mindedness. I'm just trying to stop the worst from happening."

"The worst has already happened. You can call off the whole thing, but that won't stop a few morons from running around the city saying the patricians killed Gerhard."

Johann started to speak, then breathed out slowly and shook his head.

"I agree with you," Matthias assured him. "We can't let it come to a bloodbath. But we've gone too far. There was a point when we could have turned back, but we passed that long ago."

"With Gerhard."

"Precisely. With Gerhard. Gerhard is dead. There was a witness. Agreed, not everything has gone as planned, but if we give up now, everything will have been in vain. The people will have died in vain. Gerhard will have died in vain."

Johann remained silent.

Matthias sat down and looked at them one after the other. "I think there is one chance. If we can show that the redhead is a liar and a thief, then people won't believe those he's told either. That leaves just one person who's a real danger to us."

"Kuno," Daniel murmured.

All eyes turned toward him.

"You will keep quiet," growled Johann. "You've done enough damage already."

Daniel leaned forward. He looked terrible. His face was swollen and partly covered in blue bruises, his nose just a shapeless lump. But the gleam of hatred in his eyes was unchanged.

"I know what I've done," he said calmly. "Nevertheless, if Matthias goes to see Urquhart, he should impress on him the need to get rid of Kuno."

"We're not going to sacrifice another person just to please you!" Johann shouted. "Once and for all, there have been enough—"

"That is precisely what we will do," Matthias interrupted. "For once I agree with Daniel. If Kuno decides to give evidence against us, we really do have a problem, a bloody big problem."

"Why should Kuno do that?" asked Heinrich.

Daniel gave a hoarse laugh. "Why? Because I damn near killed him, that's why."

"As long as I preside over this alliance—" Johann began to say.

Matthias shot up. "But you no longer preside over it."

"I don't? Who says so?"

"I do. If there's anyone to whom we owe responsibility, it's your mother, Blithildis."

"As if that meant anything to you! I wonder now whether you ever believed in our common goal. You're not doing any of this for my mother—don't try to fool me—and even less for those who are imprisoned or banned. Everything you've done was serving your own interests and your own balance sheet."

"And whose interests are served by your sudden withdrawal, your ridiculous scruples?"

Heinrich von Mainz stood up. "I'm leaving. We're not going to come to any decision."

"No! You stay!" Matthias barked.

"I will not be—"

"Sit down!"

There was an embarrassed silence. Heinrich stared at Matthias, seething with fury. Then he lowered his eyes and sat back down on the gold-embroidered cushion.

Matthias waited a moment, but no one said anything. Then he went and stood at the farther end of the table, leaning on his knuckles, his eyes fixed on Johann.

"What we are doing is right," he insisted. "I'm not looking for a quarrel, Johann. Forgive me if I was lacking in due respect. We're in a difficult situation and I can understand if some of us feel the pressure of the last few days has been too much. But don't you agree that we have all come too far together to turn back now? One last time I beg you to vote for our plan, to trust me one last time. I beg you! Tomorrow will be a day of rejoicing, our enemies will wail and gnash their teeth, and no one will be interested in a few nobodies trying to draw attention to themselves by claiming Gerhard was pushed. Tomorrow we'll have a new world. And nothing will happen to Kuno, I promise. I will just get Urquhart to keep him quiet until it's all over. As God is my witness, there will be no more killings. Believe me! Believe in our cause, Johann, I beg you. We will triumph. We *will* triumph."

Johann rubbed his eyes and slumped back in his chair. "Where do you think Kuno and that woman will have gone to hide?" he asked.

"I don't know. His house? The dean's? Or perhaps to her house?"

"Where does she live?"

"I will find out."

"Now? It's the middle of the night. You're due to meet Urquhart."

Matthias gave a grim smile. "I have found out other things in much shorter time."

POWER

Goddert was sitting by the fire, his chin on his chest, snoring quietly. Beside him was Daniel's sword. Kuno lay unconscious on the chest between the front and back rooms. They had carefully carried him there because it was the warmest place in the house. Jaspar had managed to staunch the blood, but the young man was in a bad way.

They held out their hands to the fire, waiting for him to regain consciousness and tell them why the world was so terribly different since Gerhard's death. Outside, the wind was rattling at the shutters with undiminished violence.

"Will he pull through?" Jacob asked after a while.

"Hmm," said Jaspar.

Jacob looked up. "What does 'hmm' mean?"

"He's lost a lot of blood, but I've managed to close his wounds and it looks as if no vital organs are damaged. Otherwise he'd be dead already. Now he's in a fever. All we can do is wait."

"I hope he comes round." Richmodis sighed. "He knows the truth."

"Don't bank on it. We have to work out what's going to happen ourselves." He stroked his bald head. "What I'm asking myself is, who else is involved?"

Goddert's stomach rumbled in his sleep and he smacked his lips.

"The Devil," suggested Richmodis.

"How unimaginative," said Jaspar reproachfully. "Please think of something helpful. The Devil's behind every piece of villainy, that's nothing new."

"No, that's not what I meant. I was facing him in the old warehouse today, the stranger, I mean—the Devil seemed to be inside him. It was odd. He filled me with fear, but at the same time I had a feeling of great closeness, as if it would take almost nothing, a mere trifle to make him quite different, the complete opposite. I suddenly felt the urge—"

"Yes?" Jaspar asked, alert. "To do what?"

"Better not say. You'll be having me exorcised."

"You felt the urge to touch him."

She gave him a look of surprise and blushed.

"That's all right," said Jaspar. "Christ and Antichrist, one and the same. Do you know what makes evil so fascinating? Its tragic nature. The Devil is a fallen angel. Look at Kuno. He seems to have decided to get out of hell and become an angel again. That means it can work the other way around as well and that gives me hope. Our enemies are not only ranged against us—they're against one another, too."

"But there is a difference between fighting against men of flesh and blood and against the Devil," said Jacob. "I'm not sure who or what I saw on the scaffolding. As I said, it could have been a man, but the way he came after me was simply too fast for a man. He jumped down like a cat. It could have been a tail streaming out behind him."

"That's enough of that!" Jaspar was angry. "You're coming out with the same nonsense as all the credulous folk who go goggle-eyed as soon as the magician says *Casisa, hasisa, mesisa medantor*, or some such rigmarole. Good God, you're about as stupid as the peasant who won't slaughter a pig on Saint Gall's day for fear the meat will taste of gall. Did he have a tail, Richmodis?"

"No. His hair came down to his waist. That was the tail."

"There you are."

"But the Devil was in his eyes."

"More peasant nonsense." Jaspar groaned. "Why this relapse into ignorance? Surely you've heard me trying to demonstrate the power of reason to your father often enough. Has nothing rubbed off?"

"All right. But if you'd just let me finish—"

"And you, Jacob, you heathen. Have you ever bothered with religion, with heaven and hell? You don't even know a prayer and suddenly you start wittering on about the Devil. Do you really believe you saw the Devil up there? Or is that what you want to believe because it's nice and simple?"

Jacob and Richmodis exchanged looks. They shrugged their shoulders uncertainly. He's right, thought Jacob. It's easy to make the Devil responsible for everything. I don't really think I saw the Devil on the scaffolding. So why did I say I had?

"However," Jaspar went on in milder tones now that he saw his words were having an effect, "what we do know is that at least four members of patrician families have a finger in this particular pie. That doesn't sound like the Devil to me, more like a conspiracy."

He got up and started striding around the room, his nostrils quivering. "We have to find out what they're plotting. Find their weak spot."

Richmodis nodded slowly. "Kuno said something to Daniel about an alliance being broken, whatever he meant by that. It sounded as if they had originally been on the same side, then fallen out."

Jaspar stopped. "There you are. Just as I said."

"But it was unclear to me what he meant."

"Perhaps not to me. Think back!"

"I don't know. Everything happened so quickly. I was just terribly afraid. I think I was praying, without daring to make a sound, while Kuno kept trying to persuade Daniel of something."

"What did he say?"

"Something about a common goal and higher justice, that kind of thing. And that they had done something that was wrong."

"What?"

"They sacrificed someone—Kuno's only friend—"

"Gerhard," Jaspar cried triumphantly. "I knew it. Gerhard knew their secret, and that's why he had to die. Kuno has broken with them. He's changed sides. I knew it. I knew it."

"Wait." Her frown cleared. "There was something else. Kuno reminded Daniel of his past, of how important justice had been to him." She puckered her lips in distaste. "Strange. I can't imagine that bastard ever being concerned about justice."

"He wasn't," growled Jaspar. "Daniel was one of the youngest magistrates, a corrupt bigmouth with money but no brains. A trick Kuno tried to talk him around. Without success." He paused and slapped his forehead. "And Daniel is the son of Johann Overstolz! My God! If he's in it, too, that means we have almost all the senior members of the Overstolz clan against us. An alliance between the Overstolzes and the Kones. What could that mean? A patrician revolt?"

"Why should they plan a revolt?" Jacob asked.

"They've got reason enough."

"Why?"

"To regain their old supremacy."

Jacob glanced at Kuno. Had the man moved or was he just imagining it? "What's the point of all this, Jaspar?" he said in desperation. "It's all beyond me. I know nothing of power and politics, nothing about the patricians. I know nothing at all. How am I supposed to defend myself against something that's a complete mystery to me?"

"But you live here, in the city," said Jaspar. It didn't sound reproachful, only surprised.

"Only for the last few months. I've been away too long. Since I came back I haven't concerned myself with what's going on in Cologne. I just wanted to get on with my life."

"Have you ever really concerned yourself with anything?" asked Richmodis.

Her remark cut him to the quick. "Perhaps," he said coolly.

Jaspar came over and squatted down in front of him. "Am I wrong, or could you be running away from something?"

"You know already."

"No, I don't know. I mean something you can't escape. Always keeping your eyes closed, not facing up to things, not being interested in things, not even in your music, really, even though you play your whistle exceptionally well. There's something wrong there."

Jacob looked at him. The palms of his hands were sore. He realized he had been boring his fingernails into them and forced a grin to his lips. "Blessed are the poor in spirit. Isn't that what it says?"

"Not in Abelard."

"Oh, to hell with your Abelard."

"Fox-cub!"

"Why should the patricians plan a revolt?"

"You're changing the subject."

"Yes, I'm changing the subject," Jacob snapped. "And if I am, then it's my business alone. You said we should attack, so please enlighten me. If you can."

"Oh, I can enlighten you. Given your eagerness to learn, the basic principles will probably take a lifetime, though I wouldn't guarantee you'd understand them even then."

"Jaspar," said Jacob softly, "before I met you I may well have been stupid, but I never had the feeling I was."

"Oh, I see." Jaspar scratched the back of his head. "Sir is sorry for himself. It's certainly easier to be stupid."

"I'm not listening to this."

"Oh, we're not listening to this, are we? That's because you don't want to. You always choose the easy option. If things get hard, you give up and take to your heels. You don't want to learn, you don't want to know, not even now."

"I want the truth."

"You can't take the truth."

Jacob breathed in deeply, trying to calm himself down. Most of all he felt like ramming his fist between Jaspar's mocking eyes. Suddenly he felt Richmodis's hand ruffling his hair. "Stop that," he snapped.

"Jacob."

He tried to shake her off.

"Jacob, your hair gets even redder when you're angry. Did you know that?"

He stared at the fire in silence.

"And it sticks up like a hedgehog's." She giggled. "No, more like a cock. A little angry cock. A cockerel."

He felt his anger subside and chewed his lips. He was unhappy, and his unhappiness had nothing to do with the events of the last couple of days. "I'm the Fox," he said weakly.

"And the Fox is cunning," she said with a smile. "I'm just a silly goose, but this goose has its claws in your hair, so be careful."

Jaspar went back to sit by the fire. Jacob had the feeling he was both irritated and amused at the same time. His face was glowing with the reflection of the fire. He poked the logs, sending up a crackling shower of sparks.

"All right," said Jacob, "I know nothing. I know nothing about the emperor and the pope and what the point of an archbishop is and so on and so forth. Happy now?"

"No," said Jaspar, staring into the flames. "You've told us too much for that to be true. You know a lot. You can remember astonishing details. Up to the day you ran away from home." He turned toward him, a grin on his face. "But don't worry, Fox-cub, we're stuck in here for the next few hours, so I might as well give you the benefit of my historical knowledge in the hope of filling that hollow skull of yours to overflowing with wisdom. Interested?"

Jacob sighed. "Of course."

"Good. Basically, it all comes down to who's the boss. After the collapse of Rome the empire was split up. There followed a dark period of conflict and confusion, before it was reunited under the spiritual authority of the popes and the secular power of the emperors and kings. To general rejoicing, of course. But the immense empire proved too much for them, especially since the pope only actually rules the Vatican. People were needed to administer specific local territories, and among these were some I would call—just as a joke, God forgive me my vanity—secular clerics, representatives of the powers of the pope and of the king in the same person. These were the prince bishops and archbishops."

He paused, then went on. "Now it is in the nature of things that the powerful are constantly at each others' throats. The pope wanted to turn the empire into an ecclesiastical state under the authority of the Church. The emperor, for his part, also claimed to be God's representative—naturally, since God is *the* authority—and denied the pope any jurisdiction in political and territorial matters. Each tried to clip the other's powers and increase his own. Thus the Crusades, for example, were not holy wars, but a conflict between the secular and spiritual authorities. They agreed on a common enemy, and had a common army, but one or the other of them always came out on top, depending on circumstances. The dilemma only became public, however, when the emperor and the pope began to attack each other openly. The archbishops, being servants of two masters, couldn't really fight against themselves. They were in danger of being crushed between two stones. You're still with me?"

"Conrad von Hochstaden," Richmodis interjected, "doesn't look particularly crushed to me."

"Clever girl. That's the way things were going. The archbishops had to become more powerful. And they did so to the point where they could side with one of their masters and leave the other in dire straits. Loyalty didn't have much to do with it. Basically, the archbishops don't care one bit about the emperor or pope. They're interested in politics, not in saving souls. But their strategy worked. Over the centuries they became powerful enough to grant their support as a favor. But that led to a further dilemma. Whom does the city serve?"

"The archbishop?"

"On the one hand. He is its overlord. On the other, it also serves the emperor. It's part of the empire and the citizens are his subjects."

Jacob risked a deduction. "So if the archbishop and the pope combined against the emperor, then the city would have to oppose the emperor, willy-nilly."

"Exactly! Willy-nilly. To decide for themselves, the citizens would have to make themselves independent of the archbishop. The archbishop needs them and their money. If he is to go to war, in whoever's name, he needs well-filled coffers. So what did the archbishops do? Tried to get the cities on their side. Buttered them up. Granted privileges and promised the moon. In general they succeeded in getting absolute control over the cities. Except in Cologne."

"Why not here?"

"Why?" Jaspar raised his eyebrows. "Just look around. A rich city. Wine and textiles, goldsmiths, metalworkers, armorers. Trading to the farthest boundaries of the known world and a magnet for pilgrims. Nowhere in Christendom is there such a perfect combination of religious fervor and cold calculation. A religious center and the strongest economic power in the empire. No wonder the citizens began to question the archbishops' rule. They supported them now and again, but only when the archbishops' aims coincided with their own interests."

"I still don't understand. The archbishop rules over people who don't obey his rule. Does he rule or not?"

"Well." Jaspar leaned back and clasped his hands behind his head. "People here have problems recognizing either the pope or the emperor when they've not been involved in the election. In 1198 there was a contest for the crown that Otto IV won. Why? The decisive factor was the Cologne leadership that supported England as Otto's proposer. And why did they do that? To promote Cologne's interests in the English trade. There you have it in a nutshell. The citizens of Cologne are interested in profit, and their main concern is to get rid of the archbishops, who bleed them dry and dictate to them. But what should an archbishop do if not bleed his subjects dry and dictate to them? If he doesn't rule, he's superfluous. That's the root of the eternal conflict, even though there were times when the archbishop was quite popular with the citizens."

"When they were more Christian?" Richmodis mocked.

"Huh! The people of Cologne have always been pious, not Christian. But an archbishop like Reinhard von Dassel, who brought the bones of the Three Kings to Cologne a hundred years ago, strengthened both his own position and that of the city. Lots of pilgrims, lots of new inns, lots of money coming in. And his successor, Philip von Heinsberg, used this as a base to acquire castles, estates, and privileges. He soon became one of the most powerful princes in the empire, and everything he did increased the importance of Cologne. And once they had got that far on their archbishops' coattails, the good citizens began to think of ways of getting rid of them. So they built the walls—partly out of fear of Philip's enemies, since he was always waging war, but also because they knew there was bound to be armed conflict between the archbishop and the city eventually."

"But if Philip was so powerful," Richmodis commented, "why couldn't he impose his will on them?"

"Because his power was based on money, money he had borrowed from the Cologne merchants. As everyone knew. The emperor would never have given his blessing to a subjugation of the city by force. He wanted the foremost economic power in his empire to flourish. Philip would have risked being taken to court."

"He could have gotten the pope to support him."

"Not a hope. He had even more debts in Rome. There was nothing he could do and Cologne was quietly preparing for self-government. Then it happened. The emperor decided in favor of the city—which shows just what economic strength can do. They did have to pay a kind of fine, but they were allowed to continue building the walls. From then on the archbishops lost more and more influence, leaving the city folk facing a different problem. Namely which of them was to be boss."

Jacob thought. "You said money is power."

"Precisely. In the main, the independence movement had been driven by the patricians. But then they controlled most of the city's trade. You'll know that the two burgomasters came from their ranks. What you perhaps didn't know is that until recently one of them also had to be a magistrate. At some point it became established that every magistrate had to come from the great merchant houses, who were trying to occupy all official positions in the city. The magistrates, originally impartial judges, became the mouthpiece of the patricians, who started to raise taxes to pay for the administration, for example, the burgomasters."

"Isn't that quite reasonable?" objected Jacob.

"Perhaps. But the burgomasters naturally wanted to put on as imposing a show as possible. Latterly they took to giving glittering parties, which they claimed were essential for the work of the authorities. The authorities being the patricians, of course. This all made a big hole in the finances, so they increased the taxes. It had less and less to do with representing the interests of the inhabitants of Cologne, and the noble families, as they like to call themselves, did less and less to conceal their contempt for tradesmen and excluded them from all official positions. Though that didn't stop them from dipping into everyone's pockets and even getting themselves elected masters of the guilds."

"But why did the craftsmen put up with it?"

"Ask the opposite question. Why would patricians want to be elected guildmasters?"

"To represent the interests of the trades?"

"And weaken them politically. They promised them protection against the archbishop's jurisdiction, but then they controlled all appointments to the judiciary. Another step toward depriving the archbishop completely of power. Favors given and received, an incredible sink of corruption." Jaspar sighed. "At least, that was the situation when Conrad von Hochstaden was made archbishop."

"And he wants the old power back?"

Jaspar nodded.

"I see," said Jacob thoughtfully. It was beginning to get interesting. "But now only a few patricians are magistrates."

"They have been deposed, more or less."

"By whom?"

Jaspar looked at him. "Can't you guess?"

"Conrad?"

"Who else? Conrad's ultimate aim was to reestablish the absolute power of the archbishop, but he went about it in a roundabout way, initially cooperating with the citizens and confirming their privileges. This lasted until he opposed the emperor and, in agreement with the pope, arranged the election of an anti-king. Cologne had always been loyal to the emperor, hardly surprising since he guaranteed its economic privileges and stability. Then, although he had recognized the city's right to mint its own currency, Conrad suddenly brought out a coin of his own. It wasn't worth much, but it bore his image, the vain bastard. Not content with that, he set up new customs barriers, although it didn't lie within his powers and hit Cologne's trade where it hurt. The city protested. Conrad, unimpressed, gathered an army and besieged it. To no avail, however, since it now had its splendid walls. He had to agree to a court of arbitration under Albertus Magnus, who found against Conrad on all counts."

"The Lesser Adjudication," Richmodis murmured.

"Yes! Conrad had to cancel all the disputed measures. A farce! Five years later he started a new dispute when he accused the citizens of Cologne of having planned to assassinate him—"

"And had they?" Jacob asked.

Jaspar grinned. "Who knows? Three years ago the Kleingedancks attacked one of his relatives. Right outside his palace! While he was inside dispensing justice. It was a private feud, but Conrad presented it as an attempt on his life. So we had another war, which the patricians won, and another defeat for the archbishop. Then—"

"Richmodis!" It was Kuno whispering. All heads swung around. With great effort Kuno had raised himself a little. He was deathly pale.

Richmodis jumped up and went to support him.

"He should be lying down," said Jaspar.

Goddert smacked his lips a few times, cleared his throat, and opened his eyes. "What's going on?" he asked.

No one took any notice. They were standing around Kuno as Jaspar wiped the sweat from his brow. "Relax," he said. "You're safe here."

Kuno shook his head feebly. "No one's safe." His eyelids fluttered.

"Water," Jaspar commanded. He gently slapped Kuno's cheeks. "We don't want to lose him again."

"The alliance—" Kuno breathed.

Richmodis hurried over with a damp cloth and Jaspar wiped Kuno's face. He was seized with a fit of coughing, then sank back, breathing heavily.

"Tell us about the alliance," said Jaspar urgently.

"It's too late."

"It can't be too late as long as your lot are trying to kill us."

"Not me." Kuno's chest was heaving, as if he couldn't get his breath. "I've broken with them. I want the alliance to end. It—it is wrong."

"Gerhard's words!" exclaimed Jacob.

"It is wrong."

"Who was in the alliance?" Jaspar asked.

They waited. For a while it seemed as if Kuno had fallen asleep again. Then they heard his hoarse voice. "Heinrich von Mainz—"

"Married to Sophia Overstolz," Jaspar added. "The Overstolzes again."

"My brothers, Bruno and Hermann."

"Both in exile."

"Johann and Daniel—and Matthias Overstolz—and . . . and Theoderich—"

"So we were right. Anyone else?"

"Leave me alone. I'm tired. I—"

"Who?" Jaspar shouted. He took Kuno by the shoulders and started to shake him. Kuno groaned. Jacob grabbed Jaspar's wrists and pulled him away.

"Sorry." Jaspar rubbed his eyes.

"The witch," Kuno panted.

"Witch?"

"Blithildis. The witch. The blind witch."

Jaspar looked around, dumbfounded. "Blithildis Overstolz," he whispered. "My God, what on earth do you intend to do?"

"It was her idea." Kuno was having difficulty getting the words out. "All her idea. Cursed be that evening when we were sitting together in Rheingasse. We were going to celebrate. Enjoy ourselves—oh, God—water, I'm thirsty—so thirsty."

They handed him a mug and waited until he had drunk. It was a long time.

"We had concluded a couple of good deals," Kuno went on, his voice stronger, "the Overstolzes, the von Mainzes, and—"

"Yes? Go on."

"—and me. Deals with the English. And Johann—it was for Blithildis, to cheer her up. He said it was so long since she had been in company, sitting in her room all the time like the living dead, since God had taken her sight. I asked if I might bring Gerhard, he—he was my only friend. We were sitting there, drinking our wine when—when Blithildis suddenly sent the servants away and started to speak, full of hatred, laughing, crying, sobbing until she put a spell on us and blinded us too with bloody thoughts, and it was the evil from her lips that made us join in and—and Gerhard said—"

"What, for God's sake? He said it was wrong, didn't he?"

Kuno's features contorted, as if he wanted to cry but couldn't. "It was so sad. He tried to make us change our minds and we begged him to join us. Johann said he would respect Gerhard's honest opinion as long as he would swear to remain silent."

"And Gerhard. Could he do that?"

Kuno shook his head disconsolately. "He didn't know what to do. He owed everything to the Church, but he would have had to betray his friends to—can't you see, he had no choice?" Kuno held Jaspar tight, looking at him beseechingly, as if he could turn back the clock. "Whatever he did, in his own eyes it would have been betrayal. His honesty killed him. I pleaded with the others to trust him, without even knowing myself whether we could. He knew everything. What could have come over Blithildis, to imagine she could persuade Gerhard, the cathedral architect, to join in her plan?"

"What plan, Kuno?" asked Jaspar breathlessly.

Kuno seemed not to hear. He stared vacantly into space. Then his grasp loosed, he let go of Jaspar and sank back. "Finally we brought in Urquhart," he whispered. "We clubbed together and brought the Devil to the city."

"Urquhart?"

"He costs a pretty penny, does the Devil." Kuno gave a coarse laugh. "William of Jülich recommended someone who'd been recommended to him. A man who kills for money. That's all anyone knew about him. We assumed Urquhart was a hired killer, but—"

"Who killed Gerhard? Was it Urquhart?"

Kuno nodded. "Urquhart. Slaughters whatever's in his way. A butcher. A fiend. The Berlich whore, the beggar, the two monks—"

"Monks?"

"His—witnesses."

Jaspar threw Jacob a quick glance. "Kuno," he said, "what is Urquhart going to do? What is the aim of the alliance? Answer me, for pity's sake, answer me."

But Kuno had fallen asleep.

Goddert looked around helplessly. "Should I—"

"No," said Jaspar, "we'll let him rest awhile. He needs sleep, there's nothing I can do about that."

"What time is it?" asked Richmodis.

"I don't know. At a guess, shortly after midnight."

"I'm bloody cold," moaned Goddert.

"Don't worry," said Jaspar, "I imagine things will heat up in the course of the night."

MATTHIAS

Johann was getting weak. None of the old Overstolz spirit there.

Matthias wrinkled his nose in disgust as he fought his way through the storm. He despised weakness and he despised Johann. That odor of sentimentality he had hated all his life! Like a mold you just couldn't get rid of. There was always someone ready with sniveling comments on his plans. It's wrong. It's a sin. It's against the law of God.

It was enough to make you want to spew.

Matthias stole quietly through the alleyways around Haymarket. A man of his rank should have been on horseback, but a rider would attract attention to himself. Even in weather like this the night watchmen would be going about their business. It was not the best moment to be seen.

He had spent the last two hours finding out everything Urquhart needed to know to put an end to this mess once and for all. Matthias was under no illusion that they could silence everyone who had heard of Gerhard's violent death. All the better if they could, of course. He didn't imagine the Fox and Jaspar Rodenkirchen would have gone around telling everybody and anybody, but that was pure speculation on his part. The important thing was to eliminate Kuno. If Kuno talked, then he and his new friends had time before daybreak to ruin everything. Any influential person in Cologne would believe Kuno, and he could count on leniency from his judges if he gave evidence against them. A prattling beggar or a drunken priest, on the other hand, did not represent a serious danger to the Overstolzes.

Or, to be precise, a danger to me, thought Matthias. What are the others to me? They can lead the Kones or Heinrich, Daniel or Theoderich to the block for all I care.

In a few hours it would all be over anyway.

But first there was this night to get through. Urquhart had one more task before he could carry out the deed Matthias was longing to see. It gave him grim satisfaction to think that, however much what he was about to do ran counter to Johann's wishes, it would receive Blithildis's approval. She was the only person he really admired. She was an Overstolz, she was strength, power, even if she was blind and tied to her chair. She should have been his mother, not Johann's.

He quickly went over what he had found out. Urquhart's hostage was a Richmodis von Weiden. She lived on the Brook, together with her father. He knew the house. Jaspar von Rodenkirchen had no other relatives, only a servant, a cook, and a cleaning woman. Where the two women were, he had no idea. The servant was dead.

They were doomed. Urquhart would find them.

Suddenly Matthias felt the confidence well up inside him. Looking around to see that no one was watching, he slipped into a doorway. Beyond it yawned the emptiness of a huge courtyard. The howling storm was not so bad in the protection of its walls. By day flax and candles were sold here; now it was deserted. Heavy curtains of rain billowed before him.

He blinked and rubbed the water out of his eyes. Then he saw the immense shadow coming toward him through the downpour.

"I expected you sooner," said Urquhart. His voice was as calm as ever, almost friendly, but a hint of sharpness was still audible.

"I came as quickly as I could."

"Of course."

"Have you gotten anywhere?"

Urquhart made a dismissive gesture. "I've been to the dean's. Nobody there. They're not that stupid."

"Then go to Kuno's. No, wait, leave that till last. There are too many other people there, servants and the like."

"I wouldn't bother with Kuno's. Little Kuno escaped with the woman. Daniel—your noble family can be proud of him—was kind enough to poke a few holes in him." Urquhart gave a mocking smile and threw his head back, letting the water run down over his face. "Women are such caring creatures. Softhearted. If they find a rabbit that's been hurt they take it home and look after it."

Matthias returned his smile. "I'll tell you where to find her. Do what you can. Kill them all, if you like."

"All? I couldn't say who they all are anymore. Can you?"

"No. It's enough if you eliminate one."

"Who?" Urquhart said in the tone of a man who already knows.

Matthias spat on the ground. "The weakling."

ON THE BROOK

"And the end of the story?" asked Jacob.

"Is quickly told," said Jaspar.

Goddert gave them a disgruntled look and put a couple of logs on the fire. There was a crackling and whistling as air and moisture escaped.

"We ought to be doing something instead of philosophizing about history," he muttered.

Jaspar disagreed. "We are doing something by philosophizing about history," he said. "We know the conspirators and we know they have something planned. We still don't know what or when. The answer must lie in the recent past." He massaged the bridge of his nose. "After the Great Adjudication."

"The 'Great'?" asked Jacob.

"Yes," said Richmodis, "there was another. Two years ago, when Conrad claimed there was a plot on his life."

"Conrad would have lost that war, too," Jaspar continued. "He was forced to make peace with the patricians. But he was still dangerous. And the conflict between patricians and tradesmen had reached the point where there were frequent armed clashes. On top of that there was the threat of civil war among the patricians, since they were split between the Overstolzes and their allies and the Weises. The Weises are the oldest merchant family in Cologne; compared to them the Overstolzes are *nouveaux riches*. The two groups had never been particularly fond of each other, but as long as there was a common enemy, the archbishop, they pulled together, more or less. But as the Overstolzes' influence grew, the Weises looked for an ally. They found one in the archbishop."

"Not really," objected Goddert. "They supported the authorities. They behaved with dignity."

"With dignity? They sold themselves. Not very wise, despite their name, to trust Conrad, if you ask me."

"He's our lord and master," Goddert declared, "and it is not the place of his subjects to question his authority. Apart from his perhaps overly secular approach—"

"You're talking like a priest."

"And you are one."

"Dean, if you please. Anyway, the Weises got nothing out of their treachery."

"But—"

"Let me finish. Trusting Conrad is like holding out your hand to a mad dog. Everyone knows what happened in Neuss in 1255."

"That was never proved."

"What? It wasn't proved that Conrad set fire to the tent of the King of Holland and the papal legate when they were trying to persuade him to release the bishop of Paderborn? It wouldn't be the first time Conrad had used violence to get his way. Changing from Saul to Paul after his second big defeat was merely a tactical move. He had a trial before the Curia because of his debts and while that was taking its course he could sit back and watch the patricians falling out among themselves and with the guilds."

Jaspar paused to see if Goddert would reply, but he had obviously lost interest in the argument.

"Anyway," he went on, "the conflict between the city and Conrad about their rights and privileges wasn't over. Once more a court of arbitration was set up, once more under Albertus Magnus. To demonstrate his impartiality, he even appointed some of Conrad's supporters to it, but that didn't stop Conrad's demands on the city from being rejected once more. He must have been furious, but he had to be patient again. Albertus also criticized the sleaze and corruption among the patricians, and that gave the guilds hope. The Great Adjudication only calmed things superficially."

Jacob rested his chin on his hand. "And not for long, I assume?"

"No. Last year Conrad removed all the mint officials from office, overnight, so to speak, allegedly for exceeding their powers. That meant the city could issue no more coins. The patricians screamed bloody murder, but the guilds saw their opportunity and made an official complaint against the burgomasters and magistrates, at which Conrad removed all the magistrates but one from office. He kept on emphasizing that it did not infringe on the terms of the Great Adjudication, but then he would, wouldn't he? He decreed that in the future he would make all appointments to the council of magistrates himself. The patricians were sidelined. Only yesterday they had practically ruled the city; now they were banned from office. Conrad accused them of serious crimes and summoned them to a hearing, then outlawed twenty-five who refused to attend, including Kuno's brothers. They had to flee the city, otherwise the populace would have torn them to pieces. Then Conrad appointed new magistrates, one or two patricians among them, but mostly craftsmen and guildmasters like Bodo Schuif."

"The brewer who gave us away?"

"Yes. Unfortunately."

"And what is all that supposed to mean?" Goddert joined in the argument again, his voice quivering with rage. "What Conrad did was quite right. The patricians looked down on the guilds as if they were a herd of pigs. They taxed us till we bled. The burgomasters were corrupt through and through, the magistrates were guzzling and whoring at the expense of honest people and they twisted the laws to suit themselves. Profiteering, taking bribes, and abusing their office, that's what the patricians were good at. And some were made magistrates when they were scarcely out of their nappies, like that little thug Daniel. Conrad sat in judgment on them and a good thing, too. I support our archbishop, however much you may say he's a liar and a murderer."

"He is a liar and a murderer."

"So what?" Goddert jumped up, his face bright red. "What are your patricians? Look at me. When did I ever get anything out of my work the patricians didn't steal?"

"Father—" said Richmodis, trying to calm him down.

"No. Now it's my turn. They bled us white and they got what was coming to them. I tell you, the time will come when Cologne is run by the guilds. One day we'll get rid of all those villains on horseback in their expensive robes and furs. We'll throw them out. Conrad will throw them out so that the guilds can get what they deserve."

"What they deserve is a kick up the backside," Jaspar barked back. "Because they've sold out."

"They have not sold out."

"They haven't? Damn it all, Goddert, for once you're right. Yes, the magistrates were corrupt. Yes, they fleeced the people. Yes, yes, yes, it serves the patricians right that they're getting kicked in the teeth. But don't you see that the guilds are just an instrument in Conrad's hand? He doesn't care who helps him extend his power. Last year he was still trying to reach an accommodation with the patricians. Even after he'd dismissed them from office he promised he would allow the exiles back and God knows what else if they'd sell the city's privileges. It was only when the patricians dug their heels in that he allied himself with the weavers and other guilds against them. Open your eyes. Conrad's not the guardian angel of the guilds. He'll cheat you just as he tricked the patricians."

"He will dispense justice," Goddert stated, turning away from Jaspar.

"Oh, for goodness' sake!" Jaspar groaned. "Here we are, likely to get murdered any minute and I'm arguing about politics with a driveling old soak."

"Old soak yourself."

"Yes, but at least from my own wine."

"You can keep your goddamn wine," growled Goddert. "I've got plenty of my own."

"Really? Not that I've noticed."

Goddert took a deep breath, thought for a moment, then let it out slowly. "Errrm," he said.

Jaspar furrowed his brow. "You're surely not going to suggest we have a drink?"

"All right. Shall we have a drink?"

"Let's have a drink."

"No," said Jacob.

Jaspar stared at him in amazement. "Why ever not?"

"Because you haven't gotten to the end."

"Near enough."

"Nothing you've said tells us what the patricians have planned. I'm— I'm still afraid."

Jaspar blinked, but said nothing for a while. "So am I." He glanced at Kuno, who was lying on the bench by the fire, his chest faintly rising and falling. "Richmodis," he said quietly, "you looked into this Urquhart's eyes. Will he come?"

Richmodis nodded.

"Well, then. Everything bolted and barred, Goddert?"

"With these very hands."

"Good. We ought to be fairly safe until the morning and then there'll be enough people out in the streets." He paused.

"So. The end. At the beginning of the year all hell was let loose in the city. In the church of the White Sisters a butcher mocked a patrician,

Bruno Hardefust, because Conrad had removed him from the council of magistrates. There was an argument; Bruno drew his dagger and killed the butcher. It was a spark to a powder keg. The butchers' guild screamed for vengeance. Hordes gathered at the Hardefust house and set it on fire. Riot, pillage, you name it. Hardefust drummed up a posse of patrician friends and they laid into the craftsmen. Countless wounded, some dead. The magistrates took their time, giving the patricians plenty of opportunity to commit more murders, presumably hoping to increase the seriousness of the charges against them. They only stepped in toward evening and asked Conrad to adjudicate. He had cleverly kept out of it."

Jaspar gave a grim laugh. "His hour had come. He fined both sides, but in addition he decreed that the patricians were to kneel before him barefoot and beg forgiveness with the whole city looking on. Ha! What a humiliation! Most submitted, if reluctantly, and paraded to the howls of delight of twenty thousand people. Some fled the city; three were captured the same day, dragged back, and beheaded on the spot."

"I remember," Goddert almost purred. "It was a day of rejoicing."

"Then, Fox-cub," Jaspar went on, unmoved, "in May, shortly before you came back, the patricians brought charges against the new magistrates, demanding they be removed from office. Conrad was diplomatic. He promised justice, convened a hearing, and tried to reach a compromise. But the patricians insisted on a clear verdict. In the meantime the guilds had gathered, armed to the teeth. The patricians responded immediately. Banners unfurled, they marched to the archbishop's palace because they suspected Conrad— possibly with justification—of inciting the craftsmen against them. They set up two barricades, one in Rheingasse and another outside St. Columba's. Conrad called out his armed guard and it almost came to a pitched battle. Thank God it didn't. Conrad sent envoys to the Rheingasse barricade offering an unarmed meeting in the palace to discuss terms and claiming those at the St. Columba barricade had accepted. They used the same ploy at St. Columba's."

"Not exactly honest."

"But it worked. Conrad promised the patricians safe conduct. The patricians, in good faith, appeared unarmed and were immediately fallen upon by Conrad's men. Twenty-four were arrested and imprisoned, others fled the city. Conrad invited them to a meeting, but of course they weren't so stupid as to believe him a second time. Nor did he want them to. It gave him a good reason to outlaw them. Which he did, with the pope's blessing. And that is the situation at the moment."

Jacob went through it in his mind. A thought occurred to him. "Can the patricians expect Conrad to pardon them?"

Jaspar shook his head. "Unlikely. A few weeks ago I heard that the prisoners in Godesberg Castle had laid their distress before him and begged him to free them. His response was to impose stricter conditions of imprisonment. I believe Conrad receives almost daily pleas from the patricians to pardon those banished or imprisoned, but the failure of the request from those in Godesberg seems to have disheartened them."

"Or not, as the case may be," said Jacob deliberately.

Jaspar's head came up and he gave him a keen look. "The alliance?"

"Yes. Kuno didn't say when the meeting at which they formed the alliance was, but it must have been soon after the failure of the appeal from Godesberg."

"Well, well, well, is this my Fox-cub who knows nothing?"

Jacob shrugged his shoulders. "You've been going on about history so much, you've missed the answer to the question. I've just seen it."

"What do you mean?"

Jacob couldn't repress a smug grin. His little triumph of having beaten Jaspar to the solution was all he had at the moment, but he was determined to make the most of it. "Isn't it obvious?" he asked.

Jaspar put his head on one side. "I assume it ought to be obvious."

"Clear as the waters of the Rhine. The patricians are going—"

There was a faint but unmistakable scratching sound from the front door.

"Shh," ordered Jaspar.

They listened. All they could hear was the howling of the wind and the drumming of the rain. "It must have been the storm," said Richmodis. Her voice quivered slightly.

"No," whispered Jaspar, "that wasn't the wind. He's outside."

Jacob closed his eyes and focused all his concentration on the spot outside the door. Over the years he had of necessity learned to register every noise, every minor detail.

There it was again. Scratching. Rustling.

Then something scraped along the wall of the house. Soft, cautious steps. More scratching on the wall, higher up this time.

Goddert put his hands over his mouth and looked at them one after the other, goggle-eyed. "Oh, God," he said, half choked.

Jacob could feel his heart pounding somewhere just below his jaw. It was the same feeling as a few days ago when he was hiding in the little church watching through a tiny window the shadowy figure that was searching for him, that seemed to scent him, so that, on impulse, he had poured the holy water over himself. Figures appeared in his mind unbidden: Maria, Tilman, Rolof, and— He forced himself to stay calm. The others were looking at him expectantly, fear in their eyes, every one of them.

"Yes," he said, "Urquhart's outside."

JOHANN

The night watchmen, their voices torn by the wind, had long since called eleven o'clock, but Johann was still sitting in his study, watching the candle burn down.

The group had originally intended to spend this night together. That decision seemed years ago now. Daniel had withdrawn, Theoderich, too, Heinrich von Mainz had ridden home, and Matthias had not returned. By now any idea that they were bound by a common cause seemed absurd to Johann.

"It is right," he murmured.

But was it? The words seemed to mock him. What was right about killing people? What was right was the common goal, the sacrifices they had made. But what kind of goal was it?

He tried to recover his former clarity of vision, but he could not. He felt weary and confused, incapable of saying what they actually hoped to achieve.

And yet there had been a time when it was clear to all. Each one of them had sworn an oath because each one believed in the justness of their cause.

The cause.

He realized that for days now they had just spoken of "the cause." They never mentioned the actual purpose. There were certain words they avoided, as if they didn't want to be associated with them. They were like naughty children who keep their eyes shut tight and think no one can see them.

The cause.

There had been a common goal. Such a clear, unmistakable goal they had all accepted it without regard for their own interests.

Johann could not repress a laugh, then pressed his knuckles to his lips. Had Matthias ever done anything that ran counter to his own interests? Or Daniel? Heinrich von Mainz, at least. And Kuno!

But no, Kuno was about to betray them all. If he hadn't done so already.

Theoderich? Perhaps, but—

Johann jumped up and began to pace up and down feverishly. They had lost sight of their goal. He would never be able to sleep easily again, his peace of mind was gone. There must be some kind of justification, some absolution. What they were doing was not for themselves, but for some higher purpose.

He leaned his hands on his desk and looked inside himself.

All he saw was blackness.

THE ATTACK

"Has he gone?" asked Richmodis after a while.

"We should have put out the candle," said Goddert. There were fine beads of sweat on his brow.

Jacob shook his head. "Too late. Pointless anyway."

"I can't hear anything at all."

Jaspar placed his finger on the tip of his nose. "Does that mean he's simply given up?"

"I don't know," said Jacob.

Richmodis looked at the door. "He doesn't give up," she said softly. "He'll never give up."

"Even so, nothing much can happen to us." Goddert clenched his fists. "It's a strong house, doors and shutters barred from inside. He'd need a battering ram."

"Perhaps he's brought one."

"Nonsense."

Jacob was still listening but could not hear anything apart from the storm. Still his feeling of unease was growing. It wasn't like Urquhart to leave things undone.

"He doesn't need a battering ram," he whispered. "He's much worse without one."

"What could he do?" Jaspar wondered.

"The back door!" Richmodis exclaimed.

"What?"

"I heard it clearly. He's at the back door."

Goddert shook his head vigorously. "He can't get in there. I barred it myself, even the Devil himself couldn't get in."

"How did he get around the back?" asked Jaspar. "Over the roof?"

"How else?" replied Jacob.

Goddert looked at him in dismay.

"I've escaped over the roofs once or twice myself," Jacob explained. "If Urquhart climbed up the front—"

"It's a very narrow, very sharp roof," declared Goddert, as if that settled matters.

"So what? It would be no problem for me, even less for him."

Goddert wiped the sweat from his brow. "Still," he said, "there's nowhere he can get in."

Kuno gave a quiet groan.

There were no more sounds from the back door.

They waited.

After a while Jacob began to relax. "Looks as if he really has gone."

"I find that hard to believe."

Jaspar scratched his chin and went into the kitchen. When he came back he looked less worried. "Everything secure." He sat down beside Jacob and patted him on the shoulder. "Come on, Fox-cub, you were about to tell us something. The answer to the question from your very lips. I can't wait to hear it."

Jacob nodded, but his mind wasn't really on it. There was something he'd forgotten, something important—

"Goddert?" he whispered.

"Hmm?"

"Very quietly now. You shut everything?"

"Of course! How often do I—"

"Is there a skylight?"

Goddert stared at him. The color drained from his face. "Oh, my God!"

Jacob seemed to feel the floor tremble beneath his feet. "Take it easy," he whispered. "We've got to think of something. Urquhart's in the house already."

"But what?"

"Just keep talking as normal. Go on. About anything."

"Oh, God! Oh, God!"

Jaspar cleared his throat noisily. "If you ask me, Goddert," he said in a loud voice, his eyes fixed on Jacob, "the bastard won't be back. He'll have realized we know how to protect ourselves."

"Perhaps he got afraid and ran away," agreed Richmodis in firm tones.

Jacob wasn't listening. He was thinking feverishly. Opposing Urquhart with sheer strength was pointless. He was stronger than all of them put together and he'd be armed. He was probably sitting in the loft now, his tiny crossbow ready.

At the top of the stairs, between the parlor and the kitchen, a black rectangle yawned in the ceiling. Was he up there, listening? Would he attack immediately or keep them in suspense, wearing them down? But they were at the end of their tethers already.

For a moment Jacob thought about creeping up the stairs and facing him.

In your dreams, he told himself. Urquhart will kill you the moment your fiery mane appears in the hatchway.

Fiery mane! An idea occurred to him. He gave Goddert's sleeve a little tug. Goddert's head swung around. He looked as if he was close to cracking up. Jacob placed a finger to his lips. "Have you any lamp oil?" he asked softly.

"Whaaat?"

"Lamp oil, dammit. Or any oil. A jugful."

In bewilderment Goddert looked from Jacob to Jaspar. The dean and Richmodis were desperately trying to make normal conversation.

"Y-yes, there's a jug under the kitchen seat."

"Fetch it."

Goddert went even whiter and looked up toward the open hatch at the top of the steps. Jacob rolled his eyes and patted him on the cheek. "That's all right."

It was all a matter of luck now. He fervently hoped God would grant him just a few seconds, nothing really, just the few seconds he needed to fetch the jug. He had to pass underneath the opening in the ceiling. If Urquhart put a bolt through him, then it was all over. Jaspar was a powerful intellect, but physically he was no more a match for Urquhart than Goddert. And Richmodis might put one over on a drunken patrician, but that was all.

Lord, he thought, I don't pray to you as often as I should. Thank you for all the apples I managed to steal. Have mercy on me. Just one more time.

Have mercy on Richmodis.

"I'll get us something to drink," he said, loud and clear.

"Good idea," Jaspar cried.

He threw his shoulders back and went to the kitchen, forcing himself not to look up. Fear sent shivers of ice down his spine. There was no candle burning in the back room; it was pretty dark. He gave himself a painful knock on the edge of the table. The bench was by the window.

Jacob bent down and felt for the jug. His fingers touched something round and cool. He brought it out and smelled it. Oily. Just what he was looking for.

"I've got the wine," he shouted to those in the front room. "Was under the bench. Empty those mugs, here I come."

"They're empty already," squawked Richmodis. Her voice was too shrill.

He's noticed, thought Jacob in panic. He knows we know—

With an effort he stopped his hand trembling and strolled back, deliberately taking his time. The hatch yawned above him like the gate to hell. When he passed underneath it for the second time, his legs almost gave way, but he made it. His tongue was sticking to the roof of his mouth by the time he sat down beside Jaspar, put the jug in his hands, and whispered a few words to him. Then he picked up a piece of firewood, went over, and held it to the flames.

Richmodis and Goddert watched him, baffled. Jacob pointed silently to the ceiling and tried to work out the likelihood of his plan succeeding. Richmodis and Goddert were on the street side, therefore not in the way. Jaspar, opposite him, had stood up, clutching the jug and still chatting away. Kuno was on the fireside bench, next to the doorway to the back room and therefore closest to the hatch, but he was asleep.

It might work.

Come on, thought Jacob, where are you? Don't keep us waiting. Show yourself.

"What if he didn't—" Goddert said timidly. His hand was on the hilt of the sword, but his fingers were trembling so much that he wouldn't be able to hold it for a second.

"Shut up," hissed Jaspar.

Jacob frowned.

He suddenly felt unsure. What if Goddert was right and they were standing here like idiots for no reason? Perhaps Urquhart had decided to leave them to stew in their own juice until he'd carried out the main plan. He knew they wouldn't leave the house before it was light. Did he really know that? And who said he knew where they were hiding anyway? Even that wasn't certain. Richmodis had heard something at the back door, but it could have been the wind. And the steps outside the house? What had made him so certain it was Urquhart? Perhaps it was one of the night watchmen. Or just a dog.

Time passed at a snail's pace.

Kuno mumbled something and opened his eyes. They were unnaturally bright. The fever must have risen considerably. He leaned on his elbows.

Jacob signaled to him not to move, but Kuno didn't seem to see him. He slowly sat up and stretched out his hand as if trying to grasp something. His face was gleaming with sweat.

"Gerhard?" he asked.

"Keep down," Jacob whispered.

"Gerhard!"

With surprising nimbleness Kuno slipped off the bench and staggered to his feet. He was right in the doorway. His gaze was unfocused.

"Gerhard!" he howled.

"Away from there!" Jacob shouted. He ran over to Kuno and grabbed him by the arm to drag him away. Kuno's head whirled around. His eyes and mouth were wide open. His hands shot out and grabbed Jacob's shoulders in a viselike grip. Jacob desperately tried to free himself, but Kuno seemed not to recognize him. With the strength of madness, he held him in a grip of steel, all the time bellowing Gerhard's name until his voice cracked.

It all happened very quickly.

Jacob saw something large and black emerge from the opening and heard a snapping noise. An expression of immense astonishment appeared on Kuno's face and it was a moment before Jacob realized where the arrowhead came from that suddenly stuck out of Kuno's wide-open mouth. Then Kuno sagged, slumped into him, and pulled him to the floor.

The blazing brand slipped out of his grip and rolled away over the floorboards.

"Jaspar!" he shouted.

Urquhart appeared in his field of vision. He had a brief view of the murderer's face.

It was completely expressionless.

With a whoop, Jaspar swung the jug. The oil poured over Urquhart, who spun around and hit Jaspar with a blow that sent him flying across the room like a doll, crashing into Richmodis. Jacob had to use all his strength to push Kuno's body to one side and saw Goddert, in what must have been the bravest moment of his life, hurl himself at Urquhart, brandishing the sword in his right hand. His arthritic fingers were clenching the hilt as if no power on earth could loosen them.

Urquhart grabbed his wrist.

Goddert was panting. They stood, face-to-face, motionless as statues, while Richmodis tried in vain to push Jaspar's body off her and Jacob feverishly looked for the brand.

Goddert's eyes had a strange expression, a mixture of fury, determination, and pain. His panting turned into a groan.

"Father," Richmodis shouted. "Let go of the sword."

Urquhart's features did not register the slightest emotion. Goddert gradually slumped.

Where was that blasted brand?

There! Under the bench. In a trice Jacob was there, pulled it out, and rolled over on his back.

"Father!" Richmodis screamed again.

She had struggled free of Jaspar and now threw herself at Urquhart. Jacob saw the crossbow raised and felt his heart freeze to ice.

"No," he gasped.

Then he remembered there couldn't be a bolt in it. The next moment the bow hit Richmodis on the forehead and flung her back. Urquhart was standing like a tree trunk in the middle of the room, his fingers still locked around Goddert's wrist.

"Jaspar," Goddert whimpered. The sword slowly fell from his grip.

Jacob heard the crack of Goddert's bone at the same moment as he flung the burning brand. As it flew through the air, it hit the falling sword, which sent it spinning against Urquhart's cloak.

The oil blazed up straightaway.

Stunned, Urquhart stared at Jacob, as the flames began to envelop him. Not a sound came from his lips. The next moment he was a pillar of fire.

A pillar of fire that was rushing toward him.

Jacob's heart missed a beat. Two burning arms were stretched out. He felt them grasp him and lift him up. His own clothes started to burn. Jacob screamed, then his back was smashed against the closed window, again and again and again. He felt as if everything inside him were shattering into tiny pieces, but it was just the shutters he could hear bursting as the wood gave way under the violence of the onslaught. He shot through in a cloud of sparks and splinters, plummeting into the mud of the street.

The rain lashed at his face. He gasped for breath and looked up into a sky shot with lightning as Urquhart jumped over him.

Laboriously he rolled over onto his stomach. The blazing figure was hurtling straight toward the stream in the middle of the street. There was a splash and it disappeared.

Jacob crawled on all fours through the mud, got to his feet, and stumbled on. He'd drown him. Hold him underwater until he was dead. If it was possible to kill the monster, he would.

He knelt down where the human torch had been extinguished by the water. Dipping his hands into the dirty brown current, he felt everywhere.

"Where are you?" he panted. "Where are you?"

Nothing.

He searched like a man possessed, pulling himself this way and that on his elbows. He didn't see the doors open, a crowd appear, shouting curious questions, waving candles. He didn't see Jaspar come out, unsteady on his feet and with a bloody nose, to reassure them. He didn't see Richmodis, her arm around the trembling Goddert. All he saw was the water.

Even when it had become clear Urquhart had escaped, he kept blundering angrily on until exhaustion brought him to a halt.

Breathing heavily, he raised his hands and howled up at the heavens.

His cry was lost in the raging storm.

14 September

✠

AFTER MIDNIGHT

Jacob, dripping wet, was sitting on the fireside bench watching as Goddert's arm was put in a makeshift splint. He felt wretched, tired, and useless.

Goddert moaned softly, but he bore his injury bravely, almost with a hint of pride. The neighbors had gotten the nearest surgeon out of bed. He was more familiar with bone setting than Jaspar and was examining Goddert with a professional air, while Jaspar dealt with the large cut on Richmodis's forehead. It looked worse than it was. Apart from his bloody nose and an impressive bump, Jaspar was uninjured.

It was Jacob who was a minor miracle. He ought to have been dead, or at least had most of the bones in his body broken. He certainly felt half dead, and the fact that he had escaped with numerous bruises, grazes, and slight burns he owed solely to the state of Goddert's shutters, which were more rotten than the bones of the Three Kings.

He put his head to one side and looked around. Where the window had been a gap yawned, through which the wind whistled. Even before the neighbors had appeared, Richmodis had managed to get water from the well in the backyard to put out the fires that were flaring up. The room looked like the aftermath of a Tartar attack, overturned furniture and scorch marks everywhere.

Kuno's body was stretched out across the floor. Jacob tried to feel sorry for him but couldn't. Everything had been too much. Only his immense relief that Richmodis was safe and sound told him that he was not completely burned out inside.

There was a throng gathered outside and inside the house. They all wanted to know what had happened and Jaspar never tired of repeating his story of the mysterious crossbow murderer who, as everyone knew, had been at large in the town during the last few days. And that Kuno, a friend, well, more of an acquaintance really, should have sought refuge from the storm on this night of all nights—no, he had no idea where Kuno had been before, hadn't asked, and now it was too late, God have mercy on his soul.

Jacob didn't understand why Jaspar didn't tell the whole story, but for the moment he couldn't really care. A bowl of hot soup appeared under his nose. Bewildered, he looked up. A middle-aged woman was regarding him with sympathetic concern. "You must be frozen stiff," she said.

Jacob stared at her, uncomprehending. How long had he been sitting here? How long since—

"Are you all right?"

"What?"

"There's some soup."

"Oh—oh, thank you." He managed a smile for her, took the bowl, and set it to his lips. It was hot and did him good. It tasted of beef and vegetables. Only now did he realize how hungry he was. Greedily he emptied the bowl and held it up for the woman to take, but she had disappeared.

There was a stir outside. "The magistrates are coming," someone shouted. Magistrates? Oh, yes, Jaspar had sent someone to wake the magistrates. Had he not specifically said they should bring Bodo Schuif, the brewer?

Jacob's head was spinning; he wasn't sure of anything anymore. All he could think was that Urquhart had gotten away—he hadn't been able to drown him.

He wondered how badly injured Urquhart was. When the murderer had picked him up and rammed him against the window, he had instinctively closed his eyes against the heat. Everything had happened so quickly.

Perhaps Urquhart had gotten away with a fright and no more. Jacob wasn't even convinced it was possible to frighten Urquhart at all. His every action, even when he was enveloped in flames, indicated the workings of a coldly rational mind. Jaspar and Richmodis he had knocked to the ground; Goddert's arm was broken. When the oil blazed up he had immediately grabbed the only one who might present a danger and had used him as a battering ram to smash his way out.

And he appeared to have escaped with his crossbow. It was nowhere to be found.

He put down the empty bowl and went to join Jaspar and Richmodis. At that moment Bodo Schuif pushed his way through the bystanders and glanced around the room. He took in Goddert and the surgeon, Jaspar, Richmodis, and Jacob. Then his eye fell on Kuno. "Holy Mother of God," he mumbled.

"We were attacked—" Jaspar began.

Bodo nodded toward the door. "Outside. We have to talk."

Jaspar gave him a baffled look, shrugged his shoulders, and followed Bodo out into the street. Jacob hesitated a moment, then hurried after them.

"What've you been up to, for God's sake?" he heard Bodo asking Jaspar in vehement tones. He looked around, saw Jacob approaching, and waved him away.

"It's all right," Jaspar said. "He can hear everything."

Bodo scrutinized Jacob dubiously. "Let's go somewhere a bit quieter," he said. "Quick."

They went far enough away so no one could hear them. The wind had died down. Now there was only the rain and Jacob had stopped noticing that.

"I don't know what I'm going to do with you," Bodo barked at Jaspar. "I really don't. Tell me it's not true."

"None of us knew that monster, Bodo. He came over the roof. I've no idea what he was after, he—"

"That's not what this is all about. Dammit, Jaspar, I ran here as fast as I could. They're coming to arrest you, d'you hear? They're going to throw you in the Tower."

"Who?" Jaspar was flabbergasted.

"Theoderich Overstolz."

For a moment even Jaspar was speechless.

"How do you know?" he gasped.

"How do you know, how do you know! Is that all you're worried about? The constables had already gotten me out of bed before Goddert's neighbors turned up. I was supposed to go and meet Theoderich Overstolz in Severinstraße. They said that, following information received, your house had been searched and a dead body found. They also said you were responsible, you'd slit open the poor bugger's belly! Then these people turned up"—Bodo gestured in the general direction of the Brook—"and told me about all the fuss here, and again it was your name that was mentioned. For God's sake, Jaspar, it won't take Theoderich long to find out you're here. Now tell me what's been going on."

"Listen, Bodo," said Jaspar, as calmly as he could. "You've known me for ages. Am I the kind of man to go around slitting people's bellies open?"

"Of course not. I wouldn't be here otherwise."

"Do you remember I hinted yesterday morning that Gerhard Morart's death might not have been an accident?"

"What's that got to do with all this?"

"It would take me so long to explain, I might as well go and present myself at the Tower. It's got everything to do with it, take my word for it."

Bodo looked around nervously. "You'll have to tell me more if I'm to help you."

"You'll help us? Excellent!"

"I'll help *you*," said Bodo. "Who else?"

"Jacob here. Richmodis and Goddert. We need time."

"And how do you think you're going to get that?"

"Did Theoderich's people say anything about Richmodis or Goddert being involved?"

"Nonsense. It's just you they want. What would your relatives have to do with it?"

"All the better. Then you can do something for us. Jacob and I, we need somewhere to hide."

"Somewhere to hide?" Bodo echoed in surprise. "Just a moment, I—"

"I was thinking of Keygasse. Your brewery."

"But—"

"Now. Right away. No time to lose. Do we need a key or is somewhere open?"

"Are you out of your mind?" Bodo hissed. "When I said help, I meant I'd put in a good word for you."

"Good words are no use to us."

"Christ Almighty, Jaspar!" said Bodo despairingly. "Do you know what you're asking? If it comes out that I hid a suspected murderer, I can say good-bye to my position as magistrate."

"Yes, and you can say good-bye to your head, too. Do it anyway. Anything else would be a mistake."

Bodo gasped and held his head, as if to make sure it stayed there. "Oh, damnation!" he said.

"The keys," Jaspar repeated.

"Infernal damnation!"

"It won't help, however often you repeat it. I give you my word I didn't murder my servant. There's a foul plot going on, people have died, and someone's going to be the next if we don't stop it." He gave Bodo a meaningful look. "It might even be you."

"Me? Saints preserve us, why me?"

"Because Gerhard Morart was murdered," Jaspar whispered, "and because so far hardly anyone who knew has lived long enough to tell the tale. Now you know, too."

Bodo shook his head in disbelief.

"Quick," Jaspar urged. "Make up your mind what you're going to do, but do it!"

Bodo looked at Jacob as if he could release him from the nightmare he had blundered into. Jacob shrugged his shoulders. "Jaspar's right," he said.

Bodo's oath made the air turn blue. "I don't believe it. Here I am and—oh, bugger it! The shed next to the brewery is open. There are no barrels in it at the moment, so the dogs won't bite you. But Jaspar"—he held his fist under Jaspar's nose—"you're gone by tomorrow morning. I don't care what you do then."

Jaspar threw out his arms and, to his friend's surprise, embraced the brewer.

"And if you're having me on"—Bodo's muffled voice came from the folds of Jaspar's habit—"I'll string you up with my own hands, and that carrot-top sidekick of yours."

"Thank you, my friend."

"Is that clear?"

Jaspar gave Jacob a quick glance. "What was that nice turn of phrase you had? Clear as the waters of the Rhine. Bodo, if anyone asks, we escaped just as you were about to arrest us. Keep an eye on Goddert and Richmodis, won't you, and tell Richmodis we're safe. Keep a good eye on them."

"Of course." Bodo sighed. "Of course. And I'll carry the cathedral across the Rhine and find a wife for the pope. I must be out of my mind. You'd better clear off, before I change it."

They trotted off, not looking around once.

Some time later, just after they had passed the convent of the White Sisters and were approaching Keygasse, Jaspar turned to Jacob and said, "Just while we get our breath back, what do you think the patricians are going to do, Fox-cub?"

Jacob looked at him. "Isn't it obvious? Kill the archbishop."

RHEINGASSE

Somewhere a cock crowed.

"Too soon," muttered Johann.

He had crept up to Blithildis's room, torn between the desire to wake her up and fear of what she would say. She was asleep. Or appeared to be. She hadn't said a word nor moved when he came in, but that didn't necessarily mean anything. Often she sat listening; she could hear things in the quietness that were hidden from others. She had the gift of going inside time and hearing things. The future became the past and the past the future.

Once his eyes had adjusted to the darkness, he could observe her face. It looked more like a death mask than ever. He felt no terror at this, only sadness that God let her suffer instead of taking her to Him.

He did not want to lose her, yet he would be happy for her to be reborn in Christ, to find peace.

Or was it his own peace he hoped to find when she was taken from them?

Their goal. The cause.

It was Blithildis's idea. After Conrad had imposed stricter conditions on the imprisoned patricians it was obvious to everyone that he would never pardon them as long as he lived. And Conrad von Hochstaden was tough. His seal, showing him with God's hand poised in blessing above his head, was a reflection of his inordinate self-esteem, and he had made no secret of his profound hatred of the patricians. He was not concerned with justice. He had made an example of them as a demonstration of his power, to show anyone who challenged his authority what they could expect.

That evening Blithildis had remonstrated with them for celebrating. "How can you celebrate," she had said, "when our people go in fear of their lives, in exile or rotting away in cold, damp dungeons? How can these costly wines not turn to vinegar on your tongues when that ungodly archbishop is depriving the noble houses of their liberties, cheating them out of their privileges, plundering them, breaking his word, and dragging everyone's honor through the mud? How can you let them numb your senses when the once proud city of Cologne is being turned into a sink of fawning and treachery, ruled by fear? How can you congratulate yourselves on your business deals when no one dare speak his mind openly anymore for fear Conrad might have him taken and executed on the spot?"

She had shamed them all, then pursued her reflections to their logical conclusion. If Conrad were to die, everything would change overnight. The exiles and prisoners could return home. A new, stable order would be set up in Cologne, a patrician order, in which everyone had their place and which a new archbishop would be powerless to prevent. Did people not say that Conrad, despite his show of authority, was the last hope of the

Church in Cologne? If he did not succeed in restoring the old power of the archbishops, no successor would.

That evening the chance gathering had been molded by Blithildis into an alliance, whether they wanted it or not. They had all, apart from Gerhard, been carried away. The patricians would triumph! Yes, they had made mistakes, but you could learn from mistakes. It was a cause worth fighting for. It was even a cause worth killing an archbishop for.

At least it had been. But what was right?

"I can hear your breathing," Blithildis whispered.

So she had been awake. Was it his imagination, or did her voice sound weaker than usual?

Johann tensed. "And what does it tell you?"

"That you're still worrying."

He nodded. It was strange. He always behaved as if she could see him.

"Things have happened, Mother," he said. "You've been asleep. Matthias has been to see Urquhart. The hostage has escaped and it looks as if we have problems with Kuno as well."

"Kuno is nothing," replied Blithildis. "I know you're worrying whether the cause—"

Johann corrected her. "You mean murdering Conrad."

She paused and stuck her chin out. Her nostrils flared, as if she could smell his thoughts.

"—whether the justified execution of that whore of an archbishop will be successful. I have been praying, Johann, not sleeping, and the Lord has heard my prayer. Conrad will die, as we agreed."

For a while Johann was silent.

"Mother," he said hesitantly, "I've been thinking. Sometimes, when God wants to test our faith, he leads us astray. He clouds our thought and blinds us to the truth. We lose sight of our goal and fall victim to powers that would corrupt us. But we do not see the corruption, we take it for the expression of the Divine, just as the Israelites did when they asked Aaron to make them gods of gold. I believe it was not so much pride as uncertainty and fear that led them to make the Golden Calf. Sometimes I think they were not worthy to receive God's Commandments. Even before that they were not really following the Lord, but another golden calf by the name of Moses. But this Moses was alive, he was—at least he was someone, a personality, and he had an inner flame. The calf, on the other hand, merely glittered and Moses was right to burn it. But who knows, perhaps even without Moses they would eventually have realized that the calf could not keep them together because it was only a hollow piece of metal, lacking meaning, lacking everything that can raise men, in humility and selflessness, up to the true God. They would have realized that as soon as they became disunited, and if they had been asked then who their god was, each would have given a different answer, the one that suited them best."

He paused. Blithildis did not move.

"They would have seen that they were not following a common god," he went on, "that each had his own idea of God, different from that of all the others. They would have seen that everything they had done in the name of that god was therefore wrong. Wrong and sinful."

"You think what we are doing is wrong?" she asked bluntly.

"I don't know. I mean, in whose interest are we acting? I have come to find out whether we are following God or a golden calf. Is there a common goal uniting us, a valid goal? I have never doubted you, Mother, but—"

"Then let us pray together," she said in an almost voiceless tone. "Let us pray that Conrad will not survive the coming day. He has humiliated us before the whole of Christendom. Our house should shine in glory and splendor, not suffer exile and imprisonment. The fame of our holy city should be our fame, not that of priests and a brutal tyrant who has stolen our wealth and our property. I had hoped to end my life a proud woman able to show her pride but, thanks to Conrad, I sit here like a lost soul. He has cast me down and for that I pray that hell will devour him and that Satan and all his demons will torment him until the apocalypse. Then let him burn and his soul be consigned to oblivion."

She paused, her chest heaving. Her bony fingers were clutching the arms of her chair like claws. Gradually she relaxed and turned to Johann.

In the darkness he saw a faint smile cross her face, a face no longer made for smiling.

"Your father died so young," she said.

Johann was silent.

There was a finality in her words that left no room for reply. He looked at her and suddenly realized that revenge was all Blithildis had lived for. She was the daughter of the founding father of the Overstolz dynasty. She had been part of the glorious rise of the house, had inherited boundless self-confidence, been the very image of good fortune. But then fortune had abandoned her. Thirty years ago the husband she loved had died. Her soul had withered, her eyes lost their sight, and now the house in Rheingasse, the magnificent symbol of Overstolz greatness, looked with empty windows out onto a different Cologne and a different glory that mocked her.

There had never been a common goal. Neither Matthias nor Daniel, Hermann nor Theoderich, certainly not Blithildis and not even Kuno had sought higher justice. Daniel wanted to kill Conrad out of personal resentment for the loss of the position of magistrate. Matthias had been a magistrate, too, but all he was interested in were his trading enterprises, which required different policies from Conrad's. Theoderich was an opportunist who would jump on any bandwagon. Kuno's interest was his brothers, and his brothers wanted to return, that was all. Heinrich von Mainz was interested in his business, like Matthias; Lorenzo had been bought and Blithildis was obsessed with revenge.

And behind it all was the secret bitterness of the Overstolzes that not they were the first among the leading houses of Cologne, but the Weises. That the Weises, having sold themselves to Conrad, still dominated the *Richerzeche*, the council of the richest families in the city, while the Overstolzes were facing total defeat.

It was not the patricians who were to triumph, it was the Overstolz family. Conrad's end would be the end of the Weises, the end of the decades of conflict between the two houses.

Power at any price.

The alliance had not collapsed. It had never existed. What they had followed was the glitter of a golden calf; what had briefly united them was gold, the gold they had put together to hire a murderer, who was now teaching them a fearful lesson.

Too late to save anyone. Conrad would die, and Jacob the Fox, and Jaspar Rodenkirchen, and all those around them. Things would change, for the better for some, for the worse for others. Johann got up, went over to Blithildis, and put his arms around her. He held the frail body in his gentle embrace for a long time, surprised at how fragile and small it was, almost like a child's.

He gave her a kiss on the forehead and straightened up. "I love you, Mother. You should try to get a little sleep."

She shook her head vigorously. "I won't sleep. I will wait until they come and tell me it is done. I will be happy."

"Yes, Mother," said Johann, with a heavy heart. "You will be. Certainly you will." He closed the door softly behind him and went back to his study.

KEYGASSE

They should have taken a lantern, Jacob thought. In the shed you couldn't see the hand in front of your face. After a certain amount of stumbling around Jaspar discovered a fair-size pile of sacks, presumably for barley, and they sat down on them. They were damp and cold, but that didn't bother either of them particularly.

"Why didn't we think of it sooner?" said Jaspar, his irritation audible.

Now, in the impenetrable darkness, it struck Jacob that Jaspar's voice didn't go with his physical appearance at all. It was powerful and mellifluous, the kind of voice you would have associated with a tall, broad-shouldered man. A man of Urquhart's stature. Then it occurred to him that Jaspar matched Urquhart in stature, only it was a stature not visible to the eye.

"Perhaps we would have thought of it sooner if they hadn't kept trying to kill us," he replied.

"I'm starting to get fed up with this alliance," Jaspar grumbled. "I wouldn't be surprised if Urquhart didn't slit Rolof open for a reason. No one would think I went around shooting crossbows, but I could have stuck a knife in my servant. How convenient to have me thrown into the Tower." He gave a contemptuous snort. "And how inept to make a mess of it. Theoderich is a numskull. Should have waited till he'd gotten his hands on me before telling the world about my supposed crimes."

"That's what I still don't understand," said Jacob. "Why get you taken to court? Surely that would ensure everything came out."

"You think so?" Jaspar gave a humorless laugh. "There would have been no appearance in court. If Theoderich's plan had succeeded, I'd be in the Tower now. Where I might well break my neck before another magistrate saw me. All sorts of things can happen going up the stairs. An unfortunate accident. Or I try to escape and one of the guards draws his knife. A natural reflex. And they do say the odd prisoner dies while being questioned under torture, if the executioner goes a bit too far. But before that I might have got fed up with the red-hot pincers and betrayed you and Goddert and Richmodis. I might even tell them that Bodo Schuif knows. I might betray everyone."

Jaspar fell silent. For a while he might not have been there at all.

"So what now?" Jacob asked.

"Good question."

"Still attack, attack?"

"What else?" It sounded as if Jaspar were getting more and more angry. "I'm trying to work out how Urquhart will have planned it all."

"He'll hardly go for a walk around the archbishop's palace."

"I don't know. I'm coming to think that son of a whore's capable of anything. The thing is, it's almost impossible to get close to Conrad. He's one person who's learned from the past. The murder of Engelbert was only forty years ago. I can't remember ever having seen Conrad in public except surrounded by men in armor."

Jacob thought. "I can't remember ever having seen him."

"Of course. You've only been here a few months."

"Still. When does he show himself?"

"He doesn't."

"And when's the next time he won't show himself?"

It was meant as a joke, and not a particularly good one at that, but Jacob literally heard Jaspar's jaw drop. "You dunderhead, Rodenkirchen!" he exclaimed. "The Crusade! He's going to say mass and then preach the Crusade against the Tartars from the pulpit, as the pope ordered."

Jacob sat up. "When?"

"Tomorrow. No, in a few hours. No wonder Theoderich rushed everything like that. They're worried we might spoil things at the last minute. Their nerves must be in tatters."

Jacob swallowed. "To be honest, mine, too," he said wearily. To crown it all he was to have the honor of saving the archbishop's life. Why not the emperor's? "You should have told Bodo everything," he said. "Perhaps we could have gotten help."

"Should, should! Perhaps you should have told us about the plot against the archbishop a bit sooner, since I've obviously got a turnip on my shoulders. But even then it wouldn't have been a good idea. Theoderich would have gotten us one way or the other."

"Not if we'd run away afterward."

"What'd be the use of that? He'd just seize Richmodis and Goddert. What's this? An attempt on Conrad's life? And what does my fair lady know about it, or that old tub of lard with the twisted hands? To the Tower with them. For questioning. No, Fox-cub, as long as they are just the victims of some mysterious attack, Theoderich will have no excuse for taking them in. And we shouldn't complain. We're not in the Tower yet."

Jacob sighed. "No, we're in an ice-cold shed without the slightest idea where Urquhart will be in a few hours' time."

"Then we'll just have to find out."

"Sure. Any idea how?"

"No. You?"

Jacob lay back on the sacks with his hands behind his head. "I think Urquhart will lie in wait outside the church."

"Not necessarily. Conrad's going to say mass in the central chapel of the new cathedral. He'll deliver his sermon there, too. There are thousands more convenient places he could have chosen, but that's the chapel he wants to be buried in, so...And it'll be the first time mass will be said in the new cathedral. A huge event, therefore. Beforehand there'll be a procession from Priest Gate, along Spormacherstraße, Wappenstickerstraße, et cetera to St. Stephen's, then left down Platea Gallica and past St. Mary's-in-the-Capitol, across Haymarket, left again through Mars Gate and back to the cathedral. It'll take about an hour."

"You think Urquhart'll be waiting somewhere along the route?"

"I think it's possible."

"If Conrad's as cautious as you say, Urquhart won't be able to get very close."

Silence once more.

"What if he doesn't have to?" said Jaspar slowly.

"How do you mean?"

"Well, I would assume Urquhart is an excellent shot, even from a distance. The crossbow is a very accurate weapon, deadly accurate. At least that's what Hieronymus said, and he ought to know. Perhaps distance is Urquhart's big advantage. Something no one's thought of. Just imagine: the archbishop falls to the ground during the procession. Result, chaos. It'll be some time before anyone realizes what has happened, never mind where the bolt came from, even less that the assassin is a good way off—or, rather, was. Urquhart will be on his way before the archbishop hits the ground."

Jacob tried to visualize where Urquhart could get sufficient distance. The narrow streets lined with people, the houses immediately behind them—if anywhere, it had to be Haymarket. But there'd still be too many people between the assassin and the archbishop. And a man with a crossbow would be noticed. Even if he managed—

"A house!" he exclaimed in surprise.

"A house?" Jaspar sounded bewildered. His thoughts had clearly been going in a different direction.

"Urquhart can only get Conrad from higher up. He has to shoot over the heads of the people. He'll be in some building."

"You're probably right," Jaspar agreed reflectively. "But in that case we've a problem. We can hardly search all the houses."

"There is another way," Jacob said hesitantly. He'd have preferred to have kept it to himself. It frightened him.

"Which is?"

It frightened him because he wouldn't be able to run away. As he'd always done. As he did when—

"Come on, Fox-cub."

He breathed out slowly and pulled himself together. "I got us into this mess, so I'll go to the palace and warn Conrad."

For a moment Jaspar was speechless. "Are you out of your mind?"

"No."

"Slowly now. Of course you can try to warn Conrad, only I doubt whether he'll even give you a hearing."

"It's worth a try."

"For God's sake, Fox-cub! Who says that by now the Overstolzes haven't put the word around that you're a thief? We're both of us on the run. If they can pin a murder on me to keep me out of the way, what do you think they'll accuse you of? You stole a guilder, Matthias said. How do you know it's not a hundred, or a thousand by now? You're going to hand yourself over to the archbishop's guards voluntarily, in the hope that they'll believe you? They might just arrest you and throw you in the Tower without further ado. Who's going to trust someone like you?"

Jacob chewed his lower lip. "They'd believe you," he said.

"Yes, they'd believe me. And I'd go if that idiot Theoderich hadn't ruined everything."

Suddenly Jacob was sure Jaspar was on the wrong track. "Jaspar," he said slowly, "what would you be doing at this moment, if you were Theoderich?"

"Looking for us, probably."

"You would? Well, I'd give myself a kick up the backside and do the exact opposite."

"Why did we run aw—" Jaspar suddenly stopped and let out a soft whistle. "I see. Well, bugger me!"

"If Theoderich had got his hands on us, his plan would have worked. But he made a mess of it. His chances of finding us are minimal. If it's made public that you're wanted for Rolof's murder, then someone else is quite likely to arrest you, you'll be taken before different magistrates and he'll not be in control anymore, he'll just have to sit and listen to you spilling the beans on him. Unlike me, you're a respected citizen. They'd be all ears! What would you be doing now, in Theoderich's place?"

Jaspar gave a quiet laugh. "I'd make sure the accusation laid against Jaspar Rodenkirchen was withdrawn as quickly as possible."

"He's probably already done so."

"I'd say there'd been a mistake. Perhaps even that the real murderer had already been caught. Something like that. Damn it all, that's his only chance of getting out of the mess he's got himself into. You're right. What the alliance wants is for no one to bother with us, at least not until Urquhart's done his worst."

"Exactly. For the same reason, I don't think they'll have spread rumors about me. So I can go to the palace and see if they'll listen. If they don't, then it's their funeral—as you might say."

He drew up his knees and tried to sound firm and resolute, but the urge to run away was almost unbearable. He felt the gray chill of fear creeping up his spine, and all at once he knew it wasn't Urquhart or the Overstolzes he wanted to run away from but something quite different, something immensely greater, something that would catch up with him again, as it always had, and he would run away again, keep on running until he ran himself into the grave—

Urquhart was his personal demon. God had created a being for him alone, for his fear, and he had to face up to it if he ever wanted to be free.

"I have no choice," he said. It sounded good. It sounded brave, almost dauntless.

Jaspar said nothing.

"I have no choice," he repeated.

"Fox-cub." Jaspar cleared his throat copiously. "Didn't you tell me I had the choice of helping you or not? Fine words. You think they don't apply to you, too? Of course you have a choice. Everyone has a choice, always. What is there to keep you in Cologne? What's to stop you from simply walking away?"

Could that blasted dean read his thoughts? "And what'll happen to you and Richmodis?"

"That's not important," said Jaspar calmly.

"Of course it's important!"

"Why? Just tell yourself it was all a dream. You might find it a bit difficult at first, but if you try hard enough, Goddert, Richmodis, and I will disappear without a word of complaint into the realm of fiction. As if we were part of a story you'd heard. Delude yourself. Perhaps we are just clowns in a story. You as well! Be a figment of the imagination, Fox-cub. Figments don't have to take responsibility."

"I don't understand what you're getting at."

"I'm getting you to save your life. Run away."

"No."

"Why not?"

"I've had enough of running away," Jacob heard himself say.

There was a rustle of cloth from where Jaspar was. He'd obviously stretched out. Jacob waited for him to say something, but there was no reaction to what he'd said. He gave up.

"All right, Jaspar," he said wearily, "what is it you want to know?"

"Me?" said the dean innocently. "Nothing at all. I don't want to know anything."

They lay there in silence for a while. Jacob listened to his heartbeat. It seemed to get louder and louder until his chest resounded with hammer blows. He suddenly realized he was crying.

He was amazed and happy at the same time. Had he ever shed a tear? He couldn't remember. Overwhelmed with sorrow, flooded with sadness, he yet felt boundless relief. Puzzled and at the same time curious, he abandoned himself to this unknown emotion. And as he sobbed and sniffled, he felt as if his grief were feeding a bright, blazing fire that gradually consumed him, while a new, unknown strength began to throb in his veins. Scenes from an old story, too long repressed, rolled past his mind's eye, and with every image, every sound, every sensation his fear shrank a little more, giving way to the desire for a home.

Jaspar left him to himself.

After what seemed like an eternity, the tears dried up. He stared into the darkness. His heartbeat had slowed down, his breathing was calm and steady. In fact, he didn't feel bad at all.

"Jaspar?"

There was a quiver in his voice. Not a trace of firm resolution left. He didn't care.

"Jaspar, that time I came back—I mean when I was a boy, to my father's house—I told you there was nothing but a smoking ruin left." He paused. "There was something else."

"I know," said Jaspar, unmoved.

"You know about it?" exclaimed Jacob in surprise.

"No, Fox-cub. I know nothing, really—except that you were able to remember everything that happened before that day. Or were willing to remember. Every detail. You were a bright lad. Still are. But then one day you saw the wreckage of a house and took flight. From then on your life seems rather hazy, almost as if it was that of another person. The day before yesterday, when we talked together for the first time, I thought, if he goes on pouring out his memories like this, I'll end up pouring out the whole of my wine cellar. Then everything suddenly ended at a few smoldering timbers, and the rest was sketched in with a couple of strokes. You saw something, didn't you? Something that's been haunting you to this day? You started running away when you turned your back on the burned-down shack and you haven't stopped since. Whatever you've run away from over the years—constables, women, responsibility—basically it's that shack you've been running away from. Even now, if you run away, you'll be running away from that shack."

"How do you know all this? You hardly know me!"

"I know you quite well. I can see others in you, Fox-cub. What was it you saw?"

Jacob sat up slowly and stared at the darkness. But it was something else he saw: countryside, fields, a column of smoke—

"My father and my brother," he said.

"Dead?"

"They were lying outside the shack. It looked as if they'd been cut down. I stood there, quite a way away. I felt unable to take even one step closer. I was too cowardly to go and look them in the face. I was afraid of having their deaths confirmed. I thought if I looked away, forgot everything as quickly as possible, then it wouldn't have happened." He swallowed hard. "I turned around. But just as I looked away, I thought I saw a movement out of the corner of my eye. As if my father had waved to me."

"And still you ran away."

"Yes. I didn't have the courage to go and look. I'll never know whether I ran away from two dead bodies, or whether, in my fear, I left someone to die I could have helped. I didn't want to see if they were dead, so I never saw if they were perhaps alive."

"Do you sometimes have dreams about it?"

"Rarely. When I do, it's the wave I see. Sometimes it's the desperate wave of a dying man, sometimes a mocking farewell from the dead. That's the truth, Jaspar. I left them in the lurch, and I keep on asking myself what would happen if I had the chance to go back and start again."

"No one has that chance."

"I know. But I can't get it out of my mind. I wish I could turn the clock back."

He heard Jaspar scratching his bald head.

"No," said the dean, "that is not a good wish."

"It is. Then it wouldn't have happened."

"You think so? When they wish for things like that people deny their hopes, their convictions, their whole being. It's what indecisive and weak people wish for. Did you know that, for the whole of his life, Abelard never regretted his love for Heloise? He was cruelly punished for it, but given the chance he would always have made the same choice."

"You keep going on about this Abelard," said Jacob.

"I model myself on him," Jaspar replied. "Even though he's been dead for over a hundred years now. Peter Abelard was one of the most outstanding minds France has produced. He was humble before God, yet bold enough, when at the height of his fame, to describe himself as the greatest of all philosophers. They call disputation the clerics' joust—he was unbeaten in it. And he seemed to love making enemies. His belief that mankind possessed free will was diametrically opposed to the teachings of the Mystics. Eventually he fell in love with Heloise, a canon's niece who was his pupil. Forbidden love. There was a series of scandals that concluded with a punitive expedition to his house one night. The canon had him castrated." He gave a soft laugh. "But he could not cut off their love, nor could he stop them being buried beside each other in the end. Abelard never wished he could turn the clock back, and that was the basis of his greatness. Everything was of his own free will."

"My father," Jacob mused, "was always talking about how impotent sinful mankind was. That we had no choice to decide anything for ourselves."

"And that's what you believe, too?"

"No."

"Goddert believes that." Jaspar sighed. "And there are many like him, men who have no real convictions and confuse weakness with faith. He drifts from one view to another, picks up a bit of each, but never the real point, and patches together something out of them he likes to think of as his opinion. Oh, he enjoys an argument. We spend all the day in disputations on everything under the sun, but they never lead anywhere. It's just good fun, concealing the sad fact that Goddert has no real opinion. I know I shouldn't talk about him like that, but he's typical of the unfortunate attitude prevailing today. When people stop forming their own opinions, when they take bits for a whole and don't look for connections, then the world becomes a church with no mortar between the stones. One day it'll collapse spectacularly and people will talk of the coming of the Antichrist, whom Saint Bernard conjured up in vivid words like no one before or since. But the Antichrist is no fiendish destroyer, no horned devil, nor a beast rising from the sea. The Antichrist is a product of the Christians. He is the emptiness behind a faith that knows only inertia and punishment. And he is also the emptiness behind the fatalism you have been sucked into, the emptiness in your life. One could say the Devil's just waiting to take possession of you."

Jacob found Jaspar's words almost physically painful. "Hasn't he already?" he asked. "At our house. Aren't I lost for good?"

"No, you are not!" said Jaspar emphatically. "It's your refusal to accept that life goes on, that you can't change the past, just giving up and running away, that's what the Devil is."

"You mean he doesn't exist?" Jacob shook his head. "Not as a—being?"

"What is devilish is to deny human nature, our ability to reason, our free will, just as the blind persecution of heretics is the work of the devil. There is nothing more arrogant than fanatical humility. But reason without faith is equally devilish and every man who is enslaved, whether to reason or to faith, is blind in his own way. Christendom is being consumed by a war waged by the blind. That is what the Cistercians, what Bernard and William of Saint-Thierry mean when they talk of the impotence of sinful mankind, that we cannot act because, they say, God does not want us to act; because every independent action represents a denial of God's omnipotence and therefore heresy; and because anyone who cannot act can happily be blind, indeed must be, of necessity. But if one were to follow that idea through to its logical conclusion, the blind couldn't undertake anything of their own volition, not send the sighted, or other blind men, to the stake, not wage war, not teach in public; from the point of view of pure logic, they could not even exist. But they do exist, they talk of impotence and exercise power, they preach humility and humiliate others. What weakness of intellect! That, Fox-cub, is the Devil I believe in."

Jacob tried to digest all this. "If that's what the Devil's like," he said slowly, "then who or what is God?"

Jaspar did not answer straightaway, but when he did there was a mild undertone of mockery in his voice. "How should I know who God is?"

"No, I mean—I always thought that God and the Devil, they were—" He was struggling for words.

"You think God and the Devil are persons, in a way?"

"Yes."

"To be honest, I don't know. All I can do is tell you what God is for me, if that's what you're asking. Abelard was of the opinion that we can distinguish between what is sin and what is not. We have a choice. Of course we can't, as you so touchingly put it, turn the clock back. But we can own up to our actions and accept responsibility for them. Do you see what that implies? Everything was made by God, but perhaps not everything is willed by God. Perhaps God's will is that we should use our own willpower, that we should develop His ideas because we *are* His ideas. If God is in everything and we are therefore God, then our impotence would be God's impotence, and that is something which, with the best will in the world, I simply can't imagine. But if God is the creative principle, then, in order to carry out His will, we too must be creative, we must accept responsibility for what we do. God is the alliance between reason and the beauty of faith, what the scholars call reason illumined by faith. He is harmony; He is what connects, not separates, creation; He is creativity proceeding within time. But above all, God is the free will of the whole of creation, which is constantly re-creating itself; He is the free will of each individual. And that means you can still turn back, Jacob. You have faced up to the past. Sins can be forgiven. Forgive yourself. Stop running away, there are people who need you."

There was a soft thrum of rain on the shed. Jacob listened to the sound as if he were hearing it for the first time. He had the feeling he should go out and discover the world anew. "Thank you," he said quietly.

"Don't mention it, Fox-cub. But if you don't mind, I need to sleep for an hour or so."

"Sleep?" Jacob exclaimed in surprise. "Now?"

"Yes. Why not?"

"We have to do something. Urquhart will be—"

"Urquhart will be licking his wounds. It's the middle of the night. Do you want to get Conrad out of his bed? God knows, we need some rest. Don't worry, I'll wake you when it's time."

Uncertainly, Jacob lay down. "I won't get to sleep," he said.

"Pity."

How can I sleep, he thought, after everything that's happened? I'll lie awake, and eventually Jaspar will start snoring and sleep will be even more impossible. We ought to be making use of the time.

His thoughts turned to Richmodis.

I won't get any sleep, he thought.

JACOB

"Wake up!"

Someone was shaking him. For a moment he thought he was under his arch in the Wall, then he sat up. It was still dark, but he vaguely recognized Jaspar's silhouette. He was laughing. "So this is the lad who can't get to sleep?"

"What time is it?"

"The watchman called three o'clock not long ago. The procession starts in two hours, so you have plenty of time to ask for an audience in the archbishop's palace. Then we'll meet between the fourth and fifth hour in Seidenmachergäßchen. It's nice and quiet there on a Sunday morning. Let's say by the city weighhouse."

"Just a moment," said Jacob, rubbing his eyes. "What's all this about meeting? I thought we were going together."

"So did I. But I had an idea while you were sleeping. It's connected with your story. I'm going somewhere else."

"To Goddert's house, perhaps?"

"I'd like to."

"So would I, dammit!"

"But we'd be fools to let ourselves be seen on the Brook at this juncture. Not now. Off you go, and make sure you keep that forest fire you have on your head well covered on your way to the palace."

Jacob stood up and stretched. Tried to, at least. His body was probably black and blue from being hammered against the shutters. "What do you have in mind?" he groaned.

"I'm—" Jaspar patted him on the shoulder. "Tell you later. You know where the weighhouse is?"

"Yes."

"Good. If I don't see you there, I'll assume your mission has been successful and go along to the palace."

"Why can't you tell me where you're going?"

"Because it won't get us anywhere just now and would take too long to explain. Off you go, and keep out of Urquhart's way. He'll be blazing mad at you."

Before Jacob could say anything, Jaspar had taken him by the shoulders and pushed him out into the street. The rain had stopped, but it was still cold. Jacob looked around. There was an oil lamp swinging to and fro outside Bodo's house next to the brewery. Key House opposite was silent. There was no one about.

"Off you go," said Jaspar.

Jacob put his head back and pumped his lungs full of air till they were bursting. Although he was sore all over, he felt as if he had come alive again after a long time. Then he embraced Jaspar, pressing him so tight to his breast something cracked, and gave him a smacking kiss on his bald head. Jaspar stared at him, flabbergasted.

"Not like me." He grinned, then turned and scurried away up Keygasse.

The archbishop's palace, also known as the Hall, was on the southern side of the cathedral precinct, between Dragon Gate and Tollbooth Gate. Built a hundred years ago, it was an imposing, two-story castle with a row of arcades on double columns decorating the opulently furnished hall on the upper floor. That was where Conrad dispensed justice; it was also the place where he had outwitted the patricians when they had come for supposedly unarmed and peaceful discussions.

Conrad's private apartments were to the rear, opposite the cathedral and not visible from the street. There was no point in trying to gain admittance there. Anyone who wanted something from the archbishop had to approach his soldiers and officials, which meant humbly begging audience at the front entrance.

Jacob had avoided the main streets, weaving his way through the narrow alleys like a salamander. There was a chance the patricians were still looking for him and Jaspar, but they couldn't get into every nook and cranny, and that was where Jacob was at home.

He paused for a moment to draw breath. He was at the end of Pützgäßchen, which led into Am Hof, a broad, prestigious street with stately buildings such as the Crown House, where the dukes of Brabant held court when they were in Cologne, and the Klockring, the sheriffs' headquarters. The archbishop's palace was directly opposite. There were lights on in some of the ground-floor windows and the main door was open. A group of men in armor were talking with two night watchmen on horseback. Their muffled voices came to Jacob, but he could not tell what they were saying. With a burst of coarse laughter, the night watchmen spurred their horses and the soldiers withdrew into the building. The double doors screeched and slammed shut.

Cautiously he peered out into the broad thoroughfare. Farther up he saw a few monks scuttle through the darkness into the provost's quarters. There was garbage lying everywhere. Heavy rain, such as that during the night, swept everything the citizens threw into the street down through the steep east side of the city toward the Rhine. And there was nothing the good citizens did not throw into the street. The senses were assaulted by the mixture of the ubiquitous pig dung with an amalgam of rotting vegetable scraps and gnawed bones. Despite that, all appeals to throw everything in the cesspits were ignored, or dismissed with the irrefutable argument that the gold diggers—the local term for the unfortunates who were supposed to empty them—performed their function too rarely.

Jacob decided he had waited long enough. Making sure not a single red hair was sticking out from under his hood, he ran over to the door and knocked loudly.

Immediately a flap slid back and a pair of eyes scrutinized him. Jacob felt his hopes rise. "I have some important information for the archbishop," he said breathlessly.

"What information?"

"A matter of life and death."

"What?"

"For God's sake, just let me in before it's too late."

The flap slid to, then one of the doors opened and Jacob found himself face to face with a man in armor and helmet. There were three more behind him, regarding him with curiosity.

"The Lord be—oh, why bother?" muttered Jacob as he sketched a blessing and hurried inside. The door snapped shut behind him.

He looked around. The entrance was lit by pairs of torches in elaborate holders. At one side a broad stone staircase with a massive stone balustrade led to the upper floor. Between the torches the wall was hung with tapestries representing chimeras and Titans, sphinxes, naiads, and centaurs, beings with snakes' heads and bats' wings, manticores baring their fangs and dwarves with the faces of dogs, cyclops, scaly devils and gorgons, birds with women's heads and werewolves, forming a garland of merry horror around the ecstatic saints with eyes turned to heaven, bodies disfigured by the wounds of martyrdom, hands raised to the angels with their powerful gold-blue-and-turquoise wings and haloes. Above them all was Christ, His right hand raised, His earnest gaze directed straight ahead. The dark eyes appeared to see everything and at the same time into the heart of each and every individual. Jacob trembled. He saw the living God and felt strong, felt new courage well up inside him.

An iron-gloved hand was laid on his shoulder. He turned away from the comforting eyes of Christ and found himself looking into the soldier's.

"What's all this about, monk?" the guard barked.

Monk? Oh, of course.

"I have to speak to the archbishop," Jacob said, against all reason.

The man stared at him, then roared with laughter. The others joined in. "It's not that easy to get to speak to the archbishop, Friar Oaf. Has no one ever taught you to bow your head when you ask for audience?"

"And what have you been taught?" Jacob retorted. "Conrad von Hochstaden is in great danger and you make fun of the messenger who might save his life. Do you want to end up bowing your head on the executioner's block?"

The laughter died away. The soldier scratched his beard, unsure what to do. "What's this danger you're talking about?" he asked.

"Mortal danger!" Jacob cried. "God wither your loins if you don't take me to Conrad this instant."

"I can't take you to His Excellency," the soldier shouted back. "The archbishop is occupied with the preparations for the procession." He gave an indignant snort, then went on more calmly. "But I could call the archbishop's secretary. Would that do?"

Success!

"All right," he said with feigned sullenness, "if that's the best you can do."

The guard nodded and sent two of his comrades up the stairs. Jacob waited, hands clasped behind his back. He didn't know precisely what a secretary was, but it sounded important.

Surprisingly quickly a short, skinny man appeared with the two soldiers at the top of the stairs and descended with mincing steps. A gold chain lay resplendent on his lilac-and-black robe, his hands were in gloves of burgundy leather. A kindly face with watery blue eyes was framed by a fluffy white beard. He came up to Jacob and smiled. When he spoke, Jacob noticed the accent of some Latin country.

"The Lord be with you and with thy spirit."

Jacob sniffed in embarrassment. "Yes. Of course. Definitely."

The secretary put his head to one side. "What can I do for you, my son? I was told you had information for the archbishop, but are unwilling to say what."

"I must talk to him," said Jacob. "The archbishop is in great danger."

"Danger?" The secretary came closer and lowered his voice. "Don't speak so loudly in front of the soldiers, my son. They're loyal, but you never know. Archbishops have occasionally been murdered by their own nephews. Whisper in my ear. Who wants to harm our archbishop?"

Jacob leaned forward and whispered, "Conrad is to be killed today. I don't know if it will be during the procession or the service, but they intend to kill him."

A horrified expression appeared in the secretary's blue eyes. He clapped both hands to his mouth and took a step back. "Who intends to do that?" he breathed.

"The patricians, I'm afraid. There's a conspiracy—"

"Stop!" The secretary gave the guards a suspicious glance. "We can't discuss this here. I am staggered by what you have told me, my son, profoundly shocked. I find it unbelievable. You must tell me everything you know, everything, do you hear?"

"Most willingly."

"After that I will take you to Conrad. Follow me."

He turned around and went up the stairs. Jacob followed. Somewhat amused, he observed the secretary's affected walk. "Peacock" was the word that came to mind. Probably Italian. Bram had often told him how Italian nobles and clerics loved fine materials and had costly hats made of ermine and sable. His eye ran over the slim figure.

He almost fell down the stairs.

Trembling, he clutched the banister and wondered what to do. There must be many rich citizens in Cologne who wore expensive shoes, but so far he had only seen one pair with purple lilies on them.

Now he was seeing them again.

"Excuse me, Herr—er—" he said.

The secretary turned to face him, bathing him in a rosy glow. "My name is Lorenzo da Castellofiore, my son."

Jacob forced a smile to his lips. "Well, Lorenzo da—well, I've just remembered I have to—I have to—"

Lorenzo's eyes went on the alert. "Yes, my son? What is it?"

"My horse. I think I forgot to tether it. If you wouldn't mind waiting a moment, I'll just pop outside and—"

Lorenzo's expression froze. "Guards," he shouted, "arrest this man."

Jacob's eyes darted to the bottom of the stairs. The soldiers came on the double, swords unsheathed. For a moment he was completely at a loss. Impossible to get past the guards, and even if he did, he'd have to unbolt the door, and by the time he'd—

He swung around and slammed his elbow into Lorenzo's stomach. With a strangled cry, the secretary doubled up. Jacob grabbed him and pushed him at the soldiers. Then, without waiting to see the result, he took the last steps two at a time as the staircase echoed to the crash and clank of armor and Lorenzo's high-pitched screams.

In front of him was a corridor that ended in a wall some way ahead. On the left were two openings. Jacob hesitated for a moment, clearly long enough for the guards to get back to their feet, for he could hear them clattering up the stairs.

Without further thought he ran through one of the openings.

"Catch him," Lorenzo roared with all his might. "That bloody gang, that bunch of misbegotten layabouts! Your mother should have drowned the lot of you at birth. He mustn't escape."

Jacob did a pirouette and his eyes popped. He was in an immense, magnificent room with carved beams and pillars. The far end was entirely taken up with huge stalls of polished black wood. The floor was covered with an elaborate maze of inlay work, while the opposite wall was broken by a long balcony with trefoil windows, the middle part of which was open.

The arcades. He was in the Hall.

The soldiers appeared in the doorways, brandishing their swords menacingly, followed by a very-red-in-the-face Lorenzo. Jacob desperately looked for another way out, but there was none, only the arcade windows, and they were too high to jump down into the street. He fell back and saw the triumph in Lorenzo's eyes.

"The man who stole a guilder from Matthias Overstolz," he hissed. "How nice of you to come to see us. Better surrender if you don't want us to spread your stinking corpse all over the room. What do you think?"

The guards approached. Jacob stumbled and looked down. A jump after all? But it was too high. He'd only break his legs.

There was something rising up outside the arcades, branching out.

A tree.

He let his shoulders droop and nodded resignedly. "You've won, Lorenzo. I'll come with you."

The soldiers relaxed. Their swords sank. Lorenzo grinned. "A wise decision, my son."

"Yes," said Jacob, "I hope so." He spun around and was at the window in one leap. Lorenzo shrieked. Jacob jumped up onto the balustrade. The street yawned below. The tree was farther away than he had thought.

Too far. He wouldn't make it.

"Go on," Lorenzo shouted, "get him. You're letting him escape."

Will it never end? Jacob groaned to himself.

He bent his knees and sprang. He sailed out of the arcades and over the street. For one wonderful moment he felt light as a feather, free as a bird, as free from gravity as an angel. Then he crashed into the boughs with a snapping of twigs.

Branches tore at his face and limbs. He tried to find something to hold on to, to arrest his fall, but he just kept falling down, the tree giving him the worst thrashing he'd ever had. Something struck him a painful blow across the back and the world turned upside down. He scrabbled for the nearest branch, like a cat, and hung there for a moment, kicking his legs. Then he dropped to the ground, got to his feet, and shot down the nearest alleyway.

By the time the guards in their heavy armor had unbolted the door and dashed out into the street, he was well away.

RHEINGASSE

"You did *what*?" said Johann angrily.

Theoderich looked embarrassed.

Matthias tried to calm him down. "Urquhart told me he had made sure he left the servant looking as if the dean could have done it. That gave me the idea of increasing the pressure on this Jaspar Rodenkirchen."

Johann shook his head in disbelief. "Increasing the pressure! The last thing we need is the sheriffs hunting high and low for Rodenkirchen, and you go and increase the pressure! Why didn't you at least wait until you'd gotten him?"

"That's what I meant to do," Theoderich insisted.

"Meant to? But you'd no idea where he was."

"I thought I did."

"You thought you did. But you didn't know?"

"We assumed he was hiding with his relations. Which turned out to be the case," Matthias explained.

"Oh, well, that's different," said Johann, his voice dripping with sarcasm. "You assumed. You probably got some old witch to tell you the future from your palms. Fools!"

"We were right," Theoderich cried in fury. "How should I know he'd clear off before we got there? Someone must have warned him."

"Who, then?"

"Obvious. Bodo Schuif, of course."

"So what do you propose to do about Bodo Schuif?"

Theoderich hesitated.

"You can't do anything about him," Johann declared. "You can't do anything about anyone. Nothing we've tried has worked out. Everything's gone wrong from the word go. Marvelous! Congratulations, gentlemen."

Matthias waved Johann's objections aside. "We didn't tell anyone else Jaspar had killed his servant." He went to the window and looked out into the dark street. "Nor will we. All right, it was a mistake. So what? Urquhart's killed Kuno. That should stop them letting their tongues wag."

Johann gritted his teeth together so hard it hurt. He could not remember ever having been so angry before. "Yes, killed. Nothing but killing," he said through his clenched teeth. "We've turned into a miserable gang of butchers. You promised me—"

"What do you want me to do, for God's sake?" Matthias shouted. "You do nothing but whine on and on about your moral scruples. I'm sick of it! I'm fed up with your 'We've burdened ourselves with guilt, there's blood on our hands, blah, blah, blah.'" He thumped the windowsill with his fist. "Kuno would have betrayed us. He had to be gotten rid of. If I had my way, I'd eliminate the lot of them this very night. I'd send a few lads around to the Brook to slit the throat of that Goddert and his filly. That would be two fewer who know about it. And we'll get the others, you mark my words."

"You will not get anyone else. Enough is enough, Matthias."

"Yes, enough is enough. Just think, Johann. I'm willing to bet they've not told anyone else. They haven't had time. Let Theoderich lock up Goddert and Richmodis von Weiden in the Tower. The pretext doesn't matter. We'll invent one."

"No."

Matthias wrung his hands. "We must protect ourselves, Johann."

"I said no. Where is Urquhart?"

"What?" Matthias seemed confused. "Why? I don't know where he is. It doesn't look as if he was so badly burned he won't be able to carry out his commission. Otherwise he'd have sent word."

"And where will he be when the time comes?"

Matthias gave him a suspicious look. His lips twisted in a faint smile. "Are you thinking of—"

"Where, goddammit?!"

"In a good position."

Johann stood right in front of him. "I suppose I will not be able to stop Conrad being killed"—his voice was trembling with rage—"even though I have come to the conclusion that I have never agreed to anything more evil, more sinful than this alliance. That must take its course. But I can stop more people being killed in the name of this unholy alliance, the aim of which is nothing more than a cowardly murder to allow each of us to satisfy his personal desires. For too long I have stood idly by while each of you does what he wants. From now on every decision is in my hands. Did you hear, Matthias? Every decision. No more killings."

"You're crazy," Matthias sneered.

"Yes, I'm crazy to have listened to my mother at all. From the outset I should have—"

There was a knocking below. They fell silent and looked at each other. Further knocking, then the shuffle of footsteps as one of the maids went to see who was demanding entry at that time of the night. They heard the sound of quiet voices, then the maid came. "It's the archbishop's secretary, His Excellency Lorenzo da Castellofiore, sir."

Theoderich's jaw dropped. "What can he want?"

"Bring him up," Johann ordered brusquely. The maid gave a respectful nod and disappeared. Johann frowned, wondering what could have happened now. Theoderich was right. Lorenzo ought to be in the palace. It was irresponsible of him to be seen here.

The secretary rushed in, completely out of breath. "Wine."

"What?"

Lorenzo collapsed onto a stool. "Give me something to drink. Quickly, I can't stay long."

Matthias gave the others a bewildered look, went to the sideboard, and filled a gold goblet, which he handed to Lorenzo. The secretary tossed it down as if he were dying of thirst.

"Johann has just observed that we are a band of fools," Matthias remarked pointedly.

Lorenzo wiped his lips and stared at him. "Yes," he panted, "you can say that again."

THE SEARCH

Jaspar seemed engrossed in meditation as he crossed Haymarket with measured tread, his face in the shadow of his hood, his hands in his sleeves. At the entrance to Seidenmachergäßchen he stopped, his eyes scanning the buildings on either side. It was close to the fifth hour. People were still asleep. The furriers' and saddlers' stalls were as empty as the shops opposite. They wouldn't be selling their wares today anyway. It was the Lord's day.

To the left was the outline of the city weighhouse. Nothing moved.

He took a few steps into the alley and felt his nervousness increase. If Jacob wasn't there he'd have to go to the Hall. His absence could be a good sign. It could just as well mean he hadn't managed to get as far as the palace.

He strolled along past the crowstepped facades of the little shops, murmuring the Lord's Prayer. Immediately Jacob peered out from an entrance and waved him over. Jaspar's heart missed a beat. He forced himself to keep walking slowly, although it felt like torture, until he was standing beside Jacob.

"Persons in holy orders don't wave their arms about," he said with a note of censure, "at least not in public."

Jacob growled and looked all around. "You're bloody late."

Jaspar shrugged his shoulders. "We agreed between the fourth and fifth hour. I preferred to take it at a pace that is pleasing to the Lord. God does not like to see His servants running."

"How saintly!"

"No, just cautious. Did you get anywhere at the palace?"

"I had a go at flying."

"What?"

Jacob told him.

"Curses and double curses!" Jaspar exclaimed. "Another conspirator."

"Who is this Lorenzo?"

"He's from Milan. In Conrad's service, though he only arrived a few months ago. As far as I know, he's responsible for the correspondence. An inscrutable type, vain and unpopular, slimy, sticks to you like porridge. The patricians probably bribed him to get the details of the procession and the placement of the guards." Jaspar stamped his foot in fury. "These corrupt clerics! No wonder Christendom's in such a state when everyone can be bought."

"They must have paid him a tidy sum."

"Huh!" Jaspar snorted contemptuously. "Some'll do it for a mess of pottage. Rome's become a whore, what else can you expect?"

Jacob was downcast. "Well, we can forget about warning Conrad," he said.

"Yes," Jaspar agreed. "Probably about finding Urquhart, too. I guess they'll be gathering in the cathedral courtyard for the procession about now." He frowned. "We haven't much time."

"Let's look for him all the same," said Jacob, determination in his voice.

Jaspar nodded gloomily. "We'll start here. You take the right side of the street, I'll take the left. Head for Mars Gate in the first instance, the procession will pass through it. We'll go over the route ahead of them."

"And what are we looking for?"

"If only I knew! Open windows. Movements. Anything."

"Brilliant."

"Have you a better idea?"

"No."

"Off we go, then."

They scanned the house fronts. There wasn't much to see. The tops of the hills in the east gleamed with a pale foretoken of dawn, but it was still dark in the narrow streets. At least the clouds had dispersed. All that remained of the storm were the puddles and the churned-up mud.

"Where have you been?" Jacob asked as they went through Mars Gate.

"What?" Jaspar blinked. "Oh, I see. St. Pantaleon."

"You went back there?" Jacob cried in amazement. "Why?"

"Because—" Jaspar gave an irritated sigh. "I'll tell you later. This really isn't the moment."

"Why all the secrecy?"

"Not now."

"Is it important?"

Jaspar shook his head. He had observed a suspiciously dark opening in the upper floor of a house standing somewhat back from the street and was craning his neck.

Not an opening. Black shutters.

"Is it important?" Jacob asked again.

"It all depends."

"Depends on what?"

"Whether we find Urquhart."

"Then what?"

"Later, later." Jaspar suddenly felt at a complete loss. He stopped and looked at Jacob. "So far I've seen nowhere he might be hiding. I mean, nowhere obvious. You agree?"

"I think what we're doing is stupid," said Jacob. "He could be hiding anywhere. All the houses are high enough."

"But too near."

"Too near for what? For a crossbow shot?"

"Yes, you're right." Jaspar gave a heartfelt sigh. "Still. Let us rely on Divine Providence. If it's God's will, we'll find the murderer." He bowed his head in humble prayer. "Lord, two sinners beg your aid. Keep us in Thy favor for all eternity, but especially now. Yes, especially now, in the hour of our need, O Lord, Almighty God. Be with us and grant us a sign, amen."

He backed up his prayer with a vigorous nod and set off again.

Jacob stopped. He was looking up at the sky, obviously filled with reverence.

"What is it now?" asked Jaspar impatiently.

Jacob started. "I thought—"

"Forget it. Don't stand around. God's a very busy man."

The first people were beginning to appear in the streets, on their way to church. Nobody paid any attention to them, though Jaspar felt the way they were constantly craning their necks must make them extremely conspicuous.

With every step his hopes fell. Urquhart could be anywhere. They were behaving like children. If they did find him, then his second visit to Hieronymus would perhaps have been worthwhile. Perhaps—assuming, that is, Hieronymus hadn't simply made it all up.

But Urquhart would make sure he couldn't be found.

After a while the palace appeared in front of them again.

"Wait."

Massaging the bridge of his nose, Jaspar turned toward Jacob. "You think they might recognize you?"

"Possibly."

"I imagine they'll hardly expect you to turn up here again. Remember, you're just a monk, one of thousands. A monk has no face."

Jacob looked dubious. "You might know that, but"—he pointed at the palace—"do they?"

"You'd rather go back?"

"No," said Jacob irascibly, stepping past Jaspar out into Am Hof. Diagonally opposite was the tree through the branches of which he had come crashing down.

"Slowly," hissed Jaspar. He took Jacob's arm and drew him past the palace up toward Pfaffenstraße. They saw priests, bishops, and monks from various orders gathering in a long procession outside the cathedral cloisters. Novices were dashing to and fro, bringing crucifixes and reliquaries. Jaspar could see the top of a tall, wide baldachin. Presumably Conrad would be riding underneath it. The archbishop was not keen on going on foot.

Suddenly Jaspar had misgivings. The baldachin was huge. It would hide Conrad completely. How could Urquhart even see his target from an elevated standpoint, never mind hit it?

Or did Urquhart have something else in mind?

"But what?" he muttered to himself.

Then he had an idea, an idea that made him abandon caution and hurry along the street.

J acob would have preferred to stride out as he followed the route of the procession, but Jaspar was right. As long as they were within sight of the palace, it was best to remain as inconspicuous as possible. And most inconspicuous of all was a monk plodding slowly past.

He was starting to get hot under his habit. It couldn't be the weather. Was it fear making him sweat?

Pull yourself together, he told himself. You've been through worse than this.

His eye was caught by the gathering in front. Patches of purple, blue, and gold were picked out by the dawn light. A group of riders appeared from behind the provost's house, impressive in their gleaming armor, which shone like molten pewter in the first light of morning. For a brief moment they parted and Jacob saw another figure on horseback: slim, stiffly upright in the saddle, with a sharp, clean-shaven profile and curly gray hair. Then he was gone and a baldachin was raised. He heard the faint sound of music. The great processions were always preceded by an organ on a cart.

Jacob had seen many of these processions and the music always reminded him of the marvelous ships that had sailed across the land in honor of the fair Isabella. He felt a brief stab of melancholy.

Another time. Another man.

Jacob suddenly realized he was dog weary. It was the weariness that comes from not knowing what to do. What did they hope to achieve? Ridiculous, looking at all the houses, as if Urquhart would be leaning out of the window to give them a friendly wave. Here I am, look, up here. Great you could make it. Come up and stop me from murdering Conrad.

Too many streets. Too many buildings. If Urquhart had survived the fire in anything like one piece, the archbishop would die. They couldn't stop the murderer carrying out his commission because they couldn't find him.

He looked over at the cathedral. That was where everything had started. With a few apples. Damn the apples. They'd caused nothing but trouble since Adam and Eve.

As he surveyed the forest of spars forming the scaffolding, in his mind's eye he saw again Gerhard walking along, on the top level, and then Urquhart's black shadow—

The Shadow.

Bewildered, Jacob screwed up his eyes and looked again. For a moment it had seemed as if history were repeating itself. But that was nonsense. Nothing about the building was different from usual.

He looked away and turned his attention back to the procession.

At that moment Jaspar muttered something incomprehensible and dashed off. Jacob stared at him, openmouthed, swore softly, and hurried after him.

"Jaspar," he hissed.

The dean didn't hear. He had obviously discovered something that made him ignore his own advice. He was heading straight for the procession.

"Jas—"

The bells rang out. At once the procession began to move. Jacob ran on for a few more steps, then stopped. Jaspar had vanished among the people standing around. He probably assumed Jacob was following him.

But something rooted Jacob to the spot and forced him to turn around to look at the cathedral again.

It was the same as ever. There was nothing out of the ordinary about it. Nothing at all. The light-colored stone of the chancel. The scaffolding. No one on it. Of course not, it was too early. And, anyway, it was Sunday. Nobody would be up there today.

The sound of a hymn came from the procession, but Jacob wasn't listening. A feeling of apprehension had taken hold of him. What was wrong with the church?

Gerhard on the scaffolding. Then suddenly the Shadow. The Shadow that had appeared out of nowhere. But the Shadow had not been the Devil, it had been Urquhart, and he was a man.

Out of nowhere—

A man did not appear out of nowhere.

Undecided about what to do, Jacob looked across at the procession, trying to find Jaspar, but he had vanished. More and more people were coming out of the nearby houses, gentlemen and their wives, many in fine clothes, while others came riding up singly or in small groups to follow the procession. There were simple tradesmen there as well, maids and servants, pilgrims and peasants who had arrived in the city the previous day to take part in the celebration, sick people, layabouts, beggars, everyone.

Jacob walked slowly back past the palace, continuing until he was almost at the river, then turned left. A few steps took him to the Franks Tower, where suspects were questioned under torture and criminals handed over to the warden of the archbishop's palace.

He was to the east of the cathedral, separated from it by a large square and the smaller church of St. Mary's-on-the-Steps. Again he looked up and studied the mighty facade with its incredibly high, slender windows. He could get there from the Franks Tower without having to pass through a gate with guards.

As he crossed the square, walking at an unhurried pace, apparently deep in prayer, he suddenly knew where the Shadow had appeared from.

All at once he knew.

ll at once he knew.

He had hurried along behind the procession because he had suddenly had the idea Urquhart might have joined it, disguised as a priest, a monk, or even a horseman in armor. His progress was followed by irritated glances from those who had felt the sharpness of his elbow as he quickly made his way through the singing and praying throng. Some way ahead of him Conrad was riding underneath the baldachin, two men in armor behind, beside, and before him. His hair fluttered in the wind. His lively, bright blue eyes surmounted a nose which gave him something of the animal dignity of a falcon. The archbishop was neither tall nor strongly built, but he had a presence that dominated everything and everyone.

Urquhart was not in the procession. Jaspar felt foolish at the idea of running on in front, like a court jester, to gawp at the buildings. He looked around. It was getting more and more crowded. He tried to find Jacob.

What a fool he'd been to trot off like that, following a stupid idea. Annoyed with himself, he pushed his way through the onlookers to get back to Jacob.

"Listen," he heard a ragged woman say to the girl she was carrying, "listen to the holy men singing. That's the choir."

"The choir," the girl repeated.

The choir—

The cathedral choir! It struck Jaspar like a bolt from the blue.

He groaned. He felt a surge of nausea. Using fists and elbows this time, he started to force his way back through the crowd.

THE CATHEDRAL

Compared with what was supposed to become the most sublime church in Christendom, the choir appeared fairly modest. Gerhard had only been able to complete the ground floor with the ring of chapels around the apse and a large part of the adjoining sacristy to the north.

Compared, however, with all the other buildings in Cologne, the result was already colossal. The gigantic semicircle of the chancel joined onto what was left of the old cathedral, so that one had to pass through it to get to the interior of the new building. It made a curious picture. A few months before the foundation stone for the new cathedral had been laid, the old one, a massive basilica over a hundred yards long with chancels and transepts to the east and west, had burned down. Only the western half had been temporarily rebuilt, so that the old church looked as if it had been cut right through the middle with a blow from a huge sword. What began beyond it was not only a new house of God, but a new age.

Jacob stood and let his gaze wander over the airy structure of the scaffolding. High up he could see cranes, windlasses, and tread wheels.

It was immediately obvious that what he was looking at was not a simple semicircle. The chancel was in the shape of a horseshoe and it was only the rounded end of the horseshoe, where the chapels were, that was roofed over. When Urquhart had suddenly seemed to come from nowhere, he had not appeared by magic, he had climbed up the open interior of the horseshoe, while Gerhard had gone along the outside. He had not been waiting *on* the cathedral, but *inside*.

But how should a man who knew a lot about stealing apples and nothing about architecture be expected to realize that? Jacob had simply assumed the whole building was covered by a single, continuous roof. Instead, the interior was open to the sky. Which meant that from the top one could see, depending where one was, into each of the chapels around the apse and, with a little care, not be seen oneself. One could see—and shoot—into the chapels.

Jacob stepped under the scaffolding and laid his forehead against the cool stone. The mass was due to start at prime, at six of the clock. Conrad would enter the central chapel to deliver his sermon. Then what Jacob had prophesied would happen, only not in the street, but in the cathedral. Conrad would fall to the ground, a bolt through his heart, and no one would think of looking up. They'd search for the assassin in the crowd, while Urquhart made his escape over the roof and the outside scaffolding.

Jaspar had told them Conrad wanted to be buried in the central chapel. It looked as if he was going to die there, too. There was less than an hour to go.

Should he see if he could find one of the sheriffs? But whom could he trust, when even the archbishop's secretary turned out to be a traitor?

One hour.

Jacob caught his fingers starting to massage the bridge of his nose, as if he were Jaspar, the thinker. When would Urquhart climb the wall and where would he take up his position? Then he realized the murderer had no choice. To be able to fire into the central chapel, he had to be at one or the other of the ends of the horseshoe. But he couldn't make his escape over the southern facade because that would take him into the cathedral precinct and past the guards outside the archbishop's palace. To the north, on the other hand, was Dranckgasse, running along the cathedral building site. A much better escape route.

At the end of the north wall, then. That's where Urquhart would be waiting to kill Conrad. Unless someone tried to stop him first.

Jacob looked up again. He was standing at the side of the sacristy, where the curve of the apse began. Right in front of him was a ladder pointing upward, almost as if Providence had led him to the right place to climb up and sacrifice his life.

His life. Was that where it was all heading?

Tentatively he placed his hands on the vertical ladder that led to the lower platform. Until two-thirds of the way up the choir wall the structure of beams, sturdy reeds, and planks had been kept to the minimum necessary to allow workers to reach the upper areas. Work on the lower parts was largely completed. Higher up, on the other hand, delicate work was being done on the tracery of the windows and the supports began to get stronger, rising above the stonework in preparation for the next stage on the way to heaven.

Like the Tower of Babel.

Why not run away after all?

Before he had completed the question to himself, Jacob was already climbing. There was nobody to see him. The whole of Cologne was still watching the procession. He might find some tool up there, an axe or a crowbar, he could use to defend himself when Urquhart arrived. The murderer would hardly expect to find anyone else there. Jacob could hide in one of the tread wheels or behind a crane and attack him from behind. That was the coward's way, true, but being courageous might very quickly mean being dead. Trying to defeat Urquhart with courage was pointless.

As he climbed higher, Jacob was astonished at how huge the windows were in reality. Seen from street level, they appeared to rise to a slender, delicate beauty; from close up they looked broad and massive, the buttresses almost fortresslike. In the dim light the glass, although colored, was a black skin with veins of lead running through. He continued to climb until he reached the first walkway. He was already looking down on the roofs of the houses around.

The next ladder was right in front of him. He climbed it slowly, rung by rung. Jacob had not intended to spend longer than necessary on the scaffolding, but he was fascinated by everything he saw. Just above, the pointed arches at the tops of the windows began, filled with magnificent tracery that seemed to render the heavy stone weightless. He almost felt he could abandon the foot- and handholds to be borne up by the soaring lightness of the concept on which this church of churches was based—

Gerhard's concept. Gerhard had not soared. He had fallen.

Jacob tore his eyes away from the architecture. His hands clasped the next rung, and the next, and the next. He reached the second level and continued to climb. The edge of the roof was getting closer.

All at once he started and nearly let go, but the thing that had suddenly emerged from the stone beside him was only a grotesque gargoyle. Nothing to worry about. Not yet.

Then he had reached the top of the wall and was looking out in wonder over the great segmented curve of roofs on the chapels, gently sloping gable roofs, almost impossible to walk on. For a brief moment Jacob was reminded of a range of rolling hills with a deep, gloomy chasm yawning in the middle. Above it stretched the further landscape of the walkways and platforms of the scaffolding. Almost unreal in the distance, the towers of the old cathedral tried to assert themselves, but from this perspective they were nothing but sacred toys.

Jacob quickly climbed the last rungs to stand on the top of the scaffolding. From here narrow walkways and platforms led to all parts of the chancel.

There was nobody to be seen. Some distance away, at the northern end, he could see two tread wheels, each large enough to take two men, one beside the other. He would hide in one until Urquhart came. Poking out from behind the wheels was a low, crudely made chest. Jacob hoped it was used to keep tools in. Without some kind of weapon he might as well go straight back down.

Cautiously he made his way along the airy walkways. When he had almost reached the wheels he went to the edge and looked down inside the chancel.

It was breathtaking.

Each of the piers supporting the structure and separating the chapels seemed to be composed of many smaller columns of varying diameter, crowned by capitals of petrified foliage below the sweep of the vaults and arcades. Jacob was looking down into a ravine, as frightening as it was wonderful, an abyss containing nothing broad or bulky, only endless vertical lines.

Suddenly Jacob realized what kind of man Urquhart had pushed off the scaffolding.

His eye took in the central chapel. He could clearly see the pulpit from which Conrad was to preach. The archbishop could scarcely have chosen a better place—from the point of view of the assassin.

He took a step back and looked out over the roofs of the city to the hills of the County of Berg. The sun would soon be rising. A blur of noise reached his ear. He couldn't see the procession, the streets were too narrow, but he could hear the singing and the jostle of the crowd. The wind tousled his hair. It was beautiful up here. Had Gerhard flown, too, he wondered, the architect taking flight? Some run away, others try to soar aloft.

He leaned forward again, as far as he could. Perhaps he'd see something even more wonderful.

Come on, a voice whispered in his head, it's time you were hiding.

In a minute. It's so beautiful here.

Quick!

In a minute.

Quick!!

Yes, in a minute. I just want to—

"What a pity I can't push you over just there."

Jacob felt a thousand tiny birds take off in his stomach, fluttering their wings in panic. Before he could turn around, he was dragged back and dumped on the planks with a jolt.

Urquhart was grinning down at him. He looked terrible. The left side of his face was in a bad way, the eyebrows singed off. Not much of his blond mane was left.

"Incredible sometimes, the way old friends meet, isn't it?"

Jacob hastily slid backward and tried to get to his feet. Urquhart's arm came down. The fingers grasped his habit and lifted him up like an empty sack.

"Thought you'd gotten rid of me, did you?" Urquhart laughed. His fist came flying and a bolt of lightning flashed right through Jacob's head. He slammed painfully into the edge of the nearest tread wheel, fell to his knees, and was pulled up again.

"You thought wrong."

The next blow was to his solar plexus. Pain stabbed through every part of his body. He slumped to the floor by the wheel in a writhing heap.

"Nobody gets rid of me."

Jacob gagged. He pushed himself up on his hands and collapsed again. His mouth was filled with the metallic taste of blood. Urquhart bent down and pulled him up with both hands. Jacob's feet were off the ground. He kicked out helplessly, flailed his arms, and tried to grab Urquhart's throat.

"Nobody, do you hear?" Urquhart whispered. "I'm inside your head. You can't drive me away, can't burn me or drown me. Your hatred isn't enough to defeat me, it only makes me stronger. I feed on hatred. I am stronger than all of you, faster and cleverer. You will never get rid of me. I'm part of you. I'm inside you. Inside all of you."

Jacob felt himself being lifted up and up, above Urquhart's head, then sky and scaffolding scrambled. He flew through the air and landed on his side with a thump that made the whole structure shudder. He rolled to the edge of the platform and found himself looking down, a long way down, into Dranckgasse. His hands grabbed empty air. He was falling.

With a jerk that almost tore his scalp off, Urquhart grasped his hair and pulled him back up so vigorously he shot across the platform straight into the tread wheel.

The next moment Urquhart was there, leaning in.

"Not a good idea, to send you the same way as Gerhard," he said. His eyes gleamed with perverse amusement. "Might interfere with my mission. Cause too much of a stir to have you lying down there, don't you agree? Let's continue our chat up here—"

Jacob tried to say something. All that came out was a weak groan. His desperate fingers clutched at the axle of the wheel he was inside to pull himself up.

Urquhart drew back his fist. "—seeing it's so pleasant."

The blow almost knocked Jacob out. His head crashed against the side of the wheel.

He had to get out of it. Urquhart was about to beat him to death.

"No," he panted.

"No?" Urquhart placed his right hand on the top of the wheel. "Oh, yes."

Out, out of here, Jacob thought. I must get out. He staggered to his feet and immediately fell down again as, with a squeal of protest, the huge drum slowly started to turn. For a moment he saw his feet above his head, then he tumbled back down. The wheel started to rotate more quickly, above and below were the same. Jacob was going around and around, arms outstretched. He could hear Urquhart laughing. It seemed to be coming from all sides and everything went black.

With what remained of his strength, he braced himself with both hands, threw himself to one side, and fell out of the wheel.

His head was still going around and around. Completely disoriented, he crawled across the planks. He heard rapid steps and looked up just in time to see Urquhart's foot coming toward him. The toe of the boot struck him on the chest, sending him flat on his back.

The world around started to grow colder.

Urquhart came up to him and shook his head. "You shouldn't have come," he said. It sounded almost sympathetic.

Jacob coughed and felt the blood running down his chin. His lungs seemed unwilling to take in air. "I know that." He had to force the words out.

"I don't understand. Why didn't you just run away?"

"I was too slow."

"You're not slow."

"Oh, yes, I am." The air whistled as he sucked it in. "You're always too slow when you run away."

Urquhart hesitated. Then he gave an unexpected nod as his hand disappeared inside his cloak. When it reappeared Jacob saw the all-too-familiar little crossbow. The disfigured face twisted in a smile. "Welcome to nowhere, Jacob."

Jacob turned his head away.

A voice rang out. "Urquhart of Monadhliath!"

The effect was startling. A look of pure horror appeared on Urquhart's face. He swung around, pointing his bow with outstretched arm in the direction the voice had come from.

Jaspar's voice!

Breathing heavily, Jacob rolled onto his side and crawled on all fours to the wheel. Away from Urquhart was the only thought in his head.

But the murderer seemed to have forgotten him. He was looking around wildly for Jaspar, who was nowhere to be seen, though his voice was still to be heard.

"Do you remember the children, Urquhart? What they did to the children? You wanted to stop them. Remember?"

It came from below. Jaspar must be somewhere on the scaffolding. Gasping with pain, Jacob pulled himself up and stood there, swaying. Urquhart leaped across to the side of the scaffolding and looked down into Dranckgasse. At the same time Jaspar's head appeared farther away.

"But you couldn't stop them," he cried.

With a scream of fury, Urquhart whirled around toward him. But Jaspar had disappeared again.

"Lies!" he shouted. "Lies! I wasn't there when it happened."

From below came a clattering, like footsteps running, then it faded. Urquhart took a step forward, but there was nothing there. No boards, no struts, no rails. Urquhart drew back.

Then he turned to face Jacob again. His eyes had lost their icy coldness. All they registered was pure horror. The bolt was aimed at Jacob's forehead.

"Do you sometimes dream of the children?" came Jaspar's voice, echoing across the roof.

Urquhart's hand started to tremble. The next moment he was running along the planks away from Jacob. He leaped the gap to the next platform, ran to the edge and—staggered. He doubled up. The arm with the cross-bow sank, his free hand went to his head.

Jacob held his breath.

Jaspar appeared on the rungs, directly in front of Urquhart. He looked tense. After a quick glance at Jacob, he clambered onto the platform. His eyes were flickering with fear, but his voice was steady, each word cutting like a sword.

"You are Urquhart, duke of Monadhliath," he said.

Urquhart drew back a step.

"You came down from the Scottish Highlands to join Louis of France in the sixth Crusade. You wanted to serve the Lord your God and win back the Holy Land, but what you saw after you took Damietta was the face of Satan."

Urquhart did not move.

"Remember Damietta."

Jacob watched in disbelief as Jaspar went up to the huge figure and slowly stretched out his hand. He must be out of his mind!

"You butchered the Egyptians. First the men. Then Louis's soldiers fell on the women. I know you were against it, Urquhart. You did not want God's name dishonored, you used all your influence, but in vain. You arrived too late." Jaspar paused. "And then Louis's bully-boys herded the children together. You remember?"

"No," Urquhart mumbled.

Now Jaspar's hand was trembling. He tried to take the crossbow. Urquhart gave a groan and jumped back. They made a grotesque picture, as if the two disparate figures were performing some mysterious heathen dance on the edge of an abyss.

"Think of the children," Jaspar insisted. "The soldiers—"

"No. No!"

"Listen to me. You're going to listen to me." Jaspar clenched his fist and came closer. "Just as you were forced to listen when the French king joked about their whimpering, when he said it reminded him of the mewing of seagulls, just as you were forced to look on as the swords descended, chopping them into pieces, just as you were forced to watch as their bellies were slit open while they were still alive, Urquhart, they were still alive, and it drove you mad, and—"

A scream came from Urquhart such as Jacob had never heard from a human throat before.

Jaspar tried to grab the crossbow.

And failed.

Jacob saw Urquhart straighten up. Everything seemed to happen excruciatingly slowly. His arm started to rise, the tip of the bolt came up, and the realization that he had lost showed in Jaspar's eyes. The muscles of his face relaxed. With a smile he looked up to heaven.

Jaspar had given up. He was accepting his fate.

It was absurd.

Not a sound passed Jacob's lips as he launched himself. He forgot his pain. He forgot his fear. He forgot Goddert and Richmodis, Maria, Tilman, Rolof, and Kuno. He forgot everything that had happened in the last few days.

Then he forgot the smoking ruins of the shack, forgot his father and his brother.

All he saw was Urquhart and Jaspar.

Long strides took him toward them. There seemed an eternity between each heartbeat. Centuries rolled past. As if in a dream, Jacob floated over the scaffolding while the crossbow still rose, higher and higher, until it came to a halt, pointing at Jaspar's breast.

Somehow he managed to cross the gap to the next platform. He kept going.

Urquhart's index finger tightened.

Time stood still.

Jacob stretched out his arms and put all the strength left in his body into one last leap. He felt a wonderful lightness. The impact, when he hit Urquhart, was almost soft. He grasped the arm of the duke of Monadhliath as if he were taking him home, pushed him over the edge of the scaffolding, and followed him readily.

Urquhart had been right. They had become one.

Perhaps they could rise up together. Without the hatred and the fear and the terrible memories.

Joy welled up inside him and he closed his eyes.

"It's simply beyond belief," said Jaspar.

Jacob blinked.

He was hanging over Dranckgasse. Far below a dog was sniffing at Urquhart's corpse.

Nonplussed, he turned his head and found himself looking into Jaspar's haggard face. The dean was grasping him firmly with both hands, his brow gleaming with sweat.

"This really is the most stupid fox I've ever caught." He sniffed. "Genuinely thinks he can fly."

THE CITY WALL

No one ever heard what was agreed between Jaspar Rodenkirchen and Johann Overstolz on that morning of 14 September in the year of our Lord 1260. At the end of the discussion, however, the threat had disappeared and, in return, there had never been an alliance. Gerhard's death was an accident and poor Rolof had been attacked by thieves. Once they'd agreed to each other's lies, everything was right with the world again.

Conrad said mass at prime and preached another holy Crusade, without ever learning what a close escape he had had. The body of an unknown man, with burns to the face and chest, was found in Dranckgasse. The weapon beside him left no doubt that he was the crossbow murderer who had killed at least three people in the city. No one knew his name, where he came from, or what his motives for the killings were, so the knacker took him away on his cart and buried him in a common grave, where he was soon forgotten.

Goddert was bursting with pride. He displayed his splint as if it were a piece of knightly armor. Soon the whole district knew that he had crossed swords with a mighty opponent and, well, if not exactly driven the intruder out, still, he had given him something to think about.

Richmodis smiled and said not a word.

And Jacob disappeared.

It was early evening when Jaspar finally found him. He was up on the city wall, not far from his tumbledown shack under the arch, leaning on the parapet, gazing out over the fields. He looked as if a herd of cows had trampled over him, but his expression was one of almost serene calm.

Without a word, Jaspar stood beside him. Together they watched the sunset. After a while Jacob turned to face him. "Is Richmodis all right?"

Jaspar smiled. "Why don't you ask her yourself?"

Jacob was silent.

"Are you thinking of running away again?"

"No."

"You've nothing to fear, Fox-cub. Johann rattled his saber, and so did I. We each promised the other we'd make his life hell on earth if there wasn't peace immediately." Jaspar smiled smugly. "I had to cheat a bit. But only a bit."

"What did you tell him?"

"That's water under the bridge. Better nobody knows. I believe in knowledge, but too much can sometimes cause trouble."

"What you found out about Urquhart didn't. Quite the opposite."

"It was your story, Fox-cub," Jaspar explained. "I couldn't get it out of my mind. I kept asking myself what could have made such an intelligent and cultured man as Urquhart into what he was. Suddenly I had the idea he must be like you, with a curse on him that lay somewhere in his past. I went back to St. Pantaleon to talk to Hieronymus again. Now I knew the murderer's name. It was only a vague hope and not without its tragic aspect, forcing a dying man to rack his brains for me."

"That's why you were late?"

"Hieronymus couldn't remember a man with long blond hair because at that time Urquhart didn't have long blond hair. But the name rang a bell. At the end I knew what Urquhart really was."

"And what was he?"

Jaspar gazed reflectively over the fields gilded by the setting sun. "He was a victim," he said after a while.

"A victim?" Jacob mused. "And did you find the culprit?"

"War, Fox-cub. The thing that kills us at the moment when we kill. Urquhart was duke of Monadhliath in Scotland. His castle rises above Loch Ness. But he was not one of those clan chiefs who was a crude butcher. He had been to Paris and well taught there. Hieronymus described him as a man both noble and bold. Quick to take up his sword, but just as quick with words. A man who loved duels, but not slaughter. Among the nobles who led the Crusade, he was counted as one of the most honorable, although like so many he had succumbed to the mistaken belief that God's seed can flourish in blood-soaked soil. Then Louis's troops captured Damietta. And something happened he could not understand. Slaughter. Louis had hundreds of children herded together to demonstrate once and for all what he thought of the infidel. They were tortured and butchered, so that many of the men, even the toughest and cruelest among them, turned away in horror."

Jaspar sighed.

"The mighty ignore condemnations of war with contempt, intellectuals with a shrug of the shoulders, because they say nothing new or original. But they will remain true as long as we continue to wage war. We will have dominion over the whole of creation in a way God never dreamed of. We will not be dwarves on the shoulders of giants, but a race of giants, each outgrowing the other much too quickly—but when it comes to the crunch, we'll still smash one another's skulls in as in the darkest of dark ages. When they slaughtered the children in Damietta, something changed inside Urquhart. War has more subtle methods of destroying people than just killing them. He fell into a fit of demented rage. And his heart began to freeze to ice. Eventually they were all afraid of him, even Louis. He sent a dozen of his best men to Urquhart's tent. They crept in at night to kill him while he slept."

"What happened?"

"Only one came out. Crawled out on his belly. His last words were that it wasn't a man they'd found in the tent, but a beast, and that beast had been the Devil. The next morning Urquhart was gone. He had run away, just like you. From himself, from what could not be altered. And unlike you, who eventually managed to come to terms with it, Urquhart gave himself up to the dark side. The evil, that he believed he was fighting against, became his nature. Urquhart no longer recognized himself, otherwise he would have realized that one can always turn back."

For a while Jacob said nothing. Then, "No," he said, "I don't think he could turn back."

"But you did."

"I had help."

"Hmm." Jaspar massaged the bridge of his nose. For a long time there was silence.

"What are you going to do now?" he eventually asked.

"Don't know. Think. Play my whistle. Not run away, that's for sure."

"Very worthy. Now I'm not trying to talk you into anything you don't want, but—well, as far as dyeing's concerned, Goddert will have to call it a day, and Richmodis—well, I think I can say she quite likes you..."

"I more than quite like Richmodis."

"Well, there you are!" Jaspar slapped the stone parapet. "What are we waiting for?"

"Jaspar." Jacob shook his head and smiled for the first time. "You can run away by staying where you are. I need to be alone with myself for a while. It isn't all over for me yet. What I mean is, saying Urquhart's dead and the alliance dissolved is not the end of the story. I'm still the man who looked away too quickly. Once. Give me time."

Jaspar looked at him for a long time. "Will you go away?"

Jacob shrugged his shoulders. "Perhaps. In a way we were similar. Urquhart no longer knew who he was, and I've been running away for so long that over the years I've lost myself. Do you think Richmodis could be happy with a man who doesn't know who he is?"

Jaspar thought about it. "No," he admitted quietly. Suddenly he felt sad. And at the same time a little proud of his Fox.

The sky was turning pink. A flight of swallows skimmed over their heads. Soon they would be gone, too.

"But if you go searching—"

Jacob looked at him.

"—and find what you're looking for—" Jaspar spread his arms wide. "I mean, you have a choice."

Jacob nodded. "Abelard," he said, smiling.

Jaspar's grin was broad. Dammit, another reason to be proud.

"Yes," he said. "Abelard."

Author's Note

✠

Conrad von Hochstaden died on 28 September 1261, without having pardoned the imprisoned patricians. All pleas were in vain. Whether there were further plans to assassinate him is not known. What is known is that he reestablished—for one last time—the power of the archbishops of Cologne. He was buried first of all in the old cathedral, then in the axial chapel of the new cathedral. Today his tomb is in the chapel of St. John, while the axial chapel is devoted to the memory of the Three Kings—and, in a way, to Gerhard, the cathedral's first architect. If you look up along the arch to the point of the center window, you will see a carved head with long, curly hair and an open mouth, as if he were still calling out his instructions to the stonemasons. Whether it is the place where Gerhard fell to his death and whether it is actually a portrait of him has never been established for certain.

Conrad's successor, Engelbert von Falkenburg, dashed the patricians' hopes of release so that they took the matter into their own hands and escaped. Following some large-scale horse-trading, the patricians were supposed to be allowed to return, for which Engelbert was to receive 1,500 marks. At the same time the number of complaints of corruption and excess against the new council of magistrates increased. Engelbert, however, did not keep his promise to reinstate the patricians in the city administration; instead he ruled as a tyrant and had Bayen Tower and Kunibert Tower converted into real fortresses. As a consequence, the patricians, guilds, and citizens banded together again and war broke out. Engelbert besieged the city, but without success. The bishop of Liège and the count of Geldern came to resolve the conflict, at the end of which Engelbert was compelled to recognize, as had Conrad before him, the Great Adjudication of 1258, and the patricians and former magistrates finally returned.

Engelbert's power had gone. He could not even stop himself from being imprisoned for twenty days by the citizens for supposedly hatching an armed plot against the patricians. The pope, Urban IV, more and more concerned by the city's efforts to achieve independence, attempted to intervene several times, despite his low opinion of Engelbert. The latter tried everything, including stirring up the guilds, who were defeated by the patricians in a bloody conflict. At last the ensuing arbitration made the patricians go barefoot to beg the archbishop's forgiveness once again. Under Conrad that had been the beginning of a nightmare for them; under Engelbert it led to farce. The archbishop again tried to subdue Cologne by force of arms and instigated an intrigue that was a complete failure, compelling him to flee to Bonn. There was the usual reconciliation, but while outwardly Engelbert was all sweetness and light, in secret he was stirring up the old antipathies between the noble families, inciting the Weises against the Overstolzes. At the last moment open conflict was avoided through the mediation of Count William of Jülich, the old enemy of Conrad and of the archbishops in general. Engelbert then took up arms against William, devastated his territory, and spent the next three and a half years imprisoned in Jülich.

In the meantime William's efforts were proving vain—the Weises and the Overstolzes were at each other's throats. Ludwig Weise, the burgomaster, and Matthias Overstolz came to blows. Weise was killed and the rest of the family sought asylum with the Church. Only the hasty arrival of William of Jülich stopped the Overstolzes from wiping out the Weises. The latter were expelled from the city and the Overstolzes took over.

Time for a new intrigue. Engelbert, lord of the city on paper alone, formed an alliance with the Weises and the tradesmen. Money was spent and a tunnel was dug under the city walls through which the Weises intended to return. This plan also came to naught. Although the Weises entered the town, they were driven out again in a bloody battle. Among the dead was Matthias Overstolz.

In 1271 Engelbert returned from imprisonment. A changed man, he made peace with the city. Three years later he died.

His successor, Siegfried von Westerburg, once more tried to reestablish the power Conrad had achieved. He saw himself as a warlord and remained on reasonably good terms with the citizens until they tired of financing his constant feuds. But Siegfried was cleverer than Engelbert. Having made himself the strongest force on the lower Rhine, he managed for a long time to walk the tightrope between tyranny and tolerance, until his plans came into terminal conflict with the city's desire for independence. In the famous battle of Worringen he was defeated by the citizens and their allies. He made one more attempt to assert himself, which led to his conclusive defeat. Cologne became a free imperial city. The power of the archbishops was broken for good.

In another land another power came to an end. Castle Urquhart in Scotland was destroyed. The duke of Monadhliath did not return from the Crusades, and the land was leaderless.

The castle on the shores of Loch Ness remains for all to see—unlike the celebrated monster. A few years ago the Catholic Church sent an exorcist to deal with it. He sprinkled holy water on the waves and recited a large number of prayers. Effective ones, apparently. The monster has not been seen since.